ILLUMINATION

RICHARD LAZAROFF

LifeRich Publishing is a registered trademark of The Reader's Digest Association, Inc.

LifeRich Publishing books may be ordered through booksellers or by contacting:

LifeRich Publishing
1663 Liberty Drive
Bloomington, IN 47403
www.liferichpublishing.com
844-686-9607

Because of the dynamic nature of the Internet, any web addresses or links contained in this book may have changed since publication and may no longer be valid. The views expressed in this work are solely those of the author and do not necessarily reflect the views of the publisher, and the publisher hereby disclaims any responsibility for them.

Any people depicted in stock imagery provided by Getty Images are models, and such images are being used for illustrative purposes only. Certain stock imagery © Getty Images.

ISBN: 978-1-4897-4087-8 (sc)
ISBN: 978-1-4897-4088-5 (hc)
ISBN: 978-1-4897-4086-1 (e)

Library of Congress Control Number: 2022904982

Print information available on the last page.

LifeRich Publishing rev. date: 07/21/2022

CONTENTS

PROLOGUE

The Baron de Hirsch Fund was established in 1891 with a mission to get Jews out of Eastern Europe and Russia by promoting the development of Jewish settlements and trade schools. To this day the Fund survives providing services and assisting Jewish immigrants to integrate successfully in the United States.

"What is more natural than that I should find my highest purpose in bringing to the followers of Judaism, who have been oppressed for a thousand years, who are starving in misery, the possibilities of a physical and moral regeneration?" The Baron de Hirsch, Paris 1891

THE FAMILY TREE

Samuel Goldman & Helen Glickman

Children—Jacob (b.1909)—Isaac (b.1912)—**Charlotte** (Lottie b.1918)

Charlotte Goldman & Daniel Zlatkin

Children—Jack (b.1942)—**Joan** (b.1946)—Alan (b.1948)

Joan Zlatkin & Joseph Levitt

Children—Paul (b.1965)—Michele (b.1967)—**Rachel** (b.1972)

Rachel Levitt & Bill Walsh

Children—Andrew (b.2002)—Hannah (b.2004)

SUMMER 2016—
SOUTH HAVEN,
MICHIGAN

It was truly the best ten minutes of each and every week for as long as Rachel could remember. Her life was good, happy—though sometimes conflicts and disappointments seemed to cloud over even the best moments. And she was always rushing. Rushing to her pediatric office or home to Bill and the kids. Therefore, the simplicity of taking out her candlesticks, alone, lighting both of them and saying a Hebrew prayer she had been taught as a child was just the break she needed. She did not consider herself a religious person, but Rachel did believe there had to be something greater going on. She remembered a college course she took freshman year at Brown where the professor talked about Abraham Joshua Heschel and his description of the ineffable. It was something about parting company with words...a "tangent to the curve of the human experience." Yes, she believed strongly in something greater, something one could not explain. But just as Heschel described the ineffable, the arc of her life and her acceptance of faith might be described as two parallel lines never to intersect. Lately, this caused her to feel as if there were a hole inside, at the core of her being. As if the parallel lines ran along each side of her body leaving a gaping space between.

Rachel had married outside her faith and chosen to accede to her husband's strong devotion to the Catholic church. Or was her husband's faith simply the result of growing up in a small town where Catholicism ran unopposed? In any event, they committed to raising their children in a single religious tradition. Still, those ten minutes every Friday night when she lit the Sabbath lights were almost like Transcendental Meditation in the sixties or the Mindfulness Movement of the current day—just her and her great-grandmother's candlesticks. Though Rachel had never met the woman, the candlesticks were a palpable link to her past.

Rachel was a pediatrician. It often took several hours after finishing at the office for her mind to settle down and leave the problems of her patients behind. Every day was long and pretty similar to the previous one. She called those Groundhog Days, like the movie.

Just occasionally, there was an opportunity to shine and the day her partner called her in to examine a two-year-old child was one of them. The child had a hard, red, swollen cheek and Rachel listened while her partner explained his diagnosis of buccal cellulitis. He was nearly certain but wanted Rachel's corroboration. If he were correct, the child had a serious bacterial infection requiring admission to the hospital and a septic work-up involving pain, many needle sticks and even a spinal tap.

As her partner finished his explanation, Rachel turned her attention from him to the child, and then to the child's parents who were standing anxiously by the examination table. The importance of establishing facts for herself had been drilled into her during medical school and reinforced in residency training. At the back of her mind, she could hear her mentor, Dr. Phillips, saying to make a correct diagnosis you must start with a "good history followed by a thorough physical examination." She questioned them, her manner brisk but kind. What had the child been doing in the last twenty-four hours? Where had he played? What had he eaten? It turned out the child didn't need all that poking and prodding. His parents just needed to avoid giving him popsicles in the future.

Who would have thought she would ever see a case of popsicle panniculitis, inflamed inner cheeks from cold exposure, in her career?

Usually, pediatrics was less glamorous, full of blocking and tackling to see thirty patients a day with common colds, diarrhea, rashes, and school avoidance. And the phone calls. Parents were anxious; helicoptering was the term in vogue. Who could blame them with social media having so many wrong answers swirling at their fingertips. This hovering over their children, ready to intervene before physical or emotional injury had an opportunity to occur, had become the new normal in parenting, reinforced by pressure from friends and grandparents alike.

The practice she chose to join in South Haven was exhausting and not what she had expected after finishing her hospital residency training in Ann Arbor. There, the focus was on sick children—Rachel being taught to order as many tests as necessary to quickly and accurately make a diagnosis and follow clinically proven treatment protocols. But the practice of pediatrics away from a university teaching hospital was quite different. The children she saw were rarely so sick that they needed to be admitted. No, their presenting problems were subtle and rarely solved by a knee-jerk reaction to perform more tests.

Though it had taken a couple of years to become proficient, honing her skills of listening and observing, she was now an excellent clinician—seeing herself as part detective, part social worker, and part psychologist. No longer was a physician expected to be paternalistic, calling all the shots at times without a patient's explicit consent. Best practices called for shared medical decision making where a doctor needed to, first, educate patients about the science behind a diagnosis in order to next, together, make the best treatment choices in an efficient and compassionate manner. Though more time consuming, Rachel liked practicing in this manner. If she were not a doctor herself, it was how she would expect to be treated when someone in her family was ill.

Rachel continued to gaze at the candlesticks allowing her mind to wander further. Somehow over the last twenty years, in addition to establishing a thriving pediatric practice, she had caught up socially, married Bill, and pushed out a son and a daughter.

Today, the kids were still at soccer practice and Bill was picking them up after his full day teaching biology at a local high school. She wondered how they were doing as parents. After all, on a daily basis she saw all kinds of parenting adventures of both the good and not so good variety. So far, their mistakes did not seem too awful. But could she see herself and Bill honestly?

Thinking about the future had interrupted her meditative moment with the candles and the respite she needed. Maybe if she could somehow manage to cook dinner for the kids and get them started on their homework, her mother might come over to the rescue. The kids loved NaNa who wouldn't mind having a few minutes alone with them, so perhaps she and Bill could still make an eight o'clock movie.

As the candles burned, Rachel wondered how different her life must be than the one her great-grandmother had lived. How did emigrants survive the trauma of leaving everything behind? Why had her family chosen to settle in Southwestern Michigan? How did her family go from farming to resorts, to her life as a physician all without leaving a fifteen-mile radius from her current home on North Shore Drive? And what role had their faith played in sustaining them? Though in the past she had never seen her own identity through a Jewish lens, Rachel now wondered what part Judaism could play in her life if she chose to accept it.

Just then, the back door opened and in ran the troops. "Hi Mom," Hannah screamed out. "Andrew got a C on his biology test."

"What!" Rachel exclaimed. "Andrew! I thought you wanted to be a doctor someday?"

It was too late. The words were out of her mouth. It was a déjà vu moment courtesy of her temporal lobe. Home from college for winter break one year, her mother Joan asked Rachel, "Are your grades going to be good enough to get into med school?" Almost as a reflex, she responded, "Go fuck yourself." Even back then she never doubted her mother meant well, pushing and striving for her to succeed. Her mother "decided" she should become a doctor after her seventh-grade national test scores in math and science were in the top one percentile. "I think you should go into medicine," her mother said on the way home in the car after being informed of her scores in the school counsellor's office. "Probably pediatrics. You're a natural with young kids."

Perhaps this extra gear Jewish mothers were perceived to possess was a myth, an unfair attribution attached to her mother's generation as they battled to both resist and, at times, pursue assimilation of their families into American culture. In any event, at the time it left Rachel in a conundrum about her true interest in medicine. Now, as a mother of tweens, she shuddered at the thought of the profanity she had thrown so effortlessly at her mother and wondered how long it would be until her children inevitably returned the same.

"I'm sorry, Mom. I should have studied harder," said Andrew lowering his chin so that the brim of his baseball hat partially covered his now wet eyes.

Rachel looked at her son's all too familiar face and could see only shame. "I'm sorry too," said Rachel. "I didn't need to yell at you."

Sometimes her ten minutes only felt like five.

1892—KIEV, RUSSIA

Helen Glickman, a fourteen-year-old Russian girl living in Kiev, had just been told by her father that the family would be leaving at first opportunity for America. Ever since she could remember, her parents discussed this being a probability.

She was too young to have any personal recall of the events ten years ago now referred to as the "Storms in the South." These pogroms against the Jews, triggered by rumors that they were behind the assassination of Czar Alexander in March 1881, resulted in Jewish homes and businesses being burned to the ground. Though able to rebuild their home, it became clear to Helen's father that the Russian government either couldn't stop, or wouldn't stop, antisemitism from affecting their everyday lives. Her father was particularly upset about the May laws of 1882 restricting his daughter's chance to attend secondary schools.

"I am sorry," he told his wife and daughter, "but we must leave behind our lives here in Kiev. I can no longer live in a ghetto and in fear of potential violence towards our family and fellow Jews. I want my daughter to study and pursue a vocation of her choosing. Do you remember my friend Herman who left several years ago for the United States? He writes of the land he farms with other Russian Jews as a colony in Bad Axe, Michigan. It's part of the Am Olam, Eternal People movement. He received a loan from the Baron de Hirsch and was able to repay it after the first year's harvest. It's near a great lake,

Lake Huron. I know I've always made my living as a carpenter, but farming is part of our ancestral past. I think we can be successful. I think we will like it there. Start considering what you must take with us. We can't carry a lot and I believe we must leave soon."

"Mother," said Helen. "Are you sure we must go?"

"Your father and I wish for a better life for you and ourselves," said her mother. "We're no longer safe here because we are Jews. We must look forward, never back. It's been that way for Jews for thousands of years."

"I know father says we can't take very much. I'll start packing my things."

Helen stared at the small piece of luggage her mother had placed on her bed. She didn't agonize over which items of clothing to take with her to America, possessing little more than the basics anyway. But what did she need to bring with her to remind her of home? She'd outgrown her favorite dolls and her books were too bulky. Maybe her mother would let her take the family's candlesticks. They would pack easily and certainly remind her of home. She approached her mother in the kitchen with tears in her eyes.

"Do you think I can take your candlesticks with me to America?"

"Of course."

"Do I need to hide them? They have the Star of David on the base. If someone sees them, they'll know we're Jewish."

"We are going to America for religious freedom. They're a perfect choice."

FALL, 2016—
SOUTH HAVEN

Wednesdays were always Rachel's day off. She woke up with her usual sense of both dread and pleasure because Daniel, her personal trainer, would be ringing the doorbell at nine o'clock sharp.

Daniel was a great guy, always allowing her to win at her workouts. Rachel defined winning as being alive at the end and completing most of whatever he asked her to do. Daniel seemed to sense the days when her best was not very good and he would cut the workout back ever so slightly. She knew it. He knew it. But they did not discuss it.

Daniel did have an annoying habit of pairing words together she felt incompatible—like, "Now we will do 15 push-ups on the exercise ball" or "I need side planks with one arm in the air for a minute." It reminded her of a friend who recently took a vacation to Greece and was badly injured riding a donkey. "Riding a donkey" was another set of words that did not belong together. They portended doom. Why would anyone even want to ride a donkey?

Rachel kept her Wednesday appointments with the trainer on a weekly basis to stay honest about her efforts the rest of the week, but she wasn't addicted to exercising like Bill, who claimed to get that running high.

"Good morning, Rachel," said Daniel a little too cheerfully for 9 a.m. "Are you ready to get after it?"

"You sound too much like Bill does in the morning after his run to the lighthouse and back. Discipline could be his middle name."

Her husband liked structure even more than she did and Rachel appreciated that quality. In fact, it was near the top of the list of reasons why she married him. At the Walsh house, the trains ran on time, the house was always clean, and the family sat down for dinner together every night.

"Isn't it amazing how we choose our marital partners," Daniel said. "Some people say it's just random. A matter of good or bad luck."

"Well, I don't believe that. Did you ever see the Woody Allen movie, Zelig?"

"Are you kidding? How old do you think I am? The only thing I know about Woody Allen is he married his adopted daughter. I'm not sure he's an authority to be trusted on anything."

"Good point, but I do think he got it right in this movie. It's a mockumentary film where Allen portrays a chameleon-type of person taking on the characteristics of people he admires. At one point in the film, he takes on the persona of a famous psychiatrist and hypothesizes that people seek out a marital partner who can bring to the table all the good things they remember from their childhood but also the capacity to undo some of the bad. Bill does that for me."

"How so?" Daniel asked as he handed her the dumbbells to perform forearm curls on the bench.

"For example—he was raised to express love with the currency of daily actions rather than money and over the top gifts. Actions like doing an equal share of the work around the house. And when he does give me a gift on holidays or birthdays, they are thoughtful and may or may not be expensive. This certainly is different from the way it was in my house growing up and it never felt quite right."

"Well, what is the good stuff Bill reinforces?"

"That's easy to answer. It's the importance he places on family. He's especially attentive to my extended family—all the way down to nieces and nephews. This was an important quality of my childhood and I wish for my children to experience it as well."

"I love our workouts together. They are so different from most of my other clients' sessions. We talk about real stuff."

Exhausted, Rachel sat on the stool at the kitchen counter to write Daniel a check. She popped open a Diet Coke just to pimp him about his theories on nutrition. She smiled.

"I know," she said. "You are what you eat."

"Why work out?" Daniel asked.

"Look, I'm happy if my weight stays around 130, my cholesterol less than 200, HDL's above 60, and my BP around 120/80. And honestly, I love Diet Coke. Now if you really want me to upset you, it was Dads and Donuts Day at Hannah's school today. Can you believe they still do this? Couldn't they have stopped it after kindergarten?"

"What are they thinking?" replied Daniel.

"They're not thinking. As a pediatrician, I'm preaching daily about healthy choices for nutrition. Donuts never make the list. But more significant is that some school events, like this one, leave kids feeling excluded. What if they're living in single parent home with no Dad in the picture? Even worse are those gender-based school events to discuss sex. Mother-daughter teas and father-son dinners, in my opinion, reinforce a locker room mentality about sex. Is there not a more important topic for an adolescent to hear about with both parents present? No wonder teens are having sex without understanding intimacy. After talking to them in my office, I have come to conclude that for them, sex is just a physical act devoid of any personal growth for either partner and rarely real pleasure, and by that I mean orgasm, for the girls."

"See what I'm talking about. Our workouts are different. We went from kids eating donuts to having a conversation about teens having sex."

Rachel laughed. Their relationship had moved into the friendship zone. They played Words with Friends online together and suggested books and movies to each other as well. She had no doubt she could reach out to Daniel, and he to her, should either of them need support or help through a major life event, though thankfully, that hadn't happened to either of them since meeting.

✳ ✳ ✳

The most valuable commodity in Rachel's life was time. Most Wednesdays, she chose to spend some of it with her grandmother Lottie. Now ninety-nine years old, Lottie shut it down physically in her seventies, rarely exercising as she did in her youth, developing senile dementia. What remained was a most difficult life for those around her to watch. However, it was not clear if Lottie found her current state difficult at all. She still ate three square meals a day prepared by her caregivers, moved her bowels regularly, and never seemed in pain. But Rachel often wondered about psychic pain and the trauma the mind experienced when life became so small and inconsequential. Part of her motivation in working out regularly with Daniel was to stave off dementia and not end up like her grandmother.

"Hi, Grandma," said Rachel.

"Look," Lottie said to Sally, the nurse's aide. "That's my bubbala."

"What are you watching on the television this morning?" said Rachel.

"I'm not sure." Lottie was clearly confused. Though she seemed alert and aware when Rachel entered, Lottie was not always capable of following or processing what she had, just moments ago, been actively doing.

"I brought you some pictures. This one is of Hannah playing soccer."

"What's his name?"

Though never sure she should correct her, Rachel responded "That's Hannah playing on the girls soccer team. Don't you love how cute she looks with a ponytail?"

Rachel wished the nursing home would bring in a speaker to offer family members information on how to manage day-to-day interactions when a loved one experienced memory loss. Though not sure what science and memory specialists would recommend, Rachel had settled on good old-fashioned conversation, forcing Lottie to follow and occasionally lead.

"Your grandmother was just telling me that she used to be a nurse's aide just like me," said Sally.

"No grandma, that's not correct. You ran a resort business. Sally, her parents, Helen and Samuel Goldman, immigrated separately to Southwestern Michigan in the 1890s. They met, married, and started to farm before moving into the resort industry. Most women my grandmother's age didn't have the benefit of a college education, but Lottie's parents were insistent she go. She was a strong math student and received a degree in accounting. She took over the business in the forties, expanded it in the fifties, and then turned it over to my mother who later handed it over to my brother Paul.

"That's amazing," said Sally.

"When my brother took over, he put all the finances on the computer. But he'd be the first to tell you, she might have managed it better with her calculations on carbon paper. Grandma, do you remember what you told me once in fourth grade when I got an A in math on my report card? You said 'numeracy is an inherited Jewish trait similar to my fairly large nose. You, my bubbala, seem to have my skill with numbers but, thankfully, a beautiful nose.'"

They all laughed. Especially Lottie.

The woman she described to Sally was the one Rachel elected to see on these visits, though increasingly, it took a lot of imagination. There were pictures around the room of Lottie and her parents. Rachel used to quiz her grandmother about her great grandmother and how she emigrated from Russia. But today when she showed Lottie those same pictures, there was just a blank stare, not too different from the ones in the photograph of Helen and Samuel standing erect by the weathered red barn. They were fairly small, dressed in simple clothing, and looked determined to succeed.

"Back then, the growing season was short, but my great-grandparents still produced an awful lot of blueberries and raised enough chickens to provide for a family of five," Rachel said to Sally.

While Rachel was absorbed by the photograph, her grandmother had fallen asleep. She made a note on her iPhone to bring some blueberries on her next visit.

✳   ✳   ✳

After visiting Lottie, Rachel still had a couple of hours to burn before school let out. Though not hungry, she drove up Dychman on her way home so she could pop into North Side Memories. It was a convenience store that sold snacks, last minute essentials like milk, a dozen eggs, or a bottle of wine. But the store most importantly in her opinion had the best ice cream in town, though many of her friends would disagree and insist Sherman's Dairy Bar was better.

Rachel recognized the young woman behind the counter as one of her patients. She treated kids until age twenty-two or when they graduated from college. Some kids with special needs might even stay longer. Not all pediatricians chose to keep patients that long but Rachel knew these were critical years and the relationship she built with her patients was too valuable to throw away.

"Hi, Dr. Walsh. It is nice to see you outside the office. It must be your day off," said Mary.

"It is. I really worked out hard this morning with my trainer. Hard enough to treat myself to an ice cream," Rachel answered, smiling as she said it.

"By the way, Dr. Walsh, thanks for keeping that matter confidential last month." Mary glanced around the empty store and looked down at the floor. "My parents would have been so mad. You helped me make the right decision and I could tell you cared." She looked back directly into Rachel's eyes. "What would you like today?"

"I do care about you, Mary, and I'm glad my advice was helpful. OK, I'll have Mackinaw Island Fudge on a waffle cone and make it a two scooper." She was nothing if not decisive when it came to her favorite ice cream. As a kid, she and her grandmother would walk down here, get a cone, and go sit on the bench across the street to gaze at the lake. Grandma would ask her a lot of questions and talk some about the past. They called themselves the ice cream girls.

Today, rather than getting right back into the car, Rachel walked two blocks west towards Lake Michigan, allowing herself to daydream. It was a beautiful fall day, glimmering in oranges and reds. The city was quiet now. The vacationers cleared out several weeks ago presumably back to their Midwestern homes, living their Midwestern lives. She approached the old green wood bench in Packard Beach Park where she and her grandmother would sit and Rachel felt overcome by the memory of those visits with Lottie. They would sit directly in front of a monument entitled "Jewish Resorts" registering the area as a Michigan Historic Site. Today, she read the plaque describing how the area came to be known as "The Catskills of the Midwest". Her great-grandmother and grandmother had played a big role in this part of South Haven's history. Rachel was proud of her ancestry but growing up heard little from her parents about the role Judaism had played in South Haven's history. It jarred something inside her.

How small Rachel felt staring out at the vastness of Lake Michigan. It got her to thinking how ephemeral a single human life seemed. She wondered if her chosen path was meaningful enough. She helped others every day in her practice, but it was her job. She loved being a mother as well and knew that part of her legacy would manifest itself in the contributions her children would one day make in their communities. But staring at the enormous lake, her life seemed so insignificant, especially when considering the breadth it occupied in space and time. These thoughts, and the plaque recognizing South Haven's Jewish history, had Rachel thinking again about how small a role she allowed religion to play in her life.

Coincidentally, her musings were interrupted by a man approaching. It was someone she knew.

"Rabbi Weinstein," she said. "It's been months since I last saw you at the Meijer's grocery. You probably didn't even know who I was when I said hello that day."

"Of course I did Rachel. Your wedding was one I cannot easily forget—sharing the stage with a priest. Generally, I don't like to split top billing with anyone and that includes my wife of forty-five years."

Rachel warmed to his smile.

Her wedding had been memorable. Rabbi Weinstein and Father O'Connor could have been cast by a Hollywood producer. The rabbi was small, balding, with a Jewish nose and a gait with a bounce, radiating confidence. The priest, a young Irishman with wavy red hair and a gentle smile, had served in the parish when Bill was a teenager. Several years after the wedding, Bill and Rachel learned that Father O'Connor had doubts about his calling and left the priesthood to marry.

They had written their own vows and stood in her backyard under a chuppah their fathers constructed together. She was touched by Bill's father's willingness to help out and honor one of her religious traditions. The chuppah was a tent with four poles and openings on all sides. The tent itself was representative of a home, empty but for, and defined by, the people who would live there and the lives they would lead. The sides were symbolic of the tent of Abraham, always open for visitors and hospitality. And a linen sheet covered the top, serving as a roof, an allusion to God, and signifying that marriage had divine origin and God's blessing.

At the end of the ceremony, Bill stomped on a wine glass which had been placed in a small cloth bag. Scholars debate the meaning of this particular tradition. It either referred to the destruction of the Temple in 70 AD or to the imperfections of all marriages and the commitment to stick it out in good times and in bad.

The wedding was large by anyone's standards with over three hundred people present. Rachel remembered the walk down the aisle on her father's arm, seeing how proudly he held his head and feeling the depth of his pride in her, his daughter, the doctor. It was clear for all to see. Her sister, the maid of honor, stood up front as did Bill's father, who served as best man. Bill waited beside his father with the smile on his face Rachel had always imagined and dreamed her chosen husband would have on their wedding day. All went as planned until torrential rain in the early evening sent everyone scurrying home from the wooden dance floor built under a weeping willow tree to accommodate a six-piece band.

"Do you mind if I sit down?" the rabbi asked. He was showing more age than Rachel remembered, a seasoned look that probably reassured his congregants that he had the experience to help them no matter what troubles they were facing, though it made her a little sad as well.

Often a rabbi, or any religious leader for that matter, is the embodiment of an entire community. This was true of Rabbi Weinstein and the local Jewish community of South Haven. Though vibrant, it wasn't a large group of people and definitely smaller than when she was a child. Interfaith marriages, like her own, were becoming more common and faith was under constant attack with articles like, Is God Dead, often screaming at her from the magazine racks while standing in the grocery store check-out lines. Still, many of her childhood friends practiced Judaism and she knew the rabbi was well-respected.

She couldn't ignore the signs—she'd been feeling empty lately, reminded by the monument of the role Judaism played in South Haven's unique history of farming and resort development, and now running into the rabbi.

"Of course not, Rabbi Weinstein," answered Rachel. "I'm glad you happened by. Something has been on my mind lately. Do you have a few minutes to talk about it now?"

1895—BAD AXE, MICHIGAN

Sixty-two hundred kilometers away from Kiev, near Bad Axe, Michigan, Helen was working in the field with her father. It was an unrelenting grind, but with some luck they would have a good crop of peaches to sell later that summer. She was twenty-two years old and starting to enjoy her new country. She'd made several friends and even met a boy who seemed to like her.

The Glickmans farmed the land as part of a colony. The group named themselves "Palestine" and received financial support, seeds, and needed supplies from the support of Jews residing in Detroit and the Baron de Hirsch fund. The conditions were harsh but they were free of persecution and free to practice their religion, though Sabbath services could only be held in a simple shack until a proper Talmud Torah building was erected.

One afternoon, while eating lunch during a break from the fields, Helen asked her parents "would it be possible for Samuel to join us for dinner after the Sabbath services?"

"Is Samuel the Goldman boy?" her mother asked.

"Yes, he is. His family arrived in the United States during the same month we did. We think we may have passed each other at Ellis Island. When they arrived, his mother had cholera and was required to remain quarantined for a month. Samuel, along with his father and siblings, stayed with relatives in New York City until she was released.

17

I'm pretty sure you know his parents. They joined the colony right after we did. I think you will like him. Samuel is a serious boy who planned to become a rabbi back in Russia, but all that changed when his parents decided to leave Odessa."

Her father, Jacob, answered, "Yes. That would be fine. Sarah, do we have any meat to serve? We must have meat and some wine if we're to have a guest for our Sabbath meal. And Helen, can you polish the candlesticks you brought with you from Kiev? We want the boy to feel most welcome in our home and to understand we remain observant Jews. It is a central to our life here in America and we strongly believe it will serve you well if it remains so in your life as well."

FALL, 2016—
SOUTH HAVEN

"Hi, Honey," said Rachel, storming into the kitchen as if she intended to put out a fire. "The Richardsons will be here in an hour. I need to light the Shabbat candles, take a shower, change clothes, and straighten the house a little. Do you have the food and wine covered?"

"Yes ma'am," replied Bill. "I'm at your service. I'd be happy to help with your shower if you'd allow me to join you, but I'll let you do the other stuff on your own. I've already prepared some appetizers and the wine is chilling."

Rachel knew Bill had learned to steer clear of her for the first thirty or so minutes every night upon her arriving home. It took her that long, and some, to slow down and decompress. This was par for the course with or without company coming over.

Rachel's practice hired a new associate, Sarah Richardson, who started with her group back on July 1st. Nationally, doctors finished their residency training on that date; and if you wanted to hire the best candidate, one needed to start looking and interviewing before Thanksgiving of the prior year. Sarah trained in St. Louis but came from Michigan and was eager to return to her roots. She was married but yet to start a family.

The practice paired one of the partners to mentor a new physician and Rachel was the natural choice as this would be the second woman in a group of five. Mentoring meant setting expectations. Rachel and her partners had been on the hamster wheel since college and didn't know how to stop. A new partner would be expected to keep up with the fastest partner, always in pursuit of perfection—anything less was bad for the patients and a possible malpractice risk. The fact that this type of culture eventually produced burnout wasn't lost on Rachel, but she consciously chose not to examine this conclusion.

Rachel had been meeting with Sarah on a weekly basis since she started and both agreed it was time to get together and meet each other's spouses, hence, tonight's barbecue at the Walsh's house. Sarah and her husband John arrived at seven PM sharp. Many times Bill told Rachel how annoying this punctuality thing was that doctors expected of themselves and everyone socially attached to them. "I think you guys are part of a different species," Bill liked to say.

When Rachel answered the door, she was startled. The couple were casually dressed in shorts and polo shirts, not matching, but some effort seemed to have been made to be coordinated.

"I love your patio and garden," said Sarah. "Who is the gardener? You or Bill?"

"It's Bill. Gardening was one of his many talents that went undetected during our courtship."

"How did you guys meet?" Sarah asked.

"I was finishing my pediatric residency and he was getting his master's in education at the University of Michigan. A mutual acquaintance fixed us up. We agreed to a 'first date' at a local park to play tennis. There was some immediate chemistry and, after two sets, we decided to go have a drink."

"Have you always wanted to be a doctor, Rachel?" asked John.

"I can't believe you asked that question. It's one of the two big conundrums of my life. It's all I ever heard about from my mother after taking some dumb tests in seventh grade and acing them. As a teenager, I thought about becoming a rabbi. I enjoyed preparing and performing for my Bat Mitzvah at age thirteen. And I was close to my grandmother, who came from a fiercely religious background, and fascinated by her family's history of emigration from Russia to leave the pogroms behind. However, one Saturday morning at religious school about fifty kids and I were taken downstairs to the temple's basement auditorium to watch grainy black and white films of emaciated men, women, and children in striped clothing with Jewish stars on their shirts." And OMG, the conveyor belts with pale bones tumbling down.

"Either my parents never knew I had seen these films or they didn't know what to say about them when I came home. Talk about traumatic." The word Holocaust wasn't even in her vocabulary until that morning.

"I wasn't sure I even wanted to be a Jew anymore, let alone a rabbi, though my birth to a Jewish mother would hardly give me a chance to deny it if another holocaust ever came to America. For a week or two in high school, I was writing my name—RACHAEL—as only the Jewish girls spelled the name without an "A." When my mother found out, I was grounded for a week."

"So, then you decided to become a doctor?" said John leaning in and tilting his head off to the side.

"Not really. In college, I thought about becoming an architect. It seemed to be a profession where I could use my strengths to problem solve and see tangible results from my work. Sophomore year at Brown, I took a trip to visit my roommate's brother who was attending architecture school at Harvard. Each student had a large personal workspace in a spectacular layered glass building where they were designing an entire campus for a school to be built in Connecticut. The students had traveled to the proposed site and made extensive measurements of the property, interviewed members of the school board, and reviewed the finances to understand the budgetary constraints. I was astonished at the different approaches each student applied to the project as I moved from one workspace to the next. I decided this would be my career path if I didn't get into med school."

Rachel had loved her art history class and wondered if becoming an architect might satisfy her analytic mind and creative side that was interested in art. She thought it would be incredible to design and build personalized projects like Frank Lloyd Wright's Taliesin, his home and studio in Wisconsin. Her parents had taken her to see it when she was a young girl and her father had gone on and on about it being a "representation of the Prairie School as the building merged into the flatness of the plains." She'd never been able to look at another building again without considering how it compared to her memory of Wright's vision.

"I am fascinated by architecture and its passion," John said. "I imagine you read The Fountainhead—what an important book."

"And a great love story," Rachel said blushing. "Oh, I'm sorry. That was so lame."

"I thought it was a great love story too," Bill said with a smile.

"Anyway, in the end I got into med school and became a doctor. You know the drill from there. The first two years were a drudgery, night after night of study and memorization. Our school had a very traditional curriculum. It was quite far afield from the actual practice of medicine. But the last two years were great. I loved being thrown into the fray of clinical rotations in the hospital. On my first day I was given five patients to follow. I didn't get home until ten that night as I read each patient's chart in entirety so that I would be ready for morning rounds the next day. My confidence was low, and my medical experience was even lower. But that all changed over the last two years and I became a capable and competent physician. Sarah, did you feel that way when you finished medical school?"

"Definitely. But my personal development took a beating. I felt totally out of touch with the world around me. I had little time to stay abreast of cultural landmarks and current events," said Sarah.

"I felt the same way. I was aware that George W. Bush was elected President, but I only recently learned that his election was contested and ultimately decided by the Supreme Court over recount issues in the state of Florida. Another time, while I was working at the nurse's station, I overheard a couple of the nurses discussing Eminem. I thought they were talking about M&M's and was totally confused when I realized the subject was music. I was even more confused to find out later that night when I looked him up online that he was a white rapper."

"Clearly you're not into music. What's your thing?" asked John.

"Back then, and even now, all I had time for was baseball. I'm a huge Tigers fan, passed down from my maternal grandfather. I enjoy seeing baseball as a metaphor for life."

"I'm still waiting to hear what the other big conundrum is in your life?" Sarah asked.

"Now we're getting personal. I'm Jewish, but I was raised in a pretty secular home. I have strong feelings about Judaism. I studied it in college. I'm just not sure how to integrate it into my life. The Holocaust looms large in my psyche. And my career path is all about science. I know they can coexist but..." Rachel just stopped mid-sentence. "Anyway, that's the other big conundrum, what role religion should, or could, play in my life."

"We're not very religious," said Sarah quietly.

"Well, I'm a pretty devout Catholic," said Bill "but it wasn't going to be a deal breaker. When you meet a bright, beautiful woman, who also knows enough baseball to play the inside game, sometimes you have to overlook minor flaws. I'd been on plenty of fix-ups before, but I was smitten. I wasn't going to let her get away."

"Really?" Rachel said. "Tell them what you said at the end of the first date then when the check arrived?"

"Well, she kind of fought me for the check. I told her it was on me, but if she wanted to go out again she could call, invite me out, and she could pay."

"Yup, that's what he said. Sure, he wasn't going to let me get away," said Rachel laughing.

"So, what happened?" said Sarah and John in unison.

"I told him. 'That works for me. Let's save a phone call. I'm off next Tuesday. How about a movie on me?' We hardly spent a day apart after that second date."

"What about the religion thing?" asked Sarah.

"We're raising our family in the Catholic faith," said Bill. "We both agreed it seemed to be the best path. We still expose the kids to Jewish traditions, but outside of lighting her great-grandmother's candles each Friday night and celebrating some of the major holidays, Rachel is pretty secular in her beliefs."

Rachel shuddered. She hoped Bill and her company hadn't noticed. When she reflected on this decision over the years, Rachel came to feel that Bill assumed her religion wasn't important to her. She could understand why he thought that to be true, but it never summed up her feelings. It was simply the best choice for their family. A decision needed to be made—religion was crucial in her mind. But it was a sacrifice for Rachel. One she kept to herself.

The evening with the Richardsons proved to be an enjoyable one. On the way out as the couple was leaving, Sarah noticed Rachel's candles still burning and commented on the beauty of her candlesticks. It pleased Rachel that she noticed, but she didn't go into details about how they made their way from Russia to her living room in South Haven.

Later, while doing the dishes, Rachel chided herself for talking too much during dinner. In social settings, she often forgot how much her job reinforced the sense that everyone needed and wanted to hear her opinion on all things, big and small. One had to be awfully self-aware to recognize when it was time to shut-up and be a better listener. She made a mental note to bring this up with Sarah at their next mentoring session. It might benefit her as well to remember this when moving back and forth between her professional and private persona.

Rachel looked in on the kids, who were already asleep, and then sat down in her small dressing room to get ready for bed. The conversation with the Richardsons got Rachel thinking about when she first met Bill. Early in their relationship, Bill did vocalize that dating a resident wasn't without its drawbacks. Her call schedule was arduous and, though actually home two out of three nights, she was a zombie on one of those evenings, often recovering from being awake thirty-six hours straight. She and Bill would eat dinner together and then she would usually fall asleep on the sofa while he did the dishes and listened to a Tigers, Pistons, or Red Wings game on the radio.

Baseball was definitely a common interest for them but Bill had grown up in rural Missouri in the heart of Cardinal Nation. He never liked American League baseball with its designated hitter rule, but he loved sports and a Tigers game on the radio provided his needed fix. Sometimes when Rachel was on-call at the hospital, she would phone Bill at home only to hear the baseball game blasting on the radio in the background.

One night, early on in their relationship, while laying together in bed after having sex, Rachel looked Bill directly in his eyes and said "I love you. I'm committed to you. But you need to know, I'm also committed to making you a Tiger's fan."

"I know all of those statements to be true," Bill had answered. "But we both know the last will never happen. Once a Cardinals fan, always a Cardinals fan."

Bill's mother was a teacher and his father owned a limestone business providing agricultural products for the fields and rock for roadwork. Though he was close to both his parents, his mother's love of education and reading caught Bill's attention early on. Family members liked to say he was always with a book or a ball of some kind in his hands, graduating near the top of his high school class, and lettering in three separate sports.

Bill chose to attend the University of Michigan. It was the best Midwestern school that accepted him. He didn't look at some of the elite colleges on the East or West coasts since he wanted to attend a school away from home, but not too far away. But like many college students, the campus became home before he knew it and, after taking a summer job as a swimming instructor at Camp Mininoma, he felt like a lifelong Michigan resident.

Rachel had never dated a grad student. Bill told her it was more like a job and less like being a student. He told her he was experiencing pressure in writing his thesis on "Autism Awareness in the Classroom." But it started to come together, coincidentally, at the same time they started dating. One evening, when he thought she was soundly asleep on the sofa, Rachel overheard him tell his mother the same thing in an uncharacteristically bubbly voice. It made her feel good to know she was involved with a man who wasn't afraid to show his feelings even to his own mother.

They each had their own version on how they finally decided to get married. Rachel denied Bill's story to be the accurate one. "You're just confabulating," she would say when he told the story to friends.

They were out for a casual "date" one evening and got to talking about the future and possibly moving in together.

"My parents would frown upon that type of arrangement," said Bill.

"Well, we could get married," said Rachel.

Before the night was out, it was a done deal. Like one of the Three Stooges, Bill would tell their friends over the years,—"I was trapped like a rat." He chose to take a local job teaching in Ann Arbor until Rachel finished her residency and, together, they decided to return to her three-generational roots in South Haven. Rachel was offered an outstanding practice opportunity and there was a job opening, teaching biology, at one of the local high schools. Now some fifteen years later, they were settled, a word evoking a feeling that both their teenage selves wouldn't have been able to get their heads around.

To an outsider, their lives looked pretty perfect. But though Rachel and Bill were generally forthcoming with friends and family, they did have a scare three years ago that they kept to themselves. Bill had been diagnosed with malignant melanoma. The doctors believed they had caught it early when removing a mole that had changed in color on his back. No additional therapy was needed or advised.

Bill lived his life like nothing happened. He told Rachel it was all part of God's plan for him, something she was gradually becoming accustomed to him saying when faced with adversity. For Rachel, with a physician's orientation, his diagnosis didn't start and end with God's plan. She wished it could. It was better defined in numbers for remission, recurrence, and hopefully cure. With each passing day since receiving this diagnosis, however, Rachel was starting to believe the latter had occurred. Yet it still remained one of the main reasons she wished to give faith a second look.

* * *

For Rachel, Saturday was a day to catch up on her home life if she wasn't on call. She might start at the kitchen counter after sleeping in and pay a few bills. Bill and the kids liked to call her "Lazy Bones Jones" on the days when she didn't appear until after nine o'clock. Secretly, she liked it when they teased her. Usually the childish name calling was Bill's space with the kids, and though she accepted being excluded, it made her feel like part of the gang when they included her. After two cups of coffee, she planned to go the grocery store, pick up the cleaning, stop in to check on her parents, and possibly get a manicure. She needed to be home by noon since Saturday afternoons were devoted to basketball practice for Bill and Andrew.

Rachel sometimes stopped in with Hannah to watch practice. Today, they sat high up in the bleachers, out of site, hoping Bill would join in on the court during scrimmage time. It thrilled them and the team when he would drain the occasional three-pointer.

Andrew had just celebrated his fourteenth birthday and Bill had been coaching his youth league basketball team for four years now. Rachel enjoyed hearing Bill talk about basketball, but though he was a good athlete, he was never quite tall enough or quick enough to crack the starting lineup in high school. His record vertical leap might have exceeded 28 centimeters, but not the 28 inches needed that would have allowed him to star for his high school team or get the attention of college recruiters. Bill's love of basketball extended to his endless knowledge of basketball trivia and, to Bill, what better way was there to spend a lazy, rainy Saturday afternoon than on the family room sofa watching Hoosiers again or the more esoteric Inside Moves?

But he also craved watching the game played at the highest levels and, last year, he took Andrew and the entire team to Chicago to see the Bulls. Not the Michael Jordan Bulls that he used to go see with his dad, but it was still great fun. Andrew told his mother about Bill's pulling out several hundred-dollar bills from his wallet on the way out after the game and then asking the team "does anyone want to buy a Bull's T-shirt before we leave?" It was no wonder the team loved him.

Bill enjoyed coaching Andrew. Actually, he told Rachel he enjoyed coaching all the kids. Over the four years he had come to know each of them and their families pretty well. He was used to being seen as a trusted adult at the high school but confided to Rachel that he felt these kids were more malleable. He thought he could help them become better players on the court, but more importantly, better people off it. He recognized one couldn't predict who would grow tall enough or work hard enough to become a good ballplayer. Therefore, Bill decided early on to put an equal amount of energy into each kid trying to make sure that by the end of the season they had improved something—their shooting, dribbling, passing, or rebounding skills. However, since it was unlikely any of the kids would become basketball stars, Rachel knew he focused more on the benefits of teamwork, self-esteem, and leadership.

As she watched, she recognized a familiar rhythm to the practice. The kids would start out just horsing around and shooting from their favorite spots on the court. This was followed by a set of defensive drills, a scrimmage, running the lines, and no player would be allowed to leave the gym until they made an extra twenty-five free throws.

She snapped out of her reverie with the harsh sound of the whistle blowing.

"All right, everyone over here and take a knee. Today we are going to become better, smarter players. We played poorly in our last game and we need to get back to basics. When the ball is passed to you, I want to see you in the triple threat position—both hands on the ball with your knees bent, back straight, and head up eyeing the basket. From this position comes everything in basketball—shooting, passing, or dribbling in for a lay-up. If I blow the whistle, someone forgot the triple threat position and that means all of you get some extra exercise."

A collective groan could be heard from the kids but when the whistle blew, the kids stopped playing, dropped the ball in mid-dribble, and took a lap around the court.

Rachel imagined that coaching your own kid was not, pardon the phrase, a lay-up. You didn't want to favor him or have him take more than his share of grief from the coach. Bill and Andrew had by now reached some kind of equilibrium and both seemed to enjoy their shared interest in the game and time spent together.

Bill blew his whistle again to get everyone's attention. "Great effort guys. Before each of you shoot your free throws, I want to put in a special play for end of the game situations. It's called The Picket Fence. Maybe you guys saw it used by Jimmy Chitwood to nail the winner in the movie Hoosiers."

Bill walked the starters through their responsibilities, all to set up a fifteen-footer for Gary Gainer to drain. Rachel assumed most of the kids had probably seen the movie as they were smiling as all this was going on.

When the players left the gym to take a shower, Rachel approached Bill from behind and gave him a big bearhug.

"Good practice, Coach," she said. "The kids really seemed to enjoy your putting in that special play at the end."

"Didn't Andrew look good today in practice, giving up the ball when he should, but taking the open shots when he had them. I was pleased to see him going about his business on the court enthusiastically, given he managed to produce the most dreaded of all basketball performances in the last game. I'm not sure in my playing days that I ever had a game where I put up a Blutarsky—zero points, rebounds, and assists."

"Bill, don't let Andrew hear you say that. You may think it's funny using that crap from Animal House, but I don't, and I'm certain he wouldn't either."

"You're right. Again."

* * *

It was Bill's night to be responsible for dinner. If there was a single takeaway from their Pre-Cana classes the Catholic church had insisted on prior to marriage, it was a mutual desire to eat together every night as a family. Growing up, this was the norm for both of them and Rachel was always harping on this with patients at her office. There was real data to support the benefits of family meals including improved school performance, fewer teen pregnancies, lower rates of substance abuse, and higher self-esteem.

Bill prepared what he liked to call his "Illegible Signature Dish", lasagna, that morning having learned to make it during his bachelor days from the "I Hate to Cook" cookbook. In fact, a worn, tomato sauce-stained paperback copy was still on the kitchen shelf alongside Rachel's "Joy of Cooking". Everyone loved his lasagna. It was of the meat lovers' type with a pasta sauce improved by a bottle of beer. But the real secret was in the presentation, for after preparing it, Bill would freeze the lasagna for a couple of hours and then cut it into perfect squares. Only then would he let it come back to room temperature before popping it in the oven for about forty-five minutes at 375 degrees. All this effort so that when it was served, the lasagna didn't run and ooze out the sides.

"Can you come down here and make the salad for dinner?" Bill yelled out to no one in particular. "And I also need someone to set the table."

Tonight, the dinner conversation turned to the presidential election and the inexplicable behavior of one of the candidates. It seemed this man, a reality television personality and social media influencer, intended to singlehandedly lower the national standard of common decency. It seemed improbable that he would be elected president as all the presidents in Bill and Rachel's lifetime had, at least on a personal scale, been admirable no matter which political party they identified with or what policies they advanced. All the same, it was a healthy reminder that their children's values would need to come from them, and perhaps their extended family, not from the icons of sports, entertainment, or politics. Yet filtering or being alert to all the garbage their children were being exposed to, like the candidate's bizarre ramblings of today, was a daunting task.

"What did he say this time?" asked Rachel.

"He went off on some Muslim," said Andrew. The kids had never knowingly attended school with a Muslim child and wanted to know if Muslims believed in God in the same way Catholics did.

"They believe in one God (Allah) and use the Quran as a guide," answered Bill.

"Is that so different from being Catholic?" asked Hannah. Her daughter's question put Rachel on edge, something that happened whenever her family's Catholic faith took center stage. It made her feel like an outsider, and, at times, she questioned her decision to raise the kids exclusively in her husband's faith.

"No, it's not very different." Bill steered the conversation to tolerance and respecting others' beliefs.

Rachel settled back into the family flow quickly, agreeing with Bill on tolerance and respect. Yes, Rachel was born of a different faith, yet she and Bill always seemed to share the same values. To this point in her adult life and in their marriage, she rarely practiced her Judaism in any public manner, not even joining the Temple in town. A month ago, Rabbi Weinstein had offered, while they sat on the bench, to meet with her on a regular basis. He hoped that together, they could explore Judaism and what faith might offer her, but to date, she hadn't prioritized getting started. She had to admit, at times, to feeling pretty empty inside and wondered if Bill, or other believers, ever felt the same way. These thoughts made her feel uncomfortable again and she got up to do the dishes, hoping to distract herself.

1898—BENTON HARBOR, MICHIGAN

The Sabbath begins a few minutes before sunset on Friday night and ends with the appearance of three stars in the night sky on Saturday evening. Candles, such as the ones Helen lights in the candlesticks she brought from Russia, are lit by the woman who runs the household, at the beginning of the Sabbath.

Helen Glickstein and Samuel Goldman resettled in Benton Harbor, finding work on a farm owned by one of Samuel's acquaintances from Odessa. The Palestine colony, where their parents remained until its ultimate demise in 1899, was done in, not by a lack of effort but by poor weather leading to a lack of agricultural success. With mounting debt in 1897, the Baron de Hirsch Fund declined to provide additional funds to sustain the community.

Helen and Samuel married two years earlier but had yet to start a family. She was only twenty now and they aspired to own a farm as soon as possible. Together, they prioritized making money which required both of them to work the fields. This wasn't a sacrifice for Helen. While working alongside her father in Bad Axe, she had become passionate about farming. Helen saw it as an economic opportunity to ensure success in her new country, and though Samuel didn't share her fervor for farming, they were in agreement about their faith and the central part it would play in their family's life. In Samuel Goldman, Helen had married a devout man and she was pleased to know they would rely on their religion to be an anchor.

The parcel of land they'd been hired to work on in Benton Harbor was being utilized for fruit farming. The owner of the land, Mr. Rosenberg, seemed grateful to have Samuel and Helen under employment. "In the past," Mr. Rosenberg said. "I have only hired non-Jews and found their work often to be unsatisfactory. The two of you are intelligent problem solvers, hard-working, and don't drink but for a few sips of wine on the Sabbath and holidays. I'm so glad to have a young Jewish couple like yourselves working for me."

Samuel bowed his head and looked down at his shoes with abashment, but Helen stood a little taller and, looking straight at Mr. Rosenberg said "Thank you for the compliment."

Several other Jewish families owned land nearby. Despite not having a synagogue for them to assemble, the group remained observant of religious traditions, gathering at one home or another every Friday night for Sabbath services and celebrating the holidays together as well. Sukkot, the holiday of the Tabernacles, was especially festive. Often, it fell to Samuel, with his background of Torah study while in Russia, to lead the families in services.

These relationships with other Jews farming nearby were crucial to Helen as she still felt the sting of loneliness from having left Kiev. Her feelings of isolation were magnified now that her parents had moved to Detroit after the Palestine colony in Bad Axe failed. She was living at a distance from them for the first time in her life.

Many of the other Jewish farmers were new to America as well, having left behind relatives in Russia or Eastern Europe. They clung to each other and their shared Jewish faith fiercely, practicing their religion with utmost devotion. And though they didn't actively reject cultural assimilation, they were, like most immigrants, slow to assume the English language and the American way of life. They felt more comfortable with their own traditions, language, music, and books. The most important of the latter were the Torah and the Talmud.

It was a Tuesday afternoon in May when a representative from the Jewish Colonization Association (JCA), Saul Bernstein, came by to visit the Rosenberg farm where Samuel and Helen were working.

"Good morning," the short man with an unkempt dark beard said to announce himself.

Helen, in Hebrew replied, *"Boker tov."*

"So, you do not speak much English. That's okay. We'll carry on in Hebrew or Yiddish if you prefer. I wish to teach both of you today what I know about fruit farming and perhaps learn a little from you as well."

These field instruction visits by the JCA were invaluable to all and a central component to the success of the early Jewish farmers in Southwestern Michigan and throughout the country. Nothing was a substitute for good land and a relentless spirit but advice about successful farming techniques were useful as most Jewish farmers were novices. In addition, these visits, with a mission to share information between the separate farms, engendered an esprit de corps across the entire Jewish population of the area.

"So, you now understand the importance of pruning the apple and peach trees," said the JCA man. "The former in spring before any new growth starts. The latter, the peaches, in early spring before the sap runs but without its foliage present. It is easier to see the tree's natural shape and not interfere with any new growth. Unfortunately, as you know, you shouldn't plant a bare-rooted tree while the ground is still frozen, so your window to prune is quite short. Now, what can you teach me?" he asked in a manner suggesting to Helen that he didn't expect to learn anything from an inexperienced couple.

Samuel stood by attentively but remained quiet. Some in their community actually thought he might be mute until he stepped up to lead services. Fortunately, Helen could talk enough in social situations for both of them. She started in, "We've been experimenting with blueberries. Of course, this farmland isn't ours, but we hope one day to own a farm. Behind the small building we live in, Mr. Rosenberg allowed us to start a little blueberry patch. We think we have found two things to be helpful. The plants need air and ventilation, so we trim the branches not to touch each other. And flowers, like lilacs, provide shade and their scent attracts the bees and butterflies, helping with pollination. It will take a couple of years though to be certain."

"Hm. You probably know that I'm based in Chicago but travel all around Southwestern Michigan. There is land north of here that might work for blueberries if you are interested. Around our office there is talk of merging the JCA with the Baron de Hirsch Fund to form a new organization that will have money to lend at favorable rates. Can we stay in touch Mrs. Goldman?"

"Sure, I'm *kvelling*," replied Helen bursting with pride and a wink of her right eye.

Saul Bernstein paused to collect himself. Perhaps he was uncertain if the wink was a tic or simply flirting.

"We plan to stop working in a few minutes," said Helen. "It'll be the Sabbath soon. Would you like to join us for Sabbath dinner?"

"Of course," answered Saul. "It's generous of you to ask."

❋ ❋ ❋

A pot roast was already cooking and the aroma filled the kitchen as the three of them came into the house. Saul looked around the room. It was small, simple, and clean. Helen walked over to a cabinet and pulled out her candlesticks.

"My, those are quite beautiful," Saul exclaimed.

"Thank you. They were my mother's. When we left Russia, my father allowed me to take one extra item from the house. I chose the candlesticks. For me, they embody the two pillars in my life: family and religion. I hope to give them to a daughter one day and to have them handled down in our family forever," said Helen, who winked again at him.

"A wonderful idea," answered Saul.

"Helen, will you light the Sabbath candles so that our new friend here can enjoy the roast?" said Samuel.

Barukh ata Adonai Eloheinu, Melekh ha'olam, asher kid'shanu b'mitzvotav v'tzivanu l'hadlik ner shel Shabbat.

Blessed are You, God, Ruler of the universe, who sanctified us with the commandment of lighting Shabbat candles.

I knew bringing my candlesticks would remind me of home. Yet I do believe, I am home now in America. (From the translated diary of Helen Glickman Goldman)

WINTER 2016—
SOUTH HAVEN

Winter seemed to be lasting forever and this was viewed as a good thing in the Walsh household. The kids, when younger, enjoyed building snowmen and forts for snowball fights. Now as teens, they loved to ride with Bill and Rachel on snowmobiles and cross-country ski—the latter being a sport, a way to exercise, and, occasionally, the fastest method of transportation. But Hannah's passion was ice skating.

It started over an infatuation with a dumb movie called The Cutting Edge. It was one of those movies that seemed to be running on one cable channel or another every Saturday afternoon and Hannah and her mother would snuggle together on the couch, gleefully watching. The story line was a repetitious formula with a small-minded stage father of a young female Olympic hopeful recruiting a handsome injured hockey player to become her pairs skating partner. The couple go on to win the gold medal and fall in love. Hannah first saw this movie around eight years of age, but by now, she had watched it dozens of times.

That she would excel at skating didn't come as a complete surprise to either Bill or Rachel. As a two-year-old, she received a hot-pink scooter for her birthday. Bill and Rachel weren't even certain she would be able to ride it, but she quickly mastered the technique. Mesmerized, they would watch her ride it on the tennis court of

Rachel's brother's cottage resort at the end of Lakeshore Drive. Hannah would fly down the baseline and gracefully maneuver to the right around the net post, all the while gazing off to the left. It seemed to defy gravity and their imagination. They choose to call it The Butterfly and would call out to her, "Do The Butterfly again!" Though not a skating term, like a toe-loop or a Lutz, it became her signature move on the ice as well, taking her coach, Greta, by surprise the first time Hannah executed it. Now, Greta took Hannah's grace and balance as something expected—one less thing a coach needed to spend time teaching a student, as if this were a skill a skater could be taught in the first place.

"I don't get this sport," Bill said to Rachel as they watched their first skating event. "I know it's a competition and the kids are trained athletes but the winner is judged to have won. The scoreboard doesn't indicate you kicked their butt or you're ahead but there are two minutes left in the game."

"I get where you're coming from. I skied as a kid. Fastest one down the hill got the medal. But Hannah loves this and she's good at it. You can't let her know you think it is a stupid sport," Rachel said. "There are technical elements she must execute and the artistic part takes a lot of practice."

"It reminds me of a beauty contest with the elaborate outfits. And she's too young to be wearing make-up. Thank god Andrew doesn't like to skate except for pick-up hockey. I can't imagine him in sequins and tight form-fitting black pants. I know it is OK, even more than OK for the boys to wear that stuff and compete, but I'm still glad he doesn't."

Skating lessons were expensive and Hannah's coach, Greta, insisted on three one-hour sessions per week. Actually, Bill had no idea if the lessons were expensive or not. He left daily money matters to Rachel. She left him to worry about the macro-money decisions that needed to be made in their household, but she knew that dealing with the smaller, micro money matters of daily living would only drive him crazy.

Rachel was perfectly fine with this arrangement and when he

occasionally slipped up and asked what something cost, she gave him a canned response—"It cost less than I thought it might." Rachel knew that one day, when Hannah got married, that was the answer she would give him about the cost of the flowers, the dress, the band, the dinner, the...In the end, it was simply another illustration of how they successfully navigated their marriage.

Rachel took a seat on the bleachers as Hannah's lesson was coming to an end. She'd done a few single rotation axels to perfection. The axel, to Hannah, was kind of like The Butterfly in that you looked the other way while moving forward into the jump. But now, she was trying a double axel and she landed hard on the ice again and again. The last attempt resulted in a particularly violent fall bringing Rachel to her feet. But as Rachel started toward the ice, Hannah was back up again heading down the rink. Rachel could tell she was taking more speed into the jump allowing her to land it proudly.

"All right. Let's call it a day," barked Greta.

"Just one more," Hannah yelled, not waiting for permission. The final attempt was even better than the last. She skated to the door to get off the ice and looking up, saw her mother in the stands and smiled at her.

When they got in the car, Hannah collapsed into her seat. Rachel wasn't the least bit startled. Ever since she was young, Hannah went all in when learning a new skill but would be spent afterwards. Just as with sports, it was the same when Hannah studied hard or made a concerted effort to be sociable with her peers. After Hannah's five-year-old birthday party at Chucky Cheese, she came home and fell asleep on the couch. They had to carry her into bed. She skipped dinner and slept until morning. It was just too much effort for Hannah, a shy child, to greet everyone when they arrived and thank them for her gifts as they were leaving. This awkwardness with friends was something Rachel knew worried Bill more than herself.

"I think it's our fault," said Bill to Rachel, the night of her birthday party. "We have always done too much of her social work after we foolishly labeled her as shy."

"Look, Bill," responded Rachel. "Everything will be our fault if you think that way. But we're doing our best. I see this all the time in my office. Parents blaming themselves for their perception of a child's shortcomings. Parents need to accept a child for who they are and not judge them for what they wish they might be. Maybe you were more social as a child. But she isn't. Give it a rest. It is what it is."

❋   ❋   ❋

Rachel nudged Hannah to wake-up. She wanted to seize this one-on-one time with her daughter and make the most of it. The rink was on the outskirts of town on land that was once the Rosenthal's farm. As they were driving by Rachel said, "I remember coming out here with my aunt to pick blueberries when I was around six years old. I filled my little green basket, but I also ate many of them while picking and came home with blue lips and a blue mouth. Your grandmother thought something terrible was the matter with me, threw me in the car, and raced to the ER. They laughed at her for freaking out, thinking I was hypoxic, needing oxygen, instead of just being a dumb kid who ate too many blueberries, and being a slob at that!"

"That's pretty funny," said Hannah. "Mom, I thought Dad was going to pick me up today. I planned to ask him to increase my allowance."

"You can ask me. Dad and I work together you know."

"Oh, I know. When I was little, I learned pretty early on to ask Dad first when I wanted a new privilege, a later bedtime, or permission to go to a friend's house. He never says no about anything. One time I asked you for something, I don't even remember what it was. You said no, so I went to Dad. He asked me if I'd already asked you. He backed you up but added, 'Next time, ask me first if you want a different answer.'"

"He said that? Well, your father and I need to have a conversation. Anyway, what sort of increase are you looking for, now that you are twelve-years-old?"

"I was thinking about an extra two dollars a week."

"Done."

"Really, Mom? That's an extra one hundred and four dollars a year!"

It was just like Hannah to do all the math. Rachel wondered if every twelve-year-old calculated the exact annual increase after working their parents so easily?

"I think it's reasonable," responded Rachel. "But it's still something I need to talk to your father about. It's just how we do things in our house—at least it's how we're supposed to."

"Wow. That was easier than it usually is when I ask you for something. You must of had a good day," said Hannah.

"Hey, don't push your luck, young lady. And it's not 'must of'. It's 'must've'. Short for 'must have had a good day,'" replied Rachel, smiling.

✳   ✳   ✳

When they walked into the house, they found Bill and Andrew watching a basketball game. Bill was calling Andrew's attention to a pick and roll the team in dark uniforms had just executed.

"Hi, Hannah," Bill said, without even looking away from the television. "Hi, Honey. How was your skating lesson, Hannah?"

"Great. I worked on my axels. Dad, can I ask you a question?"

"Sure," Bill answered.

"At school today, Joey said that Jesus was Jewish. Is that true?"

Now that the kids were getting older, Bill and Rachel enjoyed it when either of them brought up a subject they could talk about intelligently. Over the last five plus years, the kids' interests were often about books in the fantasy vein of which they knew nothing, or some on-line phenomenon that, by the time they began to understand it, it was too late and the kids had moved on to something else.

"I'm surprised this isn't something you've already discussed at religious school. Maybe you just happened to miss it," he teased.

"Dad, I pay attention, even at religious school," said Hannah.

Rachel was used to hearing Bill say that kids in his classes got caught up, often, in the minutia of a subject, missing the main point entirely. However, it caught him off-guard when the same thing occurred with their own children at home.

She knew Bill liked to start at the ten-thousand-foot level when discussing important issues with their kids before attempting to land the plane and become more granular. Rachel wondered how he intended to answer this one.

"A few months ago, we talked about Muslims and whether they were so different from Catholics. Do you know what the word 'monotheistic' means?" Bill asked.

Hannah gave him puzzled look.

He went on.

"All the major religious faiths, Jewish, Christian, and Muslim are monotheistic. They believe in one God. Each of these religions have more in common than people realize. Yes, Jesus was born of the Jewish faith. When he lived, people considered him a rabbi. The Last Supper, some scholars believe, was a celebration of the Jewish Passover. Jesus and his disciples drank wine and shared matzo just as we do every year with Mom's family. It is hard to deny this history when considering what we do at church when partaking of the Eucharist."

"Cool," she said and left to go up to her room. Her pink backpack was bulging with books and her skates dangled from her hand.

"Mom," asked Andrew. "Does it bother you when we take communion?"

"Yes, and no," she replied. "I only go to church with our family on Easter and Christmas. It isn't something I see or wrestle with daily." Rachel paused. "To be honest with you, Andrew, it's strange at times for me to feel so apart from my own family. Watching people take communion is an alien experience to me. But I'm glad your father and I made the call to do something definitive about religion for you kids. Faith gives you a mooring. Is that a word you understand?"

"I think so," he answered. "Kind of something to hold on to. Right?"

"Yes."

"But don't you need a mooring also, Mom?" Andrew asked moving slightly closer to his mother.

Rachel could see the concern in his face. "Of course I do. You don't see me in temple like you guys attending church, but my faith exists. In fact, lately it seems more important to me than in a long time."

"I better get upstairs and start on my homework," said Andrew. "Dad, thanks for watching the game with me. And Mom, thanks for treating me like an adult just now. I didn't realize religion was something you even thought about."

Rachel watched him run up the stairs two at a time. What impression had she given her children about the role of faith in her life? Did they think she had abandoned it or that it had nothing to offer? And how might their impression affect their own commitment to a Catholic upbringing?

"Rachel," said Bill. "I'm sorry you feel isolated at times. We can always make some changes in how we're raising them."

"No. That's not necessary. I still think we made the right choice for them. We gave them a construct to embrace—in something greater than themselves. At the moment, it's more a matter of what I need. I'm working on it. By the way, on the way home Hannah hit me up for a two dollar a week increase in her allowance. You should've heard her work me. OK with you?"

"Sure," Bill answered.

"Bill," said Rachel. "I love them both so much. How will we ever be prepared to leave them someday?"

"I don't know," answered Bill. "It is something I hate thinking about."

"Speaking of not wanting to ever leave them, I noticed the sunscreen by your bathroom sink has hardly been used. You think just because it's winter that you don't need it. I'd rather you not die on me any sooner than necessary—even though you don't worry about your melanoma diagnosis, I do. Promise me you'll start using it again—everyday?"

"I'm sorry. I will."

"I care about you but I also care about the kids and myself. I can be a selfish person. I need you around here. Use the sunscreen. I'll be checking. And while you're at the sink, maybe you can use your toothbrush and dental floss a little more regularly as well."

"As you wish."

"Oh Christ, I hate that line—it's from the from that dumb movie The Princess Bride, isn't it?"

"It is and I'm not fond of you using the Lord's name in vain, either."

"Sorry, Honey. I mean it. I'm very sorry."

The Jewish people were geographically dispersed in Diaspora, a Biblical term used to describe the Jews being exiled from Israel by the Romans after the Temple was destroyed in 70 AD. This situation resulted in Jews always living in countries as a minority with little control over their fate or treatment until 1948 when the state of Israel was created.

For centuries, many Jews were farmers. Some chose to convert to other religions rather than sacrifice the money required to educate their children and not use them in the fields. But for those families who remained Jews, their children were required to study. Study and literacy became the backbone or calling card of the Jewish people. Over time, these skills took them away from the fields into cities to work as craftsman, shopkeepers, physicians, and scholars. By the 13th century, moneylending and finance became a most desirable vocation and Jews were uniquely qualified to excel. It was Judaism's focus on study while in Diaspora that prepared them so well.

Saul Bernstein assisted the Goldmans in finding a perfect parcel of land to purchase in South Haven. He'd been swept up by Helen's passion within minutes of their first meeting and told some of his associates in Chicago about the Goldmans when he returned from his rounds in Southwestern Michigan.

Two years passed. Saul made these trips each spring and was looking forward to stopping by the Goldmans' farm to see what progress they had made. When he arrived, he found Helen and Samuel working side-by-side, preparing the fields for planting.

"Good morning," said Saul striding up to the couple. "It's a beautiful day to be working on your own farm."

"We can't thank you enough for your help," said Samuel.

"Well, when I returned to Chicago after the first time we met, I remember telling the others at the Jewish Agricultural Society (JAS) about a couple who I thought could make it with a little help. That's what our loan program is all about. It was something in Helen's eyes, an inner light, the passion of possibility, that sold me."

The JAS was an organization formed to provide education to Jewish immigrants and emerged after receiving grants from both the Baron de Hirsch Fund and the Jewish Colonization Association. The branch in Chicago was founded by Rabbi A. R. Levy whose mission was to relocate immigrants pouring into Chicago from Eastern Europe and Russia from crowded tenement buildings in the city to nearby rural areas to farm.

The Goldmans felt fortunate to be recipients of a loan from the JAS with easy installments. They were confident that they could make the payments and still save a little before starting a family. Between themselves, Helen and Samuel playfully referred to Saul as the man with the unkempt beard. But they didn't underestimate the value he brought to their dream of farm ownership, holding their hands throughout the entire process and extending himself even further—assisting them in choosing the land they ultimately purchased, the equipment they would need, and the seed to get started.

"I know you can do it," Saul said.

"*Mir kennen*, we can. We will fruit farm but I'd like to get involved in poultry as well. I want to hedge our bets. My husband and I are determined to be successful in this country. I read everything I can get my hands on about farming. I subscribe to the Jewish Farmer and plan to attend the meeting of the Federation of Jewish Farmers later this year in New York City, that is, if I haven't already delivered the baby," said Helen, placing her hands on her belly.

Samuel had been eager to start a family ever since they married, but Helen had other ideas and could be inflexible. She told Samuel they would have to wait until they were on their feet financially. But now that they "owned" their farm, she was ready for motherhood.

"*Mazel tov,*" Bernstein exclaimed.

"Thank you, Saul. When she told me about her pregnancy a few weeks ago, I could hardly contain myself," said Samuel raising his arms enthusiastically, as if reaching to the heavens. "I hope it is a boy. He could help me with the farming when he gets big enough."

"You can hope all you want, Sam, but it is up to God. A girl can do the work just as well, maybe even better," Helen said with a look intended to signal the conversation had moved in a direction he wouldn't win if he pushed it too far. They both knew that, to date, she had contributed as much as he, if not more, to their farming success.

"Well, when my first child was born, it transformed how I saw my marriage and my life. Our house became a home. My focus was no longer on myself and my wife, Shirley. It was on my son, what he could become, and what I hoped he would contribute one day to his community. He's starting to read now. Helen, you mentioned being an avid reader. I read everything I can. I think of it as part of our Jewish heritage. Study is a fundamental component of the Jewish faith."

"My father and my grandfather often said the same thing to me when we still lived in Russia," said Samuel. "They told me that prior to the destruction of the Second Temple by the Romans in 70 AD the foundation of Judaism was built on two distinct pillars. First, the sacrifices and services at the Temple. And second, the study of the Torah, but always by a limited number of rabbis. After the temple was destroyed, Jews lived in Diaspora and study of the Torah became something every household needed to do on their own."

Helen heard Samuel describe this history before when other Jewish farmers gathered for Sabbath services. Not all of them had been schooled while still living in Russia, as Samuel had, in Judaic history. After the Temple was destroyed, Judaism's survival became dependent on the single pillar of study. It wasn't enough to have only a few rabbis studying. All Jews needed to study the Torah and, after it was written, the arguments of the Talmud as well.

But Helen remembered what Samuel would say, "Jews can control their private lives." To that end, the rabbis debated and decided on how to perform even the most inconsequential chores of daily life, rendering their exact performance crucial. The intent was to make it difficult to be a Jew, requiring followers to perform and study the rabbis' decisions on simple tasks like how one should eat bread, place a napkin, or light the candles—these efforts resulting in every home striving to be a temple.

"Remember, you and I are here in America because of one man, the Baron de Hirsch," said Saul. "He accumulated a large fortune in banking and chose to leave it in trusts to benefit Jews around the world in distress. His money helped your family escape from persecution in Kiev and Odessa, and mine from Warsaw."

"I know," said Helen. "Samuel and I arrived separately in America but met in Bad Axe, Michigan where our parents were part of the Palestine colony. The Baron de Hirsch supported the colony financially until, ultimately, it failed."

"Are your parents still farming?" Samuel asked Helen.

"No. It never suited my father. After Bad Axe, they moved to Detroit. He is very skilled with his hands and took a job with the Ford Motor Company. He is working on the Model T. They plan to make 10,000 cars this year. More and more Jewish families are living in Detroit and they enjoy being a part of a strong religious community."

"Have you told them about the pregnancy?" asked Saul.

"Of course," answered Helen. "They are eager to become grandparents. They are planning to visit soon. They've been on Samuel's side about starting a family since we married. They're hopeful we can be successful here in South Haven, but they worry about us having a strong enough Jewish community here for support and to share our religious practices."

"My travel this time of year includes several Jewish families that are farming nearby. Each received loans from the JAS and indirectly from the Baron. I'll make sure to tell them about your family. I know you will study hard to be successful at farming, but your children can become anything in America. They too must focus on study. It's what Jews do. It is what Judaism has taught us to do to survive."

"A *shaynem dank,* thank you, Mr. Bernstein," said Samuel. "We will work hard and study hard for ourselves and our baby. We have always put our religion first. Our children will be raised in the Jewish faith. They will study the Torah. Any boys we have will perform Bar Mitzvah, we will keep the Sabbath, and we will honor the Commandments. But I'll make you a promise in gratitude for all you have done for us. This child Helen is now carrying, and any future children we are blessed to have, will have the finest education possible."

Helen nodded in agreement while taking her candlesticks out of the cabinet and starting to polish them. She felt so fortunate to have these two men in her life. They both were men of faith and she knew they each believed in her.

"You mentioned to me the last time we were together that you plan to pass down those candlesticks to your daughter someday, but what if you have many girls, or none at all?" asked Saul.

"Well, if I have none, I suppose I will give them to a daughter-in-law," said Helen. "And if I have more than one daughter, I will give them to the youngest."

She started to cry.

"I'm sorry," said Saul. "Did I say something that upset you?"

"No. It's these pregnancy 'humors'. My emotions are difficult to control at times. I'm sure your wife, when pregnant, also cried at times for no reason as well." Helen regained her composure. "Saul, can you join us for dinner again tonight?"

I like that Saul Bernstein. He reminds me of my Samuel. Study and religious practice come first. (From the translated diary of Helen Glickman Goldman)

49

WINTER 2016/17—
SOUTH HAVEN

Rachel arrived promptly at 1 PM. She was nervous. She was never nervous. Deciding to call Rabbi Weinstein's office last week was definitely one of those spur-of-the-moment impulse things. She had thought about doing so ever since their chance meeting several months ago on the bench. Rachel had discussed the idea with her sister Michelle, but no one else, not even Bill.

Religion. Religious faith. Religion and Science. It seemed to Rachel that religion and science were set against one another without a middle ground. For the last twenty years, her working hours were almost exclusively dedicated to observation, careful examination, and arriving at logical conclusions. For the last several centuries, mankind seemed to have done the same, often literally fighting religious institutions as would-be scientists looked critically at the laws of the universe, the principle of evolution, and the treatment of disease.

But did the two have to be in conflict? Was there no middle ground? Were they even considering the same subjects or problems? Science attempted to study, measure, and even predict, physical phenomenon; whereas Religion tried to help mankind understand moral dilemmas, serve as a lens to understand the beauty of the universe, and provide comfort when pondering the brevity of an individual's time on earth. But that there was conflict was undeniable in Rachel's mind. She couldn't reconcile the discovery of atomic energy and the invention, and ultimate use, of the Atomic Bomb—or the work of the microbiologist Louis Pasteur and the development of biochemical warfare.

Rachel's anxiety was becoming almost physiologic, her heart seemed to be racing and her palms were sweaty. She took a final deep breath, trying to collect herself and put all her earlier negative thoughts away.

"I'm so glad you are here," started in Rabbi Weinstein. "It's not that this type of visit never happens, but it is not a frequent occurrence either. Your generation has moved away from their Judaic upbringing. In fact, I can generalize by saying that your entire generation has moved away from all faiths and organized religions. I suppose they are not seen as relevant. Perhaps the collective clergy could sell it better. Our culture mandates that children attend school and we examine their proficiencies in acquiring information about the arts and sciences. Maybe we could require a religious education for all and test students to enforce learning. It might serve our society well if young people were challenged to consider how religion has many answers to their questions in life. Oh look, I haven't even let you settle into your chair. I'm just so excited to have you here."

Rachel looked around the small room and took in that old book smell with a faint vanilla tinge. Books had disappeared from her pediatric office shelves. Everything was online. She still preferred to print pertinent articles she found on the internet and read them on paper. After all, this was how she had done all her learning. She could touch the words, make notations in the margins, and then file articles in a metal cabinet in her study at home. Would filing cabinets go away someday, an anachronism in her own lifetime?

"Have you read all these books?" she asked.

"Of course not," Rabbi Weinstein said with a warm smile. "Most of them where here when I started at the congregation twenty-plus years ago. Actually, it might surprise you, but I prefer to listen to books on tape—the more theatrical the reader, the better. Before we start in, perhaps you can tell me a little about how you practice your faith at the moment."

"Well," said Rachel. "We celebrate the holidays as a family and I light the Sabbath candles every Friday night, but usually alone. I love saying the prayer and having a moment to just put my life on pause."

"That's an interesting way to describe your experience. Abraham Heschel, the great theologian, spoke of the importance of the Sabbath in a similar vein. He worried that American culture and modern-day life placed too much value on dominating 'space'—acquiring stuff if you will, big and small. The Sabbath allows us to rein in something more invaluable, time—to stop and consider what we can do for others. All that we acquire will perish. Only God's presence is infinite."

Rabbi Weinstein paused. He came out from behind his desk and sat in the chair right next to Rachel. "Now, we talked quite a while that day on the bench sharing an ice cream, but I don't remember all the details of our conversation. I'm pretty sure I asked you to google the Baron de Hirsch to give you some background on how your family may have settled here in South Haven. But you had some bigger questions about your faith. Remind me, what is it you would like to accomplish together?" he asked.

Rachel took a deep breath. "In college, I took an independent study senior year with a Judaic studies professor. I had to write a proposal for him to approve. I told him I knew I didn't want to write any term papers but I would read anything he recommended. It's funny that you mentioned Heschel. I read him in that very independent study class. I wanted to understand the foundations of Judaism. I wanted to learn more about the Torah, the Talmud, the role of Mysticism, the history of the Holocaust, and Zionism with its culmination in statehood for Israel. I also wished to learn about the emigration of Jews from Eastern Europe and Russia, perhaps some of the specifics about families like my own that immigrated here to Southwestern Michigan.

"The professor and I met at his home on a weekly basis for dinner," Rachel continued. "It was a great academic experience, but I was unable, or didn't apply my studies properly, to discover how becoming a practicing Jew might inform me to be a better person and accept life being finite. I suppose I was too young and immature. But a lot of my angst was, and still is, about the Holocaust. For me, and I think for many Jews, it is the recent past. I think non-Jews see it as ancient history—no longer relevant today. I worry it could happen again most anywhere in the world.

"It is something I used to discuss with my grandmother." Rachel wasn't finished yet. "Her struggles were even more personal. She felt guilty that her relatives left Russia in the 1890's and didn't perish like so many Jews who either chose not to leave or didn't have an opportunity to do so. Her survival felt like an accident. A good one, but something she struggled to reconcile with belief in God."

"So, you're the kind of girl who can drop a lot on a guy on the first date," the rabbi said with the twinkle in his eye she remembered from her wedding.

"Bill used almost those exact words on our first date," replied Rachel. "And that has worked out well."

"You didn't mention exploring your interfaith marriage or your decision to raise your children as Catholics," the rabbi said.

"Well, I'm good with all of that. Occasionally, or perhaps often, I feel like I'm on the outside looking in, but I'm a big girl. It was a decision I was 100% committed to at the time and I still am. No, I'm here for myself. I'm not sure living without an anchor works. Sure, I'm anchored to Bill, my work, and my children, but as I grow older, I'm pretty sure that isn't enough."

They spoke for another half an hour about how to make this work. How often would they meet? Where would they start? Did anyone else know she was here today with this difficult request? The rabbi gave her the English translation of the Torah portion for the coming week. He also asked her to purchase a new book out about the Holocaust—"Why/Explaining the Holocaust"and a second about Israel's modern history, "My Promised Land".

"You know Rachel, Judaism is a very special religion. It isn't for everyone. God chose us and, though similar, Judaism does start from a different point of view than your husband's faith. Perhaps because the Jews lived in Diaspora from 70 AD until 1948, being Jewish has more to do with how you live your life, how you conduct yourself with others, and even with the minutiae we will learn together while studying the Talmud—how to eat, dress, and pray. As to the Holocaust, I'm not sure that I also don't have more questions than answers. Let's just say for now, we will do our best."

"That sounds good to me," said Rachel. "By the way, thanks for the tip to research the Baron de Hirsch. It is quite a story—one of the richest men in the world with no living heirs and choosing to dedicate his personal fortune to relocating Jews suffering from persecution all around the world. It led me to read about all sorts of events over the last century and how they affected Jews living in America. I hope we can touch on some of these events as well."

"I'm sure we can. It's going to be fun," said Rabbi Weinstein with a twinkle in his eye that Rachel had heard her friends talk so much about.

✳ ✳ ✳

She left the temple exhilarated. Gone was the anxiety with which Rachel had arrived. By no means did she know where this would take her. It reminded her of a line from a television show her father recently made her watch with him on Netflix, The Little Rascals. They were on a runaway kid-built taxi when one of the characters exclaimed "I don't know where we are going but we are on our way."

Her path in life had always been so programmed. When together with friends whose careers had many twists and turns, the necessary decisions she had made to date seemed a straight line—college, med school, residency, private practice, marriage, kids. But she had definitely neglected any spiritual choices. Had she neglected them or ignored them intentionally? She was ready now to at least look at the issues that bothered her about her faith—God's role in the Holocaust, the disconnect American Jews feel about allegiance to Israel and being an observant Jew, the pressure to conform to both community and family expectations of a Jewish life, and the question of an afterlife.

1909—SOUTH HAVEN

To those living in New York City, Jews were known to be merchants, not farmers. But the Agricultural Fair in 1909 gave Jewish farmers an opportunity to display both their produce and their agricultural techniques. The exhibits laid out fruits and vegetables, but also printed pamphlets about how to successfully farm. The Baron de Hirsch Agricultural School, which had been established in 1895 in nearby Woodbine, assisted with staging the event.

It was a crisp September morning and Helen was leaving by train for New York City. She was seven months pregnant and knew Samuel would have preferred her not to go. But if he hadn't already learned over their ten-plus years of marriage that when her mind was made up it was useless arguing with her, she couldn't expect him to understand today either.

The first meeting of The Federation of Jewish Farmers of America would take place in New York City on October 3rd for three days as part of an Agricultural Fair coordinated by Jewish farmers. Helen was the elected delegate from the local farmers' organization in Southwestern Michigan. Thirteen delegates from Jewish farming organizations around the country were planning to gather along with representatives from distinguished agricultural universities, including Cornell University.

"Please nap at least twice a day," pleaded Samuel.

"I will be there beside her the entire time," said her mother. "Why do you think I *schlepped* up here from Detroit? I couldn't care less about seeing New York City again. It's crowded and reeks. Helen says it's nicer near East Broadway and Jefferson where they will hold this fair, but I doubt it. Samuel, I promise the baby won't come early. I know you're worried but I've been praying ever since I heard about Helen's plans to attend this conference. The baby will wait until we get home."

"Just make sure she doesn't overdo it, then," said Samuel.

"I'll nap. I promise Samuel," said Helen. "Mom, do you think I should bring my candlesticks with us?"

"Absolutely. We will be in New York over the Sabbath. It'll make it feel more like home."

✳ ✳ ✳

While in attendance at the fair, the Federation delegates spent most of their time in meetings discussing education. One afternoon while gathered around a small table with the other thirteen delegates, Helen spoke up. "I want to bring practical knowledge and modern thinking to farmers throughout the country. And maybe we can find jobs for graduates of the de Hirsch School. If we accomplish anything this week, it must be to develop specific plans to educate as many farmers as possible. It needs to be a central part of our mission."

"We have limited funds to place graduates about the country. And not every community looks with favor upon Jewish farmers teaching them anything," said John Rubenstein, a farmer from upstate New York.

"I've heard that before. I'm from Southwestern Michigan. The Jewish farmers are a small contingent in that area of the country but we're starting to get noticed. We're uniquely positioned to be successful having emigrated from difficult living conditions in Eastern Europe and Russia. We're hard workers. We study. And our Jewish faith gives us the strength to handle disappointment and adversity, both common experiences when one farms. Many of my friends back home received help from the JAS out of Chicago. We can ask the de Hirsch Fund for more assistance. I think I can make a strong argument to support how it will pay off. And there is one last thing I'd like to bring up—currently the Baron de Hirsch Agricultural School in Woodbine only teaches the female students home economics and nursing. I would like to see that change as well—why can't women be taught to farm?"

After the meeting broke up, Helen was approached by a well-dressed man holding a derby in his hand. "A fine speech you made, young lady. My name is Willet Hays. I am the Assistant Secretary of Agriculture for the United Sates Government. I agree with you about educating farmers. But I was most impressed by your obvious passion and your impending motherhood." He nodded, his eyes on the expansive dress revealed by her open coat. "Where does your enthusiasm for education come from?"

"I suppose my parents and our heritage, Mr. Hays. The Jewish people value education. While living in Russia, parents aspired for their children to be rabbis. A rabbi must study. Jews in America are getting used to our new country. I doubt my children will be rabbis," she said, resting her hand on her front. "But with a good education, perhaps a doctor or a lawyer would be nice."

"But many people shy away from farming. It is hard work and a thin line exists between success and failure," said the Secretary. "I did a lot of work on breeding successful plant species before getting into government—trying to make failure less likely. But effort is still the name of the game as far as things you can control."

"Well, I am serious about two things, my farming and my religion. They share something in common—faith," Helen said. She smiled, serene.

"You will probably be after my job someday," he answered.

"How much does it pay?" she responded.

"Actually, not very much," said Assistant Secretary Hays.

"Then I doubt I'll be after your job. I love farming. I do it because I enjoy it. It gives me satisfaction. But like everyone I have met in

America, I also do it to feed and provide for my family. If I ever think I can do better in some other line of work, it'll get my serious attention and best efforts as well," Helen said.

"Why don't I doubt that? It was so nice to meet you and good luck with the baby."

I believe our skill and chutzpah took those city dwellers by surprise.
(From the translated diary of Helen Glickman Goldman)

NOVEMBER 2016—
SOUTH HAVEN

Rachel and her mother were cleaning out her grandmother's room at the nursing home. There wasn't much to deal with. Lottie had lived there over the last five years and her personal possessions filled just a couple of boxes that Rachel would donate later to a local charity. The "good stuff" she'd accumulated over her lifetime had been divided up between her children and grandchildren long ago. Rachel ran her fingertips around the edge of the framed photo on Lottie's nightstand as she gazed at the blank expressions of her sturdy great grandparents, Samuel and Helen. She visualized it on her dining room breakfront, next to the candlesticks her great-grandmother brought from Russia and laid it gently on the top of her bag.

Lottie's dementia accelerated over the last month of her life. In the end, she simply stopped eating. Rachel had sat with her at times in the past when, though religious, Lottie had talked of her fear of death. Like most things about her grandmother, this made a big impression on Rachel. But she saw that, despite her grandmother's fears, at the end, Lottie seemed to embrace the inevitability of death, racing towards the finish line. On one of her last visits, Rachel came upon her grandmother staring blankly out the window. After kissing Lottie's cheek from behind her grandmother said in a lucid moment, "I've come to wonder if things are better, you know, after..." simply leaving the words hanging for maybe Rachel to consider, but perhaps herself as well.

Rachel was at Lottie's side on her last day of life. Her mother Joan was vacationing in Florida and her uncles, Jack and Alan, were tied up with work. Rachel's sister, Michelle, had come to town upon hearing that Lottie was near the end and Rachel was relieved to have her company.

"Does everyone breathe so hard and made that noisy rattle when dying?" asked Michelle.

Despite her medical training, Rachel had witnessed no deaths. Not one. But she heard the crack in her sister's voice and stretching out an arm, pulled her close.

"It's all right, Sis. Her system is just shutting down, bit by bit. The act of dying shows us just how much effort we have to put into living."

When Lottie finally did stop breathing, Rachel felt an uncomfortable chill, like something had been torn out of her own chest. She sat in a chair by Lottie's bedside motionless, holding her grandmother's hand for almost an hour until it grew cold, relieved to know that Michelle was there and able to make the necessary phone calls to have their grandmother's body taken to the funeral home. Rachel was too distraught to take on this additional task.

✳   ✳   ✳

Normally, a Jewish funeral would occur within one or two days, but with Rachel's mother in Florida, the family decided to wait almost two weeks before having a service. The funeral was better attended than Rachel expected it to be for a ninety-nine-year-old woman. The sanctuary was full of friends lending their support to different members of the family spanning four generations. Rachel even noticed her trainer Daniel sitting in the back.

Just as the guests were due, her uncle Jack rushed up with a stack of service booklets under one arm and waving one with an indignant hand. "Can you believe this, Rachel? The printer got Mom's name wrong. It says, Charlotte Zlatkin."

"Let me see," said Rachel. "Did they misspell it? Zlatkin is a tough name to say or spell."

"No! No! They got her first name wrong. It's not Charlotte. It's Lottie."

"Of course it is, Uncle Jack. You're her son. How could you not know that? Everyone called her Lottie but her 'real' name was Charlotte."

"How come I never knew that?" said an obviously confused Uncle Jack walking away flabbergasted.

Rachel stood at the front of the chapel watching as Bill and some of the other spouses greeted the mourners as they prepared to be seated. One woman caught Rachel's attention: elderly, perhaps nearly as old as her grandmother but she strode to her seat with the fluid movement of a much younger woman and her back was straight, her head held high. Rachel couldn't recall ever seeing her before and was curious how this lady knew her grandmother.

After the service ended, the woman walked directly up to Rachel. The service booklet was clutched to her chest and a photo of Lottie, taken at midlife, smiled at Rachel from under the woman's hand.

"I'm sorry for your loss," she said, holding out her free hand. "I'm Dottie Schneider."

"Hello," said Rachel. The woman's hand was firm, for all its gnarled appearance. "You must have known my grandmother well?"

"We certainly did, a long time ago. She and I were members of the Women of Reform Judaism (WRJ) and marched together in Selma, Alabama in 1965. She was ten years older than me and I really looked up to her. We crossed, or tried to cross, the Edmund Pettus Bridge along with five hundred or so people. What a day! Your grandmother was a spitfire about that Voting Rights issue. By the way, she would have loved the service. The rabbi did a fine job. I mentioned Voting Rights being important to your grandmother but fighting for all types of social justice was just a manifestation of her strong religious faith. When we made that road trip to Selma, I remember Lottie opening her suitcase on the Sabbath and pulling out her candlesticks and lighting them. We talked that night, and often over the years, about faith and the role it played in each of our family's odyssey here in America. Her greatest regret was never traveling to Israel, though she preferred to call it Palestine. She said it made her feel safe to know that her family always had a place to go if needed."

"Grandma never told me about marching in Selma. I wish she had. She did mention her feelings about Israel. Thanks so much for being here today and sharing. I admired her greatly, but some of what you told me, I've never heard before."

"I believe Lottie and Daniel were having some issues back then. Actually, let's be truthful here. I know they were. I helped get them back together. I'm not surprised that she chose to skip that chapter of her life when talking with her granddaughter."

"No," said Rachel. She was thoughtful. "I suppose Lottie couldn't have talked to me about it. I wonder what my mother could tell me, but I think today isn't the right day to ask."

"I believe you are right on that one," Dottie said with a nod of her head and a wink that reminded Rachel of her grandmother.

The eulogies given by Rachel's mother and her mother's siblings were touching but it was the presence of the rabbi and the ethereal cadence of the familiar mourner's prayer, the Kaddish, that brought Rachel the most comfort. Despite one's loss and grief, the prayer spoke of still praising God. And though the service at the graveside that followed was quite short, the Jewish tradition of friends and family filling the grave, each with three shovels of dirt using the backside of the tool, brought Rachel a sense of closure.

❃ ❃ ❃

"Mom," said Rachel, as Joan and she carried the two boxes out of the nursing home. "Are you okay?"

Joan laid her box in the back of Rachel's car and rubbed at her temples. "It's so final. The day of her funeral was difficult, but we had so many people around us, supporting us, calling attention to what a great life Mom lived. Today, I'm feeling the underbelly of death—I'm feeling vulnerable. It'll be my turn next. My life reduced to a couple of boxes of old clothes."

She wiped her eye with the back of her hand.

"Mom, I'm sorry you feel that way. Truthfully, I'm scared too. I don't know about you, but I got a lot of support from the religious rituals the day of the funeral. I wished I'd talked to my kids more about it. I wonder what they took away from the service. They've attended a Catholic wake and burial before, but this was their first Jewish funeral and Grandma was a big part of their lives. My focus, when the kids were younger, was for them to simply learn about death's permanence, but even more importantly, to appreciate the lifetime lived. I hope their faith gave them comfort."

"Honey," said Joan. "I've rarely heard you talk about your Jewish faith, but I know you'll talk to them about it if it is important to you. It's the kind of mother you are. I admire that in you."

"Hey, what are those dusty old books in the box?"

"Your grandmother kept a diary," answered Joan. "I can't remember the last time I saw her write in it. Your great-grandmother's diary is in there too, but it's written in all Hebrew."

"Do you think I could have them both? Maybe the rabbi could translate the Hebrew. I'll bet they're full of fascinating stuff."

"You know I'm not much for looking at the past. My mother always said I took after my father when it came to not wanting to look back. They fought about it sometimes. She would call him the 'great assimilator'. Sure, go ahead and take them. You've been a big help today. Now, let's get out of here."

"Sure, Mom. How about a stop at North Side Memories for a cone? I'm certain it would please Grandma."

SPRING 1910—
SOUTH HAVEN

Kabbalah is a term used to describe a range of mystical study with the Zohar, written in the thirteenth century, as its core text. Kabbalah attempts to drill down to a deeper, almost personal relationship to God. The Zohar stands alongside, but, most scholars would say, behind the Torah and the Talmud as the critical writings of the Jewish faith. The Torah, "The Teaching," is the first section of the Hebrew Bible and is made up of the five books of Moses handed down by God on Mount Sinai. The Talmud, which focuses primarily on domestic life and religious observance, is a book of debate, written by rabbis over many years on how to live. These instructions are to be studied, not read as one might read a novel, and were critical to survival of the Jewish race while in Diaspora.

Saul Bernstein was back in South Haven making his rounds. On a typical trip, he might visit thirteen farms in total. Each one of these farm families received their start from funds loaned by The Jewish Agricultural Aid Society. The loaning of money was just the start of a relationship with the JAS. The visits from local agents like Saul Bernstein were a vital part of the society's goal to ensure group success. The agents brought educational materials from the Baron de Hirsch Agricultural School and served as a conduit for sharing invaluable lessons learned by individual farmers to one another.

Stopping by the Goldmans farm was at the top of his list for two reasons. Saul wanted to meet Helen's son and he wished to share an article from the New York Times with Helen, about Jewish farmers.

"Good afternoon, Saul," said Helen. He was surprised by how much her English had improved.

"I thought you would never study the English language," replied Saul.

"I have a son now. He is an American. I need to be able to talk to him, someday, when he comes home from school. Samuel and I promised you. School and a good education. Who knows what he will become? He is only four months old but I think he is very bright."

"I have a gift for him," said Saul, holding out a small package.

Helen tore at the paper. "Oh, a ball!"

"No, it's not just any ball. It's a baseball. A Cubs' baseball. Can I pick him up?"

She handed him the baby as Saul pulled a newspaper from under his arm and gave it to her. "I brought you a copy of an article that ran on March 6th this year in the New York Times no less."

Helen stared at the headline. JEWISH FARMERS SUCCEED HERE. Loans To Help Their Work.

She read the subheading, hungry to know more. "Industrial Aid Society's report shows Jewish farmers are becoming skilled agriculturists. Through the Baron de Hirsch Fund, the Society has put many Jews into industrial life."

The article detailed how $141,000 was loaned to 311 farmers across the country. One paragraph caught Helen's attention:

"The report is intended as a reply to those who allege that the Jew, and more importantly the Jewish immigrant in the United States, objects to the hard manual labor involved starting agricultural pursuits."

"I could *kvetch*," said Helen with a furrowed brow. "What would the man who wrote this know of Jews? Have him come spend a day with me—he can watch me take care of my son and our farm. No one around here is afraid of hard work. My friends are proud of their farms and thankful to the Society for its help."

Saul was rocking the baby and crooning under his breath.

"What's his name?"

"Jacob." Helen was still tracing an angry forefinger down the length of the article. "It was my grandfather's name. He passed away when I was quite young. I never really knew him."

"Well, he looks just like you. I could say he is pretty, but I suppose handsome is the right word for a boy."

"Saul Bernstein." Helen tore her attention away from the newspaper. "Are you trying to tell me I'm pretty?" She was blushing.

Samuel walked in the backdoor, sweaty and dirty from his work in the field.

"Hi, Saul," said Samuel. "Good to see you. The other night at dinner Helen and I spoke of expecting a visit from you soon. I assume you're making the rounds."

"He is, Samuel." Helen had recovered herself. "But look. He brought Jacob a baseball."

"I don't know much about the game," said Samuel. "But I suppose I need to learn. Maybe Jacob will want to play. Perhaps you can explain the game to me."

"I'd be glad to. You need to come to Chicago to see a game. Maybe on a day when 'Three Finger' Brown is pitching. There is talk of building a new stadium on the North side where Clark, Addison, Waveland and Sheffield come together—they plan to call it Weeghman Park."

"Can you stay for dinner tonight?" asked Helen. "We are having a noodle kugel and chicken breast. It's one of our own chickens. We're starting to experiment with poultry. The chickens are noisy and messy but Samuel loves eating the eggs and people tell me everything they cook is better when using your own *schmaltz*. I've never had my own chicken fat to use. I'll have you know I'm the best cook in South Haven. Ask anyone."

Saul stayed for dinner. It was Friday night so Helen pulled out her candlesticks in preparation for reciting the Sabbath blessing.

"Don't you think it is one of our wonderful religious traditions that the *mitzvah* of lighting the candles belongs to women? After all, women are the backbone of a Jewish home." said Saul.

"I do," said Helen. "Let's hurry. Sunset will come soon."

She recited the Sabbath prayer and then closed her eyes for a moment. "My mother taught me to pray after lighting the candles for good health and for children to study the Torah and illuminate the world with its teachings."

"That was beautiful," said Saul. "The light is stirring."

"Though beautiful, we mustn't confuse the emitted light from our candles with Ohr Ein Sof—the infinite or divine light," said Samuel. "Do you study Kabbalah, Saul?"

"No. I never have but I think my grandfather did."

"Well, in Kabbalah, Rabbi Isaac Luria attempts to explain creation," said Samuel. "Somehow, for The Infinite One to create and coexist with a finite world It needed to first withdraw Its Infinite Light. Tzimtzum is the word used in the Kabbalah for God's withdrawing from a point of infinite power and density, the Vacated Space, but then, afterwards He returned a ray of that light back into this space. That returning light went through many reductions and concealments to hide Divinity, but even so, it was still powerful enough to have created everything that we see around us in our physical world today."

"It must have made a big bang," said Saul. "As I travel around these parts, I often see the sun rising or falling into Lake Michigan. The light warms me and fills me up. But I suppose I'm talking about physical light. This ray of unveiled light that God sent, Ohr Ein Sof, it sounds like you are saying God sent the light into a hole, Chalal, inside himself? I've never heard this before."

"Studying the Kabbalah was part of my education as a boy in Russia before coming here. I still study it when I'm not farming." Helen could see how happy Samuel was to be talking about the subject he held most dear. "Studying the Torah, the Prophets, and the Writings make me a Jew. I love to read the arguments of the Talmud.

But the Zohar, and the Kabbalah's attempt to look into the essence of God, is what I often come back to."

"Helen, can I start on the kugel?" asked Saul. "It looks delicious."

"Not just yet." Helen pointed to two loaves of challah on the table. "First we must break the Lechem Mishna, the twin loaves, and make Kiddush to bless the wine. Then we can eat. I think the 'rabbi' is done with his sermon. Am I correct, Samuel?" She laughed and winked at her husband.

__Our farmwork is all-consuming but it must come second to our faith and worship. (From the translated diary of Helen Glickman Goldman)__

SPRING 2017—
SOUTH HAVEN

It was spring and daylight saving time had recently started, giving Rachel, and everyone she knew, a lift of sorts. It was Sunday evening, a school night in their household, and the kids were upstairs. They had made a fuss about going and she hoped they were doing their homework. Hannah attended public school and the workload was light, but Andrew was attending a prep school where the teachers probably felt obligated to give three hours of homework every night to justify the tuition of nearly twenty-thousand dollars a year.

"The Kids" were how Rachel thought about them these days, in some sort of "collective" manner. But when they were babies, she and Bill had marveled at each of their unique qualities, often commenting on how their temperaments were so distinct—Hannah cautious and Andrew never meeting a stranger. They could hardly contain their love for them.

As the first-born, Andrew's early life was completely documented both in word and pictures. Bill was the writer—filling out those silly milestone books and journaling on every birthday the answers to a series of questions: foods they liked, best friend, book they wished read to them at bedtime, and their favorite stuffed animal. Though he tried to keep it up when Hannah was born, he had failed miserably. A second baby sucks up time out of all proportion to a simple doubling of effort. It seemed to Rachel that if the effort of looking after one baby was x, the formula for the second baby was x^2.

She remembered Bill saying one evening when Hannah was about four years old, "I know one day Hannah is going to talk about what lousy parents we were in the therapy she will likely need."

"Get over it, Bill," Rachel said for the umpteenth time. She hoped he was wrong but if she were honest, she did feel guilty as well. The documentation of her own early years had paled in comparison to her two older siblings. When taking inventory of her childhood to ascertain what she would choose to do differently, this was definitely on her wish list.

But she'd come to recognize it was too harsh to judge a parent's efforts as failure—the important thing was to do your best. Perhaps she should go as far to forgive her own mother and father for the angst she felt about her religion. But how could skipping Sunday school, never lighting the candles, or having a fifteen-foot Christmas tree be passed off as a parent's best effort—and to boot, no love or support after she was shown those Holocaust films!

Rachel was the photographer. It started with a current framed photo of each child on the living room mantle and a laminated copy for each parent's wallet. But now, both children had their own Facebook page where their every move could be chronicled and followed. Every now and then, while searching for something she had lost, Rachel stumbled across an old photo of a picture-perfect moment in their lives, like the time the four of them were sitting on a log near Maroon Bells in Aspen during a Walsh family picnic. It was a clear July afternoon and the entire family collected sticks for a fire Bill's dad planned to build to fry chicken. The Bells' rugged peaks were in the background and the kids had on matching Detroit Tiger sweatshirts and huge smiles—the smiles might have been even bigger if the picture was taken after lunch. Bill's father had exceeded himself. It was off the charts. The family called Bill's father "Big Daddy" because of his huge hands and bigger than life personality. And was he ever in his element that day frying chicken outdoors under the Aspen mountains, with his entire family settled in around him. Before they ate, Big Daddy said his usual grace and concluded it with a big grin and "It's great to be alive."

As they grew older, Rachel wondered if she started to think of the kids as a unit because of the financial responsibility to provide for them. This burden to make money was resulting in her spending an awful lot of hours at the office. But on more careful consideration, Rachel never really spent time worrying about providing for her family financially. She was really good at what she did, leading to her practice having grown past capacity and, in pediatrics, it was all about volume. No, what she worried about, and why she saw them as a unit these days, was related more to "the job" of guiding and watching over their emotional development and her desire to provide them with the best parenting possible, whatever that was.

From her experience in the office, this was a tricky proposition. On a daily basis, she was in the trenches trying to help families in distress. Yesterday, during Saturday office hours, a mother said her 18-month-old baby "doesn't like to sleep in his crib. I have to rock him until he falls asleep and then ever so gently put him back in the crib. Sometimes he wakes back up in the middle of the night and I have to do this all over again."

"How do you know he doesn't like his crib?" Rachel asked. "Did he send you a letter, an email, or just text you?"

"Huh?" It took the mother a moment to realize that Dr. Walsh was just trying to make light of the situation. Rachel had hastened to share some ideas on how to best fix the situation.

Sometimes the problem was simply an out of control toddler throwing too many tantrums.

"Oh, you have chosen to let the inmates run the asylum," Rachel might say to a parent, with a grin and a quick wink of her eye.

"Yes. I suppose so." This mother caught Dr. Walsh's sense of humor and Rachel was encouraged to help her more.

"Did you take any psychology classes in school and study B. F. Skinner? My Psychology 101 course at Brown was fun, especially the labs. Each of us was given a lab rat in a Skinner box. When the rat pushed the bar, a light went on and he got a Rice Krispies to eat. If we rewarded him on a variable schedule—three times, eight times, once, etc, the rat would continue to push the bar the entire hour in order to get his treat. In my experience, parents without thinking or recognizing it, give in to their child's tantrums from time to time and unintentionally reinforce the very behavior they're complaining about. Variable reinforcement is very powerful. You're not the problem here, but you are the solution," she said. Her urge to reassure was sincere but in fact, this was code for "the parents are the problem." If they couldn't begin setting limits while their children were young, all hell broke loose when they were in their teens.

Little people, little problems; big people, big problems. In Rachel's experience, this was true. The problems she was called upon to address in adolescents and young adults were more serious. There were the routine conversations about decision making: automobile safety, the use of licit and illicit drugs, and when to become sexually active. But what she really found challenging were the parents who, without acknowledging it, enabled their child's poor behavior or stepped back, allowing for the vacuum to be filled by the most permissive parents in the community who set the tone and limits for all the kids.

Rachel was determined to do better in that arena now that her kids were in their tweens. She recalled a conversation she and Bill had recently on one of their date nights.

"We need to set limits especially when it is an issue of safety. Let's observe each other, and helpfully call it out, when either of us is enabling them," said Rachel, pausing to make sure she had Bill's attention. "And striving to become our child's best friend is definitely a no-no."

"I'm down with all of that," said Bill. This line, his line, was part of an unwritten script they were each acting out. He knew this and he knew not to miss his cue.

"Yet, we must try not to be controlling. When a parent controls more than fifty percent of a particular decision a kid needs to make, the result is on them. And it's not a great way for Andrew or Hannah to learn anything and grow up. Kids need a chance to make some mistakes along the way."

"Well, if adolescents need to learn by making mistakes, I must be a fucking genius," said Bill. "I was in and out of trouble all the time growing up."

As she sat on the sofa, waiting for Bill so that they could veg in front of the television, Rachel's mind continued to wander—it settled on trust. If she couldn't trust her kids, Rachel would be miserable every time Hannah or Andrew were out in the world facing complex decisions alone. It wasn't all that different from the trust she and Bill had for each other in their marriage or she'd come to expect from her partners at work. It worked best when it was defined, so that living up to each other's expectations became second nature.

Andrew was now almost 15. He was increasingly private, or was it, withdrawn? He had grown quieter than ever at dinner. When he was a little boy, she would try at times to leave the office early to pick him up from school. He would be a chatterbox, anxious to spill every detail of his day while they drove home. But if she didn't catch him in those first fifteen minutes after school, she got very little information later. Now, Andrew often had after-school sports and Rachel usually was not out of the office before six o'clock. She wondered if that explained why she knew so little about his life at present. She tried to respect his space and wanted to attribute his silence to normal puberty, but she worried, nonetheless.

If only Andrew would occasionally throw her a bone, as she often counseled her teenage patients to do when in conflict with their own parents and give her a little information and insight into who he was becoming. His grades were good, and he never missed school which she knew to be a common marker of some type of dysfunction in a child's life. Maybe it was a girl problem? She needed to carve out some time alone with him. Maybe she should take him to the Phoenix Street Café this Saturday for breakfast.

Hannah was almost 13. She had started to run with Bill in the morning and proclaimed to being hooked on it like her father. Her grades were even better than Andrew's, perhaps too good. She seemed to have inherited her mother's perfectionistic traits. Rachel recalled a Saturday afternoon when Hannah was just five. She was outside with a basketball trying to make a shot on the ten-foot basket. Two hours later, Hannah called her mother outside to watch her make one. My goodness, the girl had perseverance.

Rachel knew Bill enjoyed running with Hannah but she wasn't showing any signs of puberty. The average mother might not have the medical background to understand the effect of energy drain on the pituitary gland, but Rachel did, knowing it prolonged the prepubertal state and could delay menstruation. She needed to talk to Bill about her concern and ask him to change their running dates to an every-other-morning thing.

It was almost time for Homeland to come on. It was one of the few shows Rachel and Bill both liked to watch. Rachel knew Bill loved all the hospital dramas, but she hated them in general and would usually leave the room for him to watch alone. The only one of this genre she enjoyed was the show House, where Dr. House's acerbic manner, and his core belief that all patients lie, was something she could relate to. She had mourned briefly when it went off the air, something Dr. House, if she'd been one of his resident's, would have made fun of her for feeling. He would have had a field day with her if he knew how much she had similarly grieved when discovering she could no longer buy Product 19 at the grocery store.

Bill walked into the den with his usual bowl of ice cream. It amused her that Bill used this little, tiny spoon when eating it—allowing his treat to last a minute or two longer and pretend he wasn't about to consume a minimum of five hundred calories.

"What flavor is it tonight?" she asked.

"Drumstick," he answered. The show started about twenty minutes ago but they had it on demand. It was definitely relaxing at the end of a long weekend to sit in front of the television with Bill, as even for her, tomorrow could be considered a school day.

1920—SOUTH HAVEN

The National Federation of Temple Sisterhoods (NFTS) first met in 1913 with a mission of advocacy—working for social action and social change in America and around the world. In addition, they championed a more prominent role for women in Jewish life. The organization morphed into Women of Reform Judaism (WRJ) in 1993.

Helen and Samuel's farm thrived and their lives were full. She loved motherhood and saw each of her kids in distinctly different ways.

Jacob was industrious, always busy with his schoolwork and chores around the farm. He was a serious child for an eleven-year-old and could be trusted to clean out the chicken coops, collect the eggs, and give the chickens whatever the latest medicines his parents read about to keep them healthy.

Like most eight-year-olds, Isaac found joy in everything he did. Though he lacked the seriousness of his older brother, it was clear he was bright and everything came easily to him. He'd started to play baseball and loved the glove Mr. Bernstein brought him from Chicago as a gift on his last birthday.

The youngest, called Lottie by everyone though her name was Charlotte, possessed a temperament that was neither serious like Jacob's or joyful like Isaac's. Lottie was busy. She was into everything, always trying to figure out how things worked. One day, Helen found her on the floor with pieces of Samuel's pocket watch scattered about. Recovering from her astonishment, Helen recalled Samuel, several months prior, trying to open the watch himself. He needed to repair it, but he'd been unable to figure out how to get started. But their Lottie, only three, had dismantled it all by herself. It gave Helen pause and she wondered how her little girl would grow up.

Helen admitted to herself that she saw Lottie differently than her two boys. She wondered if it was her busyness that worried her or if she was overprotective because Lottie was a girl. However, deep down Helen knew her worry dated back to her pregnancy and the arrival one Sunday morning of the New York Times. The headline story was about the Spanish Influenza. She had subscribed to the Times since the day Saul Bernstein brought her the newspaper story about Jewish farmers. It usually arrived a day or two late, but she wanted to stay informed. News, even if a few days old, was still news to Helen.

The edition from September 22, 1918 had a headline: SPANISH INFLUENZA MUCH LIKE GRIPPE. Underneath the headline, the U.S. Surgeon General declared that if "properly treated, the malady can be overcome without much difficulty." But Helen feared catching "the flu" before her labor began and that falling ill would injure her baby. Her fears were unfounded and Lottie arrived in November, but Helen continued to harbor a fear that Lottie might die at any moment. She knew she was being irrational, and it would do the poor child no good to be always hovering over her, so she vowed on Lottie's third birthday to overcome her fear. It wasn't going to help Lottie become strong and Helen believed her job as a mother was to raise a child, especially a girl, to have healthy amounts of self-esteem and inner-strength. This was how she was raised and, from what she could see in this new country of hers, women were pushing to have all the opportunities of men. Helen was determined for Lottie to become that kind of woman.

They poured their profits into the farm, their house, and a savings account for college at seven percent interest. They had a party-line phone and plans to add running water and electricity to the main house. For several years now, friends, and friends of friends in Chicago, scheduled summer holidays in the countryside at the Goldman farm. And Mr. Bernstein, still working with the JAS, sent people as well, wishing to show potential JAS contributors an example of a how their money was helping Jewish farmers succeed.

"I think we should take in boarders over the summer," Helen said to Samuel one night at dinner.

"Well, we already do," he answered.

"That's not what I mean. I haven't told you or shown you but for several years people have been leaving cash on the dressers in envelopes when they leave. They also leave notes raving about my cooking. I think it could be a great business. The growing season is short for our fruit, and though I think our poultry business can still grow, we need to be saving more for college now that we have three kids."

"I doubt Charlotte will go to college," said Samuel. "Girls don't go. And look how busy she is. I don't think she'll be capable of sitting still long enough to learn to read and write."

"I can't believe you just said that, Sam!" said Helen, clenching her fists at her side. "I suppose you think that you should have gone to college but not me?"

"Now wait a minute," said Sam.

"No. You wait a minute. Women are playing bigger and bigger roles in our adopted country. You were against me becoming a member of the Jewish League for Woman's Suffrage until I told you it wasn't just about political rights for women, but about women's religious rights as well. And those baseball games you have started to follow—there was a game where the Cubs you hate so much, beat the Giants at the Polo Grounds on 'Be A Suffrage Fan' day. Events like that one are pushing the issue to the forefront and women will soon have the right to vote. It was in the paper this morning—the 19th Amendment to the United States Constitution will be ratified this week."

Samuel tried to interrupt her but she wasn't going to be stopped.

"Remember back in 1913, I took Isaac with me to Cincinnati

while still breast feeding. We started the National Federation of Temple Sisterhoods and helped with relief efforts during the war. The Federation was instrumental in assisting German rabbinical students in leaving Germany for study in America. The NFTS is dedicated to social change, and when the Federation calls, I will go. But please, Samuel, don't worry, I'll always come back. Now, do you still want to talk about Lottie not going to college and whether our daughter will have an equal opportunity to our sons and any of the other boys around here?"

"OK, you've been heard. Charlotte will go to college just like her brothers. I want her to be well-educated but also strong like you are, Helen. I'm sorry. Can we get back to this business idea of yours?"

Helen reached out to take her husband's hand, held it a little longer than necessary, and allowed a warm smile to build and light up her face.

"Well, the auto industry is altering the way people live. Those Model T cars Dad is building are everywhere. People want to travel. Gas is cheap and more filling stations are popping up. More and more Jewish people are living in the big cities not too far away like Detroit, Chicago, St. Louis, and Cincinnati. They're being turned away by many of the resorts up here because they are Jewish. I've seen signs out in front of several farms that are taking in vacationers. They say "No Jews or Dogs—Gentiles Only." I think we ought to move our efforts from farming to the resort industry."

Helen had been thinking a lot about this. She was correct when saying they should get into poultry. Her relationship with Saul Bernstein continued to open up opportunities. His days as a paperboy in Chicago made him a great business partner when it came to setting up an egg delivery route there. She and Samuel were saving more money than they ever thought they would. They'd converted one of their barns into twenty rooms for guests, but there was a piece of property available at the end of Lakeshore Drive with access to the North Beach. She thought it would be a perfect location to build a large-scale hotel. Other farmers were experiencing the same phenomenon of guests wanting to come to South Haven and

Helen suspected they were considering starting this type of project themselves. If they could just get ahead of the competition, she thought, they'd have found a gold mine.

"Helen, you're what Americans call an entrepreneur. Let's buy the property and build a hotel. But first—if we want to be successful, the food we serve must be the best and it must be Kosher. And second— no one can stay overnight on the Sabbath except for a family guest or good friend. I'm not interested in sharing our Sabbath meal, our Sabbath candles, or our day of rest. It must remain a day to remember and observe."

"I agree." Helen said as she bent down to pull her candlesticks out of the hutch. "Let's just do it. Will you help me set the table? It's almost sundown and we need to light the candles."

__I am certain I chose the right man to marry. He is supportive of my rights, a woman's right to be treated equally. (From the translated diary of Helen Glickman Goldman)__

SPRING 2017—
SOUTH HAVEN

Rachel had an agenda for breakfast this morning with her son, so she chose to ignore his poor manners when Andrew didn't say hello or make eye contact with the hostess who sat them at the Phoenix Street Cafe.

It was Saturday morning and the week had flown by. All Rachel's weeks seemed to fly by. She was reminded of her mother's warning "the kids will grow up so fast. Enjoy it." Rachel used to think of this as one of those typical Jewish mother, schmaltzy proclamations, but she was coming to acknowledge the truth of it.

Before going to bed last night, she reminded Andrew he needed to be up by eight o'clock. Saturdays at the Phoenix Street Café were usually packed and they might have to wait awfully long for a table if they arrived at the restaurant any later than eight-thirty. She loved going out to breakfast. During the week, when her hospital rounds went smoothly enough, she might have an extra forty-five minutes or so before her first scheduled appointment—just enough time to enjoy breakfast alone and get her act together before facing a day of relentless parents with concerns about their children. But this morning, it was breakfast with her son. Though she had ulterior motives, she was also looking forward to simply being alone with him.

As the waitress came over to pour Rachel a cup of coffee and take their orders, she said, "I see that you're not eating alone this morning, Dr. Walsh. Isn't he a little young for you?"

"That's funny, Rhonda. This is my son, Andrew," answered Rachel.

Again, Andrew hardly looked up. When he was younger, a similarly poor social effort wouldn't go without some coaching on the spot about respectful etiquette. But though Rachel desperately wanted to give him some feedback, she chose again to let it slide today. She didn't wish to use up her good will with Andrew over Rhonda's feelings. This morning was too important, she needed to find out if something was bothering him.

"How are things going at school?" Rachel asked.

"OMG. This is going to be an inquisition." Rachel was shocked by the vehemence of Andrew's reaction. "I thought you just wanted someone to split the blueberry waffles with. I should have suspected it. A breakfast invitation for just the two of us seemed pretty random."

"I'm sorry," Rachel said. "You just don't seem yourself lately."

"I'm fine, Mom, really."

Rachel ordered the blueberry pancakes but Andrew refused to split anything. He wanted his own food. He was in a growth spurt and acted like food insecurity had come to South Haven. He wolfed down a large glass of OJ, a three-egg cheese omelet, fried potatoes, and two pieces of sourdough toast with jelly.

"Do you have a girlfriend? Or is it a matter of not having a girlfriend?" Rachel inquired.

"Look Mom, I'm good. I've got a great squad. Getting tight with a girl in my class just isn't going to happen right now. Who needs the drama!"

"I never hear you talk about Billy anymore," said Rachel.

"He's a tool. Besides, all he ever wants to do is hang with Barbara Miller. She's OK but TBH, she can be too thirsty for my taste."

"You've lost me. You're speaking in tongues. Maybe you could give me a translation of what you just said?"

Even though Rachel was a pediatrician, she never could keep up with all the current teenage slang. She knew Andrew was simply playing good defense by going on the offensive. She wasn't born yesterday. She wondered how the great Michigan football coach, Bo Schembechler, would attack? Probably just run it up the middle.

As Andrew continued to pick at his plate, Rachel started in again. "OK. I give. I'm just worried something is wrong. You've been so quiet lately. Yes, breakfast was an excuse to get you alone. I frequently advise parents to try it, but it's clearly bad parenting advice. I remember being on call once in my early years of practice when a mother called about a big goose egg on her daughter's forehead after a fall. I told her to put ice on it. She laughed and asked if I had any children myself. I got her point. I became a better doctor after you kids were born."

"Cute story, Mom. You know I get tired of your office stories, don't you? The only thing worrying me lately is when I hear Hannah on the phone with that bitch Maryanne. I think Hannah is being bullied. I told her to cut the cord. The girl is sus."

"Thanks. But that isn't your problem to solve. It's mine and your father's. We'll take care of it and your sister doesn't need to know you told me. But just to make sure this breakfast isn't a total waste, remember, you can come to me anytime with a problem."

"I know that. But no cap in the future. You can be chill when you try."

Rachel dropped Andrew off at home. She was exasperated. Breakfast had been a shit show. She was somewhat satisfied that Andrew had fenced well with a parry for each of her lunges. But Rachel needed more time than she had this moment to put the whole spectacle into proper perspective. Rachel previously told Bill that after breakfast she intended to go to the office for an hour or two to complete some of her notes. The practice had switched over to a new electronic medical record (EMR) system and it was clunky just like the last one. The training classes required two four-hour sessions. She would have rather gone to the dentist, her OB-GYN, and the electrologist all in one day.

But actually, she wasn't going to the office at all. She was going to the synagogue. Rabbi Weinstein suggested she give the Saturday morning services a try. There was no Bar Mitzvah scheduled this week so the crowd would be small and it was likely she wouldn't see anyone she knew very well.

She sat uncomfortably off to the side. The Torah portion was about the biblical character Pinchas. The rabbi indicated that Pinchas was a controversial figure in the Torah portion for spearing to death an Israelite man and a Midianite woman who were lovers. But according to the book of Joshua, Pinchas served as a peacemaker as well. The Israelite tribes of Reuben and Gad were living outside the Israel borders and were rumored to be building alters to another god. Pinchas was sent to find out what was going on. After arriving, he didn't beat around the bush but asked the tribes directly about the rumor. They informed him they weren't doing so. An altar was being built, but to the God of Israel.

The rabbi's spin on this biblical story was to be direct in all our interpersonal relationships, it was the best way to avoid conflict arising from simple misunderstandings. Rachel believed her motive this morning with Andrew was well-intentioned but, by being deceitful, she put him on the defensive. She understood her mistake, in retrospect, very clearly. Her tactics had only served to erode the very trust she and Bill were working so hard to develop with Andrew.

Often, both in and out of the office, Rachel was asked whether it was more difficult now than in the past to raise teenagers. Many of her colleagues might respond yes reflexively, similar to her tapping on a child's knee and having their leg kick out. But when the doctor checks your knee reflexes, it's just an examination of the connection between the peripheral nerves and the spinal cord. The brain is not involved at all.

When Rachel was asked this question, her brain told her the most important aspect in raising teens hadn't changed over generations despite the particular challenges of the times. Trust was timeless. It was always about parents building trust and defining what trust would look like in their home with their own children. Once made clear, it could be nurtured, allowing a family to tackle specific issues, like the ones she referred to generically in her pediatric office as sex, drugs, and rock 'n' roll.

Rachel squirmed in her seat. She needed to go to temple and hear about some obscure controversial Jew, Pinchas, to understand what Andrew had already taught her this morning at breakfast, though he didn't know it. To date, in her adult life, she had given religion short shrift. The entire morning left her wondering if there was something to be gained by attending services at the temple more regularly. Could opening herself up to faith bring answers on how to live her life more fully, to deal with her existential fear of annihilation, and to soothe her mind about her fixed time, and the fixed time of everyone she loved here on earth?

1924—SOUTH HAVEN

The word "Semitic" refers to a family of languages historically spoken in the Middle East. Anti-Semitism would refer to all these descendants. The term, however, in modern times, is primarily associated with prejudice against the Jews. For the purpose of accuracy, and to avoid confusion, many scholars prefer the word not be hyphenated or the S capitalized—antisemitism.

Samuel now performed what was left of the farm work, while Helen managed the books, ran their expanding Goldman's Kosher Resort business, and raised their three children. All this multi-tasking and rushing left Helen little time for herself.

But time wasn't her only problem—other important issues conspired to challenge Helen. One was gender. When she and Samuel married, they promised to work together toward a shared vision of their future. It was only in the synagogue where Samuel insisted on, and Helen accepted, the traditionally diminished role for women. He was supportive of her being an equal in matters of political, civil, economic, and social life, but society, as a whole, was not. Women were starting to band together and fight for the same opportunities as men in America, but change was coming too slowly for Helen who desired to see more than incremental movement. She became a suffragist and took on a leadership position in the NFTS to fight for Lottie's future and the future of all young women.

A second issue facing Helen was competition in the developing resort industry in South Haven. Though she was raised to be cooperative and to reach out to help others, the resort industry could be cutthroat at times. The Goldmans' reputation for success was built on hard work and an intuition about where the business was going. Helen enjoyed trying to stay a step ahead, but that also took its own toll. Guests always wanted another service to be added and, though they were doing well and saving money for the kids' college education, every expansion or improvement was associated with loans needing to be paid off.

However, perhaps the most annoying problem of all for Helen was the negative reaction some people harbored towards Jews. This shouldn't have been a surprise to her, even in America—it was a part of Jewish history. When living as a minority in any country, it could be expected. Antisemitism was everywhere. It wasn't just the "No Jews Allowed" signs at other resorts. It was the way she was treated when shopping in town or negotiating for supplies for the resort. Sometimes you could do business with another Jew, but often you could not, and these encounters were unpredictable at best.

She hated when her kids weren't invited to a classmate's birthday party or prohibited from joining a ball team. But the worst was when they were directly affected by such feelings. Jack's teacher called their home one day to give Helen a heads up on an "incident" that occurred on the playground with a known bully.

"What happened at school today?" asked Helen when Jack came in the door later that day.

"Jimmy called Mark a kike. He turned towards me, and before he called me one, I blurted out that I wasn't Jewish. I shouldn't have done that, but I was scared."

"Being Jewish is something to be proud of, not hide. I'm glad you told me about it. You know better now."

Helen generally felt safe in America and, though she knew such unpleasant moments would weigh on her, she vowed to never allow such thoughts to cause her to waver about her faith—it was central in all respects to how she wished her family to live.

Yes, her life was consuming—a feminist before her time, an entrepreneur, and a woman of Jewish faith in a country of religious freedom. However, it was still a country populated by many lacking in experience with those of different backgrounds leading to bias and, at times, outright antisemitism.

＊　＊　＊

Helen, fanning herself for comfort in July heat, was behind the check-in desk on Saturday night. Since the clientele were Jewish themselves, they came to expect that their rooms wouldn't be ready until after sundown. Most arrived from nearby Chicago and other large cities in the Midwest. Many booked rooms for the same week on the calendar, year after year, giving the resort an almost summer camp-like feeling.

"Hi, Sophie." Helen greeted Mrs. Shapiro from Cincinnati. "You look terrific. I hope you and your family have enjoyed a good year."

"We have, Helen. But when we pull onto Highway 31, my mood lifts and all the troubles in my life disappear. I'll bet you don't have a care in the world, living up here full-time."

"Sophie, South Haven is no different from Cincinnati. Tomorrow night, I'll sit around the bingo table with you and we can complain a little about our lives. But I'm so glad you feel that way about coming here. I hope we have a good weather week for you and your family."

"This is my sister-in-law, Betty," said Sophie. "I finally talked her into her joining us this year. She's got four kids and another child to raise in my brother, Harry."

"It's nice to meet you, Betty," said Helen.

"I've heard so much about South Haven and the Goldmans' resort. Can you tell me a little about what to expect this week?" asked Betty.

"First of all, we still work the farm, but it also serves as a small amusement park for you city dwellers wanting to have a taste of rural farm life. During the day, kids can ride the train—which means my son Jacob pulls them along behind a small tractor. In the evenings, adults come out and he does the same for them, but in hayride fashion with drinks and appetizers."

Prohibition meant no booze was served during the adult hayrides but she didn't mind looking the other way when some customers brought their own aboard.

"That sounds like fun."

"It is. While out at the farm, you can also pick fruit. We give each of you a small bucket. Most families try to do this on Monday so they can eat what they pick the rest of the week. The forecast is for warm weather. We purchased a Model T school bus this year to transport our guests to sunbathe and swim on the South Beach or you can walk down the wooden stairs right here at the resort to get to the North Beach. You won't believe the commotion down there with everyone in their bloomers wading into Lake Michigan."

"My husband Harry wanted me to ask about the fishing nearby," said Betty.

Helen told her about the Black River. It was a slow-moving channel, black because tannins leached into the water from large amounts of decaying weeds.

"We can run you over to the Black River. It's less than a mile away. Most fish for Largemouth bass. But don't worry about the color of the river, you can eat the fish. Bring them over to the kitchen when you return and we'll help you clean them and cook them however you desire for dinner the same night."

"Can I dump the kids somewhere while I fish?" asked Bill who had come up behind his wife with some of their luggage.

"Don't say it that way," said Sophie. "What's Helen going to think of us?"

"Dumping the kids off is part of the reason why you've come. I've hired counselors to plan and supervise games and crafts for the children who accompany their parents to our resort," Helen said.

"We're going to love it here. What took you so long to listen to your sister about this place anyway?" Betty asked her husband. "Typical man, don't you think?"

The weather, the lake, and the farm all attracted customers but the food was the sustaining draw. The Goldmans' resort was noted for plentiful quantities of high calorie kosher food where adding schmaltz, whether from chicken or geese, was the "secret sauce." And Helen's enlarging kitchen staff was careful to follow the strict dietary laws of the Talmud.

Guests could often be seen loitering around the kitchen taking in the aromas of baking breads and guessing what would be served at dinner: Bagels with cream cheese, blintzes, brisket, Gefilte fish, knish, latke, pastrami, Matzah ball soup, kugel, and Challah. Those lucky enough while angling to catch a fish or two had it prepared to their liking. The dining room held around one hundred people and sounded like a buzz saw while the guests enjoyed their meals, conversations, and on most nights, a solo jazz pianist.

But the dish that garnered the most attention was Helen's chopped liver. Visitors begged for the recipe. It was her mother's, but she wouldn't give it out. She planned to share it with Lottie one day when Helen was no longer able to do the work to make it.

She started by seasoning the chicken liver with Kosher salt. Next, she grilled them on high heat, turning them frequently, before mincing and mixing them with eggs. Then, she would add sweet onions to the homemade schmaltz before cooking the combination in a skillet until golden brown. After mixing these two items, Helen added extra schmaltz, a tablespoon at a time until the chopped liver was perfectly spreadable. Samuel built her a large container to hold blocks of ice and she'd leave the mixture there for five days before taking it out overnight to rest and be served. It was always a side dish. Helen couldn't remember where she first heard the saying, "What am I, chopped liver?" but it never failed to make her laugh when someone said it.

Someday, sharing her recipes with Lottie would be a pleasure. For Helen, being a Jew was part religious dogma and part culture. She would pass down her faith to Lottie through her recipes, her commitment to social activism, and her candlesticks.

Goldmans' Resort brought in guest speakers from time to time to give talks after dinner. Though controversial, Emma Goldman, no relation, came one evening to discuss birth control with the female guests. Goldman, a Jewish emigrant from Russia, went on to fame as a political anarchist and champion of social causes. Helen had become interested in these issues after reading the Weekly Woman's Page of the Jewish Daily Forward, the largest Yiddish newspaper in the world at the time. Always looking for another cause to get behind, Helen joined the American Birth Control League and had pamphlets about fighting the "Comstock" anti-obscenity laws available at the resort. After her talk one evening, Emma Goldman sat down to have coffee with the female guests.

"You have quite the resort owner here in Helen Goldman," she said. "We share a last name but, more importantly, we share a desire for more female involvement in our country. Before my little speech this evening, Helen mentioned joining The National Council of Jewish Women (NCJW). They're discussing opening birth control clinics under the name of the Mother's Health Bureaus. Many of you are from big cities like Chicago, Detroit, and St. Louis. Try getting involved. We need people to consider having only the children they can afford to raise. I've seen such terrible poverty created by large family size. Birth control information is critical for Jewish women and, for that matter, all women."

Helen looked at the rapt faces of the women around the table. "I told Samuel, in 1917, we were done having children after my little Lottie. He respects me in our business and in our personal life. Your husbands will likely listen if you give them the chance. It is only in the synagogue that we must take a back seat to the men."

"My husband hated to wear a condom," Mrs. Rubenstein said. She blushed and bit her lip. It gave her the courage to continue. "But there are new latex condoms out. He doesn't mind wearing them at all."

Not all the speakers spoke of such intimate matters. Some simply came to discuss cooking, sewing, or books in circulation. Most of the casual conversation among the women focused on their children and their fierce determination to provide them the education they'd need to ensure success in America. After dinner, while the women attended lectures, the men went outside to smoke cigars, waiting for the big band to set up and the dancing to begin under the Pavilion.

Spending a week at the Goldmans' delivered a dependable, carefree experience families could look forward to during the cold winter months. But for Helen and Samuel, their resort was a business, and like every other first-generation American family, it was a means to an end with its share of success, failure, and stress. Helen had steered them correctly from farming to resorts. It was a decision that would become their family's launching pad to financial security and an American life—a life aligned with their core values to give their children every educational opportunity possible, to freely practice their faith, and to help others in need.

Things were good for the Goldmans and the other Jewish-owned resorts in South Haven. They were developing a reputation rivaling those on the East coast and, by the end of the decade, more than sixty Jewish-owned resorts were in existence leading to its new nickname—"The Catskills of the Midwest."

I suppose if we keep to ourselves, and our own kind, we will be safe here in America and have a profitable business to rely on. (From the translated diary of Helen Glickman Goldman)

SUMMER 2017—
SOUTH HAVEN

Lecha Dodi.
> *Come, lover, to welcome the bride*
> *The face of Shabbat we will receive*
> *"Keep" and "remember" in one saying*
> *We were caused to listen by the Unified God*
> *Adonai is One, and His Name is One*
> *To His name, and to glory and to praise!*

Rachel sat patiently in a booth waiting for her sister at Captain Nemo's. It was a typical burger and fish joint that one could find by the hundreds up and down the eastern coast of Lake Michigan. Michelle didn't eat meat, but fish and chips would be fine with her.

Rachel was glad to be off today. She was still trying to process a patient encounter from the day before. She hated it when something from the office lingered in her mind. Most of her colleagues privately shared similar feelings, especially when they worried that a child could suffer injury because of their professional failures. However, that had not been the case yesterday.

A twelve-year-old boy had come into the office with torticollis, a spasm of the neck muscles that often came from sleeping in an awkward position or with sudden movement of a child's neck on the ball field. When she entered the exam room, he was sitting on the table with tears in his eyes and his head off to the left side. The muscle on the right side of his neck was tight as a rope—the sternocleidomastoid muscle runs on the side of the neck from the collar bone to the bony process behind his ear, the mastoid bone. Rachel, ever the teacher, started to explain how in college she had majored in Evolutionary Biology and learned how the mastoid bone was not prominent in apes, but fossil evidence revealed enlargement of this bony process on the skull as apes evolved into humans. A human's upright posture, as they moved out of trees, required their heads to sit directly atop the spine. "The human head can fall backwards and this muscle, attached to the mastoid bone, can pull the head forward again," she had said.

The mother of the young boy walked out, screaming that they were Fundamentalist Christians and didn't appreciate Dr. Walsh trashing their religious beliefs with talk of evolution.

At first, Rachel was furious with the mother. But on reflection, she was more angry with herself. Her available, friendly teaching style, her schtick if you will, had let her down. She didn't mean to trample on a family's religious beliefs, but inadvertently, she had. Though Rachel firmly believed in evolution, she was beginning to understand how much faith meant to some and this mother had it in spades.

Rachel was envious—wouldn't it be nice to have such strong religious beliefs? Or maybe she just needed to keep her mouth shut in the office sometimes and become one of those boring doctors who did the right thing but without trying to "connect" to her patients in some special way all the time.

Rachel's sister was on her way to pick up her girls at summer camp where they had spent the last month. Andrew and Hannah were also away but their camps had another two weeks to go before the session concluded, giving Rachel plenty of extra time today to spend with her sister.

On a recent phone call, Michelle indicated that Amanda, Eileen, and Mary were having a great summer in upper Michigan, and though they missed their friends in Chicago, they welcomed the chance to get away from the intense social scenes at their respective schools. Each of them had navigated, for the most part, well enough, but girls at these ages could be rough on each other at times and her nieces had experienced some of that garbage in the past.

Rachel assumed that Amanda, now sixteen and the oldest, was probably having the most difficulty getting through the adolescence period unscathed. Some might have chalked it up to history repeating itself as Michelle, herself an oldest child, struggled during her adolescent years with marijuana use and poor grades.

But Rachel suspected it was more complicated. Her sister, Michelle, had been pregnant once before Amanda was born and lost the baby at 12 weeks. It was a normal pregnancy until that point and the OB/GYN tried to convince her it was just not meant to be. When Michelle called Rachel crying that afternoon, Rachel, always the doctor first, told her that between "ten and twenty percent of pregnancies result in miscarriage and that it's not your fault in any way." But she did add, with her sisterly persona, how sorry she was for her loss.

Unknown to her sister, Rachel had also suffered a miscarriage before getting pregnant with Andrew and understood the hopes and dreams that exist in a woman's mind for her child's life the moment they learn of conceiving.

The following year found Michelle pregnant again and Rachel couldn't have been happier especially when her sister called about nausea early on and then feeling the baby move around eighteen weeks—the physician's medical term being "quickening." Michelle was so anxious about the pregnancy, normal for someone who had previously experienced a miscarriage, that now sixteen years later, she was still raising Amanda as if she were a fine piece of Steuben glass. Every minor illness or injury was perceived by Michelle as life threatening. She knew better intellectually but she still couldn't relax about her responsibility to keep Amanda alive and healthy. Luckily, when her two sisters came along, Amanda received a little less attention, but less of too much was still too much.

Rachel had seen, and diagnosed, what the pediatric literature called vulnerable child syndrome many times in her career. This diagnosis wasn't on the radar screen of some of her pediatric colleagues. They rarely considered the diagnosis. But it was difficult to make any diagnosis if you were never looking for it. Rachel suspected Amanda was getting therapy. Michelle had called a few months ago, having noticed her daughter had been cutting on her own forearm.

Rachel reassured her by saying, "This isn't a suicidal gesture or attempt but more often just a cry for help. Let your pediatrician know and they'll get her some help."

"Maybe I will," Michelle had responded.

Her sister looked great as she came through the door of what they affectionately called, growing up, "The Captain." Rachel often wondered where her sister got her sense of fashion since it didn't appear to get genetically passed along. She always had a print scarf around her neck, shoes that matched her blouse, and something black—shorts, a skirt, or even a pair of Lululemon pants—on the lower half of her equator. It gave her a slim look. Her jewelry was usually simple but nice: diamond studs, a gold chain necklace, a Rolex watch, and a big diamond ring. Her husband was a law partner at Skadden in Chicago and made the big bucks. Rachel made a mental note of her appearance thinking she could probably pull it off herself.

A stranger in the next booth might have thought them to be twins despite the five years difference in age. Though not a big difference now that they were adults, growing up five years apart was a significant gap. When younger, her sister showed her the ropes in their family's bed and breakfast—how to set the table, where to put out food, and how to make the beds with those hospital corners. But by her sister's fourteenth birthday, it seemed she stopped having time for Rachel. Michelle did her chores about the house quickly and then was off to join her friends downtown to shop although, Rachel now realized, it was simply a day of loitering. She reminded Michelle of this impression during their lunch and Michelle smirked at the thought of South Haven's downtown and how it compared to Chicago's Michigan Avenue.

Rachel wasn't certain if she should ask Michelle about Amanda and her other nieces. You never knew with family how deeply to go into their personal stuff. She laughed at the word itself—FAMILY. Just the word evoked so many conflicted emotions for the average person. Bill used to joke "that you have got to call it something. It's really so bizarre." But he also tried to remind her the world wasn't her office and she needed to be more self-aware before instinctively going into her pediatrician attack mode.

"Remember, it's just lunch with your sister." Bill said as she was headed out the door. "Try not to judge or give her unsolicited advice. Only give her advice if she asks for it."

She knew he was right to remind her. He meant well. Why did she hate it when he was right? And why couldn't she ever acknowledge it? She noticed the bitter smile he made before she turned to go out the door. She'd come to recognize it whenever her actions caused him disappointment. Wouldn't a little "thanks" make him feel better, validated, that she appreciated his advice? She would say it to a friend. Just another reminder—marriage was a marathon, not a simple sprint.

Michelle mostly wanted to talk about their parents. Her mother Joan still ran the bed and breakfast though it was more of a hobby and a chance to have commotion in the house. Her father was recently retired from the real estate business. Over the years, he knew everyone and every property up and down the coast from South Haven to Benton Harbor. He had done well financially, largely because affluent Jews were comfortable with him as their agent and lakefront property in Michigan never saw bad times. But Michelle worried he was bored just playing golf. She had been home now for two days, before getting back on the road to pick the girls up at camp, and thought both parents were failing.

"Mom's memory is off. Have you noticed?" Michelle asked.

"Of course, it is" replied Rachel. "She is getting older. I'm getting older. I have to leave myself post-it notes all the time."

"How often do you drop by to see them?" Michelle leaned back, crossing her arms across her chest.

"Easy for you to ask, three hours away in Chicago," answered Rachel. "Let's not make lunch about this. You know I do my best to check in on them, as does Paul. I know you're just worried about them. I am too. But right this minute, I'm just glad to have you all to myself for lunch. I miss you."

They settled into a safer rhythm—talking about their kids and their marriages. Then Michelle asked Rachel about her sessions with the rabbi.

"It's hard work, but fun in a weird sort of way. The rabbi isn't intimidating. He's kind of a regular old guy—married with three kids that are now out of the house. I know that Catholic priests say they can counsel their parishioners even though they remain celibate, but I like knowing that he has faced some of the same problems I have in my life. I spend a lot of time thinking about our ancestors and how faith must have sustained them—starting from scratch as immigrants and making a go of it in farming and then the resort business. It's an amazing story. I know we face different challenges today but they are no less real. I need some sustenance. Michelle, I'm starting to get serious about the role faith could play in my day-to-day life, but also as I think about death."

"Have you told Bill yet?" Michelle asked.

"No. I may regret it, but first, I want to be certain about what I'm doing. Religion was a big challenge when we decided to get married. We were able to resolve things as it relates to the kids and their religious upbringing, but it confuses him that I don't see the value in belief. It's a fundamental feature of his life. He'll be thrilled to see me taking a hard look at my own religion. I just don't want to tease him with a commitment that I can't see through."

"Would you be willing to join Mom and Dad tonight for Friday night services at the temple?" Michelle asked leaning in to get her sister's attention. Rachel hadn't been to services with her parents in years and she knew it would mean a lot to her parents if they all went together.

"I realize Mom and Dad go to services, but it always seemed to be a social thing—Mom wanting to see what everyone else was wearing. And though we celebrated the Jewish holidays, it paled in comparison to how we celebrated Christmas. Honestly, I hold Mom and Dad somewhat responsible for the conundrum I have about my own lack of faith."

"Look, Sis. You are a big girl now. You can blame them for everything that you don't like about yourself. I catch myself doing that at times. But you have a choice now about faith. You also have a choice to join us or not. Bill and the kids are welcome too, if you want."

Rachel replied, "I'll think about it." She hid certain things, certain feelings even from her sister. She was more than a little upset about her parents' role in her lack of religious upbringing. She was enraged. What were they thinking? As a pediatrician, she knew children needed direction. Her parents did so many things well. She gave them full credit for her self-confidence and appreciated the unconditional love she received while growing up, never lacking for their attention or their time.

So why did they drop the ball when it came to something as important as religion?

❄ ❄ ❄

Walking into the synagogue that evening with her parents and sister was more confusing than she thought it would be. Memories flooded in about her place in the family and her religious education as a child.

The service began with a song: Lecha Dodi. She recognized the words: Keep and remember. Shamor and Zachor. These words were important. Mr. Schwartz, her sixth-grade religious school teacher was fixated on them an entire year. It was why Rachel was taught to light two candles on the Shabbat. One to keep safe and one to remember.

Mr. Schwartz taught the class that God spoke to the Jewish people by giving them the Ten Commandments. Remember the Sabbath Day and make it holy was the way the fourth commandment read in Exodus, the second book of the Torah. But the Ten Commandments were recorded twice in the Torah. In the fifth book, Deuteronomy, Zachor, remember, was replaced by Shamor, keep or safeguard—to keep the Sabbath Day and make it holy. Mr. Schwartz liked to tease the class by saying, "God was speaking out of both sides of his mouth." Mr. Schwartz would just combine the two—remember the Sabbath Day and keep it holy.

Remembering, Zachor, referred to God's covenant with Abraham to be the chosen people and to never forget God's role in their exodus from Egypt. In recent times, this concept of remembering had been extended to the Holocaust education Rachel, and her contemporaries, received. After seeing those grainy black and white movies, "Never Forget" was the message the rabbi had given the group.

But Mr. Schwartz liked to focus on Shamor. To safeguard the Sabbath had more to do with it being a day of rest. God rested on the seventh day as should an observant Jew. No work was to be done. But there was an additional meaning. Jews must safeguard their future against similar threats like the Holocaust occurring again. Be Watchful.

Off to the side of the bima, Rabbi Weinstein stood up next to a woman her mother's age. She thought it may have been Mrs. Schneider but Rachel couldn't see her face very well. They lit two candles and said the blessing over the Sabbath lights. It was the same prayer Rachel said alone most Friday nights. She looked over at her sister and her parents as they mouthed the words as well:

Barukh ata Adonai Eloheinu, Melekh ha'olam, asher kid'shanu b'mitzvotav v'tzivanu l'hadlik ner shel Shabbat.

Suddenly the temple looked different to Rachel. It seemed brighter. The candles were large, but really, they couldn't be giving off that much additional light. Illumination. It wasn't just the light. The Bible talked about light and illumination being spiritual. At least for this brief moment, she was all in.

❋ ❋ ❋

Rachel wondered if her parents or her sister had noticed—if they even knew anything of Shamor and Zachor. It wasn't an accident that she had become a secular Jew. Though she received a religious education, it was rarely reinforced in her home. But hearing the Lecha Dodi tonight, watching them light the Sabbath candles, and thinking about what Mr. Schwartz taught her in class, Rachel was starting to consider what she was missing out on by not choosing to allow faith to play a bigger role in her life.

She couldn't wait to share her thoughts and emotions with Rabbi Weinstein next Wednesday.

__I'd forgotten how much I enjoyed Mr. Schwartz for a teacher. (From the diary of Rachel Levitt Walsh)__

JULY 3, 1933—CHICAGO

In 1917, a letter was written by Foreign Secretary Arthur Balfour to Britain's most famous Jewish citizen Baron Lionel Walter Rothschild. It became known as the Balfour Declaration. Great Britain was announcing its support for the establishment of a national home for the Jewish people, consistent with the ambition of the Zionist movement. After World War I ended, Britain was entrusted to administer the government of Palestine and look after the interests of Jews and Arabs alike. Since Palestine wasn't a Jewish State yet, Theodore Herzl, the father of the Zionist movement, would likely not have considered the current situation in 1933 as progress.

In March of 1933, Dachau Camp was opened to house political prisoners and in April, a formal anti-Jewish boycott of Jewish-owned businesses began. Unknown to all at the time, The Jewish Problem would evolve into the Final Solution over the ensuing years of World War II.

American immigration was cut off in 1921 and, in 1933, Jewish families like the Glickmans and the Goldmans, desiring to immigrate to America, would have been forced to consider re-settling in Palestine instead. The Aliyah Bet was the code name for a clandestine effort to get refugees illegally out of Germany into Palestine. Their route was circuitous, and some were still turned away by British authorities upon arrival. But the Fifth Aliyah, the fifth wave of Jewish immigration to

Palestine from Europe and Asia, was going strong in 1933 and would continue until the beginning of the Second World War.

When the kids were younger, Helen took them to Chicago about once a year. Their itinerary would be jam-packed.

They would start at the museums, part of her commitment to provide her children a wide-ranging education. The Field Museum was her favorite place to visit with the botany exhibits and information about medicinal plants. She wondered if she would have been a doctor if her life had been different—perhaps one of her kids or grandkids would become one someday.

Jacob preferred the paleontology section. Dinosaur bones from the Western United States were part of the permanent collection. Like most kids, he'd felt disbelief when reading about dinosaurs in school. "How could any animal be so big?" he'd asked his Mom. Yet here were these enormous bones in the museum for kids to touch and see.

"It's just like your father says about God," she would answer.

Isaac always wished to see the exhibits on flight. He was fascinated by the occasional airplane flying over South Haven and loved to read about the Wright Brothers and their first flight in the Kitty Hawk. "I just know you will fly one day," Helen would say to him.

Lottie was learning to play piano and was mesmerized when Helen took them to Orchestra Hall to see the Chicago Symphony. Any program they performed pleased Helen, but she preferred to purchase tickets when the symphony planned to play "Rhapsody in Blue," a piece she often listened to at the end of the day on the phonograph at home with Lottie sitting nearby on the sofa. Helen would remind her daughter that the piece was written by a Jewish composer, George Gershwin. "Someday I'll be able to sit here and listen to you play it," she would say.

Though Helen didn't care for shopping, the trips to Chicago were never all about the museums or the symphony. It was a necessity to find clothing for three growing children changing sizes all the time.

102

South Haven provided little in the way of children's clothing stores. Having the kids try on and pick out clothing for an entire year was a painstaking process. But if the kids were cooperative, Helen rewarded them by allowing each to pick a single item from the large toy store on Michigan Avenue before returning home.

Today's trip to Chicago was to be quite different. The city was hosting the World's Fair. Helen and Samuel were taking only Lottie with them since the boys had scheduled activities that interfered with their going.

"Samuel," yelled Helen from the porch. "Is everything in the car?"

"Yes, Helen. We're ready."

"Do you have the tickets for the show at Soldier's Field tonight?" she screamed out again from the porch.

"Yes, and Lottie is in the car. We are both ready to leave."

The tickets today weren't for a museum. They were for a performance entitled "The Romance of a People" to be held at Soldier Field—one hundred and twenty-thousand people were expected to attend. The show served as the culmination of Jewish Day at the World's Fair. Chicago was now one hundred years old and the Fair, being held along Chicago's lakefront, was entitled "A Century of Progress", with exhibits highlighting advances in technology and industry in the United States. Lottie couldn't stop talking about riding the "Sky Ride," a transporter bridge running from one end of the fair to the other.

Jewish Day was one of two dozen special ethnic days scheduled to represent the varied nationalities living in Chicago at the time who had contributed to the city's success. Debate started early on as to whether the Jews were a nationality at all. Were they better considered a race, a religion, or a nation state? However, none of the organizers disputed the role Jews played in Chicago's last one hundred years of history and, ultimately, the Jewish Agency for Palestine was chosen to sponsor the events at the Fair. Proceeds were earmarked to the Central Refugee Fund, an organization dedicated to assisting German Jews who wished to immigrate to Palestine, something that was still possible in 1933.

The show began at 8:15 p.m. and lasted ninety minutes. It was a pageant highlighting three thousand years of Jewish history. Though sleepy on the way home, Lottie couldn't stop talking about what she'd seen.

"Could you believe it when they brought out that giant Torah scroll and placed it on the stage right in the center of the stadium next to those giant candlesticks with torches for lights? And all the singers and dancers! The man sitting next to us said there were over three thousand performers in the show." Her voice was cracking with tiredness but glee kept her awake.

"Yes, it was amazing. And three thousand years of history recounted. From Abraham to the current day and the hope for a return to Zion," said Helen.

Lottie was in the backseat reading the words in the program to The Romance of a People.

> The Romance of a People" by Miriam Joyce Selker
> I hear the tread of a wandering race
> On the flat sun-sands of a desert place,
> Swaying to the beat of Assyrian drum,
> Deafened by Babylonian cities' sybaritic hum,
> Hesitating before the blue of Alexandria's sea-
> Over oriental lands the homeless people did flee!
> A century-moment Rome paused, and shackled their
> feet in her pride,
>
> And the golden Caesars lived, and they died;
> But Judea trod onward, weariness bound her stride;
> Rome fell, and the press of feet shone clear
> While the echoes of their march fell in tragic unison
> on each nation's ear.
>
> Shaded by Alhambra's pillars in Moorish reign,
> To Americus they sailed on the Spanish Main,
> Onward, on, to furthest Cossack's frozen land,

The wanderers crept far from their white desert sand:
Hunnish faces lightened at the note

The music of their steps on Visigothic soil deeply
wrote;
And vehement Gaels, slant-eyed races, dull,
The blood-rhythm of a people could not lull.

And the long long cry-north, south and west-from
eastern sands

Clasped the universe with wanderers' hands
That wavered and faltered-with sorrow they were
wrung,
But Judean song might not long remain unsung,
For the beat of the feet in endless repeat, went on to be
Sounded in every Exodus throughout eternity,

Until at last, Judea reaped seeds, by her century-sown,
And the Exodus ceased at the heart where it had
grown,
... The wanderers prayed and thanked their One God,
For they had returned-they stood on their own sod.

—And such is the Romance of a People.

"The program describes the Jews as a wandering race now to
return to their own sod. Are we wandering still now that we are here
in America?" asked Lottie.

"No, we are not wandering. Your grandparents chose to immigrate
to America. We're very settled here, but I suppose your father's parents
and mine could easily have gone to Palestine instead. But it gives me
comfort to know that we, along with all Jewish people around the
world, will always have Palestine to return to if needed. One day, I
hope to travel there."

"Why would a Jewish person need to return to Palestine?" asked Lottie.

"Well, not everywhere in the world is like America at the moment. The Jewish people are a minority in every country where they live, including here, but some places make it very difficult for Jews to live a full and free life. It can even be difficult to practice religion openly. Your grandparents left Russia after the pogroms because they didn't feel safe. Many Jews around the world don't feel safe. In Palestine, they would feel safer."

"Thanks for bringing me along tonight." Now, Lottie sounded on the verge of sleep.

"It was Dad's idea for you to come. Thank you, Samuel, for bringing us," said Helen.

Samuel didn't answer immediately. He couldn't answer.

Helen looked over—her husband had tears in his eyes. It was a night to remember the strength of their religion and the importance of the Zionist cause. Samuel was a man of great faith. Tonight was a gift to his family, and more importantly, to himself.

Finally composed, Samuel spoke. "Lottie, I hope you carry the memory of tonight forever. Judaism has a long and complex history. We are safe here in America now, but the Zionist movement hopes for the Jewish people to one day return to Palestine. I hope to see it happen in my lifetime."

Samuel supported the Zionist cause and Helen knew he kept a copy of Der Judenstaat on his desk at home, believing in what Theodore Herzl had written:

"Therefore, I believe that a wondrous generation of Jews will spring into existence. The Maccabeans will rise again. Let me repeat once more my opening words: The Jews who wish for a State will have it. We shall live at last as free men on our own soil, and die peacefully in our own homes. The world will be freed by our liberty, enriched by our wealth, magnified by our greatness. And whatever we attempt there to accomplish for our own welfare, will react powerfully and beneficially for the good of humanity."

Lottie was asleep moments later when Helen asked her husband, "Do you ever think we should go to Palestine to live?"

"I do think about it," Samuel replied.

"I'm hopeful, but uncertain, if Jews and Arabs can ever peacefully coexist in Palestine," said Samuel. "There is so little land to share. I think we are safe here and I like America. We have freedom to practice our religion. I believe our children see themselves as Americans. I hate to uproot them."

"Then we won't discuss it again," said Helen. "We are home. But the program tonight moved me. We're part of a dynamic story— thousands of years of history. The children need to know we feel this way. The Zionist cause is part of what we must one day leave them."

✳ ✳ ✳

When her alarm clock went off the following morning, Helen was startled to find herself in comfortable surroundings, relieved to discover the distress she was experiencing was simply part of a bad dream. Fragments of the dream came back to her slowly and Helen fought to pull them together into a coherent form.

In the dream, she was living in a Berlin apartment several stories above the street. A parade was in progress below her window with Nazi flags and young people marching and singing. Some were carrying signs saying, "Jews Not Welcome." Her parents were there, watching and whispering to each other—discussing whether it was time to leave Germany and go to Palestine.

Like most dreams, Helen realized this one had been triggered by events of the prior day, their trip to the World's Fair, and the stirring show put on by the Zionists. She knew from reading the daily papers that Germany was changing. In January, articles appeared announcing Hitler had been named Chancellor of the coalition government. It seemed just a matter of time before the country accepted The National Socialist German Worker Party and their vision of a new Germany. It seemed odd to Helen that these stories, detailing the changes going on in Germany, were relegated to the back pages of the New York Times, as if they were deemed less important by the Editor.

Helen sat in her bed, frozen, re-considering the dream and its significance. Her family left Russia to escape the pogroms. They were hopeful of finding a better life in America and the freedom to observe their religion. But now she worried that Germany seemed intent on solving the Jewish Question, or what some called the Jewish Problem, that had been percolating throughout Eastern Europe and Russia over the last few centuries.

✳ ✳ ✳

Seven days after returning from their trip to the World's Fair, the weekly copy of Time Magazine arrived in the Glickmans' mail. The cover featured a profile of the German Minister of Propaganda, Goebbels, with a line under his picture—"The Jews are to Blame."

The story inside the magazine detailed how the German government placed the blame for losing World War I and their ensuing financial debt to the Allies on Jewish pacifists. The article spoke of an uplifting of German spirits by the Nazi regime, a regime which placed the blame for all Germany's recent failures on the Jews. Goebbels is quoted, advising the German people to, "Never forget it, comrades, and repeat it one hundred times so you will say in your dreams—The Jews are to Blame!"

"You won't believe the article in Time magazine today," said Helen to Samuel as they sat down to dinner. "Do you remember me telling you about the dream I had after our trip to Chicago last week? Well, Goebbels, the Minister of Public Enlightenment and Propaganda, is on the cover of Time, asking the German people to dream every night of the Jews—that they are to blame for all of Germany's problems. You have to read it. Jews in Germany are in big trouble."

"Where did you set it? I'll look at it tonight," replied Samuel.

"I left it on the coffee table in the living room."

✳ ✳ ✳

That America was in denial about the plight of Jews in Germany at this time is difficult to explain. Some argue that knowledge of the death camps would be the turning point, but that would not come until many years later. Immigration policy never reflected an obvious opportunity to demonstrate the United States' humanity.

Jews who had emigrated from Russia and Eastern Europe, were safe in America, but troubled by the danger they sensed for Jews living in Germany. For the remainder of the decade, American Jews would closely follow world events and it often dominated conversations at social gatherings, though often in hushed tones so as not to frighten the children. It was 1933 and The Romance of a People was still being written.

I think going to the Fair was the best day of my life. I just wish the show about Zionism never ended. (From the diary of Lottie Goldman Zlatkin)

SUMMER & FALL, 2017—SOUTH HAVEN

It was Friday afternoon. One of the last patient visits of the day had triggered a migraine for Rachel. She tried to put the office visit, an unexpected antisemitic encounter, as far out of her mind as possible, closing the blinds, turning out the lights in her office, taking three ibuprofen, and resting her head on the desk.

Clinic hours were over, and, for Rachel, it was the end of the work week. Every third weekend, Rachel manned the Saturday office walk-in hours and took call for the practice, but this was one of her weekends off.

Rachel was professionally spent, glad that kids would be going back to school soon and the "physical season" would be over. Some aspects of her job this time of year were senseless: completing forms that schools probably filed away without a second glance. But there were two sides to every coin, the glass could be seen as half-empty or half-full—yup, for Rachel, there was an up-side to the check-up season as well.

First, these were the months when a busy pediatrician could make revenue far outweigh expenses. She liked a healthy bottom line. Making more money year after year was a sign that her practice was growing and that the attention she paid to her patients was appreciated, if not directly with a "thank you", then by referral of friends and family. Second, it presented an opportunity for a physician to really get to know the families they were taking care of. It was a privilege Rachel didn't take lightly, but it required making an effort, asking open-ended questions, and trusting parents, and, at times, the kids themselves, to be honest about what was going on in their lives. This was rarely straightforward. People held personal secrets tight to their chest, even with their doctor. It was understandable but the tendency interfered with Rachel doing her best job.

How many times did Rachel get a call from parents in November that their child was failing school, or asking if he or she might have ADHD? Rachel would look back at her notes on the computer from the most recent summer physical, just two or three months ago, and under the heading SCHOOL would be her note—DOING WELL.

Even worse was the day a mother called her, her voice frozen with grief, to say her son had died the night before from a heroin overdose. When Rachel pulled up his chart on her desktop to check his last physical exam, there was no mention of any sort of psychosocial problems and an unequivocal denial of substance use by the boy himself.

Still reeling from that call, later that same day, another adolescent came in for a court mandated medical exam. He had completed his rehab stint for drug abuse. Rachel asked him, "How would I have been able to know that you were having drug problems? You never told me a thing during your visits."

"Dr. Walsh, there was no way for you to know. I hid it from my parents. I hid it from my coaches. Why would I tell you? I like you and I know you care about me, but think about it," he said.

However, on other occasions, families would be transparent about what was really going on in their lives, sharing both their successes and failures. Some parents would comment that they trusted her more than their own internist, or family practitioner, to actually listen to their problems.

When this type of intimacy occurred, it granted Rachel something close to family, or even godlike status. They sought out her opinion when the stakes were highest. But this only happened if, during what could be considered another mundane day of endless summer physicals, her efforts to truly connect with parents and their kids were successful. The dividends from these types of relationships were priceless when the shit hit the fan, as it often did, without warning, during the teenage years. Rachel enjoyed, or maybe that was not the correct word, knowing, she was the one in the office on those days when her patients needed her the most. She had faith in her ability to have the right answers. "WWDWD?" "What Would Dr. Walsh Do", was something she heard from time to time and she believed she had earned the confidence her patients placed in her, though the phrase did make her LOL.

Connecting with families could occur in many different ways. First, and foremost, Rachel focused on maintaining eye contact and honed her listening skills. She learned to do this back in medical school when each third-year student was filmed interviewing a patient. "What a waste of time," some of her fellow students were heard to say. "What does this have to do with being a doctor?" But she had given the experience of being taped the benefit of the doubt, learning a great deal more than the simple mechanics of how she took a patient's history and performed their physical exam. Her instructor would suggest that Rachel needed to "Listen more, talk less"—a prescient take on a line in the musical Hamilton—"talk less, smile more." It made sense to Rachel and she incorporated this behavior when interacting with patients into what eventually became her style, or shtick.

Rachel made intentional efforts to relate to every kid regardless of his or her age. When a toddler was up on the exam table in her My Little Pony underwear, she might ask "do they make those in my size?" When a college-bound girl told Rachel she intended to study the law, she might recommend reading 'To Kill a Mockingbird'. One afternoon, when an eighth-grade boy told her he played the trumpet, she suggested he might wish to "listen to Kind of Blue, it's a recording some think to be the greatest in musical history. And, oh, by the way, there is a great trumpet player, Terell Stafford, coming to the Bistro next week. You ought to go see him." Amazingly, as she and Bill were sitting at their front row table the following week, waiting for the performance to start, Rachel felt a tap on the shoulder. Standing there was the twelve-year-old boy she encouraged to listen to the Miles Davis recording. He and his mother bought tickets on a school night to see Terell's quartet. When Rachel realized they were seated at a back table in the venue, she asked Bill if he would mind swapping seats with the boy who joined her for the first set.

These efforts, though rarely rewarded as directly as that particular one, ultimately made her practice spirited and gratifying. It was more than prescribing the proper antibiotic for strep throat or persuading an anti-vaccine parent to vaccinate their child for their own protection and the protection of all in their community. It was being integrated into many families' journeys as they steered their way from infancy to adulthood.

She advised parents to be intentional in their parenting choices, but to go easy on themselves. She would tell them, "Do your best and accept it. After all, some assembly is required." Absent adherence to this advice, Rachel watched helplessly as parents overcompensated for their perceived errors, often making matters worse.

Rachel had a different message for the kids themselves as they were about to leave the practice later in adolescence. It was both sarcastic and direct. "Don't end up living in your parents' basement. I call that a failure to launch. Becoming a confident and competent adult requires some failure—take reasonable chances. It is the best path to personal growth." All of this became, as her grandmother Lottie would have said, part of her spiel.

Today, three ibuprofen and sitting in the dark with her head resting on the desk hadn't made her migraine abate. Try as she might, her thoughts returned to the bizarre visit which took place earlier that afternoon. A kid named Billy Martin was brought in by his father with a baseball injury. Rachel had taken care of Billy since he was an infant but she wasn't certain if she'd ever met his father. Billy had tears in his eyes, holding his slightly deformed left arm gingerly at the wrist.

"Billy is a second baseman for the local high school team. He was turning a double play when the runner made a hard slide, completely taking him out. He landed out on his outstretched arm. I think he broke it," said the dad.

"I think you're right. When kids land on an outstretched arm, they often break both bones in their forearm. It's called a Colles' fracture. Let's get an X-ray to confirm it. It can be fixed. Billy, don't worry, you're going to be fine."

The diagnosis was clinically obvious to Rachel looking at his forearm and X-rays confirmed her diagnostic impression.

"Billy needs to see an orthopedic surgeon to have this reduced and casted. I doubt he'll need an operation to get it fixed. Billy, you're likely out for four to six weeks. I'm so sorry," Rachel said.

"Dr. Walsh," Mr. Martin said, "I don't care who you send us to see but please don't send us to a Jewish doctor."

Rachel's entire body stiffened thinking she must've misheard or misunderstood Mr. Martin. She assumed he didn't realize she was Jewish herself—Walsh wasn't a Jewish sounding name—and how startling and offensive his request had been.

It had been quite some time since Rachel was on the receiving end of an antisemitic remark or act. She once went out on a date in high school with a popular guy only to have him tell her the following Monday "my father realized you were Jewish and told me I can't ask you out again."

When she came home from school that day and told her mother what had happened, Joan offered "maybe you ought to hide your religion from the boys. That's what I used to do." Rachel had been confused, surprised, and somewhat annoyed at the time by her mother's advice.

Lately, it seemed to Rachel, the news media was reporting on more and more stories about the use of Nazi symbols, Holocaust denial, or hate crimes directed against synagogues. These events unnerved her. Antisemitism was very real to her and seemed to be on the rise in America. Maybe now was not the time to commit to her Jewish faith after all.

"You probably don't realize that I'm Jewish, Mr. Martin." Rachel could see him freeze as his eyes opened widely and his mouth fell open. "Normally I would refer you to the best specialist for a particular problem without regard to their ethnic or religious background. However, I do believe that most of the orthopedists in this immediate area can competently handle Billy's fracture, so I am going to recommend you see Dr. Anderson. I'm fairly certain he's not Jewish, though I have never asked him about his religious affiliation."

Rachel turned to Billy "You, young man, are going to be fine. By the way, are you a firecracker on the field like Billy Martin of the 50's Yankees?"

She shook her head, rolled her eyes, and turned her back to Mr. Martin. "Mr. Martin, my assistant, Susan, will get you Dr. Anderson's phone number," she said as she walked out of the examination room standing as erectly as possible.

Rachel's migraine wouldn't relent. She couldn't sit in her office forever. Rachel wondered if others, she came into contact with on a daily basis in her social and professional life, didn't realize she was Jewish. It wasn't something she hid. Or did she? Should she? The Jewish community in South Haven was small. Did neighbors or parents at her children's schools harbor similar antisemitic feelings to Mr. Martin's? Perhaps they had better manners or perhaps a similar comment could come out of any of their mouths if the wrong situation allowed such feelings to surface and be expressed so blatantly.

Rachel couldn't believe this had actually happened—playing the scene over and over again in her mind—-she had been assaulted in her own office. What was the matter with that asshole? She wanted to get home as soon as possible where she would feel safe.

__I wish I'd just punched the guy. That's probably what Bill would have done if he'd been there. (From the diary of Rachel Levitt Walsh)__

1934—SOUTH HAVEN

Hank Greenberg was a handsome, Jewish, six foot-four-inch home run hitter and two-time MVP in the American League. During the 1934 season, he led the Detroit Tigers to the World Series hitting .339 with 26 homers and 139 RBI's. And in 1938, he challenged Babe Ruth's record with 58 home runs.

During the '34 season, as the Detroit Tigers chased the pennant, Jews around the country held varied opinions about whether Greenberg should sit out the games scheduled during the High Holidays. Antisemitism in America was never higher. Jews were barred from buying certain homes and the 1924 Immigration Act had reduced the opportunity for Jews across the world to immigrate to the United States. Greenberg was personally exposed to harsh treatment frequently being called slang terms like Kike or Sheeny. And he was inundated with unsolicited advice. Even rabbis weighed in. Ultimately, he decided to play on Rosh Hashanah and hit two home runs including one in the bottom of the ninth to beat the Boston Red Sox 2-1.

September around the Goldman resort was a quiet time with only the rare, retired couple booking a few days of respite in South Haven. Often these guests were one of their regulars from the summer months, grandparents minus their brood. A few repairs needed to be done, but most of the energy about the Goldman household was in preparation for the upcoming High Holidays.

But this September was different. Samuel was a baseball fan ever since Saul Bernstein brought Jacob a ball as a baby gift. He didn't understand baseball then, but now he listened to Detroit Tiger's games on his 634A Phillips radio. Many in South Haven preferred to follow the Chicago Cubs, but for some reason even he didn't understand, Samuel hated the Cubs.

The Tigers hadn't won the pennant since 1909, prior to Samuel's interest in baseball, but they were in contention this year. They were loaded with great ballplayers including several who would later be inducted into the Hall of Fame—catcher Mickey Cochrane, second baseman Charlie Gehringer, and of course, Hank Greenberg.

More importantly to Samuel, Greenberg was Jewish, raised in an Orthodox Jewish home, and the chase for the pennant coincided with the High Holidays. Greenberg had a dilemma—should he play in a ballgame that conflicted with the these, the holiest of holidays? On Rosh Hashanah, even as the game was about to start, his teammates were uncertain if he would play.

"I suppose I'm glad Hank played today," Samuel said that night at dinner to Helen. "The Tigers need to win the pennant."

"Listen to yourself, Sam. Are you the same man I married? Our faith has always come first in this household."

"One can be an American and be a Jew. Baseball is an integral part of American culture and now we have a baseball hero who is a Jewish boy. They call him 'Hammerin' Hank and the Hebrew Hammer. It makes me feel proud. Perhaps now, some of the other resort owners up here will take down those antisemitic signs. But I'd prefer he not play on Yom Kippur—that would be too much."

"Well, I'm glad he played too, Dad," said Lottie. "They needed to win. I can't believe he hit two homers to practically win the game by himself. The Tigers might be in the World Series this year. Do you remember when I was ten years old and you took me to a game at Navin Field and we saw Babe Ruth play against the Tigers? It was 1927 and the Babe hit one of his sixty home runs that day."

"Of course. We ate Hebrew National hotdogs and you had so much ice cream that you had a tummy ache all the way home," said Samuel.

* * *

Helen's anticipation of the High Holiday season, the ten days from Rosh Hashanah through Yom Kippur, was even greater now that two of her three children no longer lived in town. Both boys were planning to return home for the holidays from Chicago where Jacob worked as an accountant and Isaac a law clerk for a judge. But they weren't the only "guests" coming in for the holidays—Jacob was bringing Rebecca Goldstein as well. He'd written to his parents about meeting her at a temple dance several months ago and his enthusiasm for the girl jumped off the page. She worked for her family who owned a successful business in the garment industry.

"Lottie," said Helen. "I need help at the store. We have so much to buy for the breakfast meal."

"Can I make the mandelbrot myself this year?" asked Lottie. "I think I know how to make them just like Dad likes—soft, but not too soft."

"I don't know why not," replied her mother. "I'm planning on chicken salad, noodle kugel, cheese blintzes, and potato pancakes with applesauce. Of course, we will have bagels too. Your kamish bread can serve as dessert."

"Sounds great, Mom. Remember, you promised this year to write down all your recipes. I'll need them someday."

* * *

Yom Kippur, the Day of Atonement, was the holiest of days on the Jewish calendar. The congregation was required to be in place at the First Hebrew Congregation on Broadway Street while it was still daylight. The temple was built five years earlier and was the center of Jewish activity in South Haven.

Jacob and Rebecca arrived earlier that afternoon. Both Helen and Samuel took an immediate liking to her. She was composed, respectful, and soft-spoken.

"My family is Jewish but, since coming to America, we are perhaps less devout than Jacob describes your family," said Rebecca. "I think I want to raise my family in a more serious Jewish home though."

"Well, tonight we're going to Kol Nidrei services," said Samuel. "Perhaps you know all this but the Kol Nidrei is spoken before sundown and repeated three times. It's not really a prayer. It's more similar to a legal oath."

In ancient times, Jews always lived as a minority in other countries and were often forced to make vows under duress to obey other gods. When they came to attend Yom Kippur services, the Kol Nidrei ceremony absolved them of these vows.

"We fast to show our devotion to God and ask repentance for the sins we may have committed over the prior year," Samuel continued. "Tomorrow, at sundown, the shofar will blow to signify the end of the holiday and God's acknowledgement of this repentance."

"Thank you, Mr. Goldman," answered Rebecca. "And thank you for letting me join your family in celebrating the holiday."

The service was well attended. The Goldman family, along with Rebecca, were seated in a single pew waiting for the Kol Nidrei service to begin when suddenly all the lights in the synagogue went out and the room was illuminated by only two candles. The rabbi, accompanied by a small group of men, walked towards the bima carrying the Torah. Solemnly, one of the men slowly and forcefully began to recite the oath three times just as Mr. Goldman had described. The service was long but quite beautiful. The rabbi spoke about sins against fellow man, but not sins against God.

It was a clear night when they walked out of the synagogue. Helen took note of Jacob and Rebecca walking beside Mr. Goldman holding hands. It pleased Helen to see her son so happy with a nice Jewish girl.

"Good evening, Samuel," said Mr. Stolar. "May you be inscribed in The Book of Life."

"You also, Harold," answered Samuel. "Yom Tov."

When they arrived back at the house, Rebecca approached Mr. Goldman.

"What did he mean when he greeted you that way about The Book of Life?"

"It's on Yom Kippur when we believe God decides who will live and who will die in the coming year. We're to be judged over the High Holy Days. Once decided, our fate is sealed in God's Book of Life on this very day. These are very serious matters. I welcome your curiosity. I hope you will be as serious about your religion as you seem to be about my Jacob. Helen and I like you very much."

*   *   *

The following day, while Samuel attended services at the temple, the rest of the family busied themselves helping Helen prepare the breakfast meal. Though they didn't attend temple services, all were fasting. Rebecca, too, came from a family that chose to fast. She knew this to be part of repentance but later at dinner she asked Samuel about the origin of this tradition.

"It comes from Leviticus. It's to be a day of self-denial."

"So, tell us more about your family, Rebecca," said Helen.

"Well, my grandparents arrived in the United States around 1895. They started out in New York on the Lower East Side. My grandfather was a tailor back in the old country and friends helped him get a start in the garment industry. They worked out of their home. My father, though he loved his parents, didn't enjoy working in such tight quarters alongside his family and decided to move to Chicago. A chance meeting with an acquaintance led to a partnership in the garment industry. I help with the books. My brothers both work there as supervisors and my mother is a teacher at a small Jewish school."

"I know all about those sweatshops in New York. I hope your grandfather isn't still working like that," asked Helen.

"No, he passed away a few years ago."

"Your father must employ a lot of people. I know they have labor unions. I assume he has to deal with them. I imagine Jacob has told you, kiddingly of course, that I'm one of the original feminists and activists. I believe union workers must be treated fairly," said Helen. "From afar, I've supported the ILGWU (International Ladies Garment Workers Union) ever since that fire in 1911 at the Triangle Shirtwaist Factory that killed one hundred and forty-six people—the majority were women and girls."

"Then you'd be pleased to know that my father never closed his shop even in the face of the huge strikes last year. From the beginning he pushed other owners to negotiate and settle with the workers. His experience in New York made him sensitive to their demands for better pay, a fixed work week, overtime pay, and four paid holidays per year. He participated in the weeklong meetings at the United States Court House to settle the disputes with the union. An article in the Chicago Tribune was very complementary of his efforts."

"Good for him and good for you," said Helen. "You must come from nice people. Jacob, you have a winner here," she offered, teasing him.

"Mom, I warned Rebecca about you, but you've outdone yourself. At least the food isn't embarrassing. The blintzes are amazing, by the way," said Jacob, whose ears had turned bright red.

"But the kamish is just a little too soft," added Samuel. "My mother's kamish was better." Helen made note of Lottie's disappointed face. Next year, they'd work on the kamish together so that Lottie could get it right.

__What a game! Thank God Hank chose to play. They couldn't win without him. (From the translated diary of Helen Glickman Goldman)__

FALL, 2017—
SOUTH HAVEN

Jewish guilt is a concept ingrained in the minds of many and cemented by references to it in literature, culture, and humor. The notion of being a Jewish mother originated in America though many of the characteristics are shared by immigrants of other ethnicities and nationalities. As for actual Judaic teaching, when we harm others and do not show true repentance, we should feel guilt.

The caller ID indicated it was her mother. Her body stiffened before picking up the phone. She was expecting the phone call after sharing breakfast this morning with her father. He clued her in on her mother's decision not to accompany him to his forty-fifth college reunion at Northwestern. Letting the phone ring for a bit, she thought back to the conversation from the morning.

"I never thought she'd hold to this stance," said Joseph. "She'll probably try to lay a guilt trip on you to come over to the house and stay."

"How long will you be gone, Dad?" asked Rachel.

"Just the weekend."

"I can do it, Dad. Do you want me to?"

"It's your call but I know her game and it's not going to work on me. I'm going. How many more years do I have left where I will feel good enough to go hangout with my old buddies and act like an adolescent for a few days? We can't drink like we used to, but we can still have a few beers and share 'war stories' about college. I'm just trying to give you a heads up—she's holding to her promise to never attend another reunion with me after she was so bored at the last one, and we both know, she hates to be alone."

* * *

Rachel picked up the phone. "Hi Mom."

"Hi Honey. How was your breakfast with Dad?"

"Great. He even let me pay for the first time ever. He was going on and on about retirement and being on a fixed income. I know you two have plenty of money socked away but I offered to pick up the bill just to shut him up and he took me up on it. He really seemed excited about his reunion this weekend."

"Honey, you know I hate to be alone, but don't worry, I'll be alright when your Dad goes down to Chicago." Joan said. "He's just going for two nights."

* * *

Why was it always the daughter who was expected to take care of a parent as they aged and became needy? Rachel knew the answer to this question. Women were stronger emotionally, less selfish, and more patient than their male counterparts. Families expected women to step-up as the caregivers, and in Rachel's case, as was true among many of her close friends, this remained the expectation in 2018 despite the fact that many of them were employed in jobs far more demanding than their male siblings. She could talk to her mother about her hours and stress as a pediatrician, but she wasn't going to play that card. Everyone thought their own work was harder and more important than other people's. Many assumed this really was true for physicians but Rachel was starting to think that doctors were too enamored with their own perception about how hard they worked.

Rachel and Joan got along well enough but neither of them would call each other a "girlfriend" or suggest they were close. Parent-child relationships could be complicated. Until one became a parent themselves, it was hard to understand the almost universal given that a parent's love was infinite and unconditional, though sometimes almost too big for comfort. But there was a flip side as well. After becoming a parent, one also comes to the realization that one is not infallible and that one's mistakes, though unintended, can create lifetime issues for one's children.

Rachel knew her mother loved her, but she resented Joan's playing favorites while she was a kid growing up in the Levitt household. She didn't think she was repeating history with Andrew and Hannah, but how they would someday remember or imagine their own childhood, was beyond her control.

Control. An interesting word in itself. Joan was a controlling parent, to a fault, in Rachel's estimation—she did it subtly, she did it the old-fashioned way, she did it with Jewish guilt. Like the time the two of them went shopping for a prom dress and everything Rachel tried on wasn't too short for the times, but it was too short for her mother's taste. Her mother asked her, "Don't you think you are sending out the wrong message to the guys?"

Was Jewish guilt an unfair stereotype of American Jewish mothers? How did it get started in the first place? Rachel had read that Jewish immigrants were prone to tell their children they worked hard so that, "You can be happy and have more opportunity than I did." This pressure to succeed often morphed into an expectation for perfection, with anything less being seen as a disappointment. But was this unique to Jews? Didn't many parents use the same line and apply the same pressures on their children?

Regardless, for Rachel, this pressure from her mother was real and didn't allow for making mistakes as a kid, when the stakes weren't nearly so high. Maybe some of the guys would have gotten the wrong impression from her too short dress. So what? Now, as an adult, there were times when she feared the results of making certain choices, resulting in a type of paralysis, just like her current dilemma over the role faith should play in her life. Though acceptable to pause and reflect, it wasn't a good thing when one was paralyzed by the thought of making an error with huge repercussions. This was the cost to Rachel, now, of her mother's Jewish guilt games.

* * *

Rachel let out a deep sigh before responding to her mother on the phone. "Mom. are you asking me to stay the whole weekend?"

"No. I'm not asking you stay at all. I'll be OK."

"Right. You remind me of that Jewish comedian and his mother who used to go on the Tonight Show with Carson. 'How many Jewish women does it take to screw in a light bulb?' he would ask his mother. 'Don't worry' his mother would answer, 'I can sit in the dark.' Mom, are you asking me to let you sit in the dark?"

"No, I just wondered if it might be fun to have a girls' weekend over here. Just the two of us. I miss having alone time with you," said Joan.

* * *

This really didn't help matters. It was such a dishonest statement. Why couldn't her mother just be honest and say, "I'm afraid to be alone" and let Rachel help? Would it be too much for her mother to admit to her neediness and then express thanks to Rachel for being willing to take time away from her family?

Their relationship was stuck in the muck, just like the book she used to read to her kids—"Duck in a Truck". Rachel had come around to accepting it, believing it would never improve. It certainly didn't seem worthy of the time or effort Rachel would need to spend in therapy to work out her own feelings. However, none of this rationalization changed the fact that her mother's dishonesty and continued attempts to manipulate her wore Rachel out.

Rachel supposed her mother would, if pressed, admit to this tried and true behavior of hers. But she would never acknowledge the other point of friction between them, which was playing favorites. Joan clung to the belief that if she had done anything well in her life, it was how she raised her children. She couldn't see, for example, what was clear to all the family, that she had a blind spot when it came to Paul. It got in Rachel's way of loving or even liking Paul, an unintended but very real consequence of her mother's inequity. Rachel wished it weren't the case and wondered if, someday, when Joan passed, she and her brother might take advantage of the opportunity for a do-over in their relationship. After all, he was a good person.

Recently, Joan asked Paul to serve as her Power of Attorney if, and when, she became incapacitated, without distinguishing who would make any medical decisions. Rachel was fine with her brother being in charge of financial matters—he was more accustomed to that world than she was. But her mother's medical decisions! Why couldn't Joan not only acknowledge, but honor her daughter's accomplishments and appoint Rachel as her Medical Power of Attorney? Had her mother forgotten that she was a physician?

Children become weary of having their achievements and capabilities ignored or remaining invisible. It left Rachel with a scar of sorts and a propensity to see all interpersonal interactions as fair or unfair, resulting in, what psychologists call, black and white thinking. Though Rachel did have some insight into this, more often she allowed this propensity to interfere in her own interpersonal relationships.

Her dissatisfaction with her mother had resurfaced when Rachel started studying with the rabbi, attempting to sort out her feelings about Judaism and her lack of faith in God. Rachel tried to give her parents, and especially her mother, the benefit of the doubt. But this wasn't an insignificant matter, like whether Joan should introduce the piano to Rachel or sign her up for girl scouts. It was more important, like a decision about swimming lessons. Learning to swim was an essential, potentially life-saving skill. There was no choice in the matter. Every parent knew their child needed to learn how to swim as soon as possible since drowning was the number one cause of death in children.

However, now, as an adult, Rachel felt that her mother had

thrown her out into a turbulent body of water without a lifejacket. A religious orientation was imperative. What was life without faith? It was insufficient to drop a kid off at Sunday School, pick them up two hours later, and return home with no questions asked.

In contrast, her secular education hadn't been handled with such a laissez-faire attitude. When she came home from school, it was more like an inquisition. "What did you learn today" had been the mantra from the start of first grade, only to be replaced by "Did you get an A on the term paper you turned in last week?" or, "Did you score 100% on your math test?"

Rachel's parents asked her if she wanted to have a bat mitzvah. She remembered it was expected of her brothers, but it was presented as an option for her. Even back then, Rachel realized she had been given a choice because she was a girl. Rachel assumed her parents didn't run that one by her grandmother, Lottie. A feminist until her last breath, she would have had a fit.

Rachel chose to go through with the tradition. Rachel and her brothers, taking a cue from their parents, approached the event ceremonially. It was about the party and the gifts, never the actual study of the Torah and what it might teach them. Traditionally, the day marked an age of maturity in the Jewish community, when one was expected to no longer be self-absorbed, but old enough to start doing good deeds for those in need, just like every other Jew. Performing mitzvot, good deeds, was an essential responsibility, commanded by God. The least her parents should have done was require her to complete some sort of service project, like the one required of her when she graduated high school. This subtle adventure in parenting made it clear to Rachel where religion ranked in her parents' hierarchy of aspirations for her, her siblings, and even themselves.

As a mother, Rachel accepted the fact that she, not Bill, was primarily responsible for her children's physical and emotional well-being. Sure, enlightened perspectives on parenting now asked fathers to step up. But Rachel was a pediatrician and saw first-hand that fathers rarely did so. Fair or not, this led Rachel to place most all of the blame on her mother for the checked-out approach to her religious upbringing.

"OK, Mom. Let's do it. A Girls' Weekend. I'll see you tomorrow night. I'm looking forward to it," said Rachel though both of them knew her last statement to be dishonest as well.

❋ ❋ ❋

Fridays at the office were always busy. Panicked parents, just thinking about the upcoming weekend, often rushed their kids in for what Rachel would call "no good reason." Her practice was open Saturday mornings until noon and she and her partners were always arranging to meet a child at the office on Sunday morning if they had an acute illness that shouldn't wait until the next day. But come Friday afternoon, some parents just couldn't help themselves.

The last kid of the day was Jonathan Miller. He was there for a check-up mandated by the high school association overseeing soccer. When kids came in for check-ups, Rachel had typical conversations reserved for such visits depending on the age of the child. This time spent with patients fell under the generic category of Preventative Maintenance. Every doctor had their own pet peeves which drove the narrative. For Rachel, when with young children, extra minutes were devoted to discussing diet, safety, and exercise. But with teens, she liked to spend her time on navigating decisions, often about privileges and independence. Parents had a choice to make. They could simply flex their muscles, making unilateral rulings, or step back only intervening when necessary and justified to prevent real harm from occurring. "Control vs Safety" was how she characterized the topic.

"Dr. Walsh," Jonathan said. "Can I ask you a question?"

"Sure," Rachel responded. "Fire away."

"My mom won't let me go to Fun Park alone at night with my friends. She says it's too dangerous."

"What are you worried about, Mrs. Miller?"

"You probably remember that incident a few years back when a Jewish kid got beat up at the park after dark," Mrs. Miller said.

"Do you really think it had anything to do with his being Jewish? I heard it was just a fight over a girl. And that was at least five years ago," answered Rachel. "Maybe the thing to do is go down there this weekend, let him hangout with his friends, and check it out yourself. Walk around, but don't stalk him and his friends. If, afterwards, you believe it is truly unsafe don't let him go back alone. When up against difficult decisions, make sure it's about real safety versus control. Control is always easier. You don't have to worry if you won't let him out of your sight. We both know that's not possible or even a good idea. At some point he will need to make his own decisions and he won't be prepared to do so if you always make them for him."

She turned from the mother to the boy.

"Jonathan, I'm curious though about something related to your mother's concerns. Have you ever been bullied by someone just because you were Jewish? Your mother would be right to worry if that ever happens."

"Maybe just once or twice. It was the same kid. His family has moved out of South Haven. I was glad to see him go," said Jonathan.

Rachel nodded, noticing that after saying this it was difficult for him to swallow.

"Good. Don't be embarrassed to tell an adult if that kind of thing ever happens again."

* * *

As soon as Jonathan was out the door, Rachel grabbed her purse and jumped into the car. The drive to her mother's house gave her the ten minutes she needed to put the last visit somewhere neat and clean in her mind.

Control had come up again. This mother wasn't using Jewish guilt but still probably two sides of the same coin. Unrelated solutions to an age-old problem—with the potential for similarly poor results—a child afraid to make mistakes. And then, to top it off, there was the question of antisemitism. Awfully tough to handle as an adult—how was a kid supposed to manage it?

"Hi, Mom," said Rachel carrying a small suitcase as she entered the house through the backdoor to the kitchen. "Where are you?"

"I'm in the bathroom," her mother hollered from somewhere down the hallway. "I'll be out when I'm finished. You know how constipated I get."

Constipated. Already complaining. Rachel thought to herself that Bill would make some kind of joke like "The weekend is shaping up to be like a trip to the proctologist."

She smiled, realizing that may be closer to what her mother actually needed right now.

There was still enough sunlight to go sit on the deck with her mother. Her parents enjoyed a home with an unobstructed view of Lake Michigan. While growing up, she loved to watch the sunset from one of the Adirondack chairs, each a different primary color, positioned perfectly to observe the minute by minute changes in the sky as the sun set. It would be blue and purple, and then only moments later, red and orange and yellow. She wondered how Monet would have seen and expressed what she saw in the light if he had the opportunity to paint this scene like others he had painted—the Rouen Cathedral, the haystacks, and the water lilies.

"Thanks for coming to spend the weekend. I could have asked your brother, but he is so busy," said Joan, as she emerged from the bathroom.

"Mom. You realize I have a pediatric practice. I'm busy too," said Rachel, clasping her mouth as she said it. "I'm sorry, Mom. I don't want to fight. I'm here now and ready to enjoy your company, but don't bring up my brother. We both know he would have an excuse for not being able to come. The responsibility always falls on the daughter, if you're lucky enough to have one. Some families have all boys. Michelle would have stayed this weekend if she didn't live in Chicago. I'm glad I will have Hannah to look after me when I get to that useless stage of life."

"So, I'm useless."

"My bad Mom. I didn't mean that at all though, now that I think about it, it sure sounded that way. You should be proud of all that you've accomplished in life. I am. You did a great job with the resorts until turning them over to Paul. I know you helped me and my siblings become the people we are today. You attended all those games and important school events. Now that I'm a mother, I appreciate more fully how you often put our needs above your own."

"Thank you for that Rachel. I did my best. I got married when I was nineteen. I was probably too young. I know you think I'm materialistic and self-absorbed, but there is more to me than you know. I do have regrets though."

"Can I ask you about something that is bothering me?" said Rachel.

"Sure."

"Why didn't religion get much attention in our house when we were growing up? It seemed to get very little consideration."

"Well, perhaps you have hit on one of my disappointments. You need to understand that I received conflicting messages as a kid myself. Your grandmother was intense. She was intense about the resort, her family, and her religion. The latter was important to her because of the support it gave our ancestors when they emigrated from Russia. She was also devoted, through the influence of your great-grandfather, to the Zionist cause and was elated when Zionism culminated, after the war, in Israel becoming a state. These two things cemented her commitment to Judaism. My mother lived by the core principles of the Judaic faith—she treated everyone with respect. Her faith carried over into her charity work and the social causes she supported throughout her life. My father, on the other hand, was a good man but a more detached individual. I suppose he resented my mother's focus and time spent outside the home, helping others. I doubt he ever saw it, or understood it to be, a fundamental expression of her religious faith. If asked, I imagine, he would have considered himself a 'Good Jew,' but he was preoccupied with embracing American culture and assimilating. I grew up in that confusing environment. Maybe I have placed too much emphasis on our lifestyle and our family's financial security and not enough on spirituality. But Rachel, I did my best."

"I've been meeting with Rabbi Weinstein for some time now. I felt empty and wondered if I was missing something in not giving religion a chance. Bill's faith is so strong. It seems to give him peace. I'm starting to feel I need it. I know my job allows me to give back to others. Though I have expressed my anger at you at times for forcing the 'you should become a doctor' thing on me, I am thankful you pushed me as hard as you did. I love my work. It allows me to provide financially for my family while helping others. And though I'm pretty good at multitasking—being a mother, a wife, and a breadwinner— I'm starting to think I need to stop rushing about and maybe hit the pause button. I want greater meaning to my life. I think I may find it in faith."

"I'm glad to hear it. See. A girls' weekend doesn't have to be so bad," said Joan.

"We have about thirty minutes until sunset. I brought my candlesticks. I guess I could have called them your candlesticks, or grandma's, or great-grandma's. Let's go light them together and then come back out for a glass of wine. What do you think, girlfriend?"

"I'd love to."

God, will you forgive me for not being able to stand her sometimes? I know she loves me, but she is so manipulative. (From the diary of Rachel Levitt Walsh)

1937—SOUTH HAVEN AND CHICAGO

Four years prior in 1933, Labor Secretary Frances Perkins rescinded Hoover's restrictions on immigration for those trying to escape racial and religious persecution, calling it an American tradition to do so. However, ever since the reversal of the policy, the US State Department had been fighting the change and, now, had won out to restrict the number of German immigrants coming to the US. State Department officials cited unemployment numbers and competition for jobs when arguing to reinstate these restrictions.

It had been the most successful summer in the Goldman Resorts' history. They were fully booked at the main hotel and the three other homes the Goldmans now owned on North Shore Drive were always rented as well. Since Jacob and Isaac no longer lived in South Haven, Lottie, along with the hired staff, had more work to do than ever.

The summer was warmer than in recent years and the North Beach was packed every day. Lottie ordered a swimsuit from the Sears catalogue that arrived at their home in the spring. It was the same suit Rose Veronica Coyle wore as she was crowned Miss America in 1936. When Lottie could find the time to sneak away from the property, she went to the beach where her legs got plenty of sun and attention.

Lottie enjoyed the resort business. It fit her temperament to be busy. There was always another bed to be made, lost children to be returned to their parents, or an extra set of hands needed in the kitchen. The Goldmans installed a tennis court over the winter and it was a huge hit with the guests and Lottie as well. She gladly filled in when a group of three players couldn't find a fourth for doubles.

Probably the most popular activity was card games. Poker, gin rummy, and knock rummy were played by the men while the women preferred Mah-Jongg. Money often changed hands, but by the end of the week, everyone was happiest when all broke even. Lottie liked to watch the bridge games, again joining in when needed and trying to learn on the fly.

One night a month the Goldmans hired a traveling big band to play at the resort. Tomorrow night, Benny Goodman, the King of Swing, was scheduled to play. Mr. Goodman appeared over the last several summers and loved coming to the South Haven. His orchestra would play outdoors on a hurriedly built dance floor complete with colored lights and a Lake Michigan sunset. Goodman would stay over an extra night just to get his fill of Helen's great kosher cooking. Though born in Chicago, Mr. Goodman's family, like Helen's, had emigrated from the Russian Empire. He grew up in extreme poverty in the Maxwell Street neighborhood, slum housing near the railroad yards. Typically, after the band was finished, Helen and Benny would share a late-night snack and serious conversation often reflecting on how America had given these two Jewish kids an opportunity to be successful.

Big band night, like tennis and cards, sometimes required Lottie to fill in, but this time as a dance partner. She was hurrying across the property, intending to quickly stop by the kitchen to see if an extra hand was needed before showering and dressing for the big night, when Mrs. Fredman, a regular guest, approached her.

"Do you think they will ever find her?" Mrs. Fredman asked.

"Who's gone missing? Is it the Goldfarb's daughter again?"

"No, Amelia Earhart. Her plane went missing in the Pacific Ocean."

"Oh, my goodness. I've not heard anything about it. What a

shame. She is one of my heroes. Strong minded I suppose, like my own mother. Though in my limited life experience, strong minded and stubborn might be on the same continuum. My brother Isaac wants to be a pilot. I think I'd be too afraid to fly."

"Well, I don't know if Amelia Earhart is stubborn or not, but she is a champion for women's rights. You mentioned your mother. You must know she worked on Women's Suffrage back in 1917. I think there is a picture in the dining room of her at a rally in 1917 pregnant out to here," she said pointing yards out front of her stomach.

"Yeah, I'm in that picture too. I was the baby inside," Lottie answered laughing.

"By the way Lottie, do you happen to know what's for dinner tonight? I came by to see if I could tell just by aromas," said Mrs. Fredman.

"I'd get in big trouble with the boss for telling. Tonight's a big surprise. Part of the dance night celebration. Mom always tries to have Mr. Goodman's favorites when he comes to play. I'll see you at dinner."

Lottie watched Mrs. Fredman walk off. The summer was moving along well and like the band playing tonight, it had its own rhythm. It was a rhythm Lottie was beginning to wonder if she could dance to forever. Perhaps running the Goldman resort was something she should consider making part of her future.

✳ ✳ ✳

The dining hall was buzzing with anticipation. When Benny Goodman arrived, the applause became deafening as he was shown to the table where Sam and Lottie were waiting. Helen would join them as soon as she finished supervising, last minute, in the kitchen. The serving staff brought out the brisket, potato pancakes and green beans—each one of Mr. Goodman's favorites. But what he enjoyed most of all was the cherry pie for dessert.

"Helen Goldman," said Benny. "What a meal. I always look forward to our stay here in South Haven."

"Will you play Let's Dance tonight?" asked Helen.

"Of course. I can't believe how popular it has become in America. But can we talk about something more serious for a moment? Have you been reading the papers and following what's going on in Germany?"

"Of course. Everything I can get my hands on. The Jews are really suffering over there. I fear the worst."

"I think it's xenophobic that our government is trying to limit the number of immigrants," said Helen.

"Listen to your vocabulary," Benny said. "I'm not sure we even have a Yiddish word for that. I feel guilty at times just being here in the United States. I am so thankful my family came over before things got so bad."

"Me too, though I'm still uncomfortable here in America at times when I witness or am the target of antisemitic behavior," Helen said.

"Do you ever read the Dearborn Independent?" said Benny. "They once had a headline about Jazz calling it Moron Music. Henry Ford owned the paper and either directed or allowed all sorts of antisemitic stories to be published."

"Of course I know of the paper! I am so glad it doesn't exist anymore," said Helen. "My father quit the Ford Motor Company over that despicable paper and that antisemite, Henry Ford."

Henry Ford, using the Dearborn Independent, had reprinted a half a million copies of a fabricated book entitled The Protocols of the Elders of Zion and distributed them throughout the United States in pamphlets as part of a series, The International Jew. The premise of the antisemitic novel was that a kabul of Jewish bankers was meeting in cemeteries in Prague and planned to overthrow the world by taking over the press and the economies and replacing Christianity with Judaism as the dominant religion.

"My dad became politically inspired, which shocked us all. He retired from Ford Motor, and joined the American League for Defense of Jewish Rights. He even attended marches with me," said Helen.

Mr. Ford ultimately apologized for his hate speech and agreed to shut down the Dearborn Independent when settling the libel case

136

Sapiro v Ford in 1927. Sapiro hired Louis Marshall, the great Jewish lawyer of the day, who argued that Ford committed libel against not only Sapiro but also the entire American Jewish community.

"I've always doubted his apology was sincere," said Helen. "He had ten million reasons, I meant to say, ten million dollars' worth of reasons, to make an apology. By the way, what kind of man doesn't like jazz? He must be a moron himself."

"Samuel," said Benny. "You married a firecracker here. What inspires her to always fight so hard against injustice?"

"I think it is a fundamental expression of our faith," answered Samuel. "The Talmud teaches us 'anyone who destroys a single life is considered to have destroyed a world, and anyone who saves a life is considered to have saved an entire world.' Helen lives her Jewish values and seeks to help those in need and not just Jews either. A few years ago we checked out Idlewild. They call it Michigan's Black Eden. It's worth the drive northeast of here to see it. Helen heard they needed a stove and we had an extra one not in use. We hauled it up there and took Charlotte with us. The folks we met were very grateful. Lottie was especially taken by the premise of an all-Black resort. Have you ever played at Idlewild in the Fiesta Room at the Paradise Club?"

"No. They won't have us up there. I don't blame them. The Jewish resorts want Jewish bands. Even though Idlewild was started by white folks, it's for Blacks only and that means Black Big Bands as well."

"You need to see the place just to watch the dancing. It's really something," said Samuel.

"Can we get back to talking about what is happening in Germany?" asked Helen. "The Nuremberg laws deny Jews basic civil rights and are likely just the tip of the iceberg. Hitler is an evil man. He has power over a nation—something that Henry Ford didn't have despite his wealth and connections. At times, I wish Roosevelt would do something. If someone doesn't stop Hitler, I fear for the lives of every Jew in Europe."

"I don't know what the President can do," replied Benny. "Germany hasn't started a war yet for us to pick sides. I'm not sure I understand the German people. Why do they follow that man? When they passed the Enabling Act, their government essentially became a dictatorship. Hitler's blaming the Jews for the economic woes of their nation is dishonest. But isn't this just another instance of history repeating itself? This isn't the first time, or the last time, Jews living as a minority in a foreign country have been singled out and harassed."

"The Jewish people need their own country," said Helen. "I joined the Mizrachi. They identify themselves as 'The Land of Israel, for the People of Israel, According to the Torah of Israel'. I believe in the Zionist cause. I hope we will see it in our lifetime. OK, enough with the serious talk. Remember tonight, you promised me you'd play Let's Dance."

"I'll tell you what. We'll play it twice," Benny said with a smile.

* * *

Lottie returned to the University of Chicago that fall for her junior year where she was majoring in finance and minoring in Art History. She was looking forward to school starting, with most of her excitement related to seeing Jonathan again. They had started dating in the spring. He was a business major and would graduate next June. He was bright, respectful, and always a gentleman; however, he wasn't Jewish. This was significant—so much so that she avoided bringing up his name at home the entire summer. Her parents definitely would not approve of her dating outside her religion.

This wasn't just supposition. Her brother Isaac was very serious about a woman in his law school class. Recently, Lottie overheard a conversation between her parents.

"What did we do wrong, Samuel?" Helen said. "Why does he need to date a shiksa? There are plenty of nice Jewish girls in Chicago. Perhaps Rebecca can fix him up with one of her friends."

"I agree," answered Sam. "I'd support the children in most things but this? I feel so strongly, I want to forbid it. But Isaac is hard-headed. The more we object, the more we might push him to stay with this woman. At least Jacob married within his religion and Lottie has always dated Jewish boys."

Religion mattered to Lottie. She attended temple services while at college. She met several Jewish guys at social events held at the temple, but Jonathan was in one of her accounting classes and she could not keep her eyes off him. Perhaps it was too forward, but one day, after class, she cornered him and asked if he would like to join her for lunch. He called her Charlotte, just like the professor did in class. She liked that. It sounded less Jewish.

She talked to her roommate, Sarah. "Perhaps he doesn't even realize I'm Jewish, though my nose is a dead giveaway. I just want to date him. He's so cute. But I know I will marry a Jewish boy."

Arriving back on campus, Lottie hoped to see Jonathan right away. Before the school year ended in June, his fraternity scheduled a dance for the first Saturday night after fall classes began. On their last date before summer recess, they spoke about going to the dance together. It was all she could think about.

"What are you planning to wear to the dance?" asked Sarah.

"Well, my sister-in-law gave me a great flowery dress. Her family is in the garment industry here in Chicago. I think Jonathan will like how I look in it."

"Are your parents OK with his not being Jewish? I know my parents wouldn't be."

"I know my parents wouldn't approve either, but I haven't told them about Jonathan. My mother is a strong independent woman and she has raised me to be the same. If I want to date him, and I do, then that is what I'll do. I'll worry about how to tell my parents when the time comes."

"Well, good luck with that conversation. But when it comes to dating outside my religion, my parents won't allow it. They just wouldn't."

"I can't figure out why he hasn't already called to formally invite me. I know what I'll do. I just read in The Daily Maroon that tonight is the Inter-fraternity Sing. I'll go and run into him there. By the way, Jonathan is a great singer."

❋ ❋ ❋

A huge crowd was gathering in the Hutchinson courtyard. Lottie could see dozens of separate fraternity groups practicing under the IF Sing banner. Jonathan was over six feet tall and stood out even from thirty or so yards away.

"Hi Jonathan," she yelled out waving and smiling as she approached his singing group.

Jonathan turned around with a surprised look on his face. "Hi Charlotte," he said. Lottie noticed immediately that he avoided looking directly into her eyes. "How was your summer back in Michigan?"

"Great, but I missed you. Are you going to invite me to the dance tomorrow night?"

"Well, I thought it was weird when you asked me not to write this summer. I couldn't understand why letters arriving at your home might be a problem."

"I just didn't want you to have to bother. Some guys don't like it when they feel they have to write letters to please a girl."

"Well, I told my mother about you and your asking me not to write. She wondered if maybe you were Jewish."

"I am. I should have told you. I don't know why I didn't."

"Anyway, I asked John, he's a Jewish guy in our accounting class. He told me you definitely were. I like you, Charlotte, but it's senior year. I need to get serious and find a girl to marry. I'm not going to date or marry a Jewish girl. I'm sorry" he said, turning his back to her and walking back to his group.

Sarah found Lottie on her bed in their dorm room later that evening. She had obviously been crying. Her flowery dress was laying on the floor in a heap.

"I know something bad must have happened with Jonathan," Sarah said. "I'm so sorry. Did he meet someone else over the summer?"

Slowly gaining her composure, Lottie answered. "He will not date a Jewish girl. It's that simple and it's not really his fault. It was mine. I should have been up front about my religion. Many of the senior guys are looking to find a wife while here at college. Many of the girls wish the same. I really like him and I am hurt, but I was never going to get too serious with someone outside my religion. I'll get over it, though

I was really looking forward to wearing this dress to the dance. I looked terrific in it when I tried it on this morning."

"We can go together—stag. I'm up for it, if you are," said Sarah.

The girls were giddy as they approached the fraternity house holding hands. Lottie recognized the boy blocking their way. It was Brad, from one of her Art History classes.

"You can't come in without an invitation. Who is your date tonight?" asked Brad.

"Well, I thought it was Jonathan. But he stood me up at the last minute. I just figured we could come anyway."

"I don't have a date," answered Brad. "And neither does my roommate. You two can be our guests if you'd like."

"Hang on a minute," said Lottie turning to speak with Sarah.

It only took a moment for Lottie and Sarah to agree. And what a night it was. Lottie put her dress and summer resort dancing practice to good use. No one could take their eyes off the stunning Jewish girl from South Haven and it gave Lottie a wicked thrill to see Jonathan look at her with chagrin, several times during the evening.

I will not hide my Jewish ancestry again. (From the diary of Charlotte Goldman Zlatkin)

OCT/NOV 2017—
SOUTH HAVEN

Baruch Atah Adonai, Eloheinu Melech haolam, asher kid'shanu b'mitzvotav v'zivanu l'hadlik ner shel Shabbat.

Blessed are You, Eternal our God, Sovereign of the universe. You hallow us with Your commandments and command us to kindle the lights of Shabbat.

Rachel noticed the yard was blanketed with leaves as she turned into the driveway. As usual, she was in a hurry to get home from the office as it was Friday night and the sun would be setting soon. She knew not to expect anyone to be there as Andrew was in soccer season and Hannah was playing field hockey. Bill would be picking them up tonight. They were planning to have neighbors over for dinner—a mirror image family with kids of identical age and sex to their own. It made for a comfortable evening.

Upon entering the house, Rachel quickly pulled out her candlesticks to light the Sabbath lights. Holding them, she thought back to last night's dinner conversation. Andrew was quite animated for a change, enthusiastically speaking about the novel Les Miserables. It was his reading assignment in French class. Rachel remembered this classic story from her own high school years—it told of Jean

Valjean and his chance encounter with Bishop Myriel. Valjean was a thief and when caught red handed by the police with stolen goods from Bishop Myriel's church, the bishop told the police he had given Valjean the items but forgot to give him the candlesticks as well, placing them in his bag. This encounter changed Valjean's life. He became dedicated to honesty and kindness to others.

Lighting her candlesticks, Rachel reflected on the story of how her great grandmother's candlesticks made their way to America and into her home. Like Valjean, the candlesticks marked a significant moment in her family's history—their immigration to America.

What made her feel so good in this moment every Friday night, alone with her candlesticks? Was it the meaning of the Hebrew words she was about to recite, or just their rhythm and flow? Perhaps it was just pausing to reflect on her life, gaining some control over the commodity of time. If she were to be totally honest with herself, it was only since starting to meet with Rabbi Weinstein that she was beginning to contemplate her relationship with God and how embracing Judaism and God's commandments might change the way she lived her life—lighting the candles was definitely taking on some spiritual meaning.

Lighting the Sabbath candles also gave her an opportunity to reflect on her ancestry. She felt fortunate they had come to America. But how many more generations would it take before the memory of their odyssey faded away, largely forgotten?

But it also marked the end of the work week—she didn't have to go back to the office or think about her practice until Monday. She could sleep in tomorrow and do nothing if she wished to.

Rachel knew she wouldn't do that, couldn't do that. She liked to be busy, always keeping a long to-do list of projects to pick from on her kitchen desk by the phone. Maybe tomorrow wouldn't be so windy and she and Hannah could rake the leaves together. As Rachel was getting older, nothing pleased her more than taking two hours and transforming a mess, any mess, into order.

Why couldn't the chaos in life be as simply solved as cleaning up the yard?

As a child, she was always happiest when having something to do. Some kids required their parents to plan their activities but Rachel did better when left to her own pursuits. She astounded her mother one afternoon when Joan returned home from the grocery store only to discover her playing the piano scales, perfectly, while at the same time reading her school assignment, "A Tree Grows in Brooklyn".

When her mother asked her what the book was about, Rachel could tell her mother was shocked when she correctly recited all the details of the story, including her favorite part where Francie lied about her name being Mary to receive the doll a rich girl was giving away, only to later learn that her real name was Mary, Mary Frances Nolan.

Rachel could multi-task before the term was even popular.

School had been a breeze for Rachel. There were times she complained about having too much homework, but she actually reveled in it, bored when it was all completed. It was only her perfectionism that resulted in her homework assignments taking a little longer to be completed in the first place.

Rachel remembered during her childhood that her mother Joan was capable of sleeping in on the weekends once resort season was over. After she got up, she would just piddle around the house the rest of the day or perhaps go shopping. Joan jokingly identified herself as a domestic goddess, making reservations for dinner instead of a roast.

But in Joan's defense, she always made it clear to Rachel that Rachel should choose a different path. Not because her own wasn't worthy or that she felt unfulfilled. Her mother simply knew Rachel would be happier being busy three hundred and sixty-five days a year and, had therefore, pushed her towards becoming a pediatrician. Rachel had issues with her mother, who doesn't? But none were about her mother's love or devotion.

Busy was her nature, but was Rachel too busy at the office to see the true needs of her patients? She relished the opportunity to make an especially obscure diagnosis or discover a piece of history the patient omitted central to their puzzling case. She was thorough, her perfectionism serving her patients well, but did it leave her enough time, or was it a matter of taking the time, to open herself up completely to the unspoken agendas many families had about their psychosocial problems?

During the last year of residency, while attending a conference at the hospital, Rachel found herself sitting next to her mentor, Dr. Phillips, who had recently retired. Usually he only talked shop and Rachel expected him to ask about her Fascinoma of the Week. But to her surprise, he didn't want to hear about some rare medical case she was attempting to diagnose and treat. No, Dr. Phillips had something else he wished to educate her about.

"Hi, Rachel," said Dr. Phillips. "How's my favorite resident?"

"I'm good and glad to run into you before I leave Ann Arbor for South Haven. I've taken a position there in practice. I can't thank you enough for everything you have taught me."

"That is very nice of you to say. But remember, being an excellent pediatrician requires one never stops learning. I received a lesson myself just last week while waiting on a car repair to be completed. I struck up a conversation with a woman sitting across from me. We were both reading the same book, Small Great Things. We talked for thirty minutes about this book on race. I took a lot away from this chance encounter with an African American woman. Only now, in retirement, do I find I have the time to actually listen to people and be open to hearing them. I wonder if I had been more open during my practice career, what more could I have offered my patients? Maybe it would have made me a better person, certainly better informed. Perhaps you listen better than I did, but if not, consider doing so. It might make a difference."

"I try to listen. But who can't do better?" she had answered. "Thank you, Dr. Phillips."

The alarm on her Apple watch went off. She always set it for ten minutes when lighting the candles, knowing this weekly practice often set her in a reflective mood so that she lost track of time. She needed to get going. Company was coming soon. OK-perhaps she could give more to others. Wasn't this a fundamental moral expression of Judaism, kindness to others? All this time spent looking at the candles burning and letting her mind wonder, she realized she had yet to recite the Sabbath prayer.

✳   ✳   ✳

The Donovans arrived around seven and it didn't take long for the kids to devour their burgers and run off to the basement, leaving the adults to settle in around the table and talk. The topic turned to how to approach the issue of sex with their kids as puberty had begun for each of them.

"I don't want to abdicate this responsibility and assign it to some random health class teacher or coach at school. If I do that, my kids will go to them in the future, not me, when they have problems or questions," said Alan.

"I agree," replied Rachel. "They'll get the facts at school, but not your values. They need both and it works best when it comes from us. Teenage boys can learn a lot when this is discussed, not just with their father, but with their mother present as well. Sometimes I think the reverse may even be more important. Studies demonstrate and my experience confirms that girls having conversations about sex with their father present are more likely to delay initiating sexual intercourse."

"Rachel, can you give us some guidance? What do you tell parents and kids in your office?" asked Alan's wife, LeAnn.

"Now you've done it," said Bill. "You put a nickel in the slot. You're about to receive more than your money's worth. What's interesting to me though is how friends at the dinner table wish to hear what Rachel, a pediatrician, has to say about tough medical topics. This is in stark contrast to dinner with our extended family where everyone is the medical expert, forgetting there is a doctor at the table."

"Enough, Bill," said LeAnn. "Can't you shut up for once? Do you always need to be the center of attention? I'm serious about wanting some help."

Rachel laughed at LeAnn's take-down of her husband. It was WWF worthy. She started in. "From the time my patients are babies,

I use anatomically correct language with parents and I continue to do so until they leave the practice. Parents learn to expect I'll do this and the kids, by the time they are adolescents, do as well. I discuss pubertal changes, feelings about sex, and why I believe adolescents aren't capable of true intimacy, a necessary component for both individuals to experience sexual pleasure. They know to trust the information I'm giving them is accurate. And when I explain these things, the language I use needs to be gender neutral. I can't assume everyone is interested in the opposite sex, or for that matter, identifies themselves with the sex they were assigned at birth."

"You've lost me" Alan exclaimed. "I need to understand what you just said before we continue."

Bill smiled. "I warned you both. This isn't my first rodeo."

After a few questions, Rachel described how these conversations went each day in the office and how her intent was to increase the chance her patients would choose abstinence as a method of birth control. She believed she was starting to have success, because over the years since she'd changed her standard spiel about sex, instead of talking only about the risk of pregnancy and sexually transmitted infections, she now spoke more about intimacy and the almost universal failure for young women in her practice to experience orgasm. After all, this was the goal of sex for most people, along with those wishing to have a child, in the first place.

Rachel knew Bill had become used to this discussion and the zombie-like expression it left on some of their friend's faces. At the end of an evening like this, he often told her how much he admired her confidence and skill in navigating these tough issues, but Bill would also express concern as to whether their own children would safely negotiate these complex issues when they were just a few years older than they were now.

"It sounds like you give your patients a lot to think about, Rachel, but we don't believe in premarital sex in the first place," said LeAnn. "I know you think we're not all that religious. Sometimes, I'm not sure if we are either. You see us at church on Easter and Christmas. We take Holy Communion and the like. Maybe participating in all the rituals leaves the door open a little wider for us to find faith someday. But in any event, in our house, we preach no sex."

"Well, I've learned to never bring up religion directly in my office, at least not my own religious feelings. The practice of pediatrics works best when the relationship between families and myself is quite intimate, but religion is out of bounds. It's not that I'm hiding my Jewish heritage, but that's parental territory—telling their kids how they expect them to live and at times make choices consistent with their own religious commitment. My job, though I strive to get quite close to my patients, is to give medical information only."

"I didn't realize with a last name like Walsh that you were Jewish, Rachel," said a clearly puzzled Alan whose nostrils seemed to flare as he said it. "Can we go check on the kids? They're awfully quiet down there."

Rachel thought the kids looked bored with each other as she followed her guests to the basement. They all had their cellphones out, dull-eyed, earbuds in, and thumbs performing a wild dance beating out messages to god knows who. Rachel forgot to ask everyone to put their cellphones in the basket in the front hall, something she started doing when company was invited over. She realized each generation has its problems, but for teens in 2018, social media and cellphone use were near the top of the list leading to disrupted sleep, FOMO (fear of missing out), physical injury due to distraction, psychological injury from cyberbullying, and unintentional social isolation. On occasion, she'd even diagnosed a case of "texting thumb" or what doctors formally called stenosing tenosynovitis caused by the repetitive motion from these dancing digital performances. But this scene in the basement—four kids sitting around and not interacting with each other made no sense to Rachel, though she knew a similar picture might be observed at any restaurant where adults were dining together.

"OK, phones down," Bill said.

Rolling their eyes, the kids put their phones away and joined the adults for a game of Cards Against Humanity. Last night, Rachel assigned the arduous task of culling the deck of inappropriate cards to

Bill. So many of the questions were hardly suitable even for adults, but Bill found a small set of cards that produced a lot of fun and awkward moments—wasn't that the idea behind the game in the first place?

When the Donovans left, the family gathered in the kitchen for a bowl of ice cream. Hannah asked, "Do we have any plans for Christmas this year"?

It wore Rachel out how Hannah always required having a plan for future events, and in the absence of such certainty, the rest of the family would have to deal with her anxiety. Rachel thought Bill catered to her when this occurred. As if on cue, Bill blurted out, reinforcing Hannah's behavior, "It would be nice to go south for a few days, maybe Disney World, if you guys don't think you're too old to go?"

The kids were instantly excited and ran upstairs to get ready for bed. Rachel realized they would indeed be "going to Disney World" just like the Super Bowl MVP announced each year immediately after the game's conclusion.

"Bill, what about Christmas mass?" asked Rachel.

"I'll find a church near the hotel. That's one of the perks of being a Catholic, the service is the same everywhere," said Bill.

"I don't know if I've ever said this to you, and I'm sorry if it sounds offensive, but it's the repetitive nature of the service that I can't understand. It's like vanilla ice cream—always the same. Often the homily is just rambling."

"Well, personally, I like that it's the same. Partaking in the Eucharist is what Jesus asks of us. Pope Francis described it as having 'compassion for others and with a commitment to sharing what we have.' And though some homilies are better than others, be honest with me, you've probably already checked-out by that point and aren't open to hearing the priest's intention to make the weekly scripture relate to our everyday lives."

"Honey, I admire your faith. My concerns are probably way off-base. It's just seems weird to me—Disney and Catholicism—I know some people consider them both to be 'religions,' but all in the same day?"

Rachel wondered if she could "let it go" like Disney's Elsa or if she needed to confront Bill now about his decision to coddle Hannah again. But before she forgot, there was one piece of unfinished business from the evening—Alan's surprise with the disclosure that Rachel was Jewish.

"Did you notice how Alan changed the subject after learning I was Jewish?" said Rachel.

"Only now that you mention it. I suspect it was harmless."

"Of course you would. You've never gotten it. You can be such an asshole at times, Bill" said Rachel who chose to ignore his flinching away from her. "Sure, Catholics get mistreated sometimes, but not like Jews and certainly not like people of color or other ethnic minorities. I sense that Alan is antisemitic. More Americans seem angry about the smallest matters than at any point I can remember in my lifetime. I worry things are going to explode. The media thrives on all the discord and the internet is filled with anonymously offered hate speech. And don't get me started on the President's role in all of this. But I noticed Alan's whole body tense up, his face turned a crimson color. It frightened me. And then, when I tell you how I feel, you blow me off."

"I'm sorry his reaction made you feel that way. And I'm truly sorry I made you feel dismissed. But I still think you're imagining things," Bill said, as he walked towards the living room.

Rachel felt a distance that she supposed all marital partners experienced from time to time in their marriage. Though she knew Bill better than anyone, she was never certain what she didn't know about him—everyone had private thoughts. This wasn't the first time he'd ever been dismissive. But it the past, it was about a less consequential matter than her feelings about being the target of antisemitism. It was discomforting, not unlike a stranger approaching her at a park. She hated it when she felt this way.

She wondered if Bill and other friends felt something similar at times about their own marital partner.

SPRING & SUMMER, 1944—SOUTH HAVEN

Following Kristallnacht, the Night of Broken Glass in 1938 when Jewish shops and houses were targets of attack in towns across Germany, the British government allowed ten thousand children, unaccompanied by their parents, to immigrate in an operation that came to be called the Kindertransport. This policy had a catch, though—the children were required to leave the United Kingdom to be reunited with their parents when the refugee crisis ended. Unfortunately, these reunions rarely occurred as most of the parents perished during the Holocaust. In addition, one out of ten of these very children were interned by the British government during the war, as antisemitic fears from British citizens lead to the conclusion that they might be Nazi sympathizers.

However, it was not until July 3rd, 1944, when the headline and sub-headline of the New York Times jumped off the page: "TWO DEATH CAMPS PLACE OF HORROR," that the world came to understand what was really going on in Nazi Germany.

Lottie and Daniel, her husband of four years, were now running the resort with ease, though having a two-year-old, Jack, in the picture, could make life more challenging. They were living in one of the rental properties along North Shore Drive that her parents acquired for overflow when business was booming, but things were quieter now with the war on and the resort was never full.

Lottie and Daniel attended the same grade school in South Haven, but they didn't date until after college. When she returned home after graduation, the pickings were pretty slim if one wished to marry within the Jewish faith. Daniel was a nice-looking guy and very attentive, but Lottie was never comfortable with his lack of passion about most anything. It caused her to wonder if she was the one out of step with the world—maybe it wasn't normal to always feel a fire burning inside, though her mother Helen seemed to have a similar orientation to life.

She returned home after graduation to help her mother with the resort. Her father Samuel suffered a stroke and, though he survived mentally intact, he could no longer use the right side of his body. This left him less able to perform many of the physical tasks required on the property. It also left him with a speech impairment. Despite these challenges, Lottie never saw him as diminished. His most important contribution to the family had always been his religiosity and he now had more time to study. And though it was hard to watch his frustration at times when attempting to communicate, he managed to get his point across when necessary.

Lottie wasn't above any job, even if it meant getting dirty or breaking a nail or two. Coming home wasn't a sacrifice. She always hoped to one day run the resort. Her education at the University of Chicago provided her with all the necessary financial skills. She majored in business and had plans for expansion when the war was over. It couldn't last forever.

Lottie's brother Jacob was still living in Chicago, but he left his accounting firm to head up his father-in-law's garment business. Since Samuel's stroke, Jacob tried to make the drive over to South Haven more frequently, usually staying at Lottie's home.

Lottie was waiting up for him late one Friday night when he pulled up to the house. After a big hug, they sat on the sofa under the warm glow from the Sabbath candles and visited.

"I wish I had grandma's candlesticks. I wonder why Mom didn't give us each one," said Jacob.

"You never light only one. You need to light two. It's the rule. Mom already informed me my youngest daughter is to have them when she marries."

"I think she loves you more than me. That's got to be it," said Jacob, shrugging his shoulders.

"Can you believe Isaac is now a captain in a paratrooper division?" said Lottie.

"He always loved airplanes as a kid," replied Jacob. "I wouldn't have been surprised if he had become a pilot, but jumping out of a plane is another matter. When he decided to enlist, I thought, being an attorney, he would sign up for some intelligence job pushing papers. But they need people in combat. Even I might still have to go. They're drafting men into their forties to serve. I'll go if it comes to that, but with two kids already, I'd rather not."

"I thought with a wife and a son he would have second thoughts about serving," said Lottie. "He seems consumed by hatred of the Nazis and National Socialists German Party. When Hitler came to power, Isaac insisted he represented more than an existential threat to Jews. He thinks Hitler will kill every Jew in Europe if he is allowed."

"I tried to write to Mom and Dad about his safety. They're frightened but proud he chose to serve. They're still pretty cool to his wife, Susan—but never to their son, Samuel. I think Isaac was trying to make up with them when he chose to name him after Dad."

"I suppose so," answered Lottie. "Marrying outside our faith is something I would never consider, but Isaac was deeply in love with Susan. He still remains an observant Jew. Sometimes I'm jealous of the passion I see in his marriage. Don't get me wrong, Daniel is a good man but I'm not sure we view life with a similar lens. I try to rationalize it. It's just not Daniel's personality to be intense about anything."

"I'm sorry to hear you say that. Rebecca and I are very happy. It seems to please her that I'm now working with her father. I don't miss my old accounting job and I know I can make more money in the garment industry. Roosevelt's War Production Board has us making uniforms for the soldiers. But after the war, things will change and our company will be well positioned. When the Allies win this war, and we will win it, America will become a dominant world power. Our economy will boom and my company will be nimble and ready to make whatever type of clothing people desire to wear. My guess is people will be ready to have fun after years of war. They'll want to buy clothing fit for a relaxed, leisurely culture. Come to think of it, the same mindset should help the family resort business. What do you think?"

"I've got my eye on a couple of properties here to expand our operation. Some of the other Jewish resort owners are getting older and not all of them have children poised to take over. I've got plans. I also wonder if the war will change our country's feeling about religious and racial differences. All those soldiers risking their lives standing next to others of different backgrounds. I think it will change our country. I think it will change the Goldman resort. I'm not sure we will be exclusively Jewish in the future. But I agree we should do well. People will be ready for some vacationing."

"We kind of got lost on business. You mentioned not always being on the same page with Daniel. Do you want to talk more about it? If it's too personal, would you rather speak to Rebecca?"

"Too personal? I guess you mean I should talk to a woman if it's about sex. No, it's not about sex. It's about commitment, not passion for each other—zeal for causes in our society like Mom always had. My life here in South Haven, and my work running the resorts, isn't enough. You mentioned Isaac's anger about the Nazis. I share it. I'm worried about Jews around the world. For me right now, with the war on against the Nazis, my religion is more than just my faith. I believe in the Zionist cause. Jews need a safe place to go. Maybe not those of us in America, but you never know. And it's not just the war that fires me up. You probably don't remember when Mom and Dad took me up to that resort for Black people a few hours north of here, Idlewild. Why can't Black people stay wherever they wish? It is no different from those signs we used to see at resorts around here screaming 'No Jews Allowed'. Dad always insisted our religion was about lifting everyone's suffering. These are the kind of things I wish concerned Daniel, but they don't."

✳ ✳ ✳

Several weeks later, Lottie was having her coffee and reading the newspaper on the porch waiting for her brother Jacob to wake up. This was the second visit he had made back to South Haven since the family learned several weeks ago of Isaac's death in combat. She tried to wait up for him last night, but she fell asleep before he arrived in from Chicago. Daniel was already out of the house attending to resort matters. It was July 3rd and the resort was full to capacity.

The Goldmans had not been notified of Isaac's death until several days after the fact. The family learned the sketchy details from newspaper accounts. US Army paratroopers descended near the town of Sainte-Mère-Église under cover of night, attempting to secure the city and nearby approaches for the planned beachhead invasion. For many, including her brother, it was their first combat experience. Each side of the conflict lost over four thousand men that day. Operation Overlord changed the course of the war and the course of world history, but it also changed everything for the Glickman family and many other families who lost a loved one.

By tradition, the resort always held a July 4th celebration. Though Lottie couldn't enjoy herself at all, she and Daniel made sure the guests enjoyed good food and the usual fireworks display. Most all the guests knew of the family's loss and expressed their sympathy. It was the first time Lottie chose to be out in public and attending the holiday events made it necessary to cut Shiva short by a couple of days, a decision her parents, Helen and Samuel, were ambivalent about.

"How do you think Mom and Dad are doing?" asked a sleepy Jacob walking out on the porch with a coffee cup in his hand.

"I'm not sure. I'm struggling so much myself. I know that sounds selfish but I'm trying to be honest. Dad seems quieter. He still talks, but his effort to be understood is less than usual since his stroke. Mom is so sad. They believe the war is being fought for good reason— but the death of their own son?" Lottie picked up her coffee cup and rolled her finger around the edges. "It's hard to accept. Mom has said as much to me, explicitly. The telegram is still sitting on the dining room table. 'The Secretary of War desires me to express his deep regret'... I cannot imagine losing my own child."

"Neither can I. I wish I were here more to help. What were you reading when I walked in?"

"The New York Times," answered Lottie. "It's one of many good habits I've acquired from Mom. There's a copy of a letter written by Eleanor Roosevelt. It speaks of the Declaration of Independence and its expression of hope. She emphasizes that the Declaration was written and signed by young men. At the end, she alludes to the ongoing war saying: 'That is what the youth of today is carrying out. God grant their elders help them'. Do you think God is involved in all this? Was he involved in Isaac's death? Could he, God, have prevented it?"

"I don't believe God works that way. He can't stop evil. Only better men can do that. I know that's what Isaac thought. He died trying to accomplish it. But my faith in God hasn't changed. I feel like something has been torn from my life in losing our brother, but I trust it will be filled again someday by my family and my faith."

"Well, her letter was only the tip of the iceberg in today's paper. Look at what's on page six."

The headline and sub-headline jumped off the page: "TWO DEATH CAMPS PLACE OF HORROR; German Establishments for Mass Killing of Jews Described by Swiss. The author of the report, Daniel Brigham, phoned this report into the Times, describing extermination camps at Auschwitz."

Lottie watched as her brother reached for a chair to sit down.

"Like you said, Jacob, God must not work amongst us here on earth. He wouldn't, couldn't, stand by watching all this. I, too, still believe, but it strengthens my resolve about the need for a safe place for Jews. I've thought this ever since Kristallnacht, the 'Night of

Broken Glass'—when they destroyed the synagogues and Jewish stores. Now, people are rumored to just disappear. I guess we now know where they took them."

Lottie and Jacob sat without speaking for minutes.

"Do you feel safe in America?" asked Jacob.

"Usually," Lottie replied. "Jacob, I know you might still get drafted, but please don't enlist. They need to pass a law prohibiting the drafting of men from a family who have already lost a loved one in war. It's too much to ask of any family, our family."

"I know you are hurting. I'll try not to go. That would please you, Mom, and my wife."

"Thanks, Jacob. I've got some lox and bagels for you before you go by to see Mom and Dad. I wish you didn't need to get back to Chicago tonight, but I understand. It's so good of you to drive all that way home for only a couple of hours with them."

Later that afternoon, Lottie stopped by her parents' home to bring dinner. While sitting shiva, the task of feeding her parents hadn't been necessary. Friends and neighbors, irrespective of their religion, had done so. The Glickmans were revered and seen as founding fathers of South Haven and news of Isaac's death spread quickly about the community. People were eager to repay the generosity Helen displayed to them over the years. Many attributed her unselfishness to her nature, but she knew better. It was commanded of her, a mitzvah, to reach out to those around her who were suffering. Helen and Samuel had been successful in farming and now the resort business. However, their life had greater meaning when they offered service to others, gemilut hasadim, acts of loving-kindness. It was something they tried to teach their children and hoped they would emulate in their own lives.

Tonight, when Lottie came in, her parents were seated together on the sofa simply holding hands. They didn't seem to hear her or notice when she noisily set the casserole dish on the kitchen counter. Lottie just listened to their sobs and her mother's voice trying to soothe her father. It was difficult to witness such suffering and intimacy between her own parents.

"Mom and Dad," Lottie said standing directly in front of them. "I brought over some dinner."

"Oh, where did you come from?" said her startled mother. "How are you doing, Charlotte?"

"I'm doing OK. I know Jacob's visit this afternoon was short, but I hope you enjoyed it. Thinking about losing Isaac is more tolerable for me when he is here. We share our loss and support each other. We try to do the same for you and Dad. We probably miss the mark, but we try."

"Charlotte, I have your father and he has me. We will move forward. But grief has its own timetable. We must give it time. One thing is for certain. I need to forgive your brother for marrying outside our faith. I need to go see Susan and young Samuel. I need to give them more of my heart. I have leftover love for Isaac to shower on them."

"I know you received word that his dog tags were found and that it helped in identifying his body. When can we have a proper funeral service?" Lottie asked.

"Grief isn't the only thing with its own timetable. I can't get straight answers from the government. I know they are doing their best but I would like closure. I would like to have his body cleansed properly and then buried with our help. Yes, a proper Jewish service."

"Mom, I need to get back home to Jack. Your resilience is inspiring." Bending down to kiss the top of her father's head and her mother's cheek, she added "Please eat the brisket and green beans I brought over. I'll see you tomorrow."

As she hurried towards the back door, she noticed the paper on the kitchen table open to the same page she showed her brother earlier this morning. DEATH CAMPS. She walked back into the den where her parents were still quietly sobbing.

"I didn't realize you saw the paper today. Is that why you are crying?" Lottie asked.

Her father Samuel tried to speak. Nothing would come out until a quite clear "Damn it." Since his stroke, it was rare for anything to be articulated precisely. It startled her. Lottie heard her father swear in the past, but she would have been hard pressed to remember the last time.

"Yes, we are crying for Isaac. We are crying for all those who have been murdered by the Nazis. Our mourning for those lost will never end and these horrendous acts must never be forgotten. Perhaps one day, those who committed these atrocities can be forgiven—perhaps not. I imagine it would be God's wish, but only after suffering the consequences of their actions."

I never imagined such evil could exist in the world. (From the diary of Lottie Goldman Zlatkin)

WINTER/CHRISTMAS 2017—SOUTH HAVEN

It was Saturday afternoon and she and Bill had just returned home from picking out a tree from the lot with the kids. She was in the garage pulling out the stored Christmas decorations in preparation for tonight's traditional evening of sipping hot chocolate, listening to Silent Night, and playing table games, but only after placing on the tree ornaments she had collected over the last twenty-plus years.

Bill and the kids were still outside giving the tree trunk a fresh cut before placing it in the stand. Disney World was a "go" for Christmas Day, but Rachel still wanted to put a tree up for Bill and the kids—and for herself. She loved the Christmas holidays.

She knew the money raised by the tree sales went to a local charity and one could expect the trees to only get more expensive year after year. However, this never stopped Bill, normally a bit of a cheapskate, from giving the teenage tree "salesman" a hundred-dollar bill for a tip. It had something to do with a complete stranger doing the same for him when working this type of lot as a kid in Missouri. It was one of those things that reinforced the feeling that she had married the right guy.

Though Rachel came from a Jewish home, her parents still chose during her childhood to celebrate Christmas and often with the tallest tree on the lot finding its way to their entrance hall up against the side of the fifteen-foot brick fireplace. In retrospect, it was a conspicuous sign to Rachel of her parents' choice to be secular Jews, more interested in assimilation than in their faith. But it was all that she knew and, consequently, celebrating Christmas with her own family didn't generate the same sense of exclusion she experienced on, for example, Easter.

Rachel opened the kitchen cabinet and pulled out the ingredients for a batch of chocolate chip cookies. Bill snuck in quietly behind her, placed his hand on her waist, and stuck his finger in the batter.

"Yum. This tastes great," said Bill.

"I can't believe you just did that. Actually, that's not an accurate statement since you do it all the time," said Rachel. Bill took his hand off her hip and took a few steps back.

"I'm sorry. Have you ever noticed that I'm always having to say I'm sorry around here? Maybe you could scold me less. You married me for better or for worse. By the way," he said with a grin on his face, "the kids and I are getting ready to put the wreath on the door, but we are thinking about adding a nativity scene in the front yard while we are at it."

"Bill Walsh. You've got to be kidding me! I do love the holidays but how far do you expect this Jewish girl to go?"

Sometimes the decorations and public anticipation of the holidays did get to Rachel. Did the Christian world think everyone wished to have their grocery stores, gas stations, and restaurants adorned with holly and pictures of Santa Claus? Her pediatric practice partners always tried to be politically or, in this case, religiously correct, by decorating the waiting room with both Christmas and Hanukkah items. She was the only Jewish partner and would acquiesce even though it bothered her to equate the two holidays. To Rachel, they weren't in the same ballpark, only sharing the same season on the calendar. One celebrated the birth of Christ—in her mind, the seminal event in Christian history. The other was in recognition of a Jewish war victory, as the Maccabees defeated their Greek-Syrian enemies in the second century BC, with the oil in the Temple lamp lasting eight days when there appeared to be only enough to last one.

Bill's family members and her friends often greeted her this time of year with a "Happy Hanukkah," but it only served to remind Rachel how conflicted her feelings were about being Jewish as a child and how they remained so to this day. Sometimes, someone she hardly knew said this to her and she wondered how they knew she was Jewish in the first place and whether they harbored any antisemitic tendencies or bias. More likely, they were nice people just trying to say the right thing.

Her confusion about the holidays was one of the issues on her mind when Rachel and the rabbi first started meeting. She had to laugh when reflecting on this—it reminded her of dating. It was by no means like the speed dating craze in vogue while she was in her early twenties—people going to a bar or bookstore and sitting across from other eligible singles and, for five minutes per table, asking a series of questions designed to expose the individual sitting across from them—assisting them in deciding whether to meet in the future for a real date. She wondered if the dating world still had these events or whether on-line dating and sites like Tinder made this an obsolete phenomenon like the slide ruler her grandfather took her to buy while taking a statistics course in high school.

Her visits with the rabbi reminded Rachel more of a television show that had been on briefly, In Treatment, showcasing weekly sessions with a therapist. Hesitant patients gradually opened up about what was bothering them and why they had come in the first place. Most of them, like Rachel, felt stuck and desired breaking through this inertia to make a difficult decision in order to move forward in their lives. It was almost universal for the patients to prefer that the therapist, Paul Weston, make the choices for them, but he pushed them to make their own, knowing that only when this occurred would a person assume real ownership of the results.

Maybe Rabbi Weinstein had seen the same show. He made it clear upfront that they would operate under such an arrangement.

She enjoyed the sessions more and more as time went by but felt very guilty about hiding the meetings from Bill. The longer she went without telling him, the more awkward it became. But there was a reason she wasn't ready to tell Bill yet. She remained uncertain of the destination these sessions would ultimately take her. It was bound to change things, maybe in a big way, and she worried that a change of any kind might drive a wedge in their marital relationship.

She and Bill briefly had a wedge moment in their marriage eight years ago when she arrived home from a girls' trip with a tattoo of a rose on her ankle. Rachel thought it was fun and part of what younger girls called being BFF. Bill was apoplectic, not speaking to her for days. When she finally coaxed him to say something, he explained how he couldn't reconcile her crazy decision with the woman he loved so much. He said he feared she was evolving into someone he wouldn't recognize and might run off ahead, leaving him behind. Though Bill claimed to be over it, she suspected it still remained an unpleasant memory for him.

"Mom," said Hannah walking into the kitchen. "Dad and Andrew are getting the tree set up. Can I help you set the table?"

"Sure," answered Rachel. "Do you know where I keep my Christmas plates? They are on the bottom shelf of the cabinet in the dining room. And get out my silver, but not the candlesticks. They are just for the Sabbath."

"It smells great in here," said Hannah. "I assume we're having the usual—green beans, twice-baked potatoes, and Filet Mignon?"

"Yup," answered Rachel.

Sometimes Rachel needed to remind herself that she never promised Bill "not to be Jewish." In fairness to him, he always wished for the family to celebrate the Jewish holidays as well. And being the cook in the house, he went so far as to spend an entire afternoon with her grandmother, Lottie, learning a bunch of Jewish recipes including one for matzo ball soup and another for potato latkes. Hearing all this, the rabbi counseled Rachel that exploring her religion would probably please Bill, not worry him, and Rabbi Weinstein encouraged her to tell him sooner than later.

But they continued to meet without his knowledge. Only her sister Michelle was aware of their sessions. Rachel needed to tell someone and who could be better than her sister to share her impressions about her journey with the rabbi?

"I'm so excited," Michelle exclaimed during one of their weekly phone calls. "Mom and Dad will be so delighted to know."

"I'll tell them when I'm ready, but not before I tell Bill," Rachel answered.

At the time, she thought about asking her sister to commit to secrecy, but knew it wasn't necessary. As kids they would commit to silence by making a pinky-promise, hooking their fifth fingers together in a type of handshake. Over the years, like many sisters, they built an inseparable bond. Secrets weren't to be shared with spouses, parents, friends, and especially not with their brother Paul who seemed unable to keep quiet about anything.

The rabbi, at first, gave her books to read about Judaism and they would come together to discuss what he had assigned. Over time, they expanded this format to include looking at the weekly Torah and Haftarah portions. Rachel performed both at her bat mitzvah, but she had completely forgotten about the Haftarah, a book of readings from The Prophets. The latter were paired each week with a Torah portion and often carried a similar message, but other times, they might share only a single word or thought.

They even dabbled at the Talmud, the book of rabbinical opinions of the Torah creating Jewish law to live by, and Kabbala, the unwritten mystical connection directly to God. Both of these were studied to appreciate the breadth of Jewish thought, though most secular Jews knew little, if anything, about either.

"I just cannot get over my fears of being Jewish," she openly offered this past Wednesday. "It seems so unfair. The kids I grew up with didn't have to wrestle with their Christian faith in the same way."

The rabbi almost scoffed at her. "Being born a Jew is a privilege. God made us his Chosen People, not that being born into another faith should be considered less significant. Do you think you chose to marry outside your religion to avoid confronting the issues of your Jewish heritage and faith?"

Rachel had been taken aback by his directness.

"I never consciously considered my faith in any manner when I chose Bill. I dated Jewish guys in the past. I always thought it was timing, meeting Bill at the right point in my life, rather than it having anything to do with avoidance. Even if true, and I doubt it, my grandmother taught me not to look back. She said it was part of our family's legacy to keep moving forward. I'm committed to examining Judaism anew and only then will I make my choices about the future role it might play in my life. But my marriage is great and Bill's religious devotion and spirituality informs me daily about the positive role faith plays. I want my life, though brief compared to how long I'll be dead, to be full and meaningful. Perhaps accepting faith will help me get there."

During prior sessions, Rabbi Weinstein spent time on Emil Fackenheim's "God's Presence in History" and it came to represent the central dilemma for Rachel when thinking about the Holocaust. Rabbi Weinstein was sensitive to Rachel's memory of being shown, as a child, actual film footage of concentration camps. She told him she felt that this traumatic experience was a big contributor to her conscious choice to be a ceremonial, and largely nonobservant Jew.

When the Holocaust came up again this week as an obstacle for Rachel, the rabbi responded, "Fackenheim's book attempts to reconcile the horrific events of the Holocaust with the notion of a provident god, but one distanced from history and the individual acts of mankind. He challenges us, as Jews, to think about the collective survival of our race and specifically to the establishment of a state of Israel. You've mentioned your grandmother more often than your parents since we started our study together. Did you discuss the Holocaust with her while she was alive?"

"Of course. She felt so guilty about her own survival, off safely in America. At her funeral, a friend of hers reminded me of her Zionist beliefs. This friend mentioned my grandmother's wish to visit Israel one day, but she never realized her dream. Towards the end of her life, I tried to engage her at times about Israel, but her dementia didn't allow her to process what was transpiring over there."

"Rachel, how do you feel about Israel?" asked the rabbi.

"Confused. The Israeli people aren't said to be all that religious. Wars break out all the time. Should the West Bank be occupied?

Should they have a two-state solution? Their government is a democracy, but a chaotic one. They have built an Atomic Bomb, but publicly deny having done so. My head rocks with confusion."

"Well, I, for one, am glad Israel exists," said Rabbi Weinstein. "Let's start with this topic next week. Remember, though geopolitical events can make it difficult, one can remain confused about Israel and still embrace your Jewish faith. I often look for more nuanced solutions when addressing many of the problems I discuss in my study with members of the congregation. Usually I'm applying this approach to those experiencing interpersonal conflicts, but I think it applies to your concerns about Israel and our faith. Don't allow this conflict to distract you right now. I'm enjoying our visits very much. I hope they're helping."

She remembered feeling numb and a bit disoriented last Wednesday sitting in the car outside the temple after their session was concluded. Inside the rabbi's study, she was contemplating issues she had put on hold too long. The upcoming holidays meant the trip to Disney World was on.

She knew it was the kind of trip any family would talk about forever, but she wanted to speak to Bill about a trip to Israel as well, as soon as she was comfortable divulging her visits with the rabbi. Such a trip would allow her to fulfill her grandmother's dream and give the kids an opportunity to see the historic sites of their own religion alongside hers. It might rival, or even surpass, Disney World as a trip the family would never forget.

It was a wonderful evening—dinner was delicious, the tree got decorated, the chocolate chip cookies were all eaten, and Andrew won the annual game of Monopoly when Bill landed on St. James Place and had to pay rent, with hotel of $950. Only two ornaments got broken—a family record. But the highlight of the evening was Bill's presentation, complete with easel and poster board, illustrating his "plan of attack" for their trip to Disney World in order to maximize their three days experience.

The kids had gone to bed and it was just the two of them, sitting by the fire. "The kids are really looking forward to the trip," said Bill reaching for her hand. "Thanks for making the evening really special. I love you."

"You're welcome," Rachel answered squeezing his hand. "By the way, I know you think wearing that Mouseketeer Ear Hat during your presentation enhanced the performance, but you look like a dope in it. Can we lose it before the trip?"

SPRING 1947— SOUTH HAVEN

The National Council of Jewish Women was increasingly committed to Israeli organizations dedicated to empowering woman in their society. They were also carefully following news surrounding statehood. Guest speakers at Helen's group spoke of a post-war world where governments were still trying to process the atrocities committed by the Nazis. The United Nations' position was to support the Balfour Declaration of 1917 calling for a Jewish home in Palestine, though they stopped short of asking for statehood. Truman, after appointing a committee to study the issue, took the latter position. Most experts believed that the UN would ultimately favor the Partition Resolution, creating both an Arab and an Israeli State thus leaving the big elephant in the room—what to do with Jerusalem? A decision needed to be made by May 1948 when the British mandate to govern the area was set to expire.

"I know you'd like it if I moved in here with your family but I'm not sure it is a good idea, Charlotte," said Helen. "I can still live on my own."

"Dad has been gone for over a year," said Lottie. "You're not eating well. Your clothes are hanging off you. I know you're supposed to be on a special diet for your diabetes. If you lived with Daniel and me, you would eat healthier and you'd be a big help with the kids. Jack is starting to be a handful and Joan is still a baby. She requires a lot of attention. You know me. I like being busy but taking care of the kids and the resort is a challenge."

"You two are doing a great job with the resort properties and with the kids. Are you thinking about having more children?"

"I'd like to. I enjoy motherhood more than I thought I would. But, it's hard to get Daniel excited about anything other than his music. I thought his playing the saxophone would be nice, a reminder of Jacob's playing when we were growing up. But it has come to signify a kind of gap between us. I can't seem to close it. My passion is for people—my kids, the people that come to the resort, and those I've come to know through the National Jewish Council of Women—not jazz. By the way, I'm so glad you got me involved with Council."

"Someday soon, maybe you can replace me on the Board of Directors. I love the work we do and, though I believe I still have something to add, I'm getting older, and you'd love the scope of our work at the Board level. Last week our speaker discussed rumors surrounding statehood," said Helen. "He thought most nations simply wanted access to the oil in the Middle East and he didn't believe they were motivated to solve the question of who has the better right to the land. Is it the Jews or the Arabs? He said his friends at the State Department have concluded that separate states would only push the Soviets to seek alliances in the Arab world and diminish US influence. My personal opinion is that Jews desperately need a homeland, but I wish for peace as well. If things aren't settled very carefully, the region will be a tinderbox."

"I'm not sure how I'd feel about Israel if their goals ever came into conflict with our own here in the United States. But the Holocaust…" Lottie paused to collect herself before continuing. "I'll just say that I too hope for the establishment of a state of Israel and a safe landing spot for the Jews around the world. But this strip of land is so small and it's a desert. How can it be developed into something successful and how can two diverse cultures coexist in a tiny city like Jerusalem?"

"That's a bigger question than you and I are going to solve today.

Let's get back to you and Daniel. Your father was a big believer in being on the same page in our marriage. We had rough spots, every marriage does. I'm worried about this distance you are feeling. Daniel seems to be a good man. He works hard around the resort and seems to adore you."

"He does. I do love him. I suppose everyone wishes they could change something about their spouse."

"Maybe you two need a date night. I'll watch the kids."

"That would be nice, Mom. It would be even nicer though, if you take up my offer and moved in."

"I know you mean well but it's not going to happen. The extra rooms at my house come in handy when your brother Jacob visits with his family or when Susan and little Samuel do the same—he reminds me so much of your brother, Isaac," said Helen. "There is another reason but I hadn't want to tell you yet. Last weekend, I didn't go to Chicago to hear the symphony with Janet. I really went alone. I met Saul Bernstein. His wife passed away several years ago. We had dinner and a lovely evening. I miss your father's companionship. Saul might start to visit here more regularly. Are you OK hearing this?"

"Wow. You've surprised me there. Does Jacob know? You said you were going to see Jacob when you were in Chicago last weekend or was that another cover for your date?" asked Lottie, swatting her mother's arm playfully.

"I saw your brother, but no, I didn't tell him. I will. You don't need to do that for me."

"Mom, I'm OK with you seeing Saul. I think Dad would be, too. He wouldn't want you lonely for companionship at the end of your life. You worked so hard caring for him after his stroke. Mr. Bernstein is a kind man. He played an awfully large role in our family's success. Dad would like you to be with someone like Saul, who lives his faith."

"You're putting the cart before the horse, young lady. I like Saul. But I don't know what he would see in me. I'm no Miss America, not like that Jewish girl from the Bronx, Bess Myerson—though you remind me of her—beauty and brains. Look, I'll babysit a little more and stay some weekend nights. You and Daniel can go out a little. See if a few 'dates' can recharge your relationship. Show some interest in the jazz music he likes. Can we just leave it there for now?"

❋   ❋   ❋

After the war ended, resorts all along the eastern shore of Lake Michigan thrived. People wanted to travel and relax. Lottie and Daniel, with her mother Helen's emotional and financial support, got out in front of the curve by investing to upgrade the resort and add rooms.

Though in competition with other resorts for guests, the Goldmans, as the family would forever be referred to, enjoyed a reputation for helping out other proprietors in a pinch. If resorts ran out of something, even an item as simple as bagels, they knew who to call.

Additionally, Lottie made arrangements with some non-Jewish resort business owners to take some of their overflow from time to time. This had not been possible before the war and, though antisemitic feelings still lingered, blatant indications like signs forbidding Jewish guests had been taken down. Some of these relationships improved to a point that the Goldmans often were the first people competitors called when wishing to sell their places and retire.

In the winter, Daniel supervised projects to improve the resort. The previous winter, he built a tower in the middle of the cottages to house a speaker system, playing music throughout the day. He replaced the old swimming pool with a more modern one. He poured concrete for shuffleboard and added a miniature golf course. He even completed Lottie's long-held wish to improve their beachfront, building a large shack to store a badminton set, some inner tubes, and a few canoes. Each improvement led to more requests from their guests and the Goldmans tried to fulfill each one of them.

Night-time activities still included dances, bingo, and a talent show. But this year they planned to add a Cowboy Night, complete with campfire, singing, and roasting marshmallows for S'mores. Lottie had learned to make S'mores at the age of ten while in the Girl

Scouts—in fact, she still had a copy of "Tramping and Trailing with the Girl Scouts" on her bookshelf.

The city of South Haven was changing as well. More stores and restaurants were opening, and though the population continued to ebb and flow between summer and winter months, there was now enough economic activity to support the city's growing business community. As a child, Lottie's clothing was purchased from catalogs or once-a-year shopping trips to Chicago with her siblings. Now, she could simply walk a few blocks into town and get whatever she needed. Prior to the war, some of the merchants had treated her poorly because she was Jewish, but this type of behavior was becoming less common, though still displayed on occasion, in post-war South Haven.

When guests from the large Midwestern urban areas checked-in over the summer, Lottie overheard conversations between them that suggested feelings towards the Jewish population where they lived were still problematic at times. She got the same impression when attending national meetings of Council and it made her sad and a bit frightened, but it also gave her some relief to know that South Haven, a much smaller city, seemed a little more immune to such problems.

Many spoke of moving to the suburbs, often to subdivisions where the majority of their neighbors were also Jewish and joining Jewish country clubs—the latter being a necessity as Jews remained excluded from established clubs. They spoke of joining hospital auxiliaries at their local Jewish hospitals. These institutions had begun popping up in major cities as Jews preferred not to be treated in largely Christian-affiliated medical centers.

And some spoke of businesses discriminating in hiring practices—a husband or wife may have been qualified for an advertised position only to be turned down when it was discovered that they were of the Jewish faith. Fortunately, this wasn't a universal experience as many in business leadership positions served in the war alongside those of different ethnic and religious backgrounds and actively disapproved of such unwritten policies.

Assimilation was on the minds of Jewish Americans was well.

Lottie witnessed this over the summer months in her clients' dress, and their interests in popular books, movies, and music. Many of the women returned to the resort having undergone plastic surgery on their noses, something Lottie thought carried things a bit too far. Food requests were less often for the classic Jewish dishes and more often for mainstream items like Beef Stroganoff and Baked Alaska. And many of their clients started to identify themselves as Reform Jews—holding to tradition, and the Torah, but wishing to have their religion keep pace with the modern world. *Tikkun olam,* repair of the world, was a central tenant of the reform movement and rabbis were pushing their membership to act on issues of social justice.

This attracted Lottie, but she also worried that Reform Judaism, along with so many things pulling at Jews in post-war America, might lead many to become simply ceremonial, with an inevitable erosion in the number of those truly observant.

❋   ❋   ❋

"Daniel," said Lottie. "My mother wants to babysit this Saturday night. I was thinking we might take in a show at the Model Theatre over on Phoenix Street. The Fabulous Dorseys is playing. It's a movie I read about in the Times. The Dorsey brothers play themselves documenting their rise to fame. I thought we could go by the Real Bakery afterwards for a donut. Maybe a 'date night' would be good for us."

"Great. I read the same article but wasn't sure you'd want to go see a jazz movie. Sometimes it seems like my bad saxophone playing is too much for you."

"You play better than you think. I know it's your passion. I think it's time I got more interested in jazz music. When I was in college, I used to move pretty well on the dance floor. I know you like to fill in with the bands in the summer, but maybe this year we could dance together a little more."

"Sure. Date nights and dance nights. Let's give both of them a shot."

* * *

"So, what did you think of the movie Lottie?" asked Daniel.

"I thought it was great. I loved the scene with that piano player and all the Dorsey brothers standing around and then joining in. His fingers were flying. I've never heard anyone play the piano quite like him."

"That was Art Tatum. He's a savant. They call what he does, 'reharmonization'. He takes the melody and then alters the harmony that typically goes along with it. He plays in Chicago from time to time. We could go see him."

Lottie did enjoy the movie. She wanted to show interest in something Daniel liked, but she worried that if she gave him an inch, he would take a mile and play his music in the house and at the resort even more. She really didn't like jazz music very much.

"I do appreciate you showing interest in my jazz. I know, at times, I get too wrapped up in it."

"Look, it's who you are. I get pretty wrapped up myself in stuff."

"But you seem to have more capacity than I do—managing the resort, the kids, and all your community activities. I can't keep up. But I'm all ears right now. Tell me a little bit about your work with the Federation. We can sit here awhile longer. Your mother has the kids and I'm pretty content eating this Long John. By the way, I think they named this type of donut after the underwear people started wearing a few years back."

"I'm not sure you're right about that," Lottie answered with a laugh. "Let's talk about the Federation some other night, if that's ok with you? I want tonight to just be a 'fun' night."

"That's fine but can I ask you one question about Israel? I know you girls with the Federation follow this more carefully than I do. How can two diverse cultures be expected to coexist in a city like Jerusalem?"

"I'm not sure myself. It's so important to both of them. My parents raised me to be a Zionist. My father used to cite from Chronicles that King Solomon quoted God as saying he gave Jerusalem to his people—the Jewish people—he brought them out of bondage from Egypt. But I'm also a realist. The Bible may not be the best or only resource to look to for answers to modern questions. The city represents so much to so many. I hope it can work. I'd like to plan a trip to go to Jerusalem someday. Daniel, thank you for such a nice evening."

"I give you all the credit. It was your idea we go out tonight."

"Not really, it was my mother's!"

Daniel paid the check, gave the young waiter a handsome tip, and then got up from the table to head out the door.

"Oh, sit down for a moment. I almost forgot to tell you something." Lottie had a big smile on her face. "I'm pregnant again. Now put your hat and coat on. It's chilly outside tonight. If we hurry, we can still catch the last set at the Pavilion. I think they still only charge twenty-five cents for three dances."

It won't be long before Israel obtains statehood. I wish Samuel were still alive to see it. (From the translated diary of Helen Glickman Goldman)

FEBRUARY 2018—
SOUTH HAVEN

It had been snowing now for days, at times even sleeting, and though the roads were a mess, Rachel was getting dressed to go out to lunch. Bethe, her best friend since grade school, had arranged for a group of old friends to get together in Saugatuck.

"You look different, but great," said Bill.

"I'm channeling my sister's fashion style. I think it works on me. I'm off to lunch at the Southerner with some high school friends."

"I'm certain you never told me about it," he paused, "or maybe you did and I didn't pay attention when you told me."

"Maybe," said Rachel, rolling her eyes as she went out the door.

Bethe told Rachel that Mary, Sarah, and Christy would make it, but she'd asked several others who were hesitant to commit. They tried to get together periodically, but as time went on, it was hit or miss, as their kids' activities always came first. Rachel found that outside of Bethe, she was losing touch with most of them. It was only natural for Bill and her to be developing closer ties to parents with kids at the same school and in the same grade as their own children—they were spending more time than she would have ever imagined watching ballgames and attending other school activities together.

Rachel and Bethe met in the fourth grade. They were rarely apart since. They went to the same Jewish Sunday school and spent two months every summer at a sleepaway camp in Wisconsin. Between school, camp, and religious school on Sundays, they saw each other nearly every day, even more often than their own parents. Bethe's kids were of slightly different ages than her own, giving them little time to visit lately, but they tried to carve out enough to make their friendship work. Rachel had a prescient feeling that this effort, and their bond, would become even more important as they grew older.

Her friends could count on Rachel being punctual, though she was never certain if this was a curse or not. When she came into the restaurant, Bethe was already sitting at the table. Rachel suspected she might have something she wished to discuss privately before the others arrived customarily late.

"Your hair looks great," said Bethe as Rachel approached the table.

"You must need to see the eye doctor, Bethe. It is untamed as usual," Rachel said. "The other day I saw myself in the mirror and thought I was looking at my own mother twenty years ago after a long day at the inn. But I am dressed a little differently—I'm ready to take this on as my new 'theme'—I borrowed it from my sister."

Rachel caught the waitress's attention as she rushed by the table and ordered a glass of white wine.

"I'm so glad you're early. I wanted to ask you about Johnny. I know you aren't technically his pediatrician, but when we decided years ago that we were too close for that relationship, you still said I could call anytime."

"You know to never think twice about asking me anything and it will stay, as Seinfeld says, in the vault."

"Johnny's having abdominal pain and vomiting. It is more common on the weekends than school days," she said. In Rachel's experience, kids with recurrent abdominal pain were more likely to be afflicted on weekdays—anxious about school or trying to get out of going for a myriad of reasons. Rachel switched into detective mode. After a series of questions, she was pretty sure she knew the answer, a diagnosis that had eluded a gastroenterologist who performed an unnecessary endoscopy on Johnny and found little.

"And Johnny spends hours taking hot baths. It is the only thing that seems to relieve the pain," continued Bethe.

"Do you think he smokes pot?" Rachel asked.

"I know he does," Bethe answered. "When we realized he was smoking almost daily, we laid down the law and he promised he would cut back, but he says it helps him to relax socially and he wasn't willing to give it up on weekends."

Rachel paused to think about how to tell her friend about her suspicions. "I think he is suffering from cannabinoid hyperemesis syndrome. Can I talk to him about his marijuana use? I'll try to persuade him to give up smoking all together. It can't be fun to puke and be in that much pain every weekend. And if he is really that anxious socially, it's time he see someone and get started on some talk therapy or medication, or better yet, both."

Bethe looked worried, but relieved as well. "Thanks. I think."

It turned out to only be the five of them at lunch. The others ordered a drink and the group decided to split two orders of fish and chips. The topic of discussion, not surprisingly, turned to their kids.

Christy mentioned her son, Tony, coming into the kitchen after school looking a bit down. When she asked him if he and his girlfriend Jennifer were getting along, he answered, "Everything is milk and cookies."

Sarah chipped in. She asked her daughter, Lisa, the same question recently about her boyfriend and was chastised with a "that's pretty random, Mom."

They took turns rattling off the language of the day—loser, hook-ups, woke, filthy, chill, hot mess, darty.

"I wonder what our kids would call Sally Fogarty these days?" asked Mary. "I remember my mother questioning me once, asking me if she was 'fast' and I had no idea what she was talking about. We just called her a slut or easy."

Bethe chimed in with a sad smile "I think Sally was simply insecure. I hope she's happy wherever she is today. We were pretty clueless back then on how to reach out to someone who might be dealing with difficult issues in their life. Last week at the Temple

Auxiliary meeting, a woman none of you know confided something very personal to me. I was more prepared to help her."

"I didn't know you practiced your faith," said Christy. "Rachel, I see you at church with Bill on holidays. You don't go to Temple though, do you?"

Rachel squirmed and answered, "I hadn't been going for a long time but recently, I've been back several times. I'm not completely sure how I feel about it."

Rachel wondered if Bethe could sense how uncomfortable she was with the subject turning to religion. Perhaps Bethe did because she changed the subject back to kid speak. "OK, who is going to spill the tea?"

Rachel glanced about the table to see if the others were as confused as she was. "We're all just chilling, having a glass of wine. No one has any tea," said Rachel laughing at herself for using the word 'chill' publicly for the first time in her life.

Bethe replied. "So, your kids don't use that expression. It's what the human race has called gossip for hundreds of years."

Mary sat up straighter in her seat. "Rumor has it that a John Jeffries and Betty McDaniel are dating. They both are recently divorced and, since they were voted cutest couple in high school, decided to get together again. I know it sounds sweet but you wouldn't catch me dead with Bobby Sandler again—nor could I see you Bethe with Michael, or Rachel with Henry, or Christy with Danny, or Mary with Steve."

"Agree," they chimed in unison.

* * *

The drive home was beautiful. The weather had cleared up and the trees were covered by a dusting. This was the Michigan only full-time residents ever saw. The fir trees lining Interstate 196 were framed by a crystal blue sky and, if she concentrated, Rachel might see several hawks on the way home.

But she was distracted by the conversation with Bethe about

Johnny and his marijuana use. It was a familiar story. When she first started in practice her days were filled with newborn baby after newborn baby. She had few adolescent patients initially to care for and none of her own at home to allow for practice or personal research. She remembered saying to Bill one date night, "I just don't get any of their psychosocial issues. It mostly seems like drama to me." But now the slew of babies had grown up, as were her own kids, and with their maturation came an expanded understanding of adolescents and the role she wished to play in their lives.

She now wanted to be the one in the office when a kid's life was in crisis believing she was well prepared to help these kids if a crucial event was playing out in their lives. Though she couldn't undo a mistake already made, she could limit the damage and assist patients, and their families, to move forward and make better choices in the future.

It was quite common for her adolescent patients to admit that they were smoking pot, but unless their lives were in danger, or they were endangering the life of someone else, she found it unethical to inform the parents and why "trash" the useful role confidentiality often played between some of the teens and herself? Her routine, around the age of twelve, included discussing the "rules" of confidentiality so that everyone knew them in advance. Smoking pot was one of many potential secrets adolescent patients asked her to keep. Parents put their trust in Rachel to counsel their children wisely when these issues came up. And though these matters did remain secret, Rachel developed, over her career, subtle methods to clue parents in that their teens were struggling. Better yet were the times she could persuade a teen to share information directly with their parents.

She looked forward to seeing Johnny. She thought he would trust her and listen seriously to the advice she would offer.

Her colleague, Randy Miller, served as Andrew and Hannah's pediatrician. In the past, she shared her concerns about Andrew's withdrawn nature. Randy listened carefully but reminded her of what she already knew, all his conversations needed to remain private, even those he had with Rachel's own children.

But now she wondered if Andrew could be smoking pot. When a parent called asking if she would screen their adolescent's urine for drugs without their knowledge, she refused. But now, hearing about Johnny, she wondered if her head was in the sand about Andrew. She never smelled it on his clothes and she hadn't witnessed him acting high, but maybe she should send a cutting of his hair into one of those labs that tested for drugs.

She checked herself. Could she really be thinking of doing something she found so abhorrent when parents in her practice resorted to these methods?

Rachel would question parents requesting non-consensual drug testing as to what they planned to do with the information if they had it or whether they ever considered just flat out asking their kid about drug use. Now faced with her own concerns about Andrew, Rachel wasn't sure what she would do about the former. As to the latter, she was fairly certain he wouldn't admit anything to her. Andrew didn't see her as Dr. Walsh, confidant, but just another intrusive mother.

Perhaps he would open up to Bill.

"I'm just freaked out by Bethe's concerns," she said out loud to herself. "I know Andrew's fine."

✳ ✳ ✳

Rachel was surprised to find Bill's car gone when the garage door opened. The television was still on loudly. There was a scrawled note lying near the kitchen phone.

You left your cell here. Tried to reach you but… Your dad passed out at temple. No other information. The kids and I are headed to the hospital.

Rachel quickly used the bathroom and then jumped back into the car for the five-minute ride to the hospital. Using her cell to call Bill, he informed her the doctors diagnosed a small stroke but her father was stable. "How's Mom?" she asked. "Actually, fairly composed," Bill replied. "Just get here and you can see it all for yourself."

Her dad was propped up by a pile of pillows, looking pale, with most of his body covered by one of those ridiculous hospital gowns. His head lolled and his eyes were shut. In fact, the only reason she assumed he was alive was the beeping of the cardiac monitor. Rachel quietly kissed his forehead before turning to Bill, the kids, her mother, and surprisingly, Rabbi Weinstein.

"He's going to be fine," Joan spoke first. "Thank goodness Rabbi Weinstein activated EMS right away. They were there in minutes."

"He was reading out loud and began to slur his speech. Then he just kind of tilted to the side," offered the rabbi. "Unfortunately for Mr. Bender, we had a dry run, if you will, last week at the temple. He didn't fare as well. I think I did a better job today with your father. By the way, I missed you this past Wednesday. It was the first time you've missed one of our appointments."

✳ ✳ ✳

"So, when were you going to tell me about your meetings with the rabbi?" Bill asked after the rabbi had left and they were sitting alone in the hospital's family lounge.

"I don't know," replied Rachel. "You know me. I need to be successful at everything I try and I didn't want to talk about it yet. I'm still struggling to understand and define what success would even look like. My world of science seems at odds with being religious. You know I'm envious of your faith and the security it seems to give you especially now that we are getting older. I wish I could believe in an afterlife. I want to believe that another holocaust won't occur in my lifetime or our children's. As a Jew, I want to believe that I, and others, will not be victimized by antisemitism. I can't bear the thought of such hatred injuring our children. You do remember me telling you, years ago, that our children, just by the fact of being born to a Jewish mother, are considered Jews regardless of how we have chosen to raise them or how they identify themselves."

"I understand that being Jewish is different from being a Christian, but I don't think accepting faith needs to be about reconciling it with science, understanding the Holocaust, or turning the other cheek to antisemitism. It is about living in a just and ethical manner. Rachel, you live that way every day. I've never regarded you as anything but a religious person."

"But what do you get out of it, your religion? What do you get out of going to church? We've talked about it before—the service is the same every time. Often when you get home and I ask you about the sermon, you might answer that you didn't even listen."

"We had the same discussion when the trip to Disney came up. Do you remember? First of all," Bill answered. "it is not a sermon, it's a homily. The priest reads a passage of scripture and then comments on it. He usually applies it to some fairly ordinary situation in life. I often find it meaningful. It's true, sometimes I don't listen. Perhaps my mind is on something else or that day I am choosing to pray for someone or something else. Rachel, if I had to put it into a single word, my faith gives me a feeling of peace. It reminds me that I am a small piece of something much larger. Even the worst of events has a purpose, God's purpose. I don't see God as being capable of preventing all bad from happening. Mankind is flawed, original sin. But my faith grounds me. In the past, you have indicated that you believe my values come from my parents, not religious dogma. I suppose there is a lot of truth to that statement. But I really can't separate how my parents raised me from their own strong religious beliefs. Does any of this help?"

"Kind of."

"Perhaps, you don't go to temple like I go to church, but..."

"But lately, I've been going to temple." Rachel interrupted. "I think I'm actually starting to get something out of it. Why should I assume to have all the answers and turn my back on the wisdom of generations and the teachings of the Torah?"

"Look, this is all a wonderful revelation. I'm glad you've been meeting with Rabbi Weinstein. Though I'm surprised you have kept this a secret, I can't wait to hear more about it. Right now, let's go back in and sit with your father. He seemed to rest more comfortably the moment you walked in and I know why. To him, you are above all else, 'my daughter, the doctor'."

They visited with her dad for another few minutes. He was awake but needed to rest. The ride home was quiet. The kids were both in the back listening to music, headphones on, looking like Will Farrell and Chris Pattan—the Roxbury guys on SNL—heads bobbing to the beat.

"He'll be ok," said Bill.

"I know," answered Rachel. "I'm just not ready to see my father growing older. I don't want to see him getting fragile and more vulnerable. It's an adjustment. My Dad was invincible in my memory from my childhood. I still want to see him that way. If I can't, then I can't think of myself as young anymore, either. Time seems to be an enemy. I'd like to hit the pause button or somehow learn to accept life's brevity."

"I get it." Bill pulled into the driveway. "I feel the same way at times. Let's get to bed. It's been a long day."

The kids had yet to notice the car had stopped. "Hey," Bill turned. "Get out of the car, you numbskulls."

❋ ❋ ❋

Rachel waited until they were undressing for bed, but she had one more thing on her mind. She looked over at Bill who was standing in his jockey shorts rubbing his neck. She knew he was tired from an exhausting day, but the memory of seeing her father lying inert on the hospital gurney was fresh. Rachel didn't wish to wait.

"I know we're both tired but there's a conversation I've been wanting to have ever since we got back from Disney World. I'd like to take you all to Israel," said Rachel.

"You want to talk about this now? Aren't you exhausted?"

"I am but it's a night like tonight that reminds me how fast life is moving. None of us know when we will lose our health. I want to fulfill my grandmother's wish. There is so much to see in Israel from both of our religions. Imagine for you, visiting the birthplace of Christ in Bethlehem, the Church of Joseph in Nazareth, the Basilica of Annunciation, Capernaum near the Sea of Galilee, and the garden of Gethsemane."

"That all sounds great."

"Good!" Rachel was relieved. "I want to see Jerusalem. I want to stand at the Western Wall, near the Foundation Stone. I know I will feel as if my grandmother Lottie will be holding my hand, standing beside me."

"I thought it was called the Wailing Wall and I've never even heard of the Foundation Stone."

"It is more properly called the Western Wall. The Western Wall is just west of the Dome of the Rock, built over the Temple Mount and the Foundation Stone. The Wall's proximity to the Temple Mount makes it the most sacred place for Jews to pray. The Dome is an Islamic shrine built between 685 and 691 CE. Jews cannot enter the Dome. The mount was where God asked Abraham to sacrifice his only son, Isaac. I think of it as God's 'ultimate ask' of Abraham to demonstrate his faith, though I find cruelty in the request, as well. I would like to see Masada, the fortress high above the Dead Sea, where 930 Jews in 73, or 74, CE committed mass suicide rather than have their families be taken captive by their Roman conquerors. Though strange to honor a mass suicide, Masada has come to represent to Israelis self-determination and the modern-day fight for national identity and nation status. Just talking about all this gives me chills."

"Start planning the trip, but I'd like to wait until the kids are old enough to appreciate what they are seeing," said Bill.

"OK, how about Christmas 2019?"

"Sounds good to me."

FALL, 1955—
SOUTH HAVEN

The papers were full of news about this tragedy in April of 1955. After receiving approval for use in the United States, several different laboratories began production of the polio vaccine. Cutter Laboratories, a California-based company, didn't properly follow the instructions Jonas Salk gave to inactivate the virus in formaldehyde resulting in 200,000 children in five Western and mid-Western states being exposed to polio. Before being halted nationally, 40,000 cases had occurred leaving 200 with some paralysis and 10 dead. Though Dr. Salk had nothing to do with this error, it resulted in his reputation being tarnished and, incredibly, he was denied the Nobel prize. The legacy of using basic laboratory science in only six years to solve a world health threat was established. But on the negative side, a skepticism about vaccine safety would begin and persist to this day.

Fall had arrived in South Haven and the colors never failed to startle Lottie year after year. Daniel was pruning the river birch in the front yard and was wearing a fleece jacket and gloves.

"Oh my goodness. I guess I'll need a jacket myself this morning," said Lottie realizing she'd underestimated the chill in the air.

"Where are you off to?" asked Daniel.

"The cemetery. It's the anniversary of Mom's death."

Lottie still wished her mother, Helen, and Saul hadn't gone out for a drive on that rainy night five years ago. But she was grateful that it was just one car involved and no one else was injured in the accident that took their lives.

"I never imagined anything like that happening to someone in our family. But your mother had a full life and enjoyed Saul's company during her last years. You've told me before that you were happy for her—that it didn't tarnish the memory of your own father."

"It was a little strange to be honest, but Mom was a force. I knew better than to think she would ever do anything she didn't want to. Her marriage to my Dad was a strong one and the time with Saul was meant to be. But today, as I reflect upon my mother's life, it's her accomplishments in business and the community of which I'm most proud. If I live long enough, maybe I can accomplish half of what she did."

"Don't forget to put a pebble on the headstone," said Daniel. "I think it's part of a Talmudic tradition. I'm not even sure how I know that fact."

"I remember my father explaining that to me when I visited the graves of my grandparents in Detroit," said Lottie. "I think you're right. It has something to do with keeping the soul of the dead down here on earth. I enjoy leaving a stone much better than flowers. A week from now, the flowers will be wilted but the pebble I leave today will still be there signaling, to others visiting their own relatives at the cemetery, that my parents are still missed."

"What else are you up to today?" asked Daniel.

"I've got appointments for the kids to get the polio vaccine this afternoon. Maybe you can make dinner?"

❊ ❊ ❊

When Lottie was a child, she hardly ever went to the doctor. Her parents only deemed it necessary when she had a fever for more than three days. There were no pediatricians in South Haven at the time, therefore, a trip to the doctor meant a trip to Benton Harbor. Dr. Knowles, a general practitioner, listened to her chest and tapped along her body with his fingers. She was never quite sure if this tapping was part of a real medical exam or simply Dr. Knowles trying to be playful with his patients. He talked about germs but when her mother quizzed him, he offered little in the way of treatment. He would simply say, "I hope it doesn't develop into something serious like pneumonia or a case of consumption."

South Haven now had a population large enough to attract a physician of its own. Lottie had been calling the doctor's office ever since reading in the *New York Times* back on April 13th about Jonas Salk and his development of a polio vaccine with the potential to save lives around the world. Polio scared everyone in the fifties, perhaps eclipsed only by fear of the Atom Bomb. And though adults could contract the disease, it was toughest on those under five, often leading to paralysis and, rarely, death. Outbreaks were more prevalent in the summer months, yet little was known about how the infection was spread. Lottie was desperate to have Jack, Joanie, and Alan vaccinated before the summer that just ended, but the Cutter Incident halted mass vaccination in the United States.

"Please sit quietly," Lottie said to no one of her three children in particular. "You're all old enough to behave better."

"Hi, Mrs. Zlatkin," said Betty Moss. "I see you have your gang in tow. I'm here with my son George. He jammed his fingers in a door hinge. I think my daughter, Allison, is in Girl Scouts with your daughter."

"Of course. I remember meeting you at Martha's house. Were you a scout as a kid? 'Respect authority, use resources wisely, and make the world a better place.'" Lottie said with a stern face. She laughed as she finished the oath.

"I was. The organization hasn't changed much, perhaps not enough."

"Honestly, I'm not sure I'll keep sending my daughter. The girls are involved in vastly different activities than the boys. I don't want Joanie limiting herself by having gender roles ingrained by the Girl

Scouts. I don't want to discuss it in front of the kids. We're here to get the polio shot. I think that is why my kids are acting up so much. I expect it from Alan. He is only seven, but Joanie is nine and Jack is thirteen. It's embarrassing."

"You really want the vaccine? Aren't you afraid they will get polio like all those kids in California this past spring? I read, they rushed the whole process for approval. I don't trust it. In fact, it'll be a long time before I give my kids a vaccine of any kind claiming to prevent a disease."

"Well, maybe I'm biased because the inventor of the polio vaccine is Jonas Salk and he is Jewish, but the newspapers said that the Cutter Laboratory didn't properly follow the instructions he gave to inactivate the virus. I won't be able to sleep at night if one of my kids gets polio and I could have prevented it."

"Well, I wouldn't be able to either if I thought I gave them polio by having them vaccinated. I've tried to read everything I could get my hands on about the vaccine. I'm no different from you, scared to death that my kids might contract polio. Who isn't? I have nothing against Dr. Salk. It's definitely not about his being Jewish. And I'm not trying to talk you out of it. I just can't get my own kids vaccinated."

"I respect what you are saying. Everyone I speak to weighs the risks differently."

✳   ✳   ✳

"How did the visit go at the doctor's office?" asked Daniel, as Lottie hurried into the house with the kids.

"Can it wait a minute, Daniel?" Lottie was gathering her candlesticks as she hurried into the house. "It's almost sundown and I need to light the Sabbath lights. Kids, come join me."

"Do we have to?" Jack said sighing heavily. "I was supposed to be with Tommy after school. I didn't realize we needed to go to the doctor. I want to call him and see if he can come over to spend the night."

"You need to set a better example for your brother and sister.

Lighting the candles is part of our faith. Remember and Keep. Your Bar Mitzvah is only two months away. It isn't about receiving a lot of gifts and having a party. It's sacred. Being Bar Mitzvah means you'll be seen as a man in the Jewish community, accountable for your actions to all and in the eyes of God."

"He's just a kid Lottie," Daniel spoke up. "Let him go call his friend."

"I most certainly will not. All of you in here at once and Alan, quit crying. Your shot can't still hurt. You may not be a man, but you're not a baby anymore either."

* * *

Daniel and Lottie hardly spoke to each other during dinner, while cleaning the dishes, or as they entertained Joanie and Alan later that evening by playing a game of Old Maid until it was their bedtime.

Jack had invited Tommy over and they played basketball in the driveway with several other boys. Lottie got Daniel to put up a regulation height basket and add some good lights so their backyard could become the center of neighborhood activity. The Zlatkins liked knowing where their kids were, especially after dark.

The kids were in bed now though Lottie could hear Jack and Tommy still talking. She eavesdropped for a bit expecting them to be talking about sports when she heard Jack say to Tommy "Wow that MaryAnn looks better to me every day." This teenage thing was going to be challenging. At the last temple auxiliary meeting, she listened to mothers with slightly older children talking about the high school years. They lamented that their adolescents were part of a separate world with its own rules, many in conflict with the very values they were attempting to teach in their own homes. She and Daniel needed to get on the same page before trying to navigate all those teenage decisions.

Tonight's argument over the Sabbath lights seemed like the tip of the iceberg for Lottie. She was willing to admit the two of them were a good business team—sharing the responsibilities around the resort and the expanding properties under management. It was her *chutzpah*, but Daniel's *matikyalas*, meticulous nature, that made them successful. However, when it came to the kids, it seemed like he took the opposite side of each decision just to bicker.

She had her doubts about his desire to develop a serious philosophy on how best to parent their children—this opinion being reinforced after she placed a copy of Dr. Spock's book on the end table next to his chair in the den and observed that it remained untouched.

Lottie found it hard to get Daniel to engage on the subjects that really mattered to her. After reading about the discovery of DNA a few years back, she started to joke with her best friend Sharon on the phone that it wasn't in Daniel's DNA to be passionate. Sharon, just like Lottie's mother, had assumed after a similar comment in the past, this was code for sex. Ever since the Kinsey report came out in the past few years, a pair of scholarly works by Alfred Kinsey on Sexual Behavior in the Human Male and Female, everyone seemed to think sex was all anybody wanted to talk about. But when Lottie complained about Daniel's lack of passion, she was referring to his lack of intensity in life. Some might have called it an easy-going nature, but it drove Lottie nuts at times and she wasn't going to tolerate it when it came to raising the children or observing their faith.

Daniel was watching *The Life of Riley* starring William Bendix when she sat down on the couch with the newspaper in hand. Riley was always making small matters into big problems through his innocent bungling.

"I know you're enjoying the show, but we need to talk," said Lottie. "I want to understand what that was all about tonight. Sometimes I think you pick fights with me for sport. You're not a mean-spirited person by nature but it's becoming a habit. Jack is hardly a boy anymore. He learns from what we say and what we do. Our religious traditions mean a lot to me. I always thought they meant a lot to us."

"I wasn't trying to pick a fight," said Daniel. "You are probably right about unconsciously wanting to argue. I'm sorry. I don't know why I do that sometimes. We work together a lot. Not every couple spends every minute of every day together. Sometimes I do feel like our religion isn't in step with all that is going on now in America. I'm less certain that being observant is meaningful."

"Well, you are missing the boat then—maybe you're getting caught up in all the things we can now afford and the advertisers are trying to sell us. As far as our religion goes, being observant is just the beginning for me. It's the acts of kindness to others, especially those in need, where I get the most out of expressing my faith. I'm not without doubts, at times, about God. But when I look out upon the lake or think back to a moment like the birth of our children, I know there is something greater going on. I feel it, inside. It illuminates my soul."

"Lottie, I hear you. I'll try harder with the kids but you need to accept me for who I am. Some of it has lost meaning for me."

"I'm sorry to hear that. When we're out of sync on something important, usually we can come to a compromise. I don't see one here. I can't drag you along to a spiritual life, but don't ruin it for our kids. They admire you. They will mimic you and your attitudes and, I believe, their lives will be empty without faith in God. This is too important to me to be willy-nilly about. I hope you've heard me clearly."

Thank God the kids finally got the polio vaccine today. I will sleep better tonight. But I don't know what to do about Daniel. (From the diary of Lottie Goldman Zlatkin)

Was the Holocaust inevitable? Many scholars write that the Holocaust was a result of independent developments colliding at the same moment in place and time. It wasn't planned. They argued that it was a heinous accident that couldn't have been avoided.

The Jews were seen throughout Europe as identifiable symbols of individual rights and wealth. They were recent beneficiaries of decisions made by European governments extricating them from social and economic confinement. For many people, not experiencing similar economic success, it became convenient to blame the Jews for their plight and their fears.

In addition, many Jews living in Germany didn't strongly resist the Nazis and those who did, or tried to appease them, died in any event. What life experiences would any of them had to suggest that all would be taken away from them, including their lives?

Countries outside of Germany were almost complicit. They didn't exactly look the other way, but there wasn't the unified condemnation seen in the post-WWII era whenever genocide was suspected. In any event, most of the Jewish deaths occurred while Germany was winning the war and the Allies either didn't know about the death camps and death marches or concluded they were powerless to stop them.

The German people embraced the National Socialists German Workers' Party as part of nationalism. They were experiencing economic and social upheaval and Adolf Hitler was an ideal messenger for the times. The Nazi party didn't rise to power with a promise to murder Jews. But they did desire to remove them from society and removing them evolved into murdering them. It was easier, more expedient.

Rachel slept in. It was Sunday. She was looking for a cup of coffee and found Bill at the kitchen table with stacks of papers strewn about.

"Good morning honey," said Rachel. "What's this chaos all about?"

"A group of my friends are gathering at The Black River Tavern this afternoon to pick our NCAA March Madness tournament teams. This is an orderly collection of the stats from the entire college basketball season. It helps me pick the best teams. I suspect you find it all childish, but it allows me to share some time with the guys. I don't mess with your girl space."

"And you better not start," Rachel smirked as she reached into the cabinet for her favorite coffee mug.

* * *

While Bill was gone, Rachel decided to look in on her parents. She didn't need to call to see if they'd be home. Her mother told her yesterday that they were planning to play bridge with their good friends, the Stolars.

Rachel spotted Mrs. Stolar trying to get her attention within moments of her coming into the living room. Nodding her head in Rachel's mother's direction, Mrs. Stolar then looked back down at her cards. Rachel, picking up on the cue, went to stand behind her mother to watch the game.

Joan opened the bidding with one No Trump. She laughed about her bid. "I hate that President Trump," she said. "But I'm to blame as much as anyone. I voted for him. Mostly I couldn't stand Hillary Clinton. She acted as if she was entitled to the Presidency—that she had somehow earned it already. But I'll admit it. I made a mistake."

Rachel saw it was the least of her mistakes at the moment. Her mother only had six points in her hand, an ace and two jacks. She was ten points shy of a no-trump opener. When Mrs. Stolar noticed Rachel's expression, she nodded again. She was such a dear friend of Rachel's mom and Rachel could tell she didn't want to make a scene.

After the hand was finished and Rachel's parents were set four tricks in a three No Trump contract, Rachel caught Mrs. Stolar's eye as the older woman excused herself to use the bathroom. This was Rachel's cue to meet her in the back hallway.

"How long has this been going on?" Rachel asked.

"Oh, a month or so. Your dad's not much better. I know you're aware, but they were awesome duplicate bridge players—using that two over one system with all those fancy conventions that go along with it. I've wanted to call you. Not being a good bridge player over time is something that happens to all of us, but Rachel, please make sure they're safe," Mrs. Stolar said.

❊ ❊ ❊

It was already evening when Bill came home. He snuck in quietly so as not to wake Rachel in case she had already gone to bed.

"How were the guys at the bar?" Rachel asked when he came in the door and walked over to kiss her. "Oh my god, you smell like smoke. I'll listen to a little about your male-bonding time but seriously, you need a shower."

"I sat down next to Randy and ordered a beer. He asked about you and then harassed me about outkicking my coverage. He called you the Trifecta of wives—beautiful, sexy, and making a lot of money. I told him that everything he said was definitely true but, if I had it to do over again, I'd place greater importance on marrying a girl who could double-bag on the golf course."

"He's smarter than I realized. And, by the way, you have to get a new line about me. That double-bagging thing is getting tired," said Rachel, shaking her head. She turned her back to him to make sure he knew he'd gone too far.

"The guys spent most of the afternoon throwing a bunch of crap at each other. I tried to bounce around the table so that I could visit with everybody. The politically correct culture would've had a fit with all the locker room talk, but we concluded they'd already gone a little insane themselves with all that woke crap."

"You boys are fortunate to have an idiot for President giving you cover every day. He's a total ass. But you know what I'm going to say—men are all unbalanced. The X and Y chromosome can't get along together. Women are better balanced with two X's."

"And you talk about me needing a new line!"

"OK, enough with the Final Four talk. Go take a shower and throw your clothes in the wash. I need to talk to you about something important."

"I'll take a shower and meet you in bed."

"Enough. Get in the shower."

❋　❋　❋

Bill was reading when she came to bed. He put his book down and was grinning like a kid waiting to open his birthday presents.

"I'm really excited to get both Duke and Auburn in my bracket. So, how long is it going to take for you to slip into something more comfortable? Maybe your doggie jammies. I assume that's why you asked me to clean up. I brushed and even flossed my teeth."

Rachel sat down on the bed next to Bill and gave him a playful shove. "How come you assumed that I didn't actually have something important to talk about?" she asked. "Sure, you're a cute guy with a nice ass but having you take a shower wasn't code for sex tonight. I need to talk to you about my parents. Mom and Dad are slipping, I stopped by this afternoon and they were playing bridge with the Stolars. I'll give you the Cliff Notes version—they didn't know what they were doing."

"Oh Rachel. I'm so sorry to hear that."

"I'm worried about their safety. I know it's more of a hobby for them now, but I'm worried about Mom's ability to manage the bed and breakfast. Dad seemed to know the bridge today was a problem. His atrial fibrillation is stable on meds so I don't believe it has anything to do with his mini-stroke. But I'm not sure Mom realizes how confused she seemed or would admit to it if she did."

"That's worrisome. People are always clamoring about how getting older is a bitch. I suppose it is inevitable, but I do dread it. Can you imagine Andrew and Hannah talking to their spouses about us someday? We'll be in denial about our capabilities, I suppose, just like your parents. Andrew will be installing grab bars in our showers. Hannah will be in charge of bowel patrol and making sure the TV's not on *Paw Patrol*."

"You're on a roll—a regular Robin Williams."

"The joking is just a defensive strategy. Kind of like playing a box and one on the basketball court. Hopefully, we are still on the front nine, but I'm looking forward to playing the back nine too—even waking up one morning to find a pretty seventy-year-old in my bed. Look honey, your concerns about their mental capabilities are too important to rush through and I'm beat. Would it be ok if we waited until tomorrow to discuss it?"

Rachel got up and went into the bathroom to put on her pajamas, wash her face, and brush her teeth. Sex might not be a bad solution to put the uneasiness she was feeling about her parents into the background for now, but when she opened the bathroom door, Bill was snoring away. His loss.

Rachel hated how easily he could fall asleep. She knew, between Bill's snoring and worrying about her parents, she'd still be up hours from now shifting her pillow for that perfect position and trying to quiet her mind enough to allow sleep to come.

She decided to head downstairs to pour herself a bowl of Rice Krispies and pull out the book on the Holocaust Rabbi Weinstein had recommended. "Why."

Several hours later, Rachel placed the book on the coffee table and wrapped herself up in her own arms. The Holocaust was the result of a convergence of multiple events at the same moment in time? Where was God when this happened? Could it happen again now? She couldn't take in any more tonight but maybe the author would provide some answers when she found the time to sit down again and read the second half of the book.

Perhaps the author was of the opinion that Zionism was the best solution. The Jews had waited nearly two thousand years to return to Israel. Having a home meant security. But the fighting over land and settlements raged on with the world seemingly more concerned about access to oil than the rights of Jews or Palestinians to inhabit their homeland and live in peace.

Rachel had a lot to talk about with the rabbi next Wednesday.

She dragged herself to bed knowing she'd have nightmares about the Holocaust. And speaking of nightmares, she chided herself, how about showing up tomorrow at the office with only three hours sleep and the usual post-weekend onslaught of anxious parents awaiting her?

As her head hit the pillow, the irony hit her. The day had started with Bill's incessant talk about March Madness and ended with a looming Monday Madness for Rachel.

I just don't know if it's worth the effort to seriously consider my Jewish faith. I'm still frightened by the Holocaust. When I talk to my non-Jewish friends, they see it as ancient history. To me, it feels like it could occur again at any moment. I'm not even sure Bill understands that I feel this way. (From the diary of Rachel Levitt Walsh)

FALL, 1960—
SOUTH HAVEN

"I have a dream that one day this nation will rise up and live out the true meaning of its creed—We hold these truths to be self-evident, that all men are created equal." Martin Luther King 1963

"I believe in an America where the separation of church and state is absolute." John F. Kennedy 1960

The issue of race had been weighing more on Lottie's mind ever since an incident at the resort this past summer involving a Black family from Detroit.

Over the years, the clientele had been exclusively Jewish but they had no formal policies prohibiting anyone else from staying. Mr. Malone represented a tire manufacturer and did business in South Haven. He thought the Goldman resort would be a perfect place to bring his wife and two small children for one of his company's two weeks off per year.

The Malones spent the first day of their vacation fishing and brought their catch around to the backdoor of the kitchen so that it could be prepared for dinner that evening. They ran into Mr. Goldberg, a fellow guest, who was waiting to do the same. Mr. Goldberg, mistaking the Malone's for "the help", pressed his fish on

Mrs. Malone and calling over his shoulder as he was walking away, said "Be sure and cook it right through."

That evening, when the Malones sat down for dinner at a table adjacent to the Goldbergs, Mr. Goldberg rose, slammed his fist on the table and shepherded his family out of the dining room. The following morning, he checked his family out. Before they left, Lottie and he had words.

"I'm sorry to hear you are leaving," she said. "You just got here. Is someone ill? We can get you into a doctor here in South Haven right away, if necessary."

"No one is sick. I've been coming here for over thirty years. My parents brought our family when I was a kid. One of the reasons we have continued to come is for the company of other Jewish families. Last night the family seated next to us in the dining room definitely weren't Jewish, they were Black. I know things are changing in our country, but it's not why we return here each summer with our family."

"I'm sorry to hear you are leaving. And I do hear you clearly. Unfortunately, I'm sorry I have. Perhaps one day you will return, perhaps not. But all families are welcome at our resort. You can tell your friends. I don't wish for them to come stay with us and be surprised."

Later that evening at dinner, Daniel asked Lottie about the incident. It had been the talk around the resort all day. "You can't let your political views affect how you treat our customers. What you did today will be bad for business."

"I guess you don't mean *all* our customers or you would also be concerned about the Malones. This isn't a matter of my political views. It's a matter of how I chose to live. I was raised to respect everyone equally. The Malones have every right to stay at our resort. How can you feel differently?"

"I know you did what you thought was right, but I just don't see it that way. Race is a problem in the South, not up here in Michigan. Blacks have resorts of their own they can stay at. This is a Jewish resort."

"Yes, a Jewish resort that my family started, not yours. And they started it when Jews had nowhere else to stay because of their ethnicity. We won't discriminate based on race."

* * *

It was now September, and the country was transfixed on the race for president. Daniel and Lottie were sitting at the kitchen table with a cup of coffee and a bagel each while sharing the newspaper.

The headline story was about the previous evening's presidential debate between Nixon and Kennedy. It was the first televised presidential debate in the country's history. The focus of the article was on how well the two candidates articulated their vision about the role of government. Though an oversimplification, Nixon preferred small central government while Kennedy saw big government as capable of solving even the most difficult of the nation's problems. The paper didn't take an editorial stance on whose position was best for the country.

Lottie took her duty to vote very seriously. After all, her mother Helen had been active in the suffrage movement. Part of Helen's legacy was to inspire her daughter to be socially conscious and Lottie was now a regional head of the National Council of Jewish Women. In this presidential election, the Council was focused on the issue of racial inequality. Kennedy, though raised in privilege, seemed the more motivated of the two candidates to tackle the problem of race in America. He believed poverty to be at the heart of the issue and thought the national government could do more to raise up Black Americans.

"Nixon really gave it to Kennedy. I plan to vote for him," said Daniel.

"You know I'm not voting for him. Why try to rile me up? Vote for whoever you wish. I think Nixon is a bright man. I expected him to be well-informed on the issues and he was. But I liked Kennedy better. It wasn't so much about how he said things, though you must agree he is very articulate. It was the substance. My views are more in line with his. By the way, and don't forget, we have an Open House at the junior high school tonight."

Joan was now in ninth grade and Alan in seventh. Jack attended the high school nearby and had already started the process of applying to colleges.

The format of Open House at the school consisted of each parent going through a compressed version of their child's schedule with ten minutes allowed for each class. When they arrived in a classroom, the teacher would welcome them and proceed to an overview of what the class would be learning over the next nine months.

Counting the time Jack spent at the junior high school, this was the sixth of these events the Zlatkins found themselves attending as they sat waiting in the gymnasium bleachers for a short address by the principal, Mr. Thomas. He was an affable man with a head of thinning blonde hair on a very athletic frame. Lottie and Daniel had heard, and assumed it to be true, that he was an outstanding college athlete playing both football and basketball.

The Zlatkins had only been called in to see the principal, Mr. Thomas, once over the years. Joanie was caught passing notes in music class in seventh grade. When they explained to Mr. Thomas they were thrilled to hear about the incident, since she was shy and their biggest worry was that she would struggle to make friends, Mr. Thomas laughed out loud. "I've never heard parents express themselves so appropriately in my office over a discipline issue. Good for you. Now get the hell out of here."

Tonight, his address was different from the ones they had heard him give in the past. "I am somewhat dispirited about the effect of the upcoming national election on our student body. Your children seem to be parroting political views being expressed in your homes. Not all of the political speech, this time around, is appropriate in my view. I was eating lunch last week in the cafeteria when two students had an argument that spilled over into a physical altercation. One of the boys said Kennedy shouldn't be elected because he was Catholic. I have decided the best course of action is to cancel the tradition of holding a mock election at the school. Things are just too divisive."

Lottie looked around to see what the reaction was among those sitting near her. It was only then she noticed that many of the parents were actually wearing buttons representing their candidates of choice. She wondered how many were feeling as ashamed as she was. She knew her kids had often heard her strident views. Even Daniel, normally less politically passionate, had occasionally been forceful in his opinions.

At the end of the evening, Daniel and Lottie were walking out with the Richardsons into the parking lot.

"What a beautiful night, Danny," said Mark Richardson. It had been quite a while since Lottie had heard anyone call him Danny, but he and Mark had been teammates on the high school baseball team.

"Isn't it?" replied Daniel as they approached their cars.

"Whoa, Nelly! What's this?" Mark stopped in surprise at Daniel's car.

"Well, I've always seen myself as a 'ragtop kind of guy.' I finally pulled the trigger. It's a Chevy Super Sport convertible. I fell in love with it. I had to get the red color. It has automatic windows and a speaker in the rear for a stereo sound."

The men, or perhaps Lottie saw them tonight more as boys, carried on about the car for another ten minutes and by the time they finished, it was getting colder, almost too cold to drive home with the top down. Lottie anticipated this might happen. She knew Daniel was excited about the car and, though she thought it ridiculous to own a convertible when living in South Haven, Michigan, she had the foresight to bring along a coat, a hat, and a pair of gloves so they wouldn't need to quarrel about a decision to put the top up or leave it down. "Choose your battles in marriage" was the advice Helen gave her on her wedding day. How smart this lesson seemed now as they often clashed over even the most insignificant things.

Mr. Thomas's comments tonight were about a divided community. The Zlatkins had a divided household. Daniel planned to vote for Richard Nixon, she for John Kennedy. Divided homes might have been more common than Lottie realized, after all, the Gallop poll predicted a rather close election with the numbers flip-flopping weekly at 48 percent and 47 percent for each candidate. She assumed Daniel's decision to vote for Nixon was part of his tendency to prefer "all" things not change. When they fought, she often resorted to calling him a "stick-in-the-mud." But even when she attempted to bait him with name calling, he either pretended not to hear or simply shrugged it off and later on, Lottie would be ashamed of her own childishness.

Lottie favored the charismatic John Kennedy for President. He was eloquent, especially last week, when responding to all the anti-Catholic rhetoric in the country. In fact, the issue of Kennedy's religion pushed her to become a volunteer for the Senator, going door-to-door to campaign on his behalf.

As they pulled out of the school parking lot, Lottie had to admit Daniel looked quite handsome behind the wheel of his new convertible as they drove across town. She both enjoyed and got tired of hearing some of her friends remark how easy he was on the eyes. She was going to hear more of this as soon as they glimpsed him about town in his new convertible.

As they turned from Broadway Street onto Dyckman Avenue, the draw bridge was slowly going up. Daniel put the car in park.

"Doesn't it bother you, Daniel, that many in the country don't want to vote for Kennedy because of his religion? What if this were a Jew running for President and the conversation was all about his religion?" said Lottie.

"Well, I'll take that as a hypothetical question since we won't see it in our lifetime. I'll even go so far as to say that a Black American will be President of the United States before a Jew."

"Personally, I couldn't care less about a candidate's race or religion or sex for that matter. I just want someone to be qualified. It's absurd to think John Kennedy would answer to the Pope. I like what Kennedy said, 'I believe in an America where the separation of church and state is absolute,' I'm certain if either of my parents were alive today, they'd be voting for Kennedy. They came to America with their parents for religious freedom and unlimited opportunity. Anyway, I prefer where he stands on the issues facing the country.

As I told you this morning, I think he will make racial inequality a priority—it's time our country tackles that problem head on."

"I'm sorry," said Daniel as the bridge started back down. "I plan to vote for Dick Nixon. He's more experienced. He's been at Ike's side for eight years. Things have been good for us. We are better off now than four years ago. Hey, I should send that phrase into the Nixon campaign. It's much better than the one they are using, 'Nixon's the One.'"

"But Eisenhower has been pretty cool to Israel. Kennedy seems more open-minded. I've heard the rumors that his father was antisemitic, but the son is not the father. Just the other night in Philadelphia, Kennedy called for the US to support all countries wishing to be free and independent and he hoped, regardless of which party won the election, that the United States would 'hold out the hand of friendship to Israel.' I may have to lock you in the bathroom on Tuesday so you can't vote."

"You're such a kidder," replied Daniel who was staring at the bridge coming back down and unable to see her whole body tense up. Why wasn't it important to him that religious freedom and racial inequality were on the ballot this election? Lottie looked over at him—he was busy adjusting the radio dials to create a stereo sensation. She wondered if there was a way she could actually pull it off—locking him up in the bathroom on Election Day.

When Kennedy won a narrow election, Lottie thought Daniel would be depressed. But like most issues, he really wasn't all that invested in the results. He was like the leaves now falling off the trees in South Haven, blowing about harmlessly, wherever the wind took them.

She spoke to the rabbi about the growing tension in their marriage and he advised counseling.

When Lottie asked Daniel to consider it, he refused, so she started going alone. The therapist casually remarked on his absence, a male's absence, being common. Lottie might have considered this an attempt to reassure her, but the therapist's lips were pressed tightly together giving rise to a bitter smile and the opposite effect. Lottie could tell the therapist saw her husband's absence as a bad sign.

FALL, 2018—
SOUTH HAVEN

Rachel sighed, stretched out in bed, and settled back into her pillow with a contented smile. Wednesday mornings gave her a feeling of freedom as if she had received a reprieve from the warden. Her long office hours inside a sterile medical building gave her a sense of incarceration and she was often envious of friends whose jobs allowed them to meet clients away from their offices for lunch or required leaving town from time to time.

If she told Bill she felt this way, he would tell her she was being overly dramatic. Rachel supposed, if honest, she would agree with him. She loved what she did for a living and couldn't imagine herself happier in another career. There was nothing better than having the opportunity to make an important diagnosis, to receive a confidential call from an adolescent with a problem, or to be called upon by a partner for a second opinion and nail the diagnosis like the day of the "Popsicles" child.

Yet when driving up to the building, especially on a pretty day, Rachel would still mutter something to herself about entering the prison walls. Her practice recently moved to a new office building and somehow her partners persuaded her to agree to the tiniest of workspaces and an office devoid of windows to gaze outside. But it wasn't just the small physical space that made Rachel feel confined. It was the singular nature of her profession.

The workload was relentless and Rachel always maintained some social distance from her staff. It only made sense—she was their boss and paid their salaries. Perhaps the only exception to this rule was her medical assistant. Rachel counted on her to keep up with the hectic pace and expectations Rachel set to provide superior care to her patients. Though Rachel was the captain, they were still a team and, because of this, Rachel, at times, chose to let her into her emotional silo.

Her partners were unavailable, each in their own safe spaces, heads down, trying to get their work done before heading home in time for dinner with their families. But never before completing every computerized office visit note, returning every phone call, and attending to every patient's medical needs without making any errors. It was a recipe for burnout, an environment of isolation.

She couldn't believe some doctors over the last ten years were marketing themselves as providing concierge care. It pissed her off. The care she provided had always been, and would always be, concierge. As far as she was concerned, paying attention to her patients' needs in a timely fashion was the essence of the job.

Watching the fan spinning over the bed, Rachel realized she had just enough time, before needing to get out of bed, to complete her mindfulness exercises. They only took ten minutes. When she started in practice, she tended to dismiss alternative forms of medical care. But after a friend struggling with chronic pain experienced great success with exercises that a therapist advised, Rachel resolved to give it the same scrutiny she might give to any medical problem and came away convinced of their value. She now did them daily, even learning to perform them most anywhere, sitting, standing, or like this morning, lying in bed. Though it never filled the gnawing hole she felt deep inside, it did settle her mind.

Rachel began by focusing on her breathing and emptying all tension in her body. Her Apple watch showed her heart rate slowing down to forty-four beats per minute. Her body felt a lightness, as if a sudden gust of wind might send her floating away. She startled when the alarm on her nightstand sounded off. She jumped up and ran to the shower. She had errands to run before meeting with Rabbi Weinstein.

Today, they would again discuss the Holocaust. Their focus would be not on why it happened or whether God had been asleep at the wheel. They had covered that ground. It would be about the future. Could it happen again—and if not, why not?

* * *

"Good morning, Rachel," the rabbi said. He stepped out from behind his study desk and pointed to a chair for her to sit.

"Hi, Rabbi Weinstein. Thanks again for helping with my father."

"How is he doing?"

"Fine," she answered.

"I enjoyed meeting your children and your husband, Bill. I guess I spilled the beans about our meetings. I didn't mean to cause you trouble. I hope it didn't?"

"We talked. We're good. Actually, Rabbi Weinstein, Bill and I are always good. I know we were supposed to discuss the Holocaust today," said Rachel. "But before we do, there is something else I wanted to talk about first, if that's okay with you? It relates to my fears of being identified as Jewish—perhaps it is two sides of the same coin.

"Recently I have been the target of a couple of antisemitic incidents. It's been quite a while since this has occurred. It's forced me to rethink my views on how enlightened our country is and how safe I am."

Rachel went on to describe her encounters with Mr. Martin and Alan Donovan. Rabbi Weinstein listened. She could see he was paying close attention. His body was tensing up as she talked.

"I'm so sorry to hear about this, though it doesn't come as a surprise. Many of my congregation have confided similar experiences to me. I will not try to suggest that these experiences of antisemitism are a precursor to the hatred or evil of the Holocaust, but I understand the fear it can place deep inside. I share this fear. Hardly a week or two goes by anymore without some ethnic or religious minority in our country or around the world being on the receiving end of such animus. I'll try to keep these recent experiences and your reactions to them in mind as we carefully tackle the Holocaust or, as I prefer the Hebrew word, *Shoah*."

"Thank you, Rabbi Weinstein. It all makes me feel kind of raw." Rachel took a deep breath and then raised her eyes to look directly at the rabbi. "The last time we talked, we concluded there was an inevitability about the Holocaust, a perfect storm, or as I prefer to call it, an imperfect storm. The Germans desired national unity. They were in crisis mode economically, and Hitler used the Jews, an identifiable minority, to blame for all their problems. Initially, he wanted to just remove them, but he came to realize it would be easier to simply kill them. If we are to accept this as a timely accident of history, why can't it happen again? As a pediatrician, I tell parents all the time that accidents happen. They bring their children in with a broken bone or a cut that needs sutures and they feel shame for looking away, even just for a moment."

"You touched on a key issue," interjected Rabbi Weinstein. "We must remain wary and alert. During our last visit, I think I mentioned having nuanced solutions to problems. The Holocaust is an exception—evil has no room for nuance. We can't look the other way for even a moment. Jews must live in this vigilant manner, but so must all citizens in any given society. Authoritarianism can creep into the most enlightened countries and seek to destroy the weak, the minorities, and the disenfranchised. We need to speak out, participate in political matters, and show concern about public policy. I hope we never see it in the United States, but we seem ripe for it."

"Why do you say that, Rabbi Weinstein?" asked Rachel twisting her wedding ring on her finger as she said it.

"Our culture is moving further away from its foundations of equality, human decency, and finding common ground to solve problems. It seems to me that many feel uncertain and threatened about their economic future and by the shift in our cultural identity— fears about race and immigrants of color—the antisemitic events you disclosed to me today are a very real example of these feelings.

Someone once said, we need to be a 'nation with the soul of a church.' I don't see or feel that anymore. I've always felt that Americans, like the Jews, were a chosen people—even Abraham Lincoln once said this. We must celebrate what we have built and come together, not be driven apart by self-serving leadership or the media."

"That sounded more like political speak than religion. My grandmother used to tell me about High Holy Day services in the sixties. She said the rabbi never wasted a full house and would use his sermons to speak of social injustice, championing the civil rights movement. My grandmother got involved. I find myself so busy in my day-to-day life—I'm ashamed to say it but taking on additional commitments outside my home or my practice would be difficult."

"I suppose in the thirties, Jews in Germany might've said something similar—simply going about their lives," said Rabbi Weinstein. "Vigilance always matters. It might matter most on a routine day when the stakes don't seem high. We can't sleepwalk through our lives, Rachel. We can't simply rush about, pursuing our careers, raising our kids, and chasing after material wants and desires. You may have the bandwidth to accomplish all these things, but if we live this way, blind to the needs and suffering of others, we aren't living the way God asks us to live."

Rachel often wondered if she could do more with her professional skills. Most of her patients had health insurance, homes, regular employment, and food on the table. Her grandmother, Lottie, always spoke to her about contributing to her community and helping those in need. There were physicians committed to caring for the indigent and some made trips to Third World countries. Perhaps she needed to rethink some of her choices.

"But the call to *Never Forget*," said Rachel trying to rearrange herself in the chair to find a comfortable position. "It sounds like we need to stand off to the side, less engaged or, worse yet, hiding. As if some group is waiting and lurking in the shadows to get us again."

"We Jews can never forget the Holocaust," said the rabbi "but it mustn't become a reason or excuse to huddle together, segregated, and never reaching out to others. We need friends. Your memories as a child of seeing films from the death camps—they frightened you as they would any child. But you're an adult woman now. These memories can block a person from trusting that the world might have changed, improved. I like to think that no country will ever again stand by and watch when genocide occurs. But in the end, I think you will regret it if your fear of another Holocaust gets in the way of accepting faith."

Rachel's foot started to bounce uncontrollably. "Well, how does Israel work into all this? Ever since I was a little girl they always seem to be at war. Does its existence make things better or worse? There's a lot for other countries to resent in Israel's success. That *Start-Up Nation* book you asked me to read was eye-opening. In some ways, Israel might be the envy of the world."

"Well, it gives me comfort that Zionism was successful. We now have a Jewish State that could be home to any of us if needed. But you and I live in the United States and our allegiance to this nation may come into conflict with the actions or goals of the state of Israel. Every country in the developed world, including the United States, takes sides now in the Middle East largely because of oil, but when oil is no longer vital, I'm uncertain if the world will care so passionately about Israel's borders, safety, or survival. I can't say I'm in lockstep with all Israeli policies or actions, but my bias is to give them the benefit of the doubt."

Again, she remembered her grandmother Lottie saying something similar before succumbing to dementia. She'd said, she wanted to see peace at any cost, even if it required two separate states.

"I recently donated money to J Street. I assume you're familiar with them. I have come to believe a two-state solution is the best chance for a lasting peace. It respects both parties, the Israelis and the Palestinians. You may be right about oil. When the day comes that oil isn't vital, and it might be sooner than we can imagine, perhaps the world will leave Israel alone and both parties will accept a resolution of their own making, to coexist. But I'm still unable to reconcile political realities and support for Israel with the issue of faith. Rabbi Weinstein, for me, though the State of Israel's existence might represent a hedge against my very real fear of annihilation, all the back and forth of current events can be a distraction."

The two of them paused for a moment. Rachel wondered what the rabbi really thought about her struggles and inertia about faith. Head slightly bowed, she fought to keep eye contact with the rabbi.

"I must tell you, Rachel, I find you to be like many Jews in post-war America—fixated on the Holocaust and Israel. They have become barometers of one's faith. But focusing on these two issues detracts from clearly seeing the fundamental message of Judaism—doing for others, being close to those suffering in our communities, and making a difference wherever possible in our world. Those who focus on the latter: I hear some in the congregation referring to them as JEWish. While those focusing on the former, who only celebrate the holidays and busy themselves with conforming to the social expectations of their family and community, are referred to as jewISH."

"I know you're right. I observe the holidays but fall short when it comes to attending temple regularly. But I'm not consumed by chasing a life of conforming to expectations. I know my angst about the Holocaust and Israel are peripheral to what I am really wrestling with—the question of whether embracing my Jewish faith will fill the hole I feel inside." Rachel said. "You must have a secret you're holding back."

"Rachel, I don't have all the answers. I imagine this might be a line you use in your office with patients as well. In Genesis, Jacob wrestles with the angel. Many assume the angel is God. Sometimes, it is only after a personal struggle that faith emerges. You, too, are wrestling. I think God expects this from most of us. When making my own life choices, the past informs me, but I try to look forward. It's how I choose to live. Though you're troubled by your past, having been raised in a secular environment and having the fear of another Holocaust instilled in you at a vulnerable age, you're living a life of good deeds in the present. That is the essence of being a religious person. What you call yourself doesn't necessarily matter. Don't be afraid of giving Judaism a chance. It has worked well for people for thousands of years. From what you have told me, it sustained your relatives when they immigrated from Russia to America—I know you feel the pull of your ancestry. Faith can also provide comfort as you grow older and face the inevitability of your own demise."

Rabbi Weinstein paused to wipe his glasses, placed them back on his nose, and then reached out to firmly place his hands upon Rachel's as a smile slowly built upon her face. "Keep studying. It's been my pleasure to walk alongside you these many weeks. Your journey has inspired me and fortified my own commitment to Judaism. I thank you for that."

The rabbi stopped and stared down at their hands for a moment and then looked into Rachel's eyes.

"Remember Rachel, *faith is a choice.*"

FEBRUARY 1965— SOUTH HAVEN, ST. LOUIS, SELMA

Lottie and Daniel had been separated for two months. There was nothing wrong with Daniel's moral compass, Lottie thought. He was a good man. He knew right from wrong. But what difference did that make if he failed to act on anything that didn't directly affect himself? She could no longer tolerate his ambivalence.

They bickered but never really fought. Perhaps Lottie wouldn't have chosen to move out of the house and into one of their rental properties if Daniel cared enough to fight about it.

She asked him to go to counseling together, but he wouldn't. "What a waste of time," Daniel said. "How is someone going to help us? Are we expected to spill our guts out in front of a perfect stranger? I'm perfectly happy with our marriage just the way it is."

"Well, you're just half of the marriage," Lottie had answered. "I'm not happy. I know you love me and I hate to do this to our children, but they're almost grown. I just can't live with your lack of passion. Things matter to me. Our religion matters to me. It asks us to be aware of other's suffering and to do something to help. I've probably waited too long to do this. The kids don't seem too committed to our religion either. I have to twist their arms to go to the synagogue with me. Look at Joan the Secular, she's starting to become your clone, thinking life is about herself, not others. Maybe seeing you and me take some time apart will result in them reassessing their own priorities. I hate to do this to you or them, but I must."

They still had to deal with each other every day, while they shared the work in running what they now called "The Goldman Resort Properties." Alan, who as the youngest was the only one still living at home, seemed to be okay with going back and forth between their homes. They were only a few blocks apart.

Most weekends, Lottie was off to another meeting in one of the larger Midwestern cities—Chicago, St. Louis, Cincinnati, Indianapolis, or down south as far as Memphis. The meetings were primarily about the Civil Rights Movement—brainstorming sessions to plan events, raise money, and pick candidates to back in upcoming elections. Lottie was most interested in discussions focused on finding solutions to improve job opportunities, access better housing, and raise educational standards for African Americans.

Kennedy had now been dead for eighteen months and Lyndon Johnson, a Southerner, was determined to do something about these issues. He was also tenacious in his pursuit of passing a Voting Rights Bill to eliminate arbitrary barriers constructed by local and state governments to make it difficult for minorities to vote.

Lottie was passionate about voting. She remembered when she was a young girl being deeply impressed when she asked her mother, Helen, about working alongside other Jewish women during the suffrage movement. Helen would reply "voting meant everything to us back then. Without the right to vote, women had no say in how our country passed laws affecting its own citizens and how the country related to the rest of the world. When we succeeded back then, all women stood a little taller." Lottie thought the same would be true for African Americans now if barriers to voting were removed.

It was at a weekend meeting in St. Louis when Lottie met Dottie Schneider. By happenstance, they were seated next to each other at a gathering of about one hundred people for a discussion of civil rights.

"Hi. I'm Lottie Zlatkin," offering her hand out to shake with the well-dressed woman sitting next to her.

"I'm Dottie Schneider," she replied. "Did you look over the program yet? The first two speakers are rabbis with personal histories of social activism. The first, a Rabbi Israel "Si" Dresner, is notorious for his distinction as the most arrested rabbi in the United States. He was first arrested during a Freedom Ride for interfaith clergy in 1961."

"I read that," answered Lottie. "Apparently the second speaker is a local St. Louis rabbi, Jerome Grollman."

"I know him well. He's my congregation's rabbi," said Dottie.

They settled into their seats. Rabbi Dresner's message at the meeting that day was about the Jewish faith and the notion that God rewards good deeds. He called upon those assembled to not sit idly by watching as the nation's laws, especially the 15th Amendment to the US Constitution guaranteeing the right to vote, were being circumvented by misguided local governments with poll taxes and literacy tests. He warned of a future where immigrants might be required to perform more rigorous and arbitrary literacy tests at the whim of the government in order to acquire citizenship.

"How would your grandparents and parents have fared if this type of discrimination had occurred when they immigrated to the United States?" he said to the thunderous applause of those in attendance.

Lottie really enjoyed Rabbi Grollman's speech about his own Bar Mitzvah. The Haftorah portion was from Leviticus. It was the part that set out the Law of Yovel, the Jubilee Year, when every fifty years, land was returned to its original owners and the people were ordered "to proclaim liberty, throughout the land, for all the inhabitants." The Jubilee Year's purpose was to avoid a permanent poor class. Rabbi Grollman found this an amazing coincidence as he now was asking for everyone present to join him the following month for a march from Selma to Montgomery, Alabama. Though slavery had been abolished after the Civil War, many African-Americans were still part of a permanent poor class and they needed support to enjoy equal voting rights.

When the speech concluded, Lottie and Dottie turned to each other.

"You said your name was Dottie when I sat down. Did I catch it right?" asked Lottie.

"Yes, Lottie and Dottie. We could be a vaudeville act. Pretty inspiring speeches, the rabbis gave. I've heard Rabbi Grollman's song and dance before. He gives a similar sermon, especially during the High Holidays, when the temple is packed and he has a captive audience. I'm not sure how the rank and file receive his passionate messages about the Civil Right movement."

"Well, I'm from South Haven, Michigan. We still don't have a full-time rabbi for our congregation. The Jewish community there is small but vibrant. However, there is rarely talk, and certainly little passion, about Civil Rights."

"My family vacationed there in the summer when I was a kid. We called it 'The Catskills of the Midwest'. I haven't been back since then. We have a place in the Ozarks—a beautiful lake, a thousand T-shirt shops, and humidity."

"Well, I run a resort in South Haven. My mother started it. My husband and I have grown it into quite a nice business," said Lottie. She looked down toward her hand and sniffled.

"I'm sorry. Did I say the wrong thing?"

"No. Daniel, my husband, and I have been separated for a couple of months. I love him dearly but his lack of passion," she looked up and decided to clarify—"not physical passion, but apathy and passivity—like the Civil Rights cause. I can't get him to even acknowledge its importance. He thinks, because we live up in a small town in Michigan, that it shouldn't be a priority in our lives. I can't let some things go once they get inside me."

"How would you like to go out to dinner tonight? We can share war stories about marriage and decide how we're going to meet and travel together to participate in the Freedom Ride," said Dottie with a little wink.

They got into Dottie's car and drove fifteen or so blocks away. As they parked, Dottie proudly announced they were in Gaslight Square. As they walked down the cobblestoned street, they passed a bar called The Crystal Palace. Lottie picked up the vibe of the area.

"I didn't realize St. Louis had anything like this. I always thought it to be a pretty dead town, not that South Haven has much of anything too exciting."

"Well, the Gaslight Square area keeps expanding. It has been around now for about five years, but lots of people in St. Louis don't know it exists. Back in 1961, that bar over there, The Crystal Palace, opened with the Smothers Brothers as headliners. You'll never guess who the warm-up act was? A little eighteen-year-old Jewish girl from New York by the name of Barbara Streisand. There's our restaurant on the right," said Dottie. "The Three Fountains."

They checked their coats and were seated at a small table each ordering a drink and a steak for dinner. Dottie offered Lottie a cigarette while they waited for their drinks.

"Are you married?" asked Lottie.

"Yes," answered Dottie. "But we hit a rough patch a while back as well. In my opinion, it's never just one person's fault. You know, it takes two to tango and my husband's a lousy dancer. Anyway, we got into a rut and stopped communicating. He had an affair with his secretary. I caught him on Valentine's Day of all times. But we got through it. Don't get me wrong, it wasn't my fault he strayed. But I accept my failure to really see him and what our lives had become. We were living in parallel. Now I see the things I hate about him are so insignificant compared to what I love about him. Maybe you need to give Donald a chance."

"It's Daniel," said Lottie. She was smiling and felt as though a weight had slipped from her shoulders. "This had been good tonight. You're a breath of fresh air. I'm angry that he is not 'seeing me' and what I care so passionately about. If he could communicate, maybe he'd say the same. Is your husband, Gary, a good communicator?"

"Honey, it's Jerry. Maybe we've had too much to drink for one night. I propose we table this meeting until tomorrow's lunch break. I'll introduce you to Rabbi Grollman and we can ask him how to go about participating in next month's march. He'll probably go on and on about the time in 1960 when Reverend King spoke at the United Hebrew Synagogue to twenty-five hundred people—his speech was entitled 'The Future of Integration.' Every Jewish person in St, Louis now claims they attended the speech just like everyone says they were at the ballpark to watch Stan Musial's last game a couple of years ago—human nature. If you count on human nature, you'll never be surprised, only disappointed—again and again and again."

*　*　*

One month later, on March 6th, 1965, the two women found themselves together in a small hotel in downtown Selma only blocks from the Brown Chapel AME Church. The church was where they were to meet others the next morning before beginning a march from Selma to Montgomery, the state capital of Alabama, to protest for voting rights. Though they'd only spent a small time together in St. Louis before deciding to make this trip, Lottie and Dottie were becoming the best of friends.

Lottie picked Dottie up in St. Louis and they made one overnight stop. Before going out to dinner that night, Lottie unpacked her candlesticks and said the Sabbath prayer.

"Those candlesticks are so beautiful," Dottie said.

"My mother brought them with her when they emigrated from Russia. They were traveling light but her father allowed her to take one more thing to always remind her of home. I will be passing them on to my daughter Joan when she marries. I just hope Joanie comes around to practicing our faith more seriously. My husband and I probably give her conflicting messages about our religion. I worry that the Reform Judaism movement is seen by Joanie and her brothers as another excuse to become assimilated. It wasn't started to encourage Jews not to be observant. It was largely about social responsibility and being more relevant in the modern world. But I've done my best. Maybe one day, with their own kids, they'll do better."

At dinner that evening, Lottie confided to Dottie that upon returning home after the St. Louis meeting, she and Daniel cleared the air and found a middle ground of mutual respect. As Dottie had suggested, they each took stock of their personal shortcomings and accepted responsibility for letting things get so bad. "I was so relieved, especially for my son Alan. A family should live under one roof," Lottie told her.

The next morning, they gathered at the church with another six hundred or so marchers. Holding hands, the group sang *We Shall Overcome* before starting out two-by-two towards the bridge.

"Your hand is so clammy," said Lottie to Dottie. She had to almost scream to be heard above the noise of the angry all-white mob gathered on both sides of the street. "Are you as nervous as I am?"

"We are just walking. So what if they scream. They will let us through," Dottie answered.

Then all hell broke loose. On Sunday, March 7, 1965, some 600 civil right demonstrators were beaten with billy clubs and tear gas as they attempted to cross the Edmund Pettus Bridge.

Lottie and Dottie were both treated in a hospital later that day for minor injuries and released. As soon as they returned to their hotel room, they each called home to reassure their husbands and, after hanging up, sat quietly side-by-side for the rest of the evening, holding each other and promising to remain close the rest of their lives.

Ten days after what would be later called "Bloody Sunday", many American cried as they watched President Johnson address Congress on TV. He introduced the Voting Rights Legislation and said to the Congress, "There is no Negro problem. There is no Southern problem. There is no Northern problem. There is only an American problem. Their cause must be our cause too. Because it is not just Negros, but really it is all of us, who must overcome the crippling legacy of bigotry and injustice. And we shall overcome."

WINTER 2018—
SOUTH HAVEN

Today, "Team Hannah" was off to a skating competition in Chicago. It was a huge event and Hannah was starting to attract attention from the pre-Olympic coaches. Andrew had a lot of homework to do and stayed behind with his grandparents.

It was just going to be a short weekend trip, but they still chose to take Rachel's SUV with its large cargo space. Each of them had a suitcase, Hannah a second one for her outfits, and a third to carry her extra pairs of skates—edges sharpened and ready to go. Rachel made a mental note of the large leather duffle—it had seen better days and a new bag for Hannah to lug her equipment around might make a good Christmas gift idea for Bill's parents or a Hanukkah present for hers.

Hannah always nailed the compulsory exercises but her performance in the free skate could be more unpredictable. She planned to skate to Taylor Swift's *Dancing With Our Hands Tied*, an anthem, of sorts, to star-crossed love. For the last six months, the song seemed to play 24/7 in her room, three minutes and thirty-one seconds at a time. On the ice, Hannah practiced endlessly, but catching an edge and falling was often the difference between a great showing and an average one.

It was also necessary to sell herself when in a skating competition. Rachel knew Hannah understood this, but she was still a young teenager, prone to moodiness that could interfere unpredictably. In any event, that was her coach's responsibility to point out, not her parents. Rachel learned this early on when, on the way home after attending a practice session, she offered both positive and negative remarks about her skate. Hannah's only takeaway was her mother's criticism.

Rachel's sister Michelle and her girls hoped to attend. They were pretty good athletes themselves though none of them skated. It was definitely one of the many "cult sports" kids could choose to participate in. And just like tennis or gymnastics, as a kid's skills progressed, the field became smaller and smaller. Hannah knew her likely competition, what types of jumps would be in the other girls' programs, and what she would have to do to beat them—execute perfectly and let her personality show.

Bill seemed tired after loading the car. Rachel wondered if maybe he hadn't wanted to come to Chicago for another one of these competitions. She knew he loved watching Hannah skate, but her ice time represented only minutes of a trip that would take three days. They would be sitting and spending time with the usual suspects of parents—most were over the top, a few Bill considered to be clinically insane. Watching the parents, one might have come away concluding that sucking up to the Olympic coaches was a competition in and of itself.

Most of the time during these trips, he tried to have his head in a book. This weekend he chose Bob Gibson's *Pitch by Pitch*. Bill told her, in the opinion of some of the talking heads on the MLB channel, it was a better book about baseball than *Ball Four*.

"No way," Rachel had responded.

"Do you mind driving?" he asked Rachel. "I feel like closing my eyes for a few minutes. I don't think I'll actually nap, but I'm tired."

"No problem," she answered. "I'll drive to New Buffalo and we can stop at Redamack's for a burger and fries. Andrew's going to be disappointed when he learns we stopped for lunch at Redamack's. It's his favorite."

They enjoyed lunch though Bill didn't finish his burger. "My stomach is just a little upset," he said. "It's been funny lately. I mentioned it to you last week and you told me to take some Pepto and it helped. Did you bring any along with you?"

They pulled into the hotel in downtown Chicago and Rachel thought Bill seemed to be laboring with the bags but he denied it. "Let the porter mess with them and go take a nap," said Rachel. "I'll run Hannah over to the rink. She has a scheduled practice skate before tomorrow's competition."

Hannah won her age group's championship, incorporating what her parents still liked to call the butterfly, looking in the opposite direction while performing her toe loop or an edge jump like a double axel. She wasn't strong enough to do any triples yet but it appeared likely she would need to add them soon if she wanted to stay at the top of the pack. Only one girl her age tried one but fell. Hannah performed her final sit spin with tremendous velocity, coming to a clean stop with a huge smile.

"Your daughter is the real deal," said one of the Olympic coaches to Bill and Rachel. "Now, it's just a matter of puberty taking over to give her a bit more size and strength. You can't coach that. You also can't coach desire, but it looks like Hannah isn't lacking in that area."

Michelle and her daughters joined the celebratory dinner that night at Ditkas. The adults and kids sat at separate tables and Rachel noticed the waiter began to avoid the girls' table with their non-stop laughing and requests for endless refills of Diet Coke. Straining to hear their conversation, Rachel concluded they were debating whether Justin Timberlake or Harry Styles was cuter. Rachel would have voted for Justin, if asked.

"So, Bill," said Michelle, "I haven't seen you since I heard you'd learned about your wife's undertaking to study Judaism."

"I'm really happy for her. You wouldn't believe our Wednesday night conversations about the religious teachings of the week. Lately, she and the rabbi have been reading the Talmud. I've learned from Rachel how obeying the Talmudic laws played a crucial role in keeping generations of Jews faithful during the Diaspora. The arc of the story of the Jewish people, especially with the recent history of the Holocaust and the establishment of the state of Israel, is compelling.

The kids don't yet know it yet," he whispered, "but we're going to take a trip to Israel during Christmas 2019. Didn't you and Gary make the same trip a few years ago?"

"We did," Michelle answered. "It was amazing. Jerusalem took my breath away."

"I'm still struggling with the Holocaust," Rachel added, "but I am starting to accept that God can't stop evil or be held responsible when it occurs. He serves as a kind of ideal for us to continuously strive to emulate, representing the beauty in the world, and the compassion we must all have for one another."

"Wow," said Michelle. "You're taking this study seriously. I guess for me it's more a cultural thing. It's who I am, how I was raised, the ritual, and the holidays. It's going to temple with Mom and Dad and remembering Passover at Grandma Lottie's home—listening to her talk about great-grandmother Helen. I try not to think about the Holocaust. I try not to contemplate the whys too much."

"Ritual can be important," said Bill. "One of the priests at my church always holds out hope that some members of our community, if they come every Sunday, will eventually slide from ritual to true belief."

"Hey," Michelle said, addressing Rachel. "Let's wrap this up. Bill seems tired. I'm coming up to South Haven next week to see Mom and Dad. You told me his atrial fibrillation is under control but Mom still seems so anxious since that trip to the ER and all the testing Dad went through at the hospital. I want to go with them next week when he sees the electrophysiologist."

"Yeah, he's stable on meds but an ablation might be recommended," added Rachel.

"Michelle is right. I'm kind of tired. I suppose it's been too much excitement with Hannah's winning today."

"OK," said Rachel. It bothered her to see, as she got up from the table, that Bill had hardly touched his dinner.

SEPTEMBER 5, 1972—
SOUTH HAVEN

The motto for the '72 Olympic Games was "Die Heiteren Spiele", or "the cheerful Games." West Germany was eager to show the world a positive face. Mark Spitz won seven gold medals at these games, but on September 5th, 1972, Spitz was hurriedly flown back to the United States over fears that he might be an additional kidnap target of terrorists due to his Jewish heritage.

On that morning, the Olympic Games were violated when the Israel Olympic team was taken hostage by of a group of eight Palestinians terrorists, part of the Black September group.

The standoff with the authorities lasted eighteen hours and culminated in what came to be called the "Munich Massacre." All the Israeli athletes and coaches died, some in a shootout at the airport after the terrorists negotiated to leave the country by air while others had already been killed and tortured when initially being taken hostage in the housing for athletes. Five of the eight kidnappers died in the attempted, but mishandled, ambush at the airport. Three were arrested and in turn released in exchange for a hijacked jetliner before becoming targets of a Mossad operation, "Operation Wrath of God."

Mossad hunted down and killed two of the three men in Operation Wrath of God. One remains at large.

For the last thirty plus years, Labor Day was the day Lottie and Daniel would go over the books to see how the business had fared. There would still be some stragglers staying in the fall, but there wasn't enough business after the holiday to keep the main lodge open, only the single-family units would be in use.

Lottie never aspired to retire, but she always appreciated that her parents turned the business over to her management while she was still in her twenties and now she and Daniel would do the same for Joan and Joseph. It sometimes confused vacationers that the Zlatkins operated Goldman Resorts. Going forward, it would be the Levitts. Maybe a family tree at the front desk, tracing the roots back to Helen Glickman, a Goldman by marriage, would help guests in sorting it all out.

Each year had its own operation's folder filled with duplicate documents made from carbon paper—until now, a copy for Lottie and one for Daniel. This year's folder had four copies so each of them could make their own notes in the margins.

"What percentage of our business is Jewish now?" asked Joseph.

The resorts weren't struggling, but they weren't flourishing either as they had been right before and after World War II. Since that time, society had opened up in so many ways and it was no longer necessary to have resorts exclusively for Jews. This was great for Jewish people who wished to see more of the country, but for Goldman Resorts, exclusivity had been a gold mine. Families returned year after year. Marketing was hardly necessary outside of making sure every guest enjoyed clean sheets, cotton towels with dense, plush loops of yarn, and three square meals a day, heavy on the *schmaltz* as tradition would have it.

"We've never asked people their religious affiliation," answered Lottie. "I never really cared. Everyone has always been welcome here. But just from the sound of their last names, I would guess that Jews might only represent 40 percent of our current customer base. When we started, I imagine it was close to 100 percent."

"Perhaps we can do a little brainstorming today," said Joan. "About how to increase our business."

226

"Maybe we need to look at our menu," said Joseph. "We can still make sure Kosher foods are available, but they don't need to dominate the menu."

"And maybe it's time to look at our changeover day," said Joan. "Mom, I know your parents wished to observe the Sabbath and make it a day of rest, but I'm not sure it meets the needs of vacationers. Most of my friends either like to start their vacation Thursday night and skip work Friday or, at the latest, Friday afternoon. Being unpacked Friday night and ready to go Saturday is what people want."

"We can't make, or won't make, these choices for the two of you," said Lottie. "It's your turn at the wheel. It would please me, if you do choose to open on Friday nights, for the two of you to have hired enough help for you to Keep and Remember the Sabbath as our religion asks. I'm certain that's what my parents would not only prefer but expect. And it will require a separate kitchen to serve both Kosher and non-Kosher foods."

"I'm good with that," Joan said, and Joseph nodded.

"Have you all been watching the Olympic games?" Joan asked. "Haven't they've been incredible? Today Mark Spitz goes after his seventh gold medal. In each of his first six events, he not only won but set new Olympic and world records in the process."

"We've been watching," said Daniel. "Your mother won't miss any of it. Over the years she has paid attention to the resort, her religion and social causes, baseball, you kids and me—in that order. But this Mark Spitz has snuck into the hierarchy. I suppose it's because he is Jewish. It's such a big deal too that the games have returned to Germany for the first time since 1936 when Jessie Owens showed up Adolph Hitler."

"Do you remember much about those games?"

Lottie answered. "Of course. We didn't know just how evil Hitler was at the time, but it was clear that he was a threat to the Jewish people. And having a Black man, back then we called them Negroes, win four gold medals. It was glorious."

"You may not know this," Joseph said affectionately to his mother-in-law. "But when Owens won his last gold medal in a relay event, he was a last-minute replacement. He and Ralph Metcalfe, both African-Americans, replaced two Jewish runners that day, Marty Glickman and Sam Stoller. It's been speculated that the decision to have replacements for these two men occurred so as not to embarrass Hitler even more than Owens already had by having two Jewish runners on the victory stand."

"Oh my." said Lottie. "I've never heard that before. I hope they don't do that with Spitz today. But it's 1972 and Germany has done much to say they're sorry about the Holocaust. Let's stop and finish our work tomorrow. I want to watch Spitz swim. He's so handsome with that mustache."

❊ ❊ ❊

"Can you believe it Mom?" Joan said walking into the kitchen with Joseph the next day. "They think some of the Israeli athletes are already dead. I can't believe security wasn't tighter, especially for the athletes from Israel."

"There have been times in my life where I have started to question God but I always come back to questioning man," said Lottie. "God gave us all these gifts, but it is still up to each individual to live and abide by His Commandments."

"Well, you know the Israeli government will not idly sit by. They will kill these men, if not today, then someday in the future," said Joseph.

"I imagine you're right about that," Lottie said. "And, I suppose, I too feel that would be justified. But we mustn't confuse our support of Israel and of these young men taken hostage with our Jewish faith. Today is a day where they appear to be in conflict. I wish we could find my Dad's old copy of Maimonides's *The Guide for the Perplexed*. My father often quoted him saying 'evil had no positive existence'. It's hard to ignore this evil today, just as it was hard to ignore what happened in Germany some thirty years ago. But our attention must never be diverted from what God asks of us and what He has given us."

"Your Mom and I part ways on some things. You both know that," said Daniel. "But over the years, she is getting to me. I don't think she expects herself, or anyone else, to turn the other cheek. But the history of the Jewish people is filled with adversity. She is trying to say that we mustn't let evil rob us of the beauty of our faith."

"Daniel, I never thought I'd see the day," said Lottie. "My friend Dottie always told me to hang in there with you. She'll have a good laugh next time we talk on the phone when I tell her about your conversion to Judaism."

"All right. Point made. Should we start on the books or put it off?" said Daniel.

"Let's put it off, Dad," said Joan. "If that's ok with you guys?"

***I don't think I'll ever be able to watch the Olympic Games again.
(From the diary of Lottie Goldman Zlatkin)***

APRIL 2019–
SOUTH HAVEN

Doctor visits had become the only reality in the Walsh household since they returned from Chicago's short trip to watch Hannah's skating competition. Bill remained fatigued and Rachel insisted he see his internist. She was worried that his melanoma had returned.

Bill wanted to put it off until after the holidays but, by the first of December, fatigue wasn't his only symptom. He was down ten pounds and starting to experience severe back pain. It had nothing to do with melanoma. A diagnosis of advanced pancreatic cancer was made quickly after his initial doctor visit, some blood tests, and a CT scan. Bill was told it was inoperable and, together, he and Rachel opted for chemotherapy and radiation. The oncologist, a man with a horrendous bedside manner and halitosis to boot, dryly offered "the statistics for chemo's efficacy are pretty dismal when pancreatic cancer is already spread to your liver and spine."

Rachel tried continuing to work. "It'll be a good distraction," her best friend Bethe offered. Bill agreed, but the decision didn't prove to work out. Her job required her best at any given moment and after she missed, what to her with hindsight was an obvious case of appendicitis in a thirteen-year-old girl, she opted to take a leave of absence. Intellectually, she knew even the most experienced and attentive physicians botch a case from time to time. The surgeon called her after the operation was finished. "It was a retrocecal appendicitis Rachel. You didn't miss anything," said Dr. Ramsey. "They're a bitch to diagnosis at times. It wasn't perforated, so I doubt it will cause any fertility problems down the line. The kid will do great. By the way, I heard about Bill. I'm so sorry."

"Thanks for taking care of Meredith's appendicitis and for your thoughts about Bill," Rachel had answered. "I'll see her in the morning when I make my rounds."

Rachel followed up on Meredith the next day, but though her body was moving and her heart was beating, she felt numb, dull, disoriented. The decision not to work proved, itself, to be hard work. Delegating every last task felt like facing a mountain. It wasn't as if she'd never been asked to cover for anyone else. Over the years, almost every member of her group faced an unexpected emergency requiring them to leave the practice for a period of time. But you still felt like a wimp when calling in favors. What was the matter with medical professionals? During their residency training, had self-flagellation been inculcated into them at the same time they received a half dozen vaccinations? Wasn't mental health something to take seriously? Med school definitely gave it too little attention.

"Bethe," said Rachel over the phone. "Do you have time for lunch tomorrow? I need to talk about everything going on. It's a shit show. I'm sleepwalking through my days and worried about myself. I'm also worried about the kids. OMG, I didn't even mention Bill. I've got to get my act together for him more than anything else. I already miss him. I'm already letting go. Some of his days are so rough. I can't stand his suffering."

"Are you still seeing Rabbi Weinstein on Wednesdays?" she replied.

"Only once since Bill received his cancer diagnosis."

"Well, I can meet you tomorrow for lunch but promise me you'll call him too. It's what the rabbi does all the time. I know he's fond of you. He mentions you all the time when I see him at temple."

"I'll call right after we get off the phone. I promise. But I'll see you tomorrow at one. Most days, Bill is napping at that time. Let's just brown bag it and meet on the bench at Packard Beach Park."

1977—SOUTH HAVEN

Lottie called the meeting of the Temple Ladies' Auxiliary to order. She was serving in her 10th year as president of the organization and assembled her group to discuss news reports of the National Socialist Party of America's (NSPA) plans for a demonstration in nearby Skokie, Illinois.

"Thanks for coming out tonight," said Lottie to the sixty-five women gathered, along with a few of their spouses. "I'd like to start by introducing a friend of mine, Dottie Schneider. She runs the United Hebrew Temple Auxiliary in St. Louis. We've been friends since the mid-sixties. Dottie has been in touch with her cousin, Jackie Goldstein, who heads up the Auxiliary of Temple Judea Mizpah in Skokie. I asked her to come tonight and say a few words about the situation there."

"Good evening and thank you, Lottie. I imagine I've met a few of you over the years during my summer visits to see Lottie and Daniel here in South Haven. I have fond memories from my childhood when my parents brought our family to vacation here back in the thirties— we would call it our Catskills. The situation in Skokie is serious. A Mr. Frank Collin of the NSPA notified the Chief of Police in Skokie of his plans to hold a free speech protest in front of Village Hall for forty Neo-Nazi members on May 1st. The Village of Skokie obtained an injunction to prevent their members from wearing Nazi uniforms and prominently displaying swastikas. The ACLU is now involved.

They are arguing that this is a First Amendment issue—that their right to free speech is being violated. Believe it or not, the attorney representing them is Jewish."

"Amazing," said one woman. "Have they no decency? And why would a Jewish lawyer take the case? Wearing the swastika is a symbol of hate and evil. It will incite a violent response—it's much worse than shouting fire in a crowded theatre. Surely it won't be allowed. I understand half the population in Skokie is Jewish and at least one out of ten of them are Holocaust survivors."

"Well, so far, both the Illinois Appellate Court and the Illinois Supreme Court refused to stay the injunction," said Lottie. "The ACLU has taken the case to the Supreme Court of the United States and a decision is likely to come down any day."

One of the men stood up, chest thrust out and legs spread wide apart—"Is it okay if I speak at your ladies' meeting?"

"Of course," answered Lottie.

"I fought in the second World War. I was in a battalion that liberated Buchenwald, one of the death camps in Germany. I'll never forget what I saw. America has been good to Jews. Since the war ended, there's less discrimination in housing and employment practices. The Jewish people in America are thriving economically, equal to their peers. But we've all seen, or occasionally been, the victim of antisemitism. I hope your Auxiliary chooses to support the Jewish community of Skokie with whatever resources and people they need. They can't be allowed to march in Skokie or anywhere else for that matter. It must be stopped with whatever means necessary."

"My heart shares all that you've said, but my head tells me that free speech is vital to our democracy," answered Lottie. "If the Supreme Court allows them to assemble, and I think they might, we need to act—but peacefully. We need to mobilize, to be seen and heard by attending the march. Antisemitism must always be opposed, but not by striking back. Can you imagine how it would reflect upon all Jews if violence erupts? It's so easy for a peaceful crowd to become a mob."

* * *

After the meeting, the gentleman who had fought in the war approached Lottie and Dottie.

"You ran a good meeting. I hope I kept my remarks brief enough. I can tell I didn't sway your opinion."

"Of course you did. You were heard. I know you are angry. I too dislike antisemitism and fear how it will affect my children and grandchildren. I don't imagine it will ever disappear—Jews will always live as a minority everywhere except in Israel. But when I marched in Selma with my friend Dottie here, the ACLU went to bat for us using the same arguments these Neo-Nazis are using now. I don't like what they wish to say or their methods for saying it, but I do like living in America where you have that right."

The man nodded slightly and then said, "We'll agree to differ on the detail but I see what you mean in the big picture." As he joined his wife and walked away, Lottie overheard him say, "Wow, that Lottie Zlatin is one tough cookie."

❋ ❋ ❋

Lottie and Dottie sat on the porch in front of the main lodge of the Goldman resort after the meeting was over. Lottie was pleased to see that Dottie had hardly changed since they first met in 1965.

"How long can you stay?" asked Lottie.

"Only a few days. I wish I could stay through July. St. Louis can be awfully hot in the summer and they are predicting record temperatures."

As they sipped some iced tea, Lottie was busy sewing name tags into her grandson Paul's underwear. It wasn't that Joan couldn't do it, but Lottie liked to sew and he needed his name placed on all his clothes for summer camp.

"Hand me a needle and thread," said Dottie. "I can help while we talk. I never sent my kids to camp. Do you think it's a good idea?"

"Absolutely. I went myself. My mother carried me during the Spanish flu pandemic. It took her a while to get over worrying that I might die. She told me that pushing herself to send me away to girl scout camp was important—it allowed me some space to grow up and develop self-esteem. Paul started going away for a month every summer last year. I pay for it because I believe in it. And Joan knows that I want her to send my grandchildren someday as well. The Goldman family will hand down certain values—religion, education, community service, and even camp. Jack, Joanie, and Alan know how strongly I feel about each of these."

"Aren't you worried about a twelve-year-old being away by himself? Like tonight. We talked about antisemitism. What if some kid says something mean to him about being Jewish?"

"Believe me, antisemitism is everywhere and tonight's meeting should remind all that attended that it must be confronted." Lottie paused and then laughed. "But he's going to Camp Tomahawk in upper Wisconsin. All the kids who go there are Jewish."

Many have a false memory of what transpired on June 14th, 1977 when the Supreme Court made a ruling in the Skokie matter. The legal precedent for the right to free speech had been established in 1967 when the court heard arguments in Brandenburg v Ohio. In that case, even extraordinarily objectionable speech was ruled allowable.

That is not what happened with Skokie. The Supreme Court of the United States didn't revisit any legal precedents on how the First Amendment applied to hate speech, be it against Jews or any other minority. Instead, they only decided that the state of Illinois must hold hearings immediately to review the allegation that an individual's free speech was being restrained or allow the march to take place.

When the Illinois Supreme Court finally complied and held these hearings, attention focused primarily on the use of the swatstika. Attorneys for the city of Skokie argued that it made citizens, especially Holocaust survivors, feel as if they were being physically attacked and its use should be prohibited. The Illinois Supreme

Court ultimately rejected this notion, allowing its use if, and when, the NSPA chose to reschedule their march.

The march never did take place in Skokie. Frank Collin chose to move the event to Chicago. Held one year later in Marquette Park, an area of predominantly white inhabitants who felt threatened by Blacks moving in, the march lasted less than an hour. The twenty-five Neo-Nazi protestors were outnumbered by two thousand Jews and Jewish sympathizers.

APRIL 2019—
SOUTH HAVEN

Rachel was waiting on the park bench. Directly behind her was a small monument celebrating South Haven's history of Jewish Resorts. Rachel walked by the small sign many times, but so many things in her life, since Bill's diagnosis, seem magnified lately. As she read the words today, memories washed over her of a day several years ago when she ran into Rabbi Weinstein at this very spot. It had sparked her journey with him to explore her faith. She smiled softly, visualizing the photographs of her ancestors and the passion of her grandmother Lottie lighting what were now her candlesticks. Briefly, she reflected on her own family's good fortune.

Rachel was eating an egg salad sandwich. It lacked *schmaltz*, even though she still used her great grandmother's recipe, handed down over the years. *Schmaltz* wasn't available anywhere in South Haven, not even at Bob's Processing. Her grandmother probably just went out back and strangled a couple of chickens, happy to donate their fat, but Rachel needed to resort to using Crisco instead.

She was eager to see Bethe. At the beginning of their friendship, when either of them were experiencing a problem, they were inconsequential matters, like the problems of most small children. But as they grew older, as one would expect, the issues they faced together were often more significant. There had been breakups with boyfriends, drama with siblings, academic disappointments, and deaths of grandparents. Rachel had been there for Bethe during her personal battle with ulcerative colitis, a colectomy, and living with an ostomy for a year before having more surgery to put what was left of her bowel back together. Bethe was resilient and Rachel imagined Bethe understood how much she was depending on her now.

Rachel wanted to get her head in the right place for the difficult weeks ahead. She was feeling so sorry for herself and all she was about to lose. Maybe being egocentric in a moment like this was part of being human, a survival instinct. You can't help others until you first help yourself. She could almost hear the stewardess say, "Should the cabin lose pressure, oxygen masks will drop from the overhead area. Please place the mask over your own mouth and nose before assisting any children traveling with you." The children—their children— Andrew and Hannah would be losing their father soon.

She found them crying alone. She found them crying together. Rachel knew this sadness was to be expected, but what she didn't know was how best to help them or how long it would last. She didn't know how long Bill would last either as he was no longer responding to his treatments.

Rachel heard them whispering in the bathroom they shared before going to bed last night.

"Do you think Dad is going to die?" Hannah asked Andrew.

"Maybe," answered Andrew. "He seems to be getting weaker. But I don't know anymore than you do. It seems Mom and Dad haven't given up. We shouldn't either. Dad is fighting this with everything he's got. If it gets worse, I think he'll tell us."

"I hope so. I'll feel terrible if I don't get a chance to say goodbye."

"Me too."

Could she handle single parenthood? If it were by choice, it would be a layup. One of her closest professional colleagues was a single mother. She'd chosen the life by going the artificial insemination route. From afar, it appeared to be a juggling act, but Rachel was curious what parenting would've been like if every decision had been her way or the highway—no one to fight, manipulate, or compromise with. There would be less drama for sure. Had she been a single parent, she knew what her parenting mantra would've been: "I will not negotiate with terrorists."

Bill was always willing to negotiate. Like most fathers, he preferred to be the fun one.

But looking back, she and Bill worked together well from the start. Like many aspects of their marriage, it seemed instinctive, second nature. They could bicker to Olympian level, but bickering wasn't fighting. The kids sometimes confused the two, becoming needlessly upset when the volume got turned up too high. There had been none of this banter lately. It was another sign that she and Bill were resigned to the seriousness of Bill's diagnosis and the certainty of his death. There wasn't enough time left together to screw around.

Bethe arrived with a casserole in a cardboard box. "My mother," she said with a slight tilt of her head. "We both know a Jewish mother's need, compulsion, an ingrained duty, to feed us when we are distressed. Do you think we'll do the same someday?"

"Probably. Your mother is the best," Rachel answered. "Thank her for me. I'll write her a note, but it may be a few days."

"She said, 'no thank you notes'. I called her yesterday right after we got off the phone. I hope you don't mind. I needed advice about how best to help you right now."

"I'd probably have done the same thing. Called your mother, not mine. I'm just kidding. So what was her advice to you?"

"You mean after telling me to come right over for a sandwich?"

Bethe paused. Rachel watched her friend's eyes rake over her. She knew she must look different: fragile, anxious. "We talked about your grandmother and mine. Mom said they were friends and competitors in the resort business. When together, they'd brag endlessly about how smart, pretty, and good we both were at soccer. The two of us would run up to them, while they sat smoking cigarettes in their lawn chairs, and they would squeeze our cheeks between their thumb and forefinger and call us their *bubbalas*."

"I remember that."

"Mom said that you are part of the Stolar family and what she wouldn't do for you if she could. But she told me just to listen. She said people feel isolated at times like these. That everyone is afraid of saying the wrong thing."

"I do feel that way. Outside of you and my trainer, Daniel, very few people really engage with me about my grief. It may surprise you to hear that Daniel has stepped up, but I always knew I could count on him. I'm still trying to work out on Wednesdays. Routine helps. I just wish I could be as consistent with my faith."

"Well, you can trust me with anything. I'll be here no matter how long your grief lasts and anytime you need me—until you are ready to move forward."

Bethe slid along the bench until she was right next to Rachel, a lump rising in the throat, as they sat quietly for a moment.

"OK, spill it out. Whatever you need to tell me," whispered Bethe. "Just talk. I'll listen and not judge."

"Bill's treatments are becoming futile," Rachel said now sobbing between her words. "And he's so weak physically. Sometimes I can't get him to eat or get out of bed. But it's amazing how strong he still seems emotionally, spiritually." Rachel paused, "I'm going to miss him so much."

Bethe focused on Rachel's honesty about her sadness and fears.

"I think I just needed some affirmation that I'm doing all I can for Bill, the kids, and myself. That I won't be alone all the time, just most of the time. You're good at this Bethe," said Rachel.

"Well, I wouldn't have been worth much without talking to my mother. Isn't it amazing? Sometimes I can't stand her and then other times she blows me away. I asked her where she gets all her advice. She said it's in the *Jewish Mother's Manual*—that she would get us both a copy. She said you need to expect a chicken casserole for dinner every Tuesday night for a while and she won't take 'no' for an answer. She said it's best to just do for someone. That I shouldn't ask, 'What can I do?' The question needs answering and so it only becomes another burden."

"She's right about that."

After a brief hug, they separated to go in opposite directions. Bethe turned around and ran back to Rachel.

"I almost forgot. My mom said to go see Rabbi Weinstein. She talked about how her own faith has seen her through the difficult moments in her own life. I told her I already gave you that piece of advice, correctly, without her help."

"He's going to see me this Sunday. What a nice man."

❋ ❋ ❋

Rachel quietly returned to the house, coming in the back door. The kids weren't due home for a while. She was glad of this. She wanted time to wash her face, have a Diet Coke, and look in on Bill.

She had asked him to spray some WD-40 on their bedroom door hinges so she could open the door without the squeak they had ignored for years. When things were normal, they couldn't be bothered to deal with a stiff but insignificant hinge but now, silencing the squeak took on enormous significance. She believed asking him to do this task would make him feel less sick, less needy, though with each passing day, these things were becoming less and less true. She was pleased to hear the door open silently as she opened it ever so slowly.

She stood at the doorway and watched him sleep. She had loved watching Bill sleep almost from the first night they met. She wasn't an "easy girl" back then, but they'd spent the night together on their second date and every night since, except for the occasional trip out of town for a pediatric meeting, a guy's golf trip for Bill, or a girl's trip for her. He always snored a little due to his large tonsils that escaped removal during his childhood, but even more now with a few extra pounds in his midsection. When Bill was gone, Rachel supposed she could sleep again without the industrial strength ear plugs the otolaryngologist had recommended for her.

She thought back to her meeting with Bethe. No one could remove her fears, but Bethe helped simply by listening to her express her feelings. She was kidding herself to think she was preoccupied by selfish thoughts. It was part of her unconscious personality trait to judge herself—all that black and white thinking. Her anxiety was reasonable. Who wouldn't feel the way she did about how to best spend the little time she and Bill had left together and then going it alone in the future?

Bill needed her help, mechanical, not spiritual. He continued to reassure her that he was "good" there. It was the physical challenges—dealing with the nausea and weakness produced by the chemotherapy, needing assistance dressing, bathing, and even eating.

But he wasn't fearful of dying. In that way, Bill reminded Rachel of his own grandmother. Rachel knew her to be absolute in her faith, that her life on earth was just a beginning. The first time she had met Grandma Walsh, Rachel walked into the living room with Bill only to find his grandmother, then ninety years old, playing the piano for her own pleasure. She was a remarkable woman, living alone, still driving her car, taking meals to the "old people" at the nursing home, and ready to go whenever God chose to take her.

In some ways, it gave Rachel the creeps when Bill told her he looked forward to seeing his grandmother in heaven—that even they, he and Rachel, would one day be together again—in heaven for eternity. When they married, she signed up for "til death do you part"; but eternity—wow, that was a long time.

And recently, it wasn't just physical assistance Bill needed of Rachel, he wanted her help with the kids. When to tell them that additional medical care was becoming futile? How to tell them he was ready to go, that they shouldn't worry about him, that he knew they would grow up to be great people with productive lives, and to look after their mother. Was all this code for saying good-bye? Did it help to say it or would writing each of them a letter be better? Would he regret it if he didn't, but more importantly, would they? She wasn't sure how to best answer any of these questions.

Quietly, she recited out loud Psalm 23. When she had called Rabbi Weinstein to make an appointment to discuss Bill's diagnosis, he had suggested she pick a prayer for these moments of sadness. She remembered it clearly from her days in Sunday School and her family's attendance during the High Holidays.

"The Lord is my shepherd; I shall not want..."

JUNE 1982—
SOUTH HAVEN

Tarot cards could be traced back to the mid-15th century when they were used to play games. They weren't part of predicting the future, divination, until late in the 18th century. Some like to see similarities between Tarot cards and the Kabbalah though scholars doubt they are truly related.

Kabbalah is the word referring to the mystical traditions and oral teachings about the relationship between man and God, the finite and the infinite. Most consider the Zohar the most important Kabalistic text, but the first known writings are contained in the Sefer Yetzirah, a somewhat mathematical theory to account for the creation of the universe. Though the author of this text remains unclear, it dates back to the 3rd or 4th century CE and suggests there were thirty-two mystical paths composed of the twenty-two letters of the Hebrew alphabet and ten numbers of the Sephriot. The ten numbers were to represent creative forces intervening between God, Ein Sof, and our world. This structure is loosely similar to the Tarot deck where ten cards make up The Tree of Life and the twenty-two, Major Arcana cards, correspond to the paths between them. Each path teaches "The Fool" life lessons so that he can become more experienced, display personal growth, and move forward to the next stage. The fifty-six Minor Arcana cards dealt with smaller day-to-day events and tribulations.

For some reason, Rachel's siblings, Michelle and Paul, rarely took advantage of the invitations Lottie made to have them spend the night. But Lottie, having herself been the youngest in the family, suspected Rachel craved the one-on-one attention that was hard to come by when you were the baby in a family of three children.

And Lottie never expected Rachel to live up to the myriad of expectations that a parent might set for their child. It was enough for Lottie for the two of them to just be together. She assumed Rachel could sense this—hoping it might lead to a special closeness from which both of them would benefit over the years.

Rachel was in the fourth grade. Lottie often bragged to friends that Rachel was "smart as a whippersnapper." Lottie didn't mean it in a derogatory fashion. She was astonished by her recall, her ability to work numbers, and her writing skills.

Her grandmother was waiting in the school parking lot for Rachel to come out and struck up a conversation with Eleanor Stolar who was waiting for her granddaughter, Bethe.

"Grandmother duty tonight?" asked Lottie.

"Yes," answered Eleanor. "It's the best, isn't it? I call it duty too, so my kids think I'm doing them a favor. But there are times I live to be with her."

"I love having Rachel without Joanie around. Don't get me wrong, I love my daughter, but it's an entirely different opportunity without her parents. I like it when Rachel and I get to choose our activities, our topics of conversation, and enjoy an evening where my rules are the only rules. Rachel's behavior is so different when it's just the two of us and Joanie isn't present. She is so confident, no shame or guilt. I suppose all the shtick between mothers and daughters that stifles them is normal, but I hate it."

"We probably made the same mistakes or worse when raising our own. I feel very similarly. I can't wait to get my hands on Bethe tonight. By the way, I understand our granddaughters are best friends. I hope they stay that way. A best friend, especially one who makes you feel good about yourself, can make a big difference in a young woman's life."

❊   ❊   ❊

"How was school today, Rachel?" asked Lottie as they pulled out of the North Shore Elementary parking lot.

"Great. The teacher timed us today to see how many of our multiplication tables we could solve in two minutes. I always complete the most, but I do feel sorry sometimes for some of the other kids who aren't as good at math. I think the teacher doesn't realize how bad they feel when they come in last all the time. I really hate it when she makes some of them try to solve problems up on the chalkboard in front of the whole class. Everyone has to do it when it is their turn, even Danny. But he can't do them. Yet he still has to take a regular turn like everyone else. Why do you think they teach that way Grandma?"

"I have no idea. I imagine you're right about how it makes some of the other kids feel. I'm proud of you for sensing that. Do you know what the vocabulary word is for what you're feeling towards the other kids?"

"No Grandma. What is it?"

"Empathy. You spell that E-M-P-A-T-H-Y. Someone like you is being empathetic."

"Well, Paul and Michelle sometimes say I'm pathetic but I know that's not a compliment."

"I'll need to speak to your mother about that. I had two brothers, Jacob and Isaac. They used to tease me also. They called it 'giving me the business.' If my mother, your great-grandmother Helen, caught them saying that kind of stuff, she called them a couple of schmucks. That's Yiddish for not being very nice."

"Didn't one of them die in the war?" asked Rachel.

"Yes. Thirty-eight years ago, next month. He was a paratrooper. He loved to fly. Many soldiers died during World War II. They were all someone's brother."

"Mom and Dad always turn off the television when they start talking about wars. I think there is a war right now in Israel."

"Rachel, I can't believe you know all this. You're just ten."

"Well, it's on the news and in the newspaper. You've always encouraged me to read the paper. Israel is fighting Lebanon and the PLO. Isn't that right?"

"Yes. It is," said Lottie.

"On television, they made it sound like it was kind of a regular thing, war in Israel."

It bothered Lottie to learn that Rachel was aware of the current conflict. But she was not all that much older in 1933 when her interest in the Zionist cause had been instilled by her own parents as she sat alongside them at Soldier's Field taking in *The Romance of a People.*

"War does little to help, Rachel," said Lottie. "Israel isn't a big country like the United States, and it's surrounded by countries that don't like the Jewish people. You're right, Israel has often been at war. I root for them to win each war, but I root harder for peace. I dream of going there one day—to stand, safely in Jerusalem, at the Western Wall, placing a prayer in a crack in the wall. We're almost home. What do you think about popping into North Side Memories for an ice cream cone? We can sit and eat it on the bench near the lake. I want to tell you about the Tarot cards. I thought tonight, we could try to read your future. Does that sound like fun?"

❅ ❅ ❅

It was Friday night and Daniel hurried into the house remembering that Lottie planned to have Rachel spend the night. He hoped Lottie would give him some space with Rachel. The two of them could be thick as thieves and it left him little opportunity to talk with her.

"I hear a little monster in the house," Daniel shouted.

"Hi PawPaw," answered Rachel.

"Daniel, dinner is ready. Please come in. Rachel and I are ready to light the Sabbath candles," said Lottie.

"Grandma, your candlesticks are so pretty," said Rachel.

"They're nice but I like your mother's better. I assume you know they were mine and, before that, your great-grandmother's. She brought them to America from Russia. One day, they will be yours. Your mother is to give them to you when you get married just as my mother did."

"Why won't she give them to my sister, Michelle?

"Because they're to go to the youngest daughter. Someday you will do the same. I hope you have a family. I hope you marry someone Jewish, but if not, I trust you'll remain Jewish yourself, honor the Sabbath, and light your candles every Friday night."

"I will, Grandma."

"Can you help me recite the prayer?"

"Sure."

Barukh ata Adonai Eloheinu, Melekh ha'olam, asher kid'shanu b'mitzvotav v'tzivanu l'hadlik ner shel Shabbat.

* * *

"Daniel, you haven't touched your carrots," said Lottie. "Please set a better example for Rachel."

"You know I hate carrots," Daniel replied.

"Quit *kvetching*. When I was a little girl, if our farm produced more carrots one year, then we ate more carrots," said Lottie.

"PawPaw," said Rachel. "At school in kindergarten they told us, you get what you get and you don't throw a fit."

Her grandfather laughed.

"I like that," said Lottie. "You're showing a little *chutzpah*."

"Well, I wonder where she inherited that, dear?" said Daniel.

"What's *chutzpah*, NaNa?"

"Self-confidence. Acting or speaking up when you need to for yourself or, more importantly, for someone who can't, or is unable."

"Will you do the dishes, Daniel? I want to show Rachel the Tarot cards and read her future."

* * *

Lottie pulled out her Rider-Waite Tarot card deck. Like her candlesticks, they'd belonged to her mother Helen. She shuffled them and placed a Tarot spread on the table. She studied the Major Arcana cards and the Minor ones, the Cups, Wands, Swords and Tentacles and then asked Rachel what she would like to know about her future.

"Well, Grandma. I'd like to know if Bethe and I will always be good friends," said Rachel.

"An excellent question, but we must phrase it differently for the deck to give us an answer. The cards don't predict the future exactly but they can instruct us on how we must act to get something we wish in life. A solid friendship for life can be invaluable. A better question for the cards about your friend Bethe might be, how must I treat Bethe if we are to remain best friends?"

Lottie paused to study the cards. "Here's an answer—the Ace of cups. You need to always be compassionate, supportive, and aware when your friend needs you."

"Is something bad going to happen to her?"

"That I can't say, but if you want to always have Bethe as a friend, use that empathy we talked about earlier today. Bad things are in all our futures. We must be ready for them, but they are outweighed by good things—like for me just being with you here tonight."

"I've got another question for the cards, Grandma," said Rachel.

"OK," answered Lottie.

"What should I be someday? What kind of job will I have?"

Lottie shuffled the cards and put out another spread, again studying them for answers. Two cards stood out. The Queen of Pentacles and the Ace of Swords. The first depicted a woman sitting on a throne with signs of material success around her, the second, a sword emerging from the sky. Both of the cards were upright.

"Well, this is interesting. The Queen tells me you will be successful financially, passionate about your work, nurturing your family while still being a working mother. And the Ace indicates your intellect, being smart, will serve you well. But there will come a day when something will happen, some type of breakthrough, where a change in your career path may make you happier."

"My Mom always tells me I should be a doctor," said Rachel. "Do the cards say I will do that?"

"It fits with financially supporting your family. But this breakthrough? I didn't see this card over here——the High Priestess. Perhaps this breakthrough will be in the realm of your spirituality, your religion."

"Really? How about this card over here, the six of swords?"

Lottie studied the card with a picture of a woman in a boat with a child beside her. She did have an intuition that it involved loss and Rachel's need, like the woman in the boat, to protect her child. They were traveling somewhere new but they would always carry their loss with them.

"I'm not sure," answered Lottie quickly deciding that a little white lie was a more appropriate answer tonight for her ten-year-old granddaughter. Lottie knew that loss was something she would wish to talk about with Rachel someday, but not quite yet.

"That was fun, Grandma," said Rachel, as they put the deck away. "You said I would have passion. Do you have passion? What are you passionate about?"

"Your grandfather would tell you I have too much passion. I am passionate for my grandchildren to have the best education possible. If you keep studying, you can be anything you want when you grow up. And I am passionate about our religion. My parents traveled here from Russia. They came to America because they could not openly practice their religion in Russia without being attacked. When they arrived, religion was their foundation. My father studied and practiced Judaism every day and my mother performed *mitzvot*, good deeds, as part of her faith. As a young woman, I followed her example and spent a lot of my time trying to make sure everyone in our country was treated equally. I still work with the Jewish Federation to do the same. God asks us to look out for those less fortunate. Do you understand what I just said?"

"I think so."

***I love the Tarot cards. They scare and delight me at the same time.
(From the diary of Lottie Goldman Zlatkin)***

Taste and See…Psalm 34 (from the diary of Rachel Levitt Walsh)

Rachel called Rabbi Weinstein's office as Bethe suggested. However, she didn't really need to be prompted by Bethe and her mother to do so. Rachel knew she needed his counsel now more than ever and his secretary indicated he would see her the following Sunday, typically a day off for a rabbi. Rachel felt guilty about taking his time on what, she assumed, would normally be a day off. A day he might use to be with his own family or for reflection and study. But Rachel guessed he understood it couldn't wait. "Dr. Rachel Walsh wishes to discuss her husband's impending death." Just like a doctor, a rabbi's job certainly included emergencies.

The Hebrew word *rabbi* means "My Master" as a student of the Torah would address his teacher. Though in school and during her residency training, Rachel had been a quick student, this ability hadn't translated over to her work on faith. She hoped the rabbi didn't find her fluctuating progress frustrating,

She and the rabbi had looked at secular literature about the Holocaust and antisemitism, weekly portions of the Torah, oral interpretations of the Torah in the Talmud and the Zohar, and even some contemporary literature about faith. Where was the light at the end of the tunnel? Now with Bill's illness gaining momentum, Rachel was desperate for guidance, enlightenment, a consciousness about meaning in life and in death. Did it really require being faced with an unimaginable life struggle, a wrestling match with God, to accept faith? If so, she found it impossible to feel grateful for the opportunity.

Rachel wasn't ready to accept losing Bill without finding faith first. Additional care had become, in medical ethics terms, futile. More chemo, or radiation, would only weaken Bill and make his remaining days more difficult to enjoy. They probably would shorten his life as well—the list of possible complications was pages long. Less quality, less quantity. It was time to concede.

But finding faith was another thing altogether. It was eluding Rachel's grasp just as the ball did for Bill Buckner as he attempted to field the slow roller off Mookie Wilson's bat in game six of the 1986 World Series. Baseball imagery was never far from her working mind. When would she just catch the ball and step on first base? Or maybe accepting faith was not akin to making or muffing a routine play. Maybe it was more like Willie Mays sprinting towards the wall with his back to home plate at the Polo Grounds and catching the ball over his shoulder. Whatever it took, she wished, if possible, to be like an athlete, reacting without thinking. But even a stranger coming into the rabbi's study would see Rachel, sitting with slumped shoulders and a too sad face, and know this young woman was weary of thinking.

"Rachel," said Rabbi Weinstein. "I'm so sorry to hear that Bill's illness has become so serious. When we first started, I wondered if someone was ill and you didn't wish to tell me. Few people come in, desiring to learn about their religion and open themselves up to accepting God, for no reason."

"Well," said Rachel. "At the beginning, I did come in because I was worried about Bill. He'd been diagnosed with malignant melanoma. But his medical issues now are completely unrelated. It's crazy—I've spent so much time in my life worrying about the bad stuff I might face at any moment—big things like someone I love or myself receiving a terminal diagnosis. But I now know, a little too late, that this was a colossal waste of time. It didn't help me at all to prepare for what I'm now feeling."

"What are you feeling?" asked the rabbi.

Rachel began to cry uncontrollably. Rabbi Weinstein sat quietly, offered her a tissue, but let her go on for several minutes. Slowly, she calmed down, took a final deep breath, and started in.

"I'm not sure I can do it, raise my kids without Bill? I worry whether I will ever feel joy again? Most importantly, whether you'll have an answer for me today about how I can accept faith? Can you appeal to my penchant for believing in things I can measure, validate, or see with my own eyes? As a scientist, I am willing to rethink my conclusions about faith, but I need new data, or a reason to believe I have misinterpreted the data I've already considered."

"I'll do the best I can, Rachel," answered the rabbi. "Let's look at two thing you can see and touch—Nature and the Torah. Maimonides wrote in the *Mishneh Torah*, an oral interpretation of the Torah, that God is eternal. Your own two eyes tell you this each and every day when you contemplate the beauty of nature. Do you recall the day we ran into each other by the bench overlooking the lake? We each remarked on the spectacular view, a view you often shared with your grandmother. What creative force can account for all this beauty?"

Rachel reflected on the rabbi's words.

"Now consider the Torah, the mind of God revealed to Moses, 'mouth to mouth' on Mount Sinai. The brilliance of God is revealed in the Torah. It's a living document, augmented over the years by oral commentary. Another palpable example of a creative force—this time guiding man to live with compassion and good will. We have been studying it. In this moment, your human experience is quite painful. But we just saw, using your own language, two data points to rethink, Nature and the Torah, each pointing to a creative force— God is near. Psalm 34:8 offers that we *Taste and See*. Think of it as a trial subscription to Netflix. An opportunity as a scientist to test an alternate hypothesis. It's a bargain. It's free."

1988—SOUTH HAVEN

Never in a million years did Rachel think she'd fail her driver's test. Not the actual driving part, she wasn't even given a chance to try that. Twenty-five stupid questions and you needed to get twenty correct. She missed passing by a single question. Who cared how many feet you needed to trail the car in front of you by if traveling fifty-five miles per hour?

She was more mad than embarrassed or ashamed. She thought, like school, she wouldn't need to study the little driver's education manual. But the questions were so arbitrary and absurd.

For as long as she could remember, Rachel was the smartest kid in the class. It wasn't simply that her grades were the highest. She could actually learn and process information so completely that good grades were a natural outcome. Her parents couldn't understand it as neither of them were ever at the top of their class, even though they were both good students. As a pre-schooler, they called her their "sponge", soaking up new words, learning the subtleties of sarcasm, displaying a sense of humor at a much earlier age than her siblings, solving puzzles, and recognizing patterns. They wondered if she had inherited a photographic memory or something similar, and though proud of her, her intellect was confusing at the same time.

Her brother and sister did well in school, but with greater effort. They were envious of how easily it came for Rachel, often making snarky comments when report cards arrived at the house like "I could make all A's too if I wanted."

Rachel threw herself into the car. Her mother had waited outside and was finishing her nails.

"Well, how did it go?" Joan asked. "You look…"

"I flunked," interrupted Rachel. "I'll never hear the end of it at home. What a birthday present!"

"Maybe that was our mistake. Everyone wants to dash right down here the day they turn sixteen."

"Give it a rest, Mom. I'm an idiot thinking I would pass like it's a school exam without at least reading the book."

"You didn't even read it?"

"Of course not. I know how to drive. I didn't realize they were going to ask insane questions."

"I assume you meant to say 'inane'."

"No, Mom, I meant 'insane'. Stopping distances and laws about driving under the influence. By the way, have I ever made anything but an A in English? Do you think I don't know the different between inane and insane? I'll tell you what. I've got one for you. What's the difference between immigrate and emigrate?"

"I guess now that you are sixteen you plan to start acting like your brother and sister, always an attitude. I suppose I did the same thing to my mother. I think I'll have to ask her next time she calls."

＊　＊　＊

Rachel went straight to her room when she returned home. She jumped on her bed, and turned on the radio. Bobby McFerrin was speaking to her:

Here's a little song I wrote

You might want to sing it note for note
Don't worry, be happy
In every life we have some trouble
But when you worry you make it double
Don't worry, be happy
Don't worry, be happy now

It was just a dumb driver's test. She would read the stupid book before returning next week and promised herself she would receive a perfect score.

Her eyes wandered to her nightstand. A small book lay on it, her assignment for Sunday School and sophomore English class. Rachel reached over and picked up *Night*, by Elie Wiesel. It was so tiny it reminded her of grade school when she first read those Dick & Jane books. *See Dick run. See Jane run. See Dick and Jane run.*

But she knew this book, though small, must be special. It wasn't every day that her Sunday School and her sophomore English class assigned the same book to read. She knew in advance it was a Holocaust story. Though now several years removed from the day she and other twelve-year-olds were taken below the synagogue to watch movies of concentration camps, the trauma still lived inside her. Perhaps it always would.

She read the entire book that afternoon in a single sitting. Once started, it compelled you to finish. The central character of the book was Eliezer, a fifteen-year-old boy living in Sighet, Transylvania. He was a happy boy who seriously studied the Talmud, and the Kabbalah, with Moshe the Beadle, an older man who befriended Eliezer. Moshe is then deported to Poland, later escapes, and returns to Sighet and tells everyone of the horrors he saw. He refers to them as "the story of his own death." Yet no one heeds his warnings. When the Germans arrive in 1944, the Jews are placed in ghettos and required to wear yellow Jewish stars on the front of their shirts or jackets. Eliezer's father says to his son "you don't die from it." Rachel knew how this story was going to unfold—families taken to Auschwitz, separated, forced into hard labor or gassed. Eliezer's loss of innocence and his faith in God, both consumed by the flames. Though Eliezer survives, liberated by the American Army at the end of the war, he no longer could recognize himself in the person he had become—changed forever by the inhumane treatment he suffered.

Rachel wanted to know more about Wiesel. She assumed "the story" was his personal story. She went downstairs to find her mother.

"Are you feeling better?" her mother asked while icing a chocolate cake for Rachel's birthday sleepover with friends.

"Sure. The driver's test is old history. But I'm a little discombobulated. I just finished a book for school entitled *Night*. Did you ever read it, Mom?" asked Rachel.

"Oh yes. I was probably around the same age you are now. It had only been out for a year or two. It seemed a strange coincidence that the writer was also about fifteen or sixteen at the time he was taken to the camps. I remember the flames. He survived but the flames took his father and robbed him of his faith in God. What I recall most about reading the book was my dad getting upset that the school required us to read such a tormenting story, yet my mother felt very differently about the assignment. I would be speaking for her if I said more. Call her. You two are close."

"I'll call her after I get ready for the party," said Rachel.

Rachel showered and washed her hair to get ready for the party. Eight girls were coming to spend the night. Rachel knew some of the boys in her class planned to crash the party. Her parents would be okay if this occurred. It was kind of an expected part of a girls' sleepover at this age and Rachel's parents always wished for her to be popular and fit in.

Having a few minutes before her friends were due to arrive, Rachel picked up the phone and dialed Grandma Lottie.

"Hello?" she answered.

"Hi, Grandma. It's Rachel."

"Happy Birthday my little *bubbala*. Sweet sixteen. How did the driver's test go?"

"Don't ask. I'm an idiot. I'm calling about my school reading assignment, *Night* by Elie Wiesel. Mom said she read it in high school and that you and Grandpa had different opinions about the school making it a required reading assignment."

"Your grandfather was just worried about the kids being mature enough to understand what they were reading. He wondered if the non-Jewish kids were old enough to have empathy for how it might affect your mother and the other Jewish kids in the class. It's a tough story about a little boy becoming a man in the worst of circumstances, in the worst of times, left to wonder where was God. For me, it was the book that turned the Holocaust into a religious event. I've heard many of my Jewish friends over the years say the same thing. Perhaps that's a good thing, perhaps not. It can divert one's attention from the real meaning of our faith."

"I read it this afternoon. Grandma, do you still have faith in God? I've never thought about my own faith 'for real.' If I had been Eliezer, I'm pretty certain that I too would have lost mine."

"Rachel, the Jewish people have survived for a very long time, often in difficult circumstances. The period of the Holocaust represents humanity at its lowest moment. Some prefer to imagine it never happened, to never read or write about it. They avoid confronting the *Shoah*. I prefer to never forget. The boy in the book, Wiesel himself, feels guilty about being unable to save his father. I feel guilty about the safety I enjoyed here in America during this horrific event. But I live with the Holocaust every day. I am thankful to Mr. Wiesel—for his courage to write his story. Does this help Rachel?"

"Yes. But you didn't answer my question about faith, faith in God."

"I'm sorry Rachel. Yes, I have faith in God. It has remained unshaken for as long as I can remember. I know I've told you before that it sustained my parents as immigrants to the United States. It was a light guiding them, illuminating their choices, and mine, to help others in need."

"Thanks, Grandma. My friends just got here for the sleepover."

"Have fun," said Lottie. "By the way, they're building a United States Holocaust Memorial Museum in Washington right now. Once it's completed, how about you and I going on a girls' trip to see it?"

"I'd love that, Grandma," answered Rachel. "Oh, I almost forgot to thank you for my birthday present. I love it. It looks kind of like your diary with my initials on the cover."

"Well, you are sixteen now. I was around that age when I started to write in mine. I still write in it—thoughts about family and events in my life. I've seen a lot over the years. Sometimes I found it painful but helpful to sort out my feelings on the page. Perhaps you will find the same to be true."

"Yehi zichro baruch"

<u>*"May his memory be a blessing." (From the diary of Rachel Levitt*</u>
<u>*Walsh)*</u>

The days right before Bill died were gruesome. Though the hospice team was in a state of constant vigilance, he still suffered and it tore Rachel apart to watch.

It was now one week since the funeral and Rachel felt as if she had been going through the motions over the last few weeks—attending events, signing papers, looking at sympathy cards.

This could not really be her life. At best, she was playing a role in some random play which she didn't audition for or wish to perform in the first place.

Like most adults, death had touched her life many times before but more peripherally. She could recount each child who had died over her career in practice. There had been an 18-month-old who drowned, two adolescent suicides, a 4-year-old in an auto accident, a young child with leukemia, and several infants born either too premature or with too many critical parts either in the wrong place or missing entirely.

Of course, she had already lost her grandparents, but her parents and siblings were still alive.

The priest knew Bill and Rachel's children well. When they met to discuss the service, little time needed to be spent on who Bill was as a person. It wouldn't be one of those situations where the clergy, when they spoke, pretended to know the deceased and how he led his life—his words would ring of authenticity.

Rachel did, however, have one unusual request.

"At a Jewish service, they always recite the Mourner's Kaddish. I don't know exactly what each word means, but the rhythm of the prayer gives me great comfort. I know it never mentions death but simply attests to the greatness of God even in the face of our faith being tested. Would you be willing to learn and recite it?" Rachel asked the priest.

The service was simple. In addition to the many couples that comprised their social life over the years, and a smattering of the older generation in the South Haven community, what really stood out were the students Bill taught over the years. The church could hardly hold them all. Several came to the lectern and reflected on how Bill had changed their lives.

Rachel sat up a bit straighter when Andrew and Hannah bravely stepped up and spoke, briefly, but beautifully, about their father. Just days before Bill passed, he and Rachel sat them down to give them the news.

"I can't explain all my feelings right now," Bill started in. "Someday, if you choose to have children, you will understand the love I have for both of you. It is unending, even after I pass. You'll be sad for a while but don't feel guilty about moving on at some point. We all need to make the most of our time. Though my life will be shorter than I wished, I've always lived a full life and I'm not regretful or afraid of dying. My faith in God carries me every day, even now. Be kind to others. Doing so will bring you success in life and personal fulfillment. Your mother will take you the rest of the way. You're in good hands."

Rachel had been so proud of her husband's strength to speak

to their children with these powerful words. She watched that day, somewhat helplessly, as the kids remained as stoic as possible, yet fighting back tears the entire time.

Towards the end of the service the priest acknowledged Rachel's request and out flowed the Mourner's Kaddish prayer.

> *Yitgadal, v'yitkadash, sh'meih raba, b'alma divra chiruteih, v'yamlich malchuteih, b'chayeichon uv'yomeichon uv'chayei d'chol beit Yisra'eil, ba'agala uviz'man kariv. V'im'ru: amein. Y'hei sh'meih raba m'varach l'alam ul'almei almaya. Yitbarach, v'yishtabach, v'yitpa'ar, v'yitromam, v'yitnasei, v'yit'hardar, v'yitaleih, v'yit'halal sh'meih d'kud'sha. B'rich hu l'eila min kol bir'chata, v'shirata, tushb'chata, v'nech'mata, da'amiran b'alma. V'im'ru: amein. Y'hei sh'lama raba min sh'maya v'chayim aleinu v'al kol Yisra'eil. V'imru: amein. Osheh shalom bim'romaav, hu ya'aseh shalom, aleinu v'al kol Yisra'eil. V'im'ru: amein.*

The prayer gave her a soft embrace. It was as if Bill was sitting beside her saying goodbye—may He create peace for us.

Can I just believe?

The words bounced about in Rachel's head.

✳ ✳ ✳

Though the service had been a wonderful celebration of Bill's life, his death was just too much, too much pain. Rachel believed in meditation and mindfulness, but when she tried these exercises, she often ended up in the fetal position on the bed and would let hours pass.

Her mother moved in temporarily to provide support. Joan busied herself cooking and cleaning and tried to stay out of Rachel's way, only coming in the bedroom to lightly tickle Rachel's spine the way she did when Rachel was little and had suffered a minor disappointment.

"Thanks, Mom," Rachel said, quietly.

Rabbi Weinstein came by the house on the following Wednesday asking if they could talk. He'd attended the service held for Bill, but Rachel had been distracted that day and hadn't see him.

"Your kids spoke so well at Bill's service. I'm never quite certain which kids can do that, and which kids can't. I always offer the option, but few take me up on it."

Rachel was glad to see the rabbi but struggled to maintain eye contact.

"Bill was really helping me, prior to his getting sick, with my struggle about the role I thought faith could play in enhancing my life. I was getting close. But the randomness of Bill's illness and the degree of his suffering has shaken my faith in God again. My grief is overwhelming. It shuts out everything."

Rabbi Weinstein paused and gently placed his hand on Rachel's arm. "Now may be the best time to open yourself up to your faith and to God, to accept even these horrible days, and remember that an afterlife awaits us all."

"But Jews don't believe in an afterlife," said Rachel.

"That isn't necessarily a true statement, though it is commonly thought to be," replied Rabbi Weinstein. "I admit it is a controversial matter in the minds of Jewish scholars, but personally, I believe there are an acceptable range of possibilities for an afterlife in Judaism. Some are similar to the Christian notion of heaven, though there isn't an alternative hell. Others believe in the soul moving on, perhaps to be reunited with the body when the Messiah comes, or in life after death, *ha'olam a'bah*, by way of our influence upon those we've touched who survive us. Some religions, the emphasis may seem to be on the life to come after death. However, for the Jew, it is our lives here on earth that must be our focus. We mustn't turn our back on making this world a better place for all, a more just world, a more peaceful world. A rabbi I knew once said this to his congregation: 'God and the world to come are not two ideas. They are two parts of the same idea. They are two facets of the same diamond, two sparks of the same fire and the same hope that bring the only enduring light to the dark night of our souls.'"

The rabbi stayed for over an hour. He asked for details about the burial. He'd heard Bill wanted to be cremated and have his ashes spread back home in Missouri as well as at the cemetery in South Haven where Rachel's family was buried.

"Yeah," Rachel replied, "the kids and I plan to get back there as soon as possible. I hope doing so will give me a sense of closure."

"People often say 'closure'," Rabbi Weinstein said. "I'm not so sure that ever happens or should happen. Bill will hopefully remain close by, all your days here on earth."

"There is something surreal about it all. The only other experience I can draw upon in my life which compares, and this may sound strange under the circumstances, was birthing my children. Neither event can be properly prepared for—one moment so exhilarating and the other so full of pain and gloom. I know birth can be explained by simple biology, as can death, but holding my children for the first time, I was awestruck by their very existence and their unlimited potential. But death is quite different. As I try to accept the finality of Bill's death, I wonder if my grief is a natural component of a spiritual odyssey we are all on—pushing me towards accepting faith."

"Rachel, searching for meaning is a good thing. It can be jarred loose by birth and death to be sure. You're not alone in feeling doubt. In rabbinical school, some of my teachers indicated that even the Torah regards skepticism as healthy. But when, and if, you're ready to choose faith, I believe it will give your day-to-day life more meaning and provide you comfort when faced with your own ultimate demise."

"Thank you for stopping by," whispered Rachel.

"*Yehi zichro baruch*," said Rabbi Weinstein. "May his memory be a blessing."

Rabbi Weinstein got up slowly and started to head out the door. "Oh," he said turning back around to race Rachel. "I keep meaning to ask you. What did you do with that diary of your great-grandmother's I translated for you after her death?"

"I've never mentioned it? I'm trying to write something fictional that would incorporate all the things she saw over her lifetime. It's a treasure of reflections on Jewish life in America. I suspect you know that though. You couldn't have translated it without a curiosity to sit down and actually read it. But I'm not a writer. For the time being, I've just reveled in the passages. I try to use my imagination to *see* her life and draw on her observations about our faith."

Rabbi Weinstein, with that twinkle in his eye and that bounce in his step, smiled and pirouetted out the doorway.

* * *

After he left, Rachel pondered all the rabbi had said, just as she did after what she had come to call their Religion 101 sessions these past months.

In her medical office, things were often best when black or white. Having the answers was her job. Uncertainty, though it did occur from time to time, wasn't in her patient's best interests. But this wasn't the rabbi's modus operandi. He challenged her to decide if and when she would choose to incorporate religious thinking into her life of science and her persistent fear of being identified as Jewish, with its associated antisemitism and existential threat of annihilation.

For Rachel, faith couldn't be measured, seen, or learned. It was more akin to watching Andrew or Hannah on the diving board around age four or so. One had to jump in. She wasn't fearful of getting wet—the moral conduct expected of those committed to any religious faith was easy, it was how Rachel could honestly say she was already living. But now, she desperately wished for what Bill believed throughout their time together, and even at the end, that he would indeed move on. That our time on earth was just a beginning, something lay ahead.

She thought back to a conversation she and Bill had several weeks before he passed. Rachel asked him about how he envisioned heaven. Would he be able to see everything she said and did? Did he think he would be playing basketball anytime if he wanted? Would he wait for her to join him or play the field until she turned up?

"I hadn't thought about playing the field, but that may not be a bad idea." He laughed. "I always wanted to date a redhead. But eternity is a really long time for you to be mad at me if I go chasing skirts for a few years. I think I'll just bach it until you show up."

They both fell quiet. It was really going to happen.

"When one goes to heaven, if you can watch and hear everything said here on earth, what do you think my grandmother and great-grandmother are thinking about our conversation just now?" Rachel had asked Bill. "I know," she had answered, before giving him chance to respond, "they'd say, Wait until we get our hands on you, Bill Walsh. You look like skin and bones. We're going to feed you like only Jewish mothers can."

AUGUST 2000—
SOUTH HAVEN

The hospital was quiet. Daniel had undergone surgery that afternoon. The surgeon hoped he would open him up and find the tumor in his liver confined to a single lobe and, therefore, resectable, however it involved all lobes.

The surgeon came out to see Lottie and suggested they see an oncologist who might have some experimental drugs to recommend. Daniel feared the surgery would be of no avail. His own father had lung cancer, probably secondary to smoking, and his work in hanging wallpaper. They'd opened and closed him also.

Lottie sat at Daniel's bedside waiting for him to wake up from the anesthesia. It would fall upon her to tell him the bad news but who better? They had been lovers, business partners, and best friends now for sixty years. Few knew of the brief period when they separated, but as Lottie looked back, if that was as bad as their life together got, they'd managed pretty well.

Earlier in the afternoon, while Daniel was still in surgery, Rabbi Weinstein dropped by the waiting room to say hello. Lottie had never stopped to consider what a rabbi's life was like. He seemed to make hospital rounds every day just like one of the doctors on staff. He did funerals, taught Bar Mitzvah students, ran daily religious services, and officiated at weddings. The High Holidays were the one time he could certainly "dazzle the congregation" but his bread-and-butter was the Sabbath services where he could expect a small but dedicated portion of the congregation to be present. Some clergy weren't allowed to marry, perhaps affording them extra time for the needs of their flock. But a rabbi could and Rabbi Weinstein's marriage, no doubt, required him to devote energy to his children and his spouse like any other married individual. He had a lot on his plate.

"Hi, Lottie," Rabbi Weinstein said, as he walked over and sat close to her. Looking at a typed sheet of paper, he said, "I see on the hospital admission list that Daniel is having surgery this afternoon. I hope it's not too serious."

"Unfortunately, it is. He has liver cancer. The surgeon offered him a small ray of hope. I'm not a pessimist by nature, but I could see it in the doctor's eyes. He was doubtful he could be helpful but thought Daniel wanted him to try even if it only offered a remote chance of success."

"What will your life be like if you lose him?"

"I'll stay busy. You know I gave up my leadership position at the Temple Auxiliary years ago but I like getting to know the younger women in the community and I'm always willing to assist them with their projects. I suppose from your perspective, finding believers isn't as easy as you'd like it to be, but the women I work with seem to get it. They enjoy helping others. I try to mentor them, telling them how it has made my life richer. I wish my own daughter, Joan, and her brothers, Jack and Allan, were more involved practicing their faith, helping others less fortunate. Perhaps my grandchildren will."

"The Mishnah speaks of *tikkum olam*—helping those in need and repairing our world. I'm glad to hear you plan to continue to work among these young women. Your leadership will be invaluable to them. And don't give up on your children or grandchildren. They may come around. Would you like me to sit with you until Daniel is out of surgery?"

"It's not necessary but this visit was wonderful. I don't expect Daniel to be getting around a lot. Will you stop in to see us at the house?"

"Of course."

"Not to be morbid, but can I ask you two questions about Jewish burials? Why do we bury our loved ones so quickly and why do we fill the grave with dirt using the backside of the shovel three times?"

"Well, the first question relates to a passage in Deuteronomy—the body of an executed man impaled on a stake must not be left overnight because it is an affront to God. It's from this passage that we still bury our dead as quickly as possible but never on the Sabbath. The backside of the shovel is to show our reluctance to say good-bye."

"I will miss my Daniel," said Lottie with a faraway look in her eyes. "I feel like my life is mirroring the Shabbat candles, burning down to the bottom. I can reflect on our time together, but it would be a mistake to live in the past. I will accept loss if it's his time and make the most of my days ahead. I will set an example for my family. Moving forward—it's what my parents taught me ever since they arrived from Russia and their lessons, and my faith, will sustain me."

Tilting his head slightly to the side Rabbi Weinstein paused to look Lottie directly in her eyes, trying to take her whole presence in. "You are an inspiration to me Lottie Zlatkin. Let's recite Psalm 20 together.

> *May the Lord answer you when you are in distress; may the name of the God of Jacob protect you. May he send you help…"*

CHRISTMAS
2019—JERUSALEM

Shema is the central prayer of Judaism and stands for its classical ethical monotheism. But it is also multivalent in Hebrew with various meanings. A person on a journey of faith not only <u>hears</u> the voice of God, they are hearkening attentively to a message. For a Jew, the message is to perform mitzvot, good deeds, to make the world a better place.

שמע ישראל יהוה אלהינו יהוה אחד.
ברוך שם כבוד מלכותו לעולם ועד.

Rachel had been awake now for almost thirty minutes. The plane was eerily quiet, not dissimilar to her mood, though several of the other passengers in business class were stirring and the stewardess was offering coffee to those already awake.

She looked across the aisle. Hannah was still sound asleep but Andrew had his headset back on, watching a movie on the tiny screen. The Walsh family, minus one, would soon be landing in Israel.

She stared at her hands, wincing as her gaze settled on Bill's running watch. She had worn it every day since his passing.

As a kid, her father played the saxophone on Sunday mornings using his Music Minus One record albums. These recordings of classic jazz tunes included an entire band without a sax player. Her father would accompany the band, making the group complete. But there was no one filling in for Bill with the Walsh family today or on any other day as far as she could see into the future.

Yet here they were, taking the trip to Israel she and Bill had committed to.

Her parents, her sister, and most of her close friends thought she and the kids were doing well. It was an immense oversimplification of the truth. In her mind, she couldn't define what well would even look or feel like after the death of a husband and a father. There were some comforting signs—their grades hadn't fallen off, Andrew was engaged in basketball, and Hannah still loved to skate. But she knew her kids would be changed forever, just as she would be. Her focus on her children was to be present, emotionally available at all times.

How many times had she written a condolence note trying to soothe someone about the loss of a loved one? She wrote these cards suspecting that she wasn't scratching the surface of their grief. She knew now, in spades, that this was true. Bill's death had exploded inside her. She cried frequently when alone, sometimes just sniffling, but other times her sobbing was violent, almost unruly.

How many times did someone say the deceased was in a better place now or how good they looked in an open casket? What were people thinking when they said this crap? Who were they kidding or protecting? Themselves?

And how was she supposed to react even now when, while out in public trying to resume her life as best she could, people were afraid to approach her, often ducking into another aisle at the grocery store hoping she hadn't seen them? Had she done this herself before in the past? She didn't think so, at least she hoped not. Her experience as a physician taught her that families often became socially isolated when dealing with difficult medical diagnoses. They weren't actual contagious diseases, but others in the community defensively behaved as if they were. Rachel tried to give people the benefit of the doubt, assuming they simply feared saying the wrong thing.

Rachel was making a concerted effort to bring Bill's presence into the house. If she missed him greatly, and she did, the kids must as well. She found it hard. You are who you are, and Rachel had a difficult time being anything other than a serious mother, doctor, daughter, and friend. These jobs always consumed her and still did. Adding the job of bringing her husband's lightness and steadfastness to her family just wasn't in her sweet spot. Change was inevitable for each of the remaining Walsh family, and whoever advanced the notion that change can be a good thing, couldn't have been considering families attempting to cope with loss.

Staring out the airplane window she wondered what to expect from this trip to Israel with her kids. She was acutely aware that something was bubbling to the surface. She felt like that four-year-old poised to jump off the diving board into the pool.

She'd already done so in her professional life, deciding to leave her private practice, and use the money from Bill's life insurance policy to purchase a building where she intended to recruit other doctors and develop a medical practice exclusively for those of lower income— joining the national group of Physicians for Social Responsibility. Rachel wished for more of her time to be spent helping others in "real" need. It was more consistent with her emerging faith. Her new professional life would allow her to perform *mitzvot* over her remaining years of practice.

Rabbi Weinstein described it as "the way God asks us to live, to make life on earth a better place for all," but it wasn't just the rabbi's instructions that moved Rachel—she knew this choice would make her Grandmother Lottie, with her passion to help others, proud. She might be confabulating, but it seemed her grandmother had actually "predicted" this career change one night when they were together reading the Tarot cards.

She couldn't wait to get started, but this trip was unfinished business, it needed to be seen through first.

Their itinerary was packed. It seemed silly to her family and friends that they would travel this far for only four days in the country, but Rachel was uncomfortable being away from home for any length of time. Just the idea flooded her with anxiety. It had only been six months since Bill's death and home was her foundation and refuge. She could get through her day at work, but she felt a furious need to return, not just to the kids, but to the house itself.

Now they would be traipsing around Israel with Rachel still uncertain about her path forward in life. What was she thinking trying to pull off such a trip?

She knew what Bill would say. "Rachel, just put on your big girl panties and get it done."

A smile creased her face—she could actually see and hear him saying it.

It wasn't long before it was time to land. Hannah was now awake and asked Rachel for some gum. She reached into her carry-on bag and dug to the bottom. Her hand slipped underneath her grandmother's candlesticks. To a stranger, bringing her candlesticks may have seemed odd, but they would be in Israel over the Sabbath. More than ever, Rachel knew she needed to draw strength from the Sabbath ritual.

They met their guide, Ayala, the afternoon they landed at Tel Aviv. She was vibrant, confident, and funny. She took them to an outdoor cafe and started telling them her personal story transposed on the narrative of Israel's history.

She was a third generation Israeli and the kids took to her immediately with questions about music, sports, and the culture. She explained what they would see together over the next several days including a trip to The Dead Sea and nearby Masada, where Jews had battled the Romans before choosing mass suicide. They would go to Bethlehem and the birthplace of Christ, Capernaum where Jesus preached in the synagogue, the Jordan River and the site of Jesus's baptism, and finally Jerusalem and the Western Wall.

Rachel started to breathe easier. Maybe she had done the right thing to bring them so soon after Bill's death. Maybe she had done the right thing for herself as well.

The trip flew by. She surrendered to Ayala's plans and began to enjoy just seeing and being. She was keenly aware of Bill at all times, knowing how much he would have enjoyed himself. He was just going to miss too much of the life they had planned together and she was going to miss too much without him.

There was a crowd when they arrived at the Western Wall. It was the last scheduled stop of their hectic tour. Looking about, Rachel tried to take it all in and process what was before her eyes. It reminded her of an archeological dig, but with modern day inhabitants occupying the space, sharing with her this historic religious ground.

The Temple Mount was nearby, and though now covered by the Dome of the Rock and the Al-Aqsa Mosque, the Mount remained the most sacred site in the world for the Jewish faith. This was where God asked Abraham to sacrifice his son Isaac, where in 900 BC God asked King David to erect an altar, and where years later David's son, King Solomon, built The First Temple. Now, all that remained was part of the Second Temple, finished in 515 BC, but destroyed in 70 AD. It was a sixty-two-foot high limestone wall, the Western Wall, built as an extension of the Temple by Herod the Great.

She was flooded with awe and wonderment—heart racing, breathing too fast, fingers tingling, and face flushed. She was keenly aware of Lottie's presence, forgetting that it was Hannah's hand she was holding, not that of her grandmother, as she squeezed it too tightly.

"Mom," said Hannah. "Are you okay?"

Fulfilling Lottie's dream, she had told Bill—it was the reason why Rachel wished to come to see Israel, once a narrow strip of arid land, now a modern day success, the product of Zionism—something her grandmother first learned as a young girl at that 1933 production of *The Romance of A People.*

But now, Rachel had traveled to Israel for herself—to *see* Jerusalem and *touch* the heart of Judaism. She wanted to experience first-hand the place of origin of the faith that had sustained her ancestors, a faith which survived the Holocaust, a faith that currently was standing up to the modern-day threats of antisemitism, and a faith that Rachel hoped could nourish her now.

While planning the trip several years ago, she couldn't anticipate that her reasons for wanting to come would change so radically.

They were to have come together with the kids. Bill would have been walking alongside her experiencing the religious history of his faith too, after all, just outside the gates to Jerusalem, on the Temple Mount, was the site of the Crucifixion of Jesus Christ. Looking at the Western Wall, Rachel knew Bill was there.

Immediately after his death, the hole inside Rachel seemed to expand exponentially. But though her sadness still had an infinite component, today, here by the Wall, the hole was filling up with all she could Taste and See.

Ayala had instructed Hannah and Rachel to wear long sleeves and longish skirts out of respect. They didn't need to cover their heads, but Ayala brought along a *yalmuka* for Andrew. He would need to go to the wall by himself as men and women were asked to approach separately.

The four of them huddled to pick a spot to gather once they were done visiting the wall, Ayala choosing to wait by the fountain to watch for their return.

As Rachel approached the wall, the light from the sun illuminated the faces of people returning from the Wall. It could have been a scene from a movie set. All ages and ethnicities were moving about in almost Brownian motion, while rabbis, in their long black coats with *tefellin* strapped to their heads and arms, were busy *shuckling* in prayer.

She felt overcome by emotion but also by an inner peace she hadn't experienced since the day they first received the news of Bill's pancreatic cancer diagnosis.

Her journey to welcoming faith was over. She was ready to choose. She stopped to search her bag for the stationary she'd taken from the hotel desk this morning and took out a pen. She wrote her prayer to God and fed the folded paper into a crevice between the stones, next to so many others.

> *I know Bill is up there in heaven. I pray you will allow me to join him one day. But I have children to raise and mitzvot to perform. So please, don't take me too soon.*

Rachel closed her eyes, kissed the wall, and slowly retreated.

AUTHOR'S NOTES

Rachel Walsh, though a fictional character, could have been an actual descendant of Russian Jews coming to America in 1892 through the generosity of the Baron de Hirsch. Some chose, ultimately, to settle in the area around South Haven, Michigan, farming at first and later pivoting into the resort business when it became a more attractive economic opportunity. As immigrants, they were a self-selected lot, emotionally and physically capable of doing whatever it took to be successful in their new homeland. But Jewish immigrants to America needed more than chutzpah and a conscious effort to never look back—what really stood out for this author were their choices to value study and the mooring of their Jewish faith.

The Baron de Hirsch, would no longer have been a young man in 1892. I imagine him sitting in a café in Paris sipping coffee, and perhaps reading a startling new play that a friend recommended. The friend would have known that Maurice, the Baron, was open-minded and expansive in his world views, but even he would have been astounded by Frühlings Erwachen's depiction of a sexually repressive culture and its effects on German youth, a book that would give rise one hundred years later to a musical, Spring Awakening.

Although the Baron de Hirsch had no living children—a daughter died in infancy and a son in his thirties—the issues raised by the playwright would have been all too familiar from his own adolescence in Bavaria. He might have been looking forward to discussing the play with his friend, but he was certainly part of a generation too repressed to think about bringing it up with anyone else except, perhaps, his wife.

The Baron was a wealthy man. In fact, he was one of the wealthiest men in all of Europe. Baron de Hirsch was born Maurice de Hirsch in Munich and both his parents came from banking families. His mother was instrumental in his receiving an education in the Hebrew language and Judaism. The Baron married Claire Bischoffsheim, the daughter of a Belgian financier, and used both his inherited wealth and her dowry to make even more money investing aggressively in the Orient Express railway, copper, and sugar.

The Baron resided in Paris. It would have surprised most of his acquaintances that only forty years later Germany would not be a safe place for a Jew to live. Baron de Hirsch had more foresight. He'd come to recognize years ago that Jews in Eastern Europe and czarist Russia needed to flee. After the pogroms, an organized massacre of Jews in Russia in the early 1880s, Rachel's family, for example, chose to escape Russia. And the Baron knew from personal experience that even in an enlightened country like France, a Jew might be respected in the banking circles where he moved, but not necessarily liked.

His business dealings and travels gave the Baron and his wife exposure to the suffering of Jews living throughout the Ottoman Empire. On a trip to Constantinople in 1887, while Clara was mourning the death of their son Lucien, she said to her husband "I am just going to wander around the city all day while you do your work here with the railroad." And she did, distributing money everywhere she went to the Jewish inhabitants living in poverty. After the trip concluded, she encouraged her husband to dedicate the remaining years of his life, and his fortune, to the oppressed Jews about the world.

Initially, he focused on education, donating huge sums of money to the Alliance Israélite Universelle, an institution formed independently in 1860 to safeguard the human rights of Jewish people around the world, who were often living as a persecuted minority in their own countries. These French-language based schools for Jewish children could be found throughout the Middle East, Mediterranean, and Ottoman Empire. The Universelle's efforts extended beyond education and trade schools to attempts to work with cooperative governments, enacting laws giving Jews full political and civil rights. Twice in the 1880s, the Baron gave gifts of one million francs to the Universelle.

During this same period, de Hirsch offered the Russian government 50 million francs to educate the Jewish people residing there, but these undertakings to improve their lot, however, were declined by the government. They demanded exclusive control of the money he planned to donate, an unacceptable condition to de Hirsch.

It was then that his focus switched to emigration and resettlement projects around the world. He told a friend one night at dinner "What is more natural than that I should find my highest purpose in bringing to the followers of Judaism, who have been oppressed for a thousand years, who are starving in misery, the possibilities of a physical and moral regeneration?"

The Baron resolved to use his financial resources to relocate Jews to the Western World and assist them in forming farming communities for the remainder of his life. To this end, he founded the Jewish Colonization Association in 1891. The association, the greatest charitable trust in the world at the time, owned land in Palestine, Canada, and Argentina and assembled a variety of services to relocate Jews including help with emigration, vocational training, and housing, and granted financial loans to buy farmland and equipment. The loans were loans, not gifts and were to be re-paid. As de Hirsch insisted:

"I contend most decidedly against the old system of alms-giving, which only makes so many more beggars; and I consider it the greatest problem in philanthropy to make human beings who are capable of work out of individuals who otherwise must become paupers, and in this way to create useful members of society."

That same year, 1891, the Baron de Hirsch Fund was established in the state of New York with an initial contribution of $2.4 million. This money was indispensable in assisting large numbers of Jews arriving from Eastern Europe and Russia. The Fund was initially earmarked to set up agricultural colonies and trade schools in the United States, but ultimately the money was spent on assisting immigrants with relocation costs, housing and legal matters.

A meeting took place in 1895 between the Baron de Hirsch and Theodor Herzl, the father of Zionism. The aim of Zionism was nothing less than to re-establish a sovereign Jewish nation in their historical home of Israel. It was early summer in Paris, probably a pleasant enough day to meet outdoors on de Hirsch's terrace overlooking his well-manicured garden.

Herzl and de Hirsch shared a common concern for the plight of Jews throughout Europe and Russia. The Jews were a minority everywhere they lived and nation states were struggling to define their legal, civil, and political rights. History now refers to these struggles as "The Jewish Problem" or the "Jewish Question." It is well-documented that Herzl thought the best solution was for Jews around the world to return to Palestine, their historic home, and establish their own country.

What we don't know is whether either man's opinion was affected by an antisemitic incident that had taken place in Paris one year before their meeting. The Dreyfuss Affair had rocked France when a Jewish French army captain, Dreyfuss, was falsely accused of spying for Germany and in the aftermath of the incident, feelings against the Jews were running very high in France.

Neither man knew if the meeting would be productive or not, though only one had an "ask" to make. What was actually said that day went unrecorded, but perhaps it went something like this. The Baron may have said, "What can I do for you Mr. Herzl? I received your letter. You said that I was the great Jew of the money and that you were the Jew of the spirit. I'm not sure if that was flattery or an insult but we share a desire for something to be done. I'm doing everything I can to resettle Jews around the world. My plan is working. My fund is on solid ground. With the loans being repaid, the Baron de Hirsch Fund should last in perpetuity. I'm not giving anyone a handout. I'm giving them a chance."

Herzl may have replied, "But it does not address the greater question, the ultimate question, of the safety of the Jewish people. We need a homeland. We should return to our ancestral home in Palestine. Help me to go the German Kaiser. I want to ask for his cooperation. I want his help and yours to establish a one billion-mark Jewish national loan fund."

The Baron must have laughed out loud. "Idealism is not what I am about. Your solution is interesting but not realistic. I don't think I can help you today."

✳   ✳   ✳

The Baron de Hirsch passed away in 1896 and his wife, Clara, the sole heir to his massive fortune, continued his charitable work. It came as no surprise to all around her as she was the one who initially pushed him towards charitable interests in the first place. The Baroness studied the plight of Jewish immigrants in New York City and set aside $1million to relocate some of them to the surrounding rural areas to relieve their cramped living conditions, $150,000 for a building to house the Baron de Hirsch Trade School to teach carpentry, plumbing, and electrical work, and $200,000 to construct the Clara de Hirsch Home for Working Girls. The home provided temporary shelter and emotional support for homeless working girls.

The Baroness would die in 1899 prior to fulfilling her intention to give all her inherited fortune away. But in her will, she still left considerable sums to the charities she and her husband started during their later years. These financial resources continue to benefit Jewish immigrants into the twenty-first century. The Fund grants money to Jewish immigrants for education to assist them in "Americanization". It also supplies money to the Jewish Agricultural and Industrial Aid Society allowing for them to provide loans to Jews purchasing farms.

✳   ✳   ✳

The author imagines when the Baron de Hirsch finished his coffee on that day in 1892, he would have tucked his book under his arm, and started to walk the three blocks to his mansion on the Rue de Elysee. He knew nothing of Michigan. He had never traveled to the United States. He had only a vague impression of the potential for success of the farming communities his money had already started in the midwestern United States and that impression was not favorable. The growing season was short. He would have been praying that the Jews who chose to resettle there would be able to turn a profit and find safety.

The Baron de Hirsch might have enjoyed reading our story that day as he sat on the Champs-Elysées sipping his coffee and wondering what would come of his unparalleled philanthropy. After all, he launched so many emigrants on their search for sanctuary, far away. He hoped to change the lives of so many families and one of those families might have been the great grandparents of a "real life" Rachel Walsh, who left behind all but their faith and a pair of candlesticks.

Two final notes need to be made about the manuscript. Both involve the chapter entitled June 2019—South Haven. The first is a quote used about the afterlife. This quote is attributable to the late Rabbi Jack Riemer.

The second is the English translation of the Mourner's Kaddish. The Kaddish, though commonly thought to be a Hebrew prayer, is actually written in Aramaic and is more properly considered an Aramaic prayer.

> *Yitgadal, v'yitkadash, sh'meih raba, b'alma divra chiruteih, v'yamlich malchuteih, b'chayeichon uv'yomeichon uv'chayei d'chol beit Yisra'eil, ba'agala uviz'man kariv. V'im'ru: amein. Y'hei sh'meih raba m'varach l'alam ul'almei almaya. Yitbarach, v'yishtabach, v'yitpa'ar, v'yitromam, v'yitnasei, v'yit'hardar, v'yitaleih, v'yit'halal sh'meih d'kud'sha. B'rich hu l'eila min kol bir'chata, v'shirata, tushb'chata, v'nech'mata, da'amiran b'alma. V'im'ru: amein. Y'hei sh'lama raba min sh'maya v'chayim aleinu v'al kol Yisra'eil. V'imru: amein. Osheh shalom bim'romaav, hu ya'aseh shalom, aleinu v'al kol Yisra'eil. V'im'ru: amein.*

Glorified and sanctified be God's great name throughout the world which He has created according to His will.

May He establish His kingdom in your lifetime and during your days, and within the life of the entire House of Israel, speedily and soon; and say, Amen.

May His great name be blessed forever and to all eternity.

Blessed and praised, glorified and exalted, extolled and honored, adored and lauded be the name of the Holy One, blessed be He, beyond all the blessings and hymns, praises and consolations that are ever spoken in the world; and say, Amen.

May there be abundant peace from heaven, and life, for us and for all Israel; and say, Amen.

He who creates peace in His celestial heights, may He create peace for us and for all Israel; and say, Amen.

ACKNOWLEDGMENTS

Writing *Illumination* helped me weather the pandemic. Hours passed in front of the computer screen without notice. I am certain the project was a key factor in preserving my mental health.

I had assistance from early readers including Betty Goran, Lynn & Carl Lyss, Pete Stecy and Diana Votaw. They encouraged me to produce chapters on a weekly basis throughout the pandemic. It allowed them to read my novel in an almost "serial format" and, in doing so, pushed me to continue to write.

Later readers, Donna Steinhoff and Bethe Growe helped to polish the manuscript into its final form—forcing me to dot each "i" and cross each "t".

Tommy Collinger shared some personal reflections on losing his wife to cancer and kaballist Susie Yehudit Schneider helped me with the concept of spiritual transformation. Tommy, Susie, and I lived four doors apart for the first twelve years of my life. Our time apart vanished as we spoke of these personal issues.

I was guided as I wrote by my certified Book Coach Michelle Melton Cox. Though I practiced pediatrics for nearly forty years, I now see myself as a writer thanks to Michelle.

One of Michelle's colleagues, Sarah Krosshell, reviewed the final manuscript from a 10,000 foot view and offered suggestions for improvement.

I thought I was done writing at that point and only needed a final line edit before seeking publication. Enter Ruth Bullivant. Ruth either really like my novel, or found it still "in need". In any event, she provided additional suggestions, many of which found their way into improving my final, final manuscript. Ruth lives in London and, though we have only met on a Zoom screen, I consider her a friend.

The final person to touch this project was Gary Huber, Rabbi Emeritus at Congregation beth tikvah in Columbus Ohio. As children, Gary and I shared carpool rides to religious school. I asked Gary to review my manuscript for accuracy. We lost contact with each other since high school, but I enjoyed renewing our friendship and chatting about some of the same topics Rachel discussed with Rabbi Weinstein. He was instrumental in some of the exchanges I wrote concerning the afterlife and even shared a quote from his mentor, the late Rabbi Jack Riemer, which I acknowledged in the Author's Notes section of my book.

Illumination is a story about faith, about Jewish history, some well-known and other pieces more obscure, but it is also a story about family. I would like to dedicate this novel of historical fiction to the nine most important people in my life, my immediate family. They inspire me daily to be the best person I can be—and at this late stage of my life, it is to be a writer.